# The Isle in the Silver Sea

## By Tasha Suri

*The Isle in the Silver Sea*

### THE BURNING KINGDOMS

*The Jasmine Throne*
*The Oleander Sword*
*The Lotus Empire*

### THE BOOKS OF AMBHA

*Empire of Sand*
*Realm of Ash*

# The Isle in the Silver Sea

## TASHA SURI

orbitbooks.net

This book is a work of fiction. Names, characters, places, and incidents are the product of the author's imagination or are used fictitiously. Any resemblance to actual events, locales, or persons, living or dead, is coincidental.

Copyright © 2025 by Natasha Suri

Cover design by Lisa Marie Pompilio
Cover art by Bridgeman, Alamy, and Shutterstock
Cover copyright © 2025 by Hachette Book Group, Inc.
Map by Tim Paul

Hachette Book Group supports the right to free expression and the value of copyright. The purpose of copyright is to encourage writers and artists to produce the creative works that enrich our culture.

The scanning, uploading, and distribution of this book without permission is a theft of the author's intellectual property. If you would like permission to use material from the book (other than for review purposes), please contact permissions@hbgusa.com. Thank you for your support of the author's rights.

Orbit
Hachette Book Group
1290 Avenue of the Americas
New York, NY 10104
orbitbooks.net

First Edition: October 2025
Simultaneously published in Great Britain by Orbit

Orbit is an imprint of Hachette Book Group.
The Orbit name and logo are registered trademarks of Little, Brown Book Group Limited.

The publisher is not responsible for websites (or their content)
that are not owned by the publisher.

The Hachette Speakers Bureau provides a wide range of authors for speaking events. To find out more, go to hachettespeakersbureau.com or email HachetteSpeakers@hbgusa.com.

Orbit books may be purchased in bulk for business, educational, or promotional use. For information, please contact your local bookseller or the Hachette Book Group Special Markets Department at special.markets@hbgusa.com.

Library of Congress Cataloging-in-Publication Data
Names: Suri, Tasha, author.
Title: The Isle in the silver sea / Tasha Suri.
Description: First edition. | New York, NY : Orbit, 2025.
Identifiers: LCCN 2025006918 | ISBN 9780316595087 (hardcover) | ISBN 9780316573160 (ebook)
Subjects: LCGFT: Fantasy fiction. | Witch fiction. | Lesbian fiction. | Novels.
Classification: LCC PR6119.U75 I85 2025 | DDC 823/.92—dc23/eng/20250214
LC record available at https://lccn.loc.gov/2025006918

ISBNs: 9780316595087 (hardcover), 9780316600668 (signed edition), 9780316573160 (ebook)

Printed in the United States of America

LSC-C

Printing 1, 2025

*for my historian*

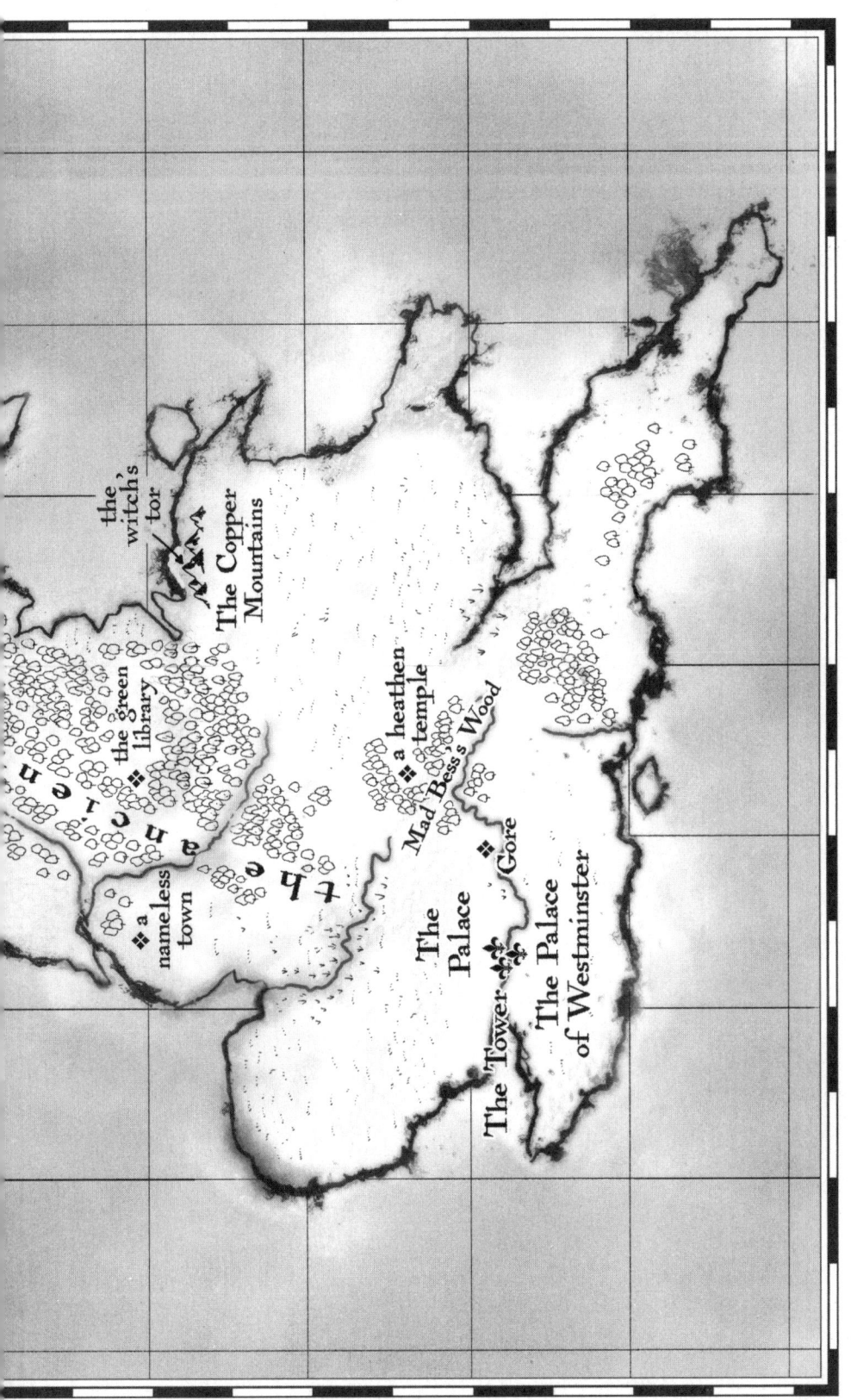
Map by Tim Paul

# The Isle in the Silver Sea

# PART ONE

[Anonymous, "The Knight and the Witch," in Laura Beaufort-Morgan (ed.), *Incarnate Tales for Children* (Chancellor Press, XVIII), pp. 22-23.]

Long ago, there lived a knight who was tasked by the Queen to kill a terrible witch.

All witches are terrible, of course, but this one was especially wicked. The witch lived upon a grand mountain range, in a sprawling palace of bronze ore. There, she spun ore into fire, and fire into scrying glass, and made great mirrors that she hung upon her mountain peaks so that she could watch the good folk of the Isle and drip evil dreams into their eyes. Every man and woman and child who glimpsed her mirrors became afflicted with nightmares so dark and so vicious that many perished from the horror of them alone.

"The witch must die," the Queen proclaimed, her white face solemn beneath her golden crown, "before she drives all the Isle to madness with her nightmares. Are you brave enough to kill her, dear knight, and pure enough of heart to survive the poison of her magic unscathed?"

The knight kneeled before the Queen and bowed his head. He was broad and tall with hair like yellow wheat and eyes as blue as the sky at midsummer, and his heart was so radiantly pure that some said light shone from his face like a beacon. He knew the witch, for they had crossed paths before, and he understood that her wickedness was as deep as his purity.

"I will not return until I have run my sword through her beating heart," the knight vowed.

He took his steed and his sword and rode for many days, from the Queen's Palace to the salt-swept coast, through forests of wizened trees and glades of fae and gnomes and all manner of trickster creatures, until he arrived at the bronze-peaked mountains of the witch's domain. He knew if he gazed into the copper light of her mirrors her poison would touch him, so he bound a cloth over his eyes and followed the guidance of his pure heart.

His heart led him upon the mountain into her palace. Around him the air smelled of meadow grass and heather, winter's mead and summer's honey, but he knew these scents were illusions and that around him lay nothing but a palace of bones, rich in the smell of smelted ore and fire and charnel smoke. He heard the whisper of silk skirts and a woman's laughter, and knew that a witch of profound ugliness had lurched toward him wearing an illusion of beauty.

He held his sword aloft, and the witch laughed again.

"You cannot kill me in my own palace, where my magic is strongest!" the witch cried.

"I can, and I shall," the knight declared. "Because my heart is pure, and I serve the Eternal Queen, who rules everlasting."

"If my magic cannot defeat you, then remove the cloth upon your eyes," commanded the witch.

The knight refused. He struck with his sword and smelled her blood on the air. It spat and sizzled where it touched the earth.

"Look at me," implored the witch before he could strike again, "and I will release all the people of the Isle enthralled by my enchantments. I vow it on my magic. May it wither if I lie to you now!"

A witch vowing on her magic is as good as a knight vowing on his honor. So the knight removed the cloth from his eyes, because he could not allow good people to suffer if it lay in his power to do aught else.

When the knight beheld the witch he saw a fair maiden with skin as white as unspoiled milk and hair spun from gold. But he knew this was an illusion, because witches are rotten by flesh and by nature.

Too late, he realized that behind her stood a vast bronze mirror inscribed with words of magic. The sight of it bled poison into his eyes and fire into his blood. With a cry, he covered his eyes once more, but it was far too late.

"It is the mirror of change," the witch gloated. "It will turn your goodness to wickedness, and the hate in your heart to love. Your own purity will destroy you and make you mine!"

Overcome, the knight went to his knees and professed his ardent love for her.

The witch kept her word and released every good Isle-blooded man and woman from her enthrallment. She considered it a worthwhile sacrifice, for she now possessed the knight, and she knew his sword would lay waste to the Isle if she only asked.

For many days the knight served the witch and committed terrible deeds on her behalf. His sword dripped blood and turned the mountain snow red. But the witch's inevitable ruin lay in the spell she had cast upon him. One day she looked into his eyes and saw her own poison of change within them reflected back at her. His love was a mirror she had foolishly gazed upon, and now it ensnared her.

In a moment, her wickedness was turned to goodness and her hate to love. And she fell into his arms and wept, repenting all the evil she had done. She kissed his eyelids and kissed his mouth as she wept, and the love in her kiss broke the enchantment upon him.

The knight remembered himself, and wept also, for the spell had transformed the witch into the fair maiden she had long pretended to be, and the sight of her made his false love into true. But he had made a vow to the Queen, and he could not break it.

He ran the sword through her heart and through his own, and they died together, the knight and the witch.

In the end, the knight acted wisely, for he knew love was the ruin of them both, and only death could set them free.

He did not know then that their love was a Great Tale—an Isle-feeding fable, a love story to nourish the forests and fields, to make the Isle's birds sing and its adders slither.

Their tale made incarnates of them, and like all incarnates they will return to live their tale and love and perish for a hundred thousand lifetimes and beyond. Indeed, they will love and die until the day comes when no more stories are born and told at all.

On that day, the Isle will crumble into the sea, and be lost forevermore.

# Chapter One

## *Simran*

*This is how it begins*
  *Long ago, a story was told, and land grew from it.*
  *Tell a tale of wolves and a girl in bloodred, and somewhere a forest will grow, sharp-toothed and open-mawed for a foolish wolf's bones. Talk of monsters slithering through the darkness, and somewhere there will be caverns to hold them. Speak a thing and make it live, on the land across the silver sea. That is a mortal gift.*
  *But those stories are hungry, and they must continue to be fed.*
  *Tell me, whisper the stories. Repeat me. Enact me. Embody me.*
  *And so we feed them. One child at a time.*

Source: *A Monograph on the Laws of the Isle* by Dr. Angharad Walsh (unpublished)

**Archivist's Ruling: Destroy. Publication barred. Interrogation recommended.**

When you live in a land that feeds on stories, you soon learn to sense when one is about to rear its head. Sometimes, if you're foolhardy enough, you can make sure to set yourself on its path. The witch from Elsewhere, with her ink-smudged brown arms and her bone compass, was not a fool, but she was hardy—a sharp, severe kind of hardness that radiated from every pore of her body. The boys who stumbled out of the Starre Tavern to smoke, soused to the gills, gave her a wide berth. Their eyes slid respectfully away from her.

Some of those boys were dressed in doublets and hose, their caps feathered. Others wore vests and pocket watches under their great surcoats, their top hats tall and black and their boots polished to a shine. Stories muddled together easily across London, but in no place better than taverns, where gossip—the most natural kind of tale-spinning—spilled as easily as drink. That kind of magic *changed* things: It made the bones of a tavern stranger, stronger, and better at luring all sorts of people in through the door. In the Starre Tavern, a boy raised to eat on a trencher and sup on mead could rub shoulders with a lad born under the shadow of coalsmoke and industry. Even an Elsewhere-born witch with ink on her skin and magic writhing under her heels—the kind of woman who belonged nowhere by design—could buy herself a pint and find herself a sticky corner of the bar to lean on.

But the witch had no plans to step through the tavern's doors tonight. Her work lay out here.

Her patience was beginning to wear thin when the cold wind finally changed, softening apple-sweet. The boys smoking outside the Starre Tavern fell silent and stubbed out their cigars and cheroots; downed their pints and stepped quietly into the pub. She watched the windows go dark as great candles of tallow were snuffed out. The door was softly closed and latched.

She was reminded of the way birds turned in a flock with the wind, or rats abandoned sinking ships. Sometimes animal instincts were the best ones.

Above her, the gas lamps dimmed, then guttered. On her palm her compass whirled, the little needle of bone spinning wildly.

Bone was a bad lodestone for direction, but it was good for snaring the edge of a tale. There was nothing a story liked more, after all, than flesh and blood.

She stepped back against the wall of the tavern. In her hastily mended cotehardie and her lambswool cloak, she was as good as written for the tale she expected to wend its way down Cloth Fair at any moment, but that did not mean she *wanted* to be seen.

They came in a group of three, as so many stories did: three knights astride three destriers, the Queen's rose pennant fluttering above them. One of them was carrying a satchel braided in gold.

Her compass needle stilled.

There.

*Do not see me*, she thought, and felt magic bubble through her flesh. She was the tavern wall, or close enough to it. Gray stone melded with her cloak. She kept her eyes on them, as the first of the horses met her trap.

"Halt," one said gruffly. "There's a fairy ring here. Toadstools."

"Fuckers," said another. "They know they're not allowed this far into London."

Under the looming checkerboard shadow of St. Bartholomew the Great Church, the riders halted. One dismounted and drew their helm from their head. The neck that was exposed was almost as dark as the witch's own—a warm tan underneath a mop of oak-brown hair. She was surprised by their face when they turned. There were darts of gold in their right ear. And the face was girlish, despite the sharpness of the jaw and cheekbones, with long-lashed eyes and a giving mouth. A handsome knight, yes. But also a pretty one. Were there many tales of pretty knights?

She knew many tales of knights, but only one that dwelled on a knight's shining beauty, and contemplating it made a kernel of poison bloom in her already rather bitter heart.

"—vinia," one knight said.

"She's not listening," said the other. "Look at her."

Something-vinia raised her head.

"Patience," she said. Her voice was a lazy curl of smoke, a rich woman's voice, beautiful and thoroughly obnoxious. She prodded the ground at the edge of the toadstool with her gloved knuckles. "Fuckers or not, I won't tread over a fairy ring without offering it silver."

"Then offer it so we can be off."

"I'm afraid I'm low on funds today," the pretty knight replied. "Care to spot me?"

The men behind her cursed, and the knight raised her head, laughing a bell-like laugh even as she stared coolly through the dark. Her eyes were the brown of a doe or hare—lustrous, wild, and canny.

In her mind, the witch from Elsewhere cursed too.

The pretty knight knew the fairy ring was false.

What mistake had revealed the illusion? She'd worked ash and water-by-moonlight together to make those toadstools; rooted them with a song and a sinewy thread. How had the knight seen through it?

"Come out," Something-vinia urged, and her voice was a hook that made the compass needle tremble.

"Who are you talking to?" another knight asked. "Vina—"

"If I place a coin in the ring, will I be snared here? You've built a clever trap." Her voice was still lazy, glass-blown at the vowels, but pitched to travel. "I'd love to hear how you did it. Come out, Lady. Speak to us."

Against the wall, the witch weighed up her options.

Something-vinia—Vina—was carrying the satchel.

One bottle of ink. That was all she needed. One bottle could stretch far in her scriptorium. The work it could bring to her door would pay her rent for a solid year.

She let the illusion around her fade and stepped forward. One of the riders made an abortive grasp for his sword, then lowered his arm with a clank of armor. Both riders looked at her and the thin, knife-whittled shadow her body threw.

"Are you a beautiful maiden wearing the guise of a hag?" the first rider asked dubiously.

"No," said Vina. "She's just a maiden." Vina's eyes hadn't strayed from hers. There was something soft in the shape of her mouth.

The witch's hood was deep, and magic held her face in shadow. And yet she had the keen sense that she was being seen and known.

"You'd know," one man chuckled.

"I would," Vina agreed, and that soft mouth bloomed into a smile. "Lady, will you lower your hood and tell us your name?"

"No, and no, fair knight," she replied.

The knight's smile did not alter one jot, but the witch thought she saw some strain in it.

"I am not fair," said the knight. "Though I am certainly a knight. And you are...?"

"Willing to let you pass in return for a tithe," said the witch.

"A tithe would be fair if you are a lady of the fae," said Vina pleasantly. "And if you were not in the Queen's city, on her soil, where fae law won't hold..."

The witch snorted.

"I've met fae in Covent Garden singing along to opera and drinking plum wine," she said. "I've watched them kill a man with burning coal shoes in Billingsgate right next to the water gate—like a *taunt*. Don't tell me what the Queen does and does not allow on her soil, knight."

"So you're not a fae after all," said Vina. She sounded smug.

The witch was immediately furious. She did not care for trickery that wasn't her own, and the knight *had* tricked her—with a soft smile, and warm eyes, and words like a slithering noose.

"You're lucky I'm no heartless maiden of the fae," the witch said sharply. "You're knights. One of you is surely an incarnate destined to wither at a fairy woman's hands—"

"No," said Vina. She shook her head. "The Tale of the Merciless Maiden isn't one of ours."

Perhaps not a one of them belonged to a tale of a knight cursed to fruitlessly love a fae woman, destined to pine their way to an early death. But there *was* a tale around them. The witch could feel it thrumming in the air—in the scent of apples and sheaves of wheat, and the slow metal-drip scent of ink. The witch could feel her compass thrumming in her palm, and something stranger still: a thrumming in her own heart, that ebbed and flowed like waves.

What tale, then? The Princess and the Dragon? Guy of Warwick and Felice? The Knight and the Wi—

She severed her own thought and thrust her left hand out, palm up.

"Ink," the witch said. "One bottle. Then you can pass."

"This ink is destined for the Queen's archives," Vina said. "We can't give any to you, Lady. What other price will allow us to pass?" She cocked her head. "A kiss?"

"I don't need to pay for kisses," the witch said. "And I would not buy them from you."

"Cut her down, Vina," one of the knights said. "We've only got until daybreak."

"Ah now," said Vina. "She means no trouble."

The witch, who absolutely did mean trouble, said, "One bottle and only one bottle. Your Queen won't miss it. You know that just as well as I do. Please."

Vina hesitated—or gave a good semblance of hesitation. Then slowly, regretfully, she shook her head.

Well, then. The witch had tried to bargain.

The witch clicked the fingers of her outstretched left hand.

Sparks of fire snapped through the air. One of the destriers lurched, rearing in panic—a fatal flaw in a warhorse, surely. On its back, its knight drew his sword, a vast and gleaming length of steel.

Vina's gloved hand shot forward and grasped her wrist. There was metal on her gloves and strength in her hand, and the vise of it stung. The witch snapped her fingers once more before Vina could close her fist over her fingers, sparks bursting anew into the air.

"Stop," Vina said, and the wildness of her eyes had deepened. "Godsblood, woman. I *know* you."

The witch wrenched her hand toward her own body and Vina

stumbled clumsily into the fairy ring. The trap sprang. Vina shuddered to a stop as webs of smoke snared her. Water, moonlight, and strings of sinew held her fast.

The second knight drew his sword.

"Draw closer and you'll have to cut through her to reach me," the witch pointed out. Quite reasonably, she thought. But the two knights on their horses obviously did not agree, and trembled with rage as motes of fire spat and singed the air around them, and made the eyes of their destriers roll wildly.

"One bottle of ink," the witch said again, meeting Vina's eyes. "Then I let you go."

"Lower your hood," Vina begged. "Let me see you so that I know you're not—not—"

It was not the witch's magic that made the motes of fire gather above them like a shared halo, cutting through the glamour of shadows beneath her hood. It was the tale that demanded it. Stories were selfish. They used anything they could grasp to feed them.

The knight was meant to see the witch's face. And the witch had been fool enough to give the knight firelight to see by.

"Isadora," Vina gasped. The name lurched out of her mouth. "*No.*"

The name wrenched at the witch like a plier pulling a tooth. The wrench echoed through her body, snaring her. She was a puppet on strings. For a brief, awful moment she was frozen. Then she found her voice once more.

"That isn't my name," the witch said sharply. She stepped into the fairy ring, her cloak brushing the knight's armor. Her own trap could not hurt her, but the knight within it could by simply being the knight. The woman could smell apples, earth. The great clang of a mirror rang in her ears, and a memory of the cold scent of snow tickled her nose. A great tale was closing its vise around them.

She'd known that stealing from knights was a dangerous business, although she had not expected *this* danger. She'd planned for a swift escape. She wore a bracelet of thread on her right wrist, bound in place with a knot stained in ashes from her home's hearth. It was a spell slumbering, waiting to be quickened. All it needed was blood, and that she could provide easily.

She raised her hand between them and saw Vina's eyes widen, fixed on both the witch and the witch's bared wrist. For a moment the knight was vulnerable, distracted, and that was enough.

With her left hand, the witch reached into the knight's satchel as she bit her own lip, blood flowering up, and pressed her mouth to the knot at her wrist.

The spell ignited. The witch sucked in a breath, threw herself forward—

—and fell with a thud onto Limehouse docks.

The Thames roared around her, briny, stinging her face with its fetid rot and salt. Her wrist ached. Her heart was beating wildly. She wasn't sure if she was breathing until the salt and sewage scent of the Thames hit her lungs and set her coughing.

She clambered to her feet. Her limbs were her own again. The ink rattled in her pocket, the bottle still whole. She'd plucked it easily from the satchel. It hadn't been hard, once she'd been close enough to touch. Limni ink wanted to be stolen.

She stomped across the dock, the wood creaking beneath her kidskin boots. They were wet. If she didn't dry them with care they'd rot, and she had no coin for new ones. An easy thing for her to be angry about; to worry over even as her compass spun and spun in wilder circles, seeking a knight's blood, *the* knight's blood, like a hungry gull.

The witch from Elsewhere began unbuttoning her long sleeves before she'd even made it to the road. Her arms, bared to the bitterly cold air, were covered in ink-black scrollwork that writhed and pulsed, flitting across her skin. At her wrist, it was winding into desperate tangles of thorns and roses. The bracelet had crumbled to dust, burned to a husk by magic.

She'd known there was a tale wending down Cloth Fair. She hadn't feared it. She'd waited for it.

She hadn't realized it was her own. If she had, she would have run, ink be damned.

\* \* \*

The witch from Elsewhere was named Simran Kaur Arora.

It said so on her arrival papers, the illuminated scroll with a facsimile of her face in silver ink, the one that had marked her as an immigrant on the hundred-and-twelfth voyage of a ship that occasionally, sullenly threatened to take the shape of the *Golden Hind*. Her silver image was a perfect re-creation of her at ten years old: tight looped braids with trailing ribbons, a round face, a belligerent mouth.

What her arrival papers did not share was how the journey had felt: the lurch of the cabins, heaving their bodies to and fro. Her father, rubbing the scar that bisected his throat, already forgetting where he'd gained it.

By the time she had been on the ship from moonrise to sunrise, her memory of home had smeared and faded too, like light and shade through glass. But she remembered fear—muddied brown water, and the sulfur of gunshot. And she knew what her mother had promised her, as she'd oiled Simran's hair on their first moonrise on the ship, her fingers drenched with the luster of night, starlight, and jasmine oil.

*We're going to a land of stories*, her mother had said. *Angrezi stories. Nothing can touch us there. We can start again.*

Why climb on a ship that shouldn't exist, and cross a shining sea to an alien and magical land, if not for that? Safety. A future. You cannot be hurt by stories that do not own you. You can live among them, a stranger and an outsider, the birth tales that made you fading like ash, and you can survive.

But Simran, breathless with wonder and too curious for her own good, had clambered onto the deck, the cold spray pricking her cheeks, and seen a woman soaked to the bone drinking a bottle of wine, her body angled precariously against the barrier rail, her blond hair long enough to snake against the boards. The woman had turned and smiled at her. Lips green as algae. Glitter of salt on her cheeks. Simran had felt something slot into place, as if a golden key had slid its way neatly into a lock that lay in her heart. And Simran had known, with a hurtling, falling-through-yourself kind of knowing, that she was changed forever. Perhaps it had not been so before she had boarded the ship, but now the woman was her, and she was the woman, and she knew she had been born and lived and died on the Isle a hundred times, a thousand times.

There would be no safety on the Isle. It would be, horribly, *home*.

"Oh," the woman had said. "It's you. I'm finally dead."

She'd sounded pleased.

There was a tangle of streets near the docks where Elsewhere folk lived. Simran's flat was on Amoy Place, where the air was always full of the fumes of the laundries: astringent lye, lavender, sweat, soap. It was late enough that nearly all the laundries were shut, and the café where most of the laundry employees bought tea and bowls of dumplings in broth was closed too. The café's glass windows were cloudy, dusk colored.

Simran rented a flat above the café. The stairway at the café's left—a winding, narrow spiral that led to her door—was lit by a single paper lamp floating by itself above the first step. The paper was blue and the light seeping through it glowed green. The light fluttered as she approached, flickering like wing-beats, like welcome.

Her trembling heartbeat settled at the sight of it. This was her shelter. Nothing could hurt her here.

She leaned down and grasped the lantern, then held it aloft and used its light to guide her up the narrow stairs.

She closed the door of her flat and immediately wrenched off the cotehardie, tugging the last of the infinitesimal rows of tiny buttons at her front and her sleeves until she slithered free. She was naked, shivering under the spill of moonlight at the window. The lantern glowed coldly, painting her inky skin deep blue.

Around her, the scriptorium was peaceful. The cat Maleficium was sleeping on a pile of open books on the table. Three clocks were ticking out of sync on the mantelpiece, and Simran's needles and inks were still locked away in their wooden boxes, the latches shaped to open only to her fingers—which they did immediately when she crossed the room and reached for them, pressing her fingers to their thumb-shaped grooves. She slid the bottle of ink into her little casket of dyes—her blues and reds, her ichor black and serpent green. Then she tucked away her bone compass, watching the needle perform a wild spin, then still.

The bedroom door was open just a crack to give Maleficium the permanent access she demanded, but the room within looked dark. Hari was probably sleeping like the dead in there. That was fine. Simran had no plans to rest tonight.

She was still shivering, but that wasn't unreasonable. She was naked and river-wet and heart-sore and the fire grate was cold. She could fix three of those things. She tugged her robe free from the pile of unwashed clothes being steadily swallowed by her sofa, shoved her feet into a pair of slippers, then lit the grate. Once the fire was burning merrily, she opened the single narrow window of her scriptorium and placed the lantern outside it. The cold stung her fresh warming skin, but this couldn't wait.

"Go on," she said. "Shoo. Tell your mistress thank you from me." A nudge of her hand and the lantern crinkled into the shape of a bird, rustled its blue-green wings, and flew obediently away. The window closed with a heavy thud behind it.

She thought about placing her kidskin boots to dry over the grate, but before she could do it, all the strength left her body and she landed on her rug arse first with an audible—and painful—thud.

After a pause, Maleficium mewed inquiringly from her perch.

"Ow," Simran said flatly. "I'm not dead, you horrid creature. You can't eat my eyeballs yet."

A little chirp was her only response. Not a single jot of noise escaped the bedroom.

Simran let herself lie back against the floorboards. She closed her eyes, letting her own teeth chatter and chatter.

*Fuck fuckity fuck.*

Simran had seen the knight. She had looked into the knight's eyes and heard her old name on the knight's lips.

*Isadora.* The knight's voice curled like fire-licked paper in her mind. *Isadora.*

Isadora was not her name anymore.

Isadora was a dead socialite. A merry, laughing, absinthe-bitter only daughter of a wealthy mill owner. She'd started life wearing ribboned gowns and sitting quietly in countryside drawing rooms, and ended it wearing dresses that were sheaths of diamonds, peacock feathers in her hair. She'd loved jewelry—garnet drop earrings, carnelian set in silver as fine as lace at her throat. Ruby bracelets shaped like vipers. When the knight had run his sword through them both, the blood had been like a starburst against her chest—prettier than any brooch she'd ever worn against her heart. So Isadora had said, smiling with all her pretty white teeth, lips pearling to a shade of ice.

"You'll love him," Isadora had said. "Oh, you'll love him so much. Wait and see."

*Him.* Isadora had been wrong about that. And Simran hadn't fallen in love with the knight either. No bolt of love had struck her heart when she'd looked into Vina's eyes. Instead, when the tale had closed its snare around her heart, she'd felt afraid.

With a start, Simran realized she had fallen so deep into her own thoughts that her clocks had all begun to chime, marking midnight. Maleficium was purring insistently, pricking her throat with slightly elongated claws and licking her ear. At some point the furry abomination had alighted from her perch in order to menace Simran's face. Simran scratched the cat's ears absently.

There was a thud from her window. Simran sat up.

The lantern bird was pecking frantically at her windowpane, its paper beak bending under the pressure. Her clocks fell abruptly silent, and a chill of warning ran down her spine.

She stood, and turned to look at her door.

A second passed. Two.

There was a hard knock.

Maleficium skittered under the sofa, flattening until only her yellow eyes were visible.

Another knock.

"I should have gotten a dog," Simran whispered viperously in the general direction of the sofa, as she hurried across the room and drew open the drawer of her work table. She rifled through papers and books until her fingers found spells on parchment, sinewy thread, and cold, hard metal. Her heart was pounding. Blood roared in her ears. "A dog would have protected me but you—you protect yourself first, don't you?" She shut the drawer. "*Stay under there*," she hissed, knowing the cat neither understood her nor had any interest in respecting her wishes. She straightened, turned, and strode toward the front door.

She wrenched it open.

Without the flying lantern's illumination, the staircase was dark. She could only see the shape of the stranger. Broad shoulders, a bowed head. Hand raised for a third knock, the knuckles red with blood.

As for his face, she could only see his eyes. They were like the Thames. Bleached unnaturally pale, not blue or green or gray, but the color of the sun against a distant shore, always out of reach.

"Scribe," he said. His voice was wavering, a roiling sea, wretched and deep. "I...I'm afraid I require your help."

# Chapter Two

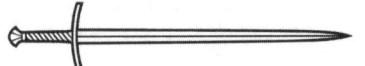

## *Vina*

*It was love. Love for Queen and country that brought the sword to his hands, and made him lay it against his love's lily-white breast. Love, that made him pierce her through.*

*There's no greater love, my brothers, than the one we have for this green and blessed land.*

Source: Parliamentary speech of MP Edward Morgan

**Archivist's Ruling: Preserve. Publication permitted. No further action required.**

When Vina was ten years old, she was examined by a scribe in her father's study.

The fire was crackling in the stone hearth. Her father's hunting dog lay asleep on the rug in front of it, snoring volubly. She stared down at her own feet, lifting and lowering her toes in her new brown brogues, the ones she'd begged for because she'd seen their thick golden buckles in the atelier's window and fallen in love with them.

Up, down. Up, down. She was already starting to crease the leather. She had not even had the chance to wear them outside yet.

*I should never have told anyone about the man crying in the orangery*, Vina thought, aggrieved. He'd been weeping a name over and over again. *Isadora, Isadora.* Vina had thought he was a burglar, or mad, or maybe both, and looking at him had made her feel as if she were floating outside her body, so she had run for help. But when she and the servants had returned, the man had been gone.

Through the crackle of flame and the dog's snores, she could hear the clink of the scribe's tools. Ink. Needle. Compass. The scribe coughed and turned, his robes rustling around him. Her father had assured her he was no *back-alley skin scribbler*, although she hadn't understood what that meant. This was a scribe from one of the best streets in Mayfair. He would look after her.

"Miss Lavinia," he said. "May I?"

She raised her head. His eyes were very blue, set in a wrinkled face. He smiled like a doctor, impersonal and kind.

"I don't know what you want me to do," she said.

"Give him your hand, Vinny," said her father. His voice boomed from behind his desk, where he sat in his large armchair. His forehead was pressed against his palm.

Vina held out her hand.

The scribe was an enormously tall man, and he loomed over as he leaned down and took her hand in his own. He held the needle aloft.

"Do you know what this is?"

Vina shook her head.

"Limni ink," he said. "The most precious of all inks, my dear. Ground from stone touched by the first incarnates, mined from the bowels of the Isle, quite precious indeed and quite finite. This bottle was taken from beneath the cavern of a witch," he told her, as he wetted his needle. The ink gathered on it like black pearls, or like the caviar the cook served at her father's dinner parties. "With this, normal ladies and gentlemen—like yourself and I—may gain the magic of a story, for a price."

With a light hand, he traced the needle in a swirl against her wrist. She tensed, expecting pain—but the needle moved so lightly it didn't cut her skin. It only left a tracery of ink behind it. The ink was in the shape of music—little flourishing notes like the ones on the book kept on the grand piano in the library.

"If you're a normal little girl, this will make you sing like an angel," the scribe said. "Of course, your voice will shrivel in your old age and take your breath with it, but such is the price of the gift of a story, my dear, it gives and it takes…"

Vina had no chance to protest. There was a sharp pain, as if a dozen needles were sliding into her skin at once. But there was only the one, driving hard into her wrist. It went in clean and oddly bloodless, as if the needle were passing through her and turning to smoke. The ink around it pulsed, shining like starlight, then abruptly dulled.

The room itself seemed to hold its breath.

Vina felt a chime in her skull. A bell ringing between her ears. Then her hand began to burn again, the pain so sharp she couldn't even scream. The ink glowed hotter and hotter, rising out of her skin—

It slithered to the floor like a ribbon and went still. The scribe leaned down and scooped it up in an empty vial.

"The tale didn't take," the scribe said, as if that meant something. "Congratulations."

Her father gave a low groan.

"Oh *hell*."

"Chin up," the scribe said to her father, slipping his vial of ink back into his pocket. "Your seat in Parliament's assured."

"Oh, I wouldn't be sure, once the papers start digging," her father muttered. He looked red and his face was damp with sweat. "Laura is going to murder me."

Laura was her father's wife. She'd always been nice enough to Vina, but Vina supposed there was probably a big difference between having your husband's bastard in your house and the papers gossiping about said bastard. And they would, when they knew what the scribe thought Vina was.

"An incarnate child is a blessing and an honor," the scribe said, reproof in his voice.

"Of course," her father agreed hastily. "But I had no reason to ever believe—that is, I thought the knight was meant to be, ah…" Her father's voice trailed off, but silence could have words in it too.

Vina looked down at her own hands. They were as brown as her mother's had been.

"Yes," the scribe said simply. "But there can be no doubt, I am afraid. Miss Lavinia is the knight who will slay the witch."

It took two hours for the others to free Vina from the witch's trap.

"Use a knife," Vina said, when they began.

"We tried the knife already," Matthias protested, as he rooted through his destrier's pack, sweaty and cursing under his breath as he drew out one talisman, then another.

"It's like getting a blade into the hinge of an oyster," she said helpfully, as Edmund dropped his sword and started waving iron and silver coins and crosses at the toadstool ring instead. "You just need to get the angle right."

They ignored her. She couldn't be angry about it, particularly. Blaming the lads for being useless was like blaming water for being wet.

"We shouldn't have let you come," Edmund said, kneeling beside her and flicking a silver coin between his fingers. He was frowning. "If we hadn't felt sorry for you—"

"I know," she sighed. "I'm nothing but trouble. Stick the knife into the toadstool to the left just to humor me, hm?"

After a good hour more of cajoling, Edmund finally tried it.

Now, Edmund and Matthias clambered onto the barge waiting for them at the edge of the Thames, sullenly untying the rope holding it against the bank and lighting the barge's torches. Vina tied up their destriers, then stood on the bank and met her own reflection in the water. Idly, she watched the way the water rippled, pushing her eyes and her mouth and her chin out of shape as the stomping of her fellow knights sent the water sloshing.

Edmund tripped lighting the last torch. He found his feet before he tipped overboard, which was a good thing. She wouldn't have wanted to watch him try to swim in full armor.

"You're an idiot, Vina, you know that?" Edmund burst out.

"Ah," she said. "Eddie, you wound me. You truly do."

Edmund gave an exasperated harrumph. "Fuck off," he said. He'd worked himself into a real lather. The knife incident must have really hurt his pride. "You had to flirt with the thief, didn't you? Had to show off and try and get into her knickers, and look where we are now. If the Queen decides we need our heads lopped off it's your fault."

"She's not going to touch my head," Vina said. "I think we'll all be fine."

"Why? Have you seduced her too?"

Godsblood, you sleep with a man's sister once, and he'll truly never forgive you.

"She's an incarnate," Matthias said. He sounded thoroughly fed up. Under his helm, she could see the twist of his mouth, the red of his cropped beard. "She's got to live to play her role."

"If it comes to it, I'll tell the Queen that I've vowed to live and die with you, or some rot like that," Vina said, grinning at Edmund, who scowled back. "She'll have to let you live, then. No need to fear for your precious neck any longer, Eddie."

"Oh, shut up," said Edmund.

"Get on here, Lavinia," Matthias ordered, knocking his shoulder softly against Edmund's. *Peace.* "The sooner we get the ink to the archives, the sooner we can go home."

She climbed onto the barge. As soon as she was onboard, the torches flickered, shivering from gold to the white-and-rose of the Queen's heraldry. The barge lurched, then began to move through the water on its own, the mirror-bright surface of the Thames splitting around it like pearls of mercury.

The city loomed around them in ripples of thatched roofs and smog-stained slate, white colonnades and stained glass windows. Usually Vina loved seeing the city like this. But tonight she wasn't herself.

She touched her gloved fingers to the satchel at her side.

It didn't feel lighter, but she knew the witch had reached into it and stolen the ink she desired. Maybe she'd only taken a single vial. That was all she'd asked for.

Vina hadn't told the others any ink had been stolen. If there was trouble at the archives over it, Vina would take responsibility. No one expected any better of her anyway.

A sense memory stole over her. The brush of the witch's breath. Her eyes, flatly furious under her own snapping firelight.

Maybe she hadn't been *the* witch. If Vina kept telling herself that, perhaps she'd soon believe it. Maybe the woman under that hood had been nothing more than a thief with a few enchantments to her name and fire in her fingertips. Maybe she'd paid a scribe to mark her up with limni ink to get all the magic she had. Maybe, maybe.

But the air had tasted like an old penny—rusty, bloody. And when Vina had met her eyes she'd seen the weeping man in the orangery so clearly that it had been as if she were ten years old again, watching him bow his head between his hands, his golden hair soaked to copper by blood, howling like a wounded animal. She'd felt a loose knot in her chest abruptly draw tight, stealing her breath. Her tale had trapped her like a noose.

*Isadora. Isadora. My love, my darling, not again, no—*

The barge jerked. She heard Edmund curse again, then settle back into silence.

She was sure he and Matthias hadn't heard her call the thief Isadora. Somehow, by luck or whatever trickery tales liked to pull, they hadn't heard the wretchedness in Vina's voice.

They didn't know her tale would soon begin, which meant they didn't pity her.

She set a hand on the edge of the barge. She was amazed at how still her hand was. She wasn't trembling at all.

The Tower soon loomed above them. Even in the shadows and torchlight of the night she could see the ravens circling overhead, their wings spread. The air seemed to grow colder as they grew closer to the gates that surrounded it. Tale-scent filled the air: iron and ink, blood and apples alike. She inhaled, and the smell of the Queen's archives filled her lungs.

As an incarnate, Vina had learned long ago that her purpose was to live out her tale. *To embody the tale is to keep it alive*, her stepmother Laura had told her gently, when Vina had first learned what she was. She'd pressed *Incarnate Tales for Children* into Vina's hands. Vina remembered, even now, the red leather of its binding, sticky from the sweat of her own hands as she'd clutched it tight. *Your value is beyond measure.*

*But tales need more than incarnates to live, darling. They need to be read. A tale read is a tale that can feast, nestling in your mind and growing strong. Read wisely, dear Lavinia. Keep the tales steadfast in your heart.*

Vina had kept that book with her when she'd been led away to her new life. And in the royal Palace, alongside her fellow knights, she'd learned that a tale told wrong was a capital crime. Changing tales, altering them—penning heresies—risked destroying the tales entirely, and the Isle with them.

To protect the Isle, the Queen's archivists maintained and preserved all canonical texts inside the Tower's walls. Every single book and newssheet published across the Isle also passed under their careful eyes before reaching people's hands.

She knew that the quiet, pervasive power of the archivists was necessary...but as she gazed up at the circling ravens, and the Queen's rose flag, dun and dark in the night's smog, she was grimly reminded that the Tower was not only an archive but a prison. Death lingered in its foundations.

When Vina had heard from Edmund's sweet, gossipy sister that he and Matthias had been given a plum quest to carry limni ink to the Tower in the dead of night...

Well, she was hardly going to let them stumble into trouble alone. She'd always had a good nose for danger, and the archives reeked of stories and danger alike. In her experience, they often went hand in hand.

Their barge led them to the Traitor's Gate, that arch of stone rising from the river. It opened at their approach with a clank and a groan. The silver water rippled around their barge as it swept beneath the darkness of the gate's arch. Beyond it, waiting on the steps, was an archivist, cowl pulled up so only her chin and the long gray braid of her hair was visible. Above her, on the walls of the Bloody Tower, perched a watchful line of ravens who cocked their heads in something like greeting.

"You're late," said the archivist.

"Entirely my fault," Vina said, jumping lightly onto the stone steps that awaited them. She bowed, then straightened. "I'm afraid we got a little caught up." She smiled.

The archivist did not smile back.

"Come with me," the archivist replied dourly, and turned. "*Quickly*, sir knights."

They followed her swiftly up the stairs and across the grounds of the Tower, beyond the Bloody Tower and Wakefield Tower alike, through the inner fortifications: gray and imposing defensive walls guarded by Yeoman Warders in their starched liveries, their faces wan and blank. Distantly, Vina could hear sobbing, high and childish. The screams and wails of the Tower's long-dead prisoners, no doubt. Matthias murmured a soft prayer under his breath.

Vina, who never prayed, started humming.

It took Matthias a full minute to realize *what* she was humming, and half a second longer to kick her in the ankle.

"You can't sing bawdy songs here," he hissed.

"It's good I wasn't saying the words, then, isn't it?" Vina replied, and resumed her efforts to psychologically torture her fellow knights with another round of "The Miller's Song."

New ghostly cries filled the air as they entered the grandest edifice on the Tower's grounds. The White Tower, as pale as its name, glowed coldly in the dark. Vina finally let her voice fade in her throat as they clambered up its many stairs, passing grim warders with their hands on their sword hilts.

"Ignore the noises," the archivist said, as ghostly wails rose up from the basement and clamored in Vina's ears. "The ghosts are bound with chains of limni ink. They can't cause us any harm."

They followed her up a narrow staircase. The higher they climbed, the more the wailing faded and the more new sound welled up in its place: shouting, running, bangs. As they reached the third narrow landing, an archivist slammed open the door ahead of them, the wood bouncing against stone.

"You have the ink?" the man snapped. "Yes? Well, come here and hand it to me!"

Matthias shoved Vina's shoulder and she strode up the stairs, taking off the satchel and handing it to the archivist. It was snatched without thanks and the man ran back into the room. The woman who had guided them up lowered her hood, revealing a tense, exhausted face, mouth wrinkled with lines of deep tension. She strode in after him.

Vina, Matthias, and Edmund exchanged looks. The archivist had not told them to follow, but she also hadn't ordered them not to. They were knights, so they did what came naturally and followed her into the fray. Matthias and Edmund drew their swords with a high-pitched whine of steel. Vina kept her own sheathed. She couldn't imagine what use a sword would be against books.

Vina was closest to the door, so she was the first to feel the gut-punch of a tale. It slammed into her, *through* her. Her mouth filled with the taste of hot pennies, and her ears filled with a buzzing: a low howl like a horde of bees, or a roaring sea; a tide of tale-spinning, rising and rising and clawing at the walls of stone and mortal flesh to force its way free. It held her frozen as Matthias and Edmund bullied their way farther into the room, leaving her by the door.

The air was howling, a tempest of wind whipping against the circular flagstone walls. Despite its ferocity, the torches hadn't guttered out. Instead they were huge wild discs of light wheeling in their sconces, billowing with the yells of the five archivists inside the chamber. They were standing in a crescent, their cowls flying behind their skulls, their eyes narrowed against the storm.

Each of the five archivists around them now held a vial of limni ink, empty vials scattered at their feet, and ribbons of ink were spinning through the air, converging on the circular table at the center of the room. With their voices and their hands, they were controlling the ink, but they were struggling to get it to obey them. Vina felt limni ink whip through the air and splatter against her exposed chin—a burn, hotter than starlight. Then it fell inert against her armor with a hiss.

"What the shit," Edmund whispered fervently. Matthias drew his shield up, angling to stand in front of them both. Vina, grimly assured now that swords weren't going to do them much good, slammed the door properly shut with her booted foot and kept her heel against the wood for good measure. Whatever was flying around this room had no business leaving it.

On the table, burning in fire that wasn't fire, in white flames that flickered in and out of existence like night terrors, lay a book.

It was an old book, an illuminated text with rich, flowing script in diamonds of bloodred and ichor black. Its binding was leather, tooled with images of rowan berries and thorns. It was open at the center, the spine cracked, the pages torn into fissures like dry earth. As Vina watched, another page began to splinter, the ink crawling from it, leeching color from the page. "*More,*" an archivist ordered, and more limni ink spooled across the page, pressing words and images back into place. "More, damn you!"

There was a blast.

The book *tore*. The sound of it was terrible, like a high scream and like flesh being pared. It did not sound like simple paper, easily mended. It sounded like death.

Ink gathered together like a cudgel and slammed its way toward the door. Matthias squared his feet against the ground, bracing his shield for the blow. Vina, thinking fast, shoved herself flat against the door. If her one job was to keep whatever lay in that book from escaping, then she was going to do it.

The ink hit them hard. This was not brief, star-sharp pain. It was all-consuming. Blackness swathed her vision, and against it she saw brief fragments of a story play out before her eyes. A fae woman in winter, cold-eyed, her heartless face lit by the brightness of new-fallen snow. A knight, kneeling at her feet, his face stricken and starved. She knew his face.

*Soren?*

Abruptly the ink—and the darkness—were gone.

She blinked. Matthias was holding one of the archivists upright. Edmund was standing in front of her, trying to shake ink from his sword. "You know, I don't think swords are meant to fight books," he muttered. "It's not right."

Small fragments of paper were flurrying through the air like snow.

Vina caught one piece on her outstretched palm. It was blank. In her mind, something was gone too—a name on the tip of her tongue, a half memory of something on a shoreline. Coastal mountains? A village?

One of the archivists laughed bitterly, hands on their knees as they bent forward.

"What do you think we've lost this time? The White Cliffs of Dover? The Forest of Arden?"

"Well, if you can remember their names—"

"We'll discuss it later," another said, and Vina felt their eyes on her. Five pairs of eyes, and a tale flickering in and out of focus behind her own.

"Vina," Edmund was saying, his voice low and alarmed. She felt Matthias's hand close around her arm. "What's wrong? *Vina?*"

She'd slumped back against the door at some point. "Terribly sorry," she said faintly. "But I don't think I can stand."

"I'll take her, sir knight," said one archivist hurriedly. He was young. There was a crack in his glasses from the storm, and the torchlight reflected strangely on it, turning one of his brown eyes into a starburst. He gave Vina a concerned smile and grasped her by the shoulders. "Come with me," he said gently. "Let's get you sat down."

He led her out of the room. He guided her carefully to the ground, letting her tip her head back.

"How do you feel, sir knight?"

"Fit as a fiddle," she said. "Just let me catch my breath."

"The ink disturbed you," the archivist murmured, brow creased. "Harmed you, I think. You're an incarnate."

"I am," Vina agreed absently, slumping into a heap. She was worried she was going to vomit. Fun.

"You were not summoned for this task," the archivist said, voice hushed. "We would never have allowed an incarnate here. You're far too sensitive to the magic of books and ink. You shouldn't touch the ink, sir knight. It causes your kind pain. There's too much tale-magic in you already."

"I came for a lark," she said weakly. "More fool me."

She sat up. Her armor felt heavier than it ever had before.

"What was that?" Vina asked. "That—wildness?"

"A tale dying," the archivist replied. He raised his hand from her shoulder and pushed his glasses up. A thumbprint of ink was left on the bridge of his nose. "You're Minister Morgan's daughter," he said. It was not a question, but archivists weren't questioners. They said how things were. Named them. *A tale dying. Minister Morgan's daughter.* But she nodded, and he nodded slowly in return, and said, "I have a message for your father. Something—private."

Private? Intriguing.

"I'll be happy to pass it on."

"Tell him to add the Tale of the Merciless Maiden to the list of the lost. And tell him... tell him he has a body to find. The body will have a circle carved into its forehead. That's how we'll know." The archivist swallowed. "Either a fae woman—he'll have to contact the Lords—or a human man. An incarnate. His name—"

"Soren," said Vina. "Soren Aldershot-Wilkins. He's—he's the incarnate of the lovelorn knight. From the Tale of the Merciless Maiden."

"Ah. Yes."

"I know him," said Vina helplessly.

"*Ah.* Then I am sorry." He patted her hand. "I'm afraid he may be—well. I'm sorry."

Her head was spinning. She wished it weren't. She did not know Soren well, but she'd still been close to him in the way only known incarnates were. Once as teenagers after a ball they'd snuck away and stolen the better part of a cask of cider, climbed on a roof, and shared secrets, apple-drunk, dancing shoes kicked off and sparkling under the moonlight. Soren had said, *I avoid the countryside because I don't want to meet her. The fae maiden who I'll die pining for. That bitch. The love of my life.*

*It's foolish perhaps, but what incarnate hasn't resisted their fate, eh, Vina?*

"I shouldn't have told you any of this," the archivist said in a rush. "But this can't be kept quiet any longer. Something has to be done."

He rose to his feet, brushing the creases from his robes with trembling hands.

"Did someone kill Soren?" Vina heard herself ask, as if from somewhere far away. "Is someone killing incarnates?"

The door opened and Matthias poked his head around the corner. "Are you feeling better, Lavinia?"

Of all the bloody timing.

"Yes," said Vina lightly. "Very much."

She looked up at the archivist. He'd taken off his glasses and was rubbing them clean on his sleeve, not looking at her.

"I'm glad to hear it," the archivist said, formal now. "The Queen's archivists thank you for your service, fair knight. If you're feeling better, we'll happily escort you back to your barge and see you on your way."

# Chapter Three

## *Simran*

*The Elsewhere population on the Isle continues to grow uncontrollably. My gentle friends, if you ever question whether the Elsewhere-born are a canker on the Isle, I encourage you to visit the slums they populate. Look at Limehouse, riddled with crime and disease. Turn your gaze on the industrious hamlets that border our capital, now infested with Elsewhere folk, who take our jobs in the factories and fields alike. It cannot be borne, friends. I ask you now: What will Parliament do to stem the tide?*

Source: Article in *The Mail*, "A Curse on Our Shores" by David Auden

**Archivist's Ruling: Preserve. Publication permitted. No further action required.**

"You don't need a scribe," Simran said. "You need a doctor."

She could hear the drip of his blood, a steady thud against the front step.

"A doctor can't fix me," he replied.

"You're bleeding," Simran said flatly. "That strikes me as a *perfect* problem for a doctor—not for me."

"Blood, I can fix myself," he said. "But I can't write a story into my own skin. For that, I need you."

"It might be worth you going to Marylebone—Harley Street's known for its scribes. I wish you luck, sir." She began to close the door.

He stumbled forward. There was no *intent* in the way he moved, even as he lumbered through the door onto his knees, then his back. He moved like the tide had brought him here, a shipwreck washing to shore—or in this case, to Simran's floorboards.

"Get up," she said, exasperated.

"I was told a scribe lived in Limehouse," he said, his face sweaty and tilted up toward her own. "An Elsewhere woman, brown-skinned. *Go to her,* I was told. *She will give you everything you need.* Please, I know you're her. Don't turn me away."

He was far enough into the room that Simran was just about able to nudge the front door shut. He lay with his head on the edge of the rug. She circled him, aware of her bare legs, the ridiculousness of her fluffy slippers—and conversely, the tangled weight of magic in the pockets of her robes, and the steady, simmering power in her blood.

For all his broadness, he looked pitiful on the floor. She wouldn't let that knock the wariness out of her.

"And what do you need a scribe for?" she asked.

"Life," he said simply.

Simran kneeled down beside him, the floor rug cushioning her knees.

"Limni ink isn't the gift you think it is," she said. "It can't mend your bones, or take the canker out of your liver. It's not the kind of magic that heals, you understand? It just stitches a little bit of a tale into you. If you want to be a better dancer, or strong as an ox—limni ink can do that for you, for a price. But it can't fix you, all right?"

Simran had given the same spiel more times than she could count. She'd seen so very many desperate people in her scriptorium, eyes liquid, hands clenched, begging her for help. She knew how this went: She was treading familiar boards, spinning familiar words by rote. So she was ready when he said, voice rough from pain, "What price?"

"The shape of your death," she replied. "Sometimes you *can* believe the rumors in the coffeehouse papers. What they say about limni ink magic is true. The gift you get from the ink will decide the way you die. You want the power of flight? You'll die falling. Want to be farsighted? Something you can't see, can't predict, will come hurtling for you on your death day. And so on." She shrugged. "Also, I take payment in cash. No bartering. If you want to come back when you're not bleeding out, we can discuss cost."

"And if I want immortality?"

"You won't find that in limni ink," she said. "You won't find that anywhere."

He rolled onto his stomach, then up onto his elbows. She heard his harsh breath. He was a strange-looking man, his face angular, his body broad-shouldered and brutish, his skin and hair as pale as limestone. His eyes were as pale as the rest of him, a silver-gold shot through with pink blood from pain or exhaustion.

"Then I'll take another gift, if you'll help me," he said.

"Go on."

Slowly, he raised his head.

"Help me, witch," he said, with liquid-eyed sincerity, "by letting me kill you."

She went very still.

She hadn't let her guard down. She'd known there was something amiss before he'd even drifted in through her door, all blood and bulk and damp eyes. But that didn't stop her stomach from plummeting, or her body going very cold, then very hot, as fear and anger started to burn up inside her. Furiously, she realized he was not really hurt at all. Beneath the blood on his knuckles, his skin was unblemished. He'd tricked her.

"Get out," she said, voice low.

"Don't reject me out of hand, witch," he said. His voice had changed—the pain in it was gone, leaving nothing but the storm-darkness beneath it. "You only know the shape of your tale, but not the way it will cut through your tendons, crack the marrow of your bones. You are just meat to be slaughtered to feed this island, but the slaughter itself—it will hurt you in ways you can't fathom. Let me kill you now, lay down your life, and I'll make it gentle."

Simran stood up. She stepped back; one step, two. She never took her eyes off him.

"If you know what I am," she said, low, "then you know what I will do to you if you don't leave now."

"Do you dream of your deaths, witch? A knife through the heart, an axe through the belly. All of them wielded by such beloved hands. I pity you. You should pity yourself." He rose to his knees, then to his feet. He wasn't swaying anymore. "Have you ever considered escaping your tale—taking a knife to your own throat, or supping from poison? Perhaps you haven't. But your life isn't your own to take. You can feel it, I'm sure—the tale's claws in your veins, holding you like a puppet on strings. If you tried, your hands would turn against your will. I followed the scent of the story on you. I know its strength." His voice made her skin crawl. The plea in it was blazing. "Let me be the hands you need."

"I don't know who you are," said Simran. "I don't know how you know me. But I will drip a curse into your eyes that makes you see waking nightmares. I will curse your footsteps with knives. I will set the teeth of imps in your veins, so you never rest. Don't fuck with a witch, you bastard. *Get out.*"

"Oh, Isadora," he said, shaking his head. "So much sharper this time than the last, aren't you? Close your eyes, I beg you. I'll free you so swiftly, it will be like sleep."

She stumbled away from him, and he moved forward, both his feet on the rug. It was enough.

She snapped her fingers and he froze. His breath left his mouth raggedly. His eyes, unblinking, were cold and wide with fury. The trap she'd drawn when she first set up her scriptorium—carved from bone-ash and thorns from grave-grown flowers, and hidden neatly beneath her rug—held him fast. At the skin of his throat, she could see the shadow of her magic ripple through his flesh.

"I told you I'd make you pay," Simran said. "Can you feel thorns under your skin, stranger? Does it hurt like a thousand knives? It should. And I can do so much more than this, if you're not honest with me. Who sent you here? Why do you want me dead?" She circled him. "Speak," she commanded, and his mouth was freed from the compulsion that held the rest of him.

"It was Bess who told me where to find you, and what you are, witch. I met her in Gore," he said. "Beneath the blackthorn tree, where the ghost deer roam and the heathen temple stands."

A punch of breath left her.

"What have you done to Bess?" she demanded.

His mouth shaped a smile.

"Let me go and I'll show you," he said. "No? Then allow me."

His arms rose up.

Magic required specific tools to be broken. Magic came from tales, and tales had *rules*. Silver to break a fairy ring. Keen eyes to find the shape of an enchantment: the illusory toadstool, or the magic door beneath the veil of an archway or a common wall. Binding vows with one singular loophole, and magic traps with lines that had to be broken to set the snared prey free.

The stranger tore through the magic trap—and the rules—as if they didn't matter at all. One sweep of his arms, and the trap was burning, the floorboards russet with embers. Simran was hit with a blast of her own magic, spelled thorns ripping through her veins in a sudden shock of bright-hot pain.

She screamed.

Maleficium skittered out from under the sofa, a many-legged, panicking pancake of fluff. Simran's heart plummeted with fear for the silly creature and she scrabbled across the floor, grabbing Mal around her ruffled middle. The stranger was moving behind her, floorboards creaking, his breath a warning at her back. But it was a noise from her bedroom that made her jerk her head up.

Hari was standing in the doorway of the bedroom, wide-eyed and open-mouthed, in nothing but his boxers and a half-open shirt.

"Shut the door," Simran snapped, and flung Maleficium at him.

Maleficium yowled, and Hari screamed, and then man and cat met in a frenzy of fur and claws. It wasn't clear if he'd caught her or if Mal had simply latched onto him with every single one of the knives in her feet, but the effect was the same. By some miracle, Hari managed to pin Maleficium safely against his chest, flail back into the bedroom, and kick the door shut as he did so.

Simran whirled around, but it was too late to react. The stranger bore down on her, slamming her to the ground. Her head hit the singed floorboards with an audible crack. She felt the shock of it reverberate through her shoulders, her spine, her hips. Then all she felt was his hands pinning her.

"A witch from *India*," he said, and the Elsewhere-name blurred and scratched at the insides of her skull. "I thought maybe you'd be different this time, that you'd found your own way out of your tale, but your scent is the same. I followed you, witch, your copper and your winter moss, your bitter snow-blood scent, *his* honey strangeness on you, and here you are. The skin changes, but you stay the same under it." He leaned closer. "I smell the knight on you," he said. "It's begun."

She struggled under him. He was immovable. One arm was in his grasp at the wrist, but the other was pinned against her side.

Her left hand was the one pinned. Thank fuck it was her left hand. She squirmed, finding the shape of her dressing gown pocket.

"I know all about you," he said. "I know all your names." He pinned her harder. She scrabbled in the pocket and metal met her fingertips. Frightened, triumphant, she grasped it.

"You shouldn't fight me," he went on, pale eyes fixed on her. "I know all your tricks, your enchantments, your magics."

"Not all of them," she said, and fired her pistol into his stomach.

The shock of the gunshot knocked her back against the floor hard and made him spasm above her, an awful, wrenching noise escaping his mouth. She scrambled out from under him, hot metal in her hand. The torn rug and burnt floorboards were splashed with blood, and Simran's hands ached.

She cocked the pistol to kill him—and froze as he began to laugh. There was no pain in his voice. His laugh was deep and pleased.

"I told you I don't need a doctor," he said. "But I admit the blood is inconvenient."

On his forehead a symbol flared, glowing a virulent red: a single empty circle. His face had been bare before, she was sure—and as she watched, the symbol faded to nothing.

She tasted a tale on the air, hot pennies on her tongue, the musk of iron-rich blood. She didn't know him—not like she'd known the knight—but she knew what he was. She couldn't help but know.

"You're an incarnate," she spat out.

He shook his head.

"You understand so little," he said. "Yourself. Me. The ink you stitch into people's skin." He took another step forward.

She shot him again in the chest. He jerked back but stayed on his feet, gaze darkening with anger. The circle flared again, blood-metal flowering on Simran's tongue in response.

"No," she said decisively. "I'm sure. You're definitely an incarnate." Her hands shook around the pistol, but she didn't need to keep her hands steady any longer. Every hidden spell in the walls and ceiling began to shine, fireless smoke rising from their surfaces. The stranger winced as her magic seared out of her wards, clasping him in golden tendrils.

Let him try and break all the magic she'd written and bled into this room; this scriptorium where she'd worked her arts for more than a year. Perhaps some would say she was arrogant and overconfident, but she didn't care. She was a scribe and a witch, and she was damnably good at being both. Inside her and beyond her skin, her magic burned hotter than sunlight.

He turned his head back, forth, wrenching against her magic. The circle on his forehead flared again. Simran *pushed*, all her strength pouring from her, and the stranger flinched and stopped trying to fight.

His gaze fixed on her again. His expression calmed. He held his hands out, palms open.

"Fine, witch," he said. "Whatever you wish. But you should have let me kill you. One day you will weep bitterly, because I did not. You would have been happier if you'd allowed it."

The magic coalesced around him, golden around his face, turning his shadow to glowing stardust. Another breath, and he was gone—banished from her home.

The scriptorium was silent. On the walls, Simran's wards dimmed. Simran took four careful steps to her desk. Placed the pistol down.

"You can come out now, Hari," she said faintly.

Then she collapsed to the ground.

She woke with Hari leaning over her. A cold wind was blowing in through the open door. Simran cleared her throat, trying to find her voice through the cotton-wool weight in her own skull.

"Why is the door...?" Simran began.

"That's my fault. I climbed out of the bedroom window and went to get some help," Hari said. "If I'd known you were going to get rid of him I would have gone out the front door obviously, but—anyway, it doesn't matter. When I ran back up the stairs, the door wasn't locked so I just left it. Lydia's coming in a second anyway and—oh *shit*, did you burn the floor?"

"Not on purpose," Simran said grouchily. She sat up, wincing. Her magic was depleted. She felt wrung out, dull, and very human.

Hari was still taking the damage in, his eyes narrowed as his gaze swept over the burnt floor, the torn rug. His focus finally landed on a hole in the wall.

"Did you shoot him?" he asked. He knew about the pistol she kept in her desk. They'd argued about it before.

*No good comes from weapons like that, Sim. They've only got one kind of tale in them, and it's one where someone ends up dead.*

*And what do you think witchcraft is, Hari? A gentle hug?*

"I did," Simran said, turning away from the troubled light in

Hari's eyes. "But I didn't kill him." She should have. She'd *tried*. "I banished him instead."

Hari lowered his voice.

"Did he get any of the ink?"

Simran shook her head. It was fair of Hari to assume the stranger had come for the limni ink. It was the only valuable thing in their whole flat.

"Right." Hari exhaled. "Do you think he'll be back?"

"If he tries to get back here on foot it'll take a while." She'd traced the traps on her walls using ash from a lusterless copse of woodland at a crossroads beyond London, where green trees met an everburning pit of factory fires. That was where the intruder had landed. He'd have a hell of a time traveling back from there, buffeted by winds of soot and navigating dying woodland. "But who knows what else he can do. Maybe he's a witch too. Is Maleficium all right?"

"I think she's scarred me for life," Hari said. "But yes, your demon from the bowels of hell is fine. I left her in the cupboard."

"Are you going to let her out?"

He shuddered.

"Maybe when she stops hissing," he said.

There was a light thud of footsteps approaching. Simran turned her head to the door.

Lydia Chen, Simran and Hari's landlady, stood at the top of the stairs. She was dressed like she'd just risen from her bed, in practical sandals over socks, a thick quilted coat, a single lantern bird perched on her shoulder. She was middle-aged, skin lightly brown and her hair more black than silver, pinned back now in a hasty bun.

Lydia had always been good in a crisis, and her expression now was calm. Her eyes scanned the room, moving from Simran to the singed floorboards to the fading glow of spells on the walls.

"Well," said Lydia. "You're going to need to pay to fix this damage, Simran, make no mistake. I told you not to put magic in the floorboards, didn't I?"

"That magic saved my life."

"And I'm glad to see you not dead," Lydia said. "But I'd be even gladder if you'd painted your trap into the rug *you* own. I'll never get those burn marks out. I'll have to take stock of the damage properly later." She crossed the room and peered down at Simran. The lantern bird rustled, preening itself. "And you?" she asked.

"My damage? I'm all right," said Simran. "Could you help me up?"

Hari and Lydia got her up onto the sofa. Lydia's forehead was creased, her mouth thin and troubled.

"Did he come for the ink? Or did he follow a curse and find you at the end of it?" Lydia demanded.

"I didn't curse him," Simran said. "If I had, I would have made sure he couldn't find me."

"He didn't take any ink," Hari said. He was by her desk, holding her unopened box of limni ink. "All's well."

Lydia's frown only deepened. Simran understood. If the man had gotten what he'd wanted, it was likely he wouldn't return. But he'd been trapped and banished with nothing to show for it. There was a big chance he'd come back, if only for revenge.

Simran owed Lydia. She and Hari had met Lydia at a molly-house in their early days in the city, when Simran had been all sharp knees and a sharper tongue, and Hari was still wearing his hair long, just in case he wanted to go home to his parents, who refused to see him for the man he was. Simran and Hari were friends. When they'd met as two lonely queer and Elsewhere-born children being raised in the same town outside London, they'd needed each other—but they'd *liked* each other too, and it was the liking that had made them leave home together to forge a new life. They'd both been lost in London, naïve and young and desperately in need of a guiding hand. Lydia had been chain-smoking, levelheaded, and unbearably kind. She was a cunning woman, a wielder of good magic and blessings. There was no one wiser in London than Lydia, who knew every cunning folk worth their salt, and gathered London's Elsewhere communities around her like kin. She'd looked at the two of them, and truly *seen* them, and welcomed them with open arms.

She'd introduced Hari to a few of the other trans boys and girls at the molly-house—"We're your family now," she'd told him—lent Simran the money for her first scribe needles, and offered them the flat at a rent they could actually afford.

Lydia was the reason Simran had a scriptorium, a warm bed, and a life she was loath to lose. So Simran meant it when she leaned forward and vowed, coldly, "I'll find him and deal with him. He won't cause any more trouble. I'll see to that."

Lydia sighed, her face softening. "Witches," she said. "You're all the same—vengeful to the core."

Her lantern bird rustled in agreement.

Cunning folk usually had little patience for witches. Simran understood that. Cunning folk were benevolent, where witches were not. But Lydia had never been dismissive of Simran, and she didn't seem inclined to start now. The hand she placed on Simran's shoulder was firm and grounding.

"You could move," she said. "Berry's got a spare room in her flat. She'd be glad of the company."

*You don't need to hunt this man down*, Lydia didn't say. But Simran understood.

"Please look after Hari for me," she said. "I won't be gone more than a week."

Simran freed Maleficium after Lydia left, and bribed the rather angry cat with slivers of baked ham. Hari made two cups of tea and sat on the floor beside her.

Hari drank deep, but Simran couldn't touch her tea. Her stomach was squirming.

"He wasn't here for the ink," said Simran.

"What did he want, then?"

She didn't reply. *He wants me because I'm an incarnate*, she thought of saying. But that was a thing she'd never shared with Hari and never wanted to.

"He mentioned Bess," said Simran finally.

His hands tightened around his mug.

"Ah," he said.

Hari had grown up with her. There were only very specific things she'd kept from him; her incarnate status was one of them. But Bess wasn't a secret. He knew Bess was an incarnate.

Bess was the one who'd helped Simran become a witch.

"Hari," she said. "I think he's done something to her. I think... I think I'm going to have to visit home."

Hari exhaled and closed his eyes.

"Well, hell," he said. "I guess we're going to Gore."

# Chapter Four

## *Vina*

What is a knight? On the Isle, we sing tales of chivalry and honor, love and duty. But I think folk don't talk enough about violence. A knight's an instrument of the State, and that instrument is used to enforce the status quo with violence. If they were just signs of purity, of goodness, they wouldn't need the big bloody swords, would they?

Source: *Arguments for Republic,* Pamphlet acquired at King's Coffee House

**Archivist's Ruling: For retention as evidence of treason. Review in 5 years. Further investigation required.**

The Palace of Westminster, like all of London, never truly slept. But it was late enough or early enough that there were only a handful of cleaners mopping the checkerboard floors. The candelabras and gas lamps were both dimmed, leaving the corridors shadow-stained.

Vina was still in her armor, and she clattered noisily through the halls, past the vine-wrought door of the House of Lords and the grand meeting hall of the House of Commons. Since there was no point in trying for stealth, she whistled tunelessly as she walked. Maybe making noise would cover her own nerves.

Her father's office stood alone at the end of a corridor lined with paintings of important, bewigged men. She rapped smartly on the door, then without further ceremony, shoved it open.

"Vinny," her father said. He pushed his glasses up his nose, blinking at her in surprise and dismay. "It's the middle of the bloody night, what are you doing here?"

Her father's office was oppressive, windowless and paneled in dark mahogany. Her father was seated in his wingback armchair, official documents in small type arranged in a pile in front of him. He grabbed a folder as she approached and unsubtly perched it on top of the mound of papers, concealing the writing from her.

"You sleep here whenever there's a crisis," Vina said, slouching back in the armchair opposite her father. It was uncomfortable, more wood and springs than upholstery, and she knew he'd designed it that way intentionally so his political guests wouldn't linger. But Vina was nothing if not stubborn, and she contorted herself with all the deranged limberness of a cat, kicking one leg over the armrest and draping her elbow over the curved chair back. "Give me the gossip. Has the Queen slept with another handsome courtier and upset the balance of power again?"

"You came to my office," her father said slowly, "to ask for gossip."

"So no one knows about her new love, then," murmured Vina, just to rile him. "Interesting."

"Lavinia," her father said, through obviously gritted teeth.

"I've just finished a quest, Father," she said. "But I heard some strange things, out at the Tower—do you know tales have been dying?"

He thinned his lips at her, which she took as a yes.

"*Why* are tales dying?" Vina asked.

"We don't know," he said, voice clipped. "What were you doing on a quest? You were expressly ordered to remain on State grounds."

"Was I? I thought it was more guidance, you know. A suggestion." She paused, relishing the twitch of his jaw. Then said, "I was given a message for you. An archivist told me—tell Minister Morgan to look for the body of a fae woman, or the knight from the Merciless Maiden. They'll have a circle carved on their brow. So here I am. Telling you."

He exhaled; a slow, long noise.

"Poor lad," he said finally. Another pause. "The archivists shouldn't have spoken to you."

*Poor lad.* It was Soren who'd died, then. The weight of that knowledge settled heavily in her chest.

Her father hadn't expected Soren's death, but he certainly wasn't surprised by it.

"Is someone killing incarnates?"

"You should never have met the archivists," said her father. "That isn't work for your kind."

"It's knightly work."

"It's not *incarnate* work, and you're only a knight by dint of your nature," said her father. "You shouldn't have known about this. You should have stayed where you were told to."

"Shouldn't I know if I'm in danger?" Vina asked. "If someone is murdering incarnates, then I *am* in danger, Father."

He said nothing.

Of course he knew she was in danger. Silly of her to point it out, really. It was clearly why she'd been ordered, in a terse missive left in her room in the royal barracks, to remain on State property: the Palace grounds, or governmental offices, or other boring buildings she had no interest in staying in.

Vina was used to being given instructions that made no real sense. What was logical about being bid to seek out questing beasts, or play riddles with elves, or save strange women from towers? Still, she should have questioned *this* order. Its very prosaicness should have raised her suspicions.

"You could have warned me," she said quietly. "Perhaps then I'd have seen the point in staying cooped up."

"There was no reason to worry you. Besides, the fewer who know, the better." He drummed his fingers anxiously against his desk.

"Soren was... It doesn't matter. You're in no danger if you stay in the royal barracks. I promise. Relax, Vinny."

"Will Soren have a funeral? No, don't tell me—I know he won't."

The death of an incarnate before their story was enacted was more than a scandal. It was a *catastrophe*. Parliament wouldn't allow the truth to get out if they could avoid it. He'd have a secret funeral. Maybe even his parents wouldn't be told.

"This killer," said Vina, leaning forward in a way that made the chair groan alarmingly. "Are they being hunted? Who have you sent after them? Forgive me for saying so, but this sounds quite worrying, Father."

"Quite worrying," he repeated. "Perhaps. But you have nothing to worry about, Vinny. We have smart folk here who'll sort this before you know it."

*Not soon enough to save Soren*, thought Vina.

"What about the witch?" Vina asked.

"The witch?"

"My witch," she clarified. "The witch to my knight. If this killer murders her, well." A shrug. "There won't be much point to me at all."

"Don't worry about the witch," he said. "Trust me, and trust your government, Vinny. Leave this be now, there's a girl."

Vina huffed, closing her eyes and tipping her head back. Behind her eyes she saw flashes of the witch's face. A dark, furious eye. Hair like a raven's wing.

Parliament, the Lords, the Queen and Court, the Royal Archivists—she wouldn't trust any of them to catch that woman, or save her. They were already keeping secrets from one another. If the right hand wasn't talking to the left, there was no chance they'd be able to get two hands around an assassin's throat.

"You look as tired as I feel," her father said into the silence. "Forget about this. Go back to the barracks. Do whatever it is you like to do—have a drink with the boys. Raise a glass to Soren if you like; he was a good lad and he deserves to be remembered."

"A drink sounds wonderful," Vina said, opening her eyes and smiling. Then she uncoiled from the chair, cracking her neck. Her father winced. "I suppose it's safe to visit you here, at least," she said. "I'll be back at some point to bother you, I'm sure."

"As much as I appreciate your visits, I'm a very busy man, Vinny. It would ease my burden to know you're safe and where you should be." He cleared his throat. Adjusted his papers. "I'll see you in a month anyway, of course. Laura's birthday."

"Of course," Vina said agreeably. She wasn't disappointed or hurt. What good would that do? "Try and get some rest, Father," she said, and went out the door.

Maybe there was a time once when Vina and her father had been close, but Vina couldn't remember it.

She and her father orbited each other like celestial bodies; he in the Palace of Westminster, and she in the barracks of the royal Palace, where the Queen's chosen knights resided under the auspices of the royal Spymaster. If she'd wanted to, Vina could have come here every day: walked the corridors with her father, and shared a meal with him in the private restaurant the ministers so loved, bonding over port and steak, or whatever those ministers liked to quaff.

But she didn't go to him, and he didn't ask for her. That was pretty reasonable, to Vina's mind. It was hard to love an incarnate child destined to die, and hard to be worthy of love when you were destined to be the kind of scum that murdered the one you loved.

She swept out of the Palace of Westminster, under the cloak of night, and headed to the royal barracks.

A crisp white letter awaited her in her room, sealed with wax. More orders? A blistering written lecture for her waywardness? She broke the seal with her belt knife and opened it.

*Her Majesty summons you.*

Vina bit back a sigh. Before her eyes, the ink began to slide out of shape, seeping into rivulets. She crumpled up the paper before the words had fully perished and tossed it onto her desk. Her room in the royal barracks was an untidy jumble of papers and books, armor polish, oiling cloths, half-full bottles of liquor and half-drunk cups of tea. One more addition to the mess wouldn't be noticed.

She left her room and went toward the Palace proper.

Black as the night was, the Palace was blazing with light.

The Palace and its grounds were a maze. So many stories had shaped it that it was prone to fracturing into new shapes with every turn of the moon. The only reliable way to navigate the grounds was to follow the light of the chandeliers and torches at every window. Vina walked through the tessellated rose gardens and the avenues of topiary, eyes on the lights, grass and gravel noisy under her feet. When the trees shifted, and the rose garden began to twist into new shapes, Vina mindfully avoided stomping through the sudden blockade of a flowerbed and worked her way around the garden's edge.

She made her way up marble steps. The corridors that greeted her were covered in white plaster and gold crenellations. As she passed through them, the plaster faded, drifting into dark stone draped in tapestries.

Only the White Hall remained steady and unchanged. Gold limned the walls. The curtains were red velvet, brocaded in golden unicorns and songbirds.

Vina entered and felt the familiar flagstones beneath her feet. She smelled the faint ever-present scent of rot on the air—the price of the Palace's closeness to the Thames. Her thoughts turned to an Isle-shaping tale about sewage in the waters.

Not all tales were glamorous. Vina knew that very well.

The stench was, apparently, a constant source of distress to the poor servants charged with caring for the Palace. The curtains were dusted daily with powdered damask-rose. Rosewater was washed into the flagstones, and candles scented with rosemary and lavender burned sweetly in broad silver stands. Those candles produced a smoke that gave the golden décor a hazy glow and made Vina's eyes water.

The throne of the Eternal Queen, on a raised platform large enough to hold both the Queen and her beloved pet, was the one thing not covered in gold, and its austerity naturally drew the eye. The seat cushion was the only touch of luxury the old thing had. It was—as was so often the case—empty.

"Her Majesty is in Nonsuch," said the royal Spymaster, naming one of the Queen's array of pleasure palaces. He was seated at the grand circular table that lay beneath the throne. Papers surrounded him in a yellowing fan of parchment. At their center lay a map of the Isle. There were gouges in the map—burns and ink stains, marking the places lost when the tales that kept them alive had died.

The map had changed since she'd last seen it. A curvature of coastline to the south was obliterated, blurred with blood-black ink. Vina remembered the loss she'd felt in the Tower—the wrenching sense of shoreline erased, a name slipping from her skull and out into nothingness. The blurred ink stared back at her like an accusation.

No one on the Isle would know the name of that coastline ever again. No one would ever walk upon it. It had died with Soren and his tale.

"Stop gawping, Lavinia," the Spymaster said. "Come closer." The light from the torches bled gold across his pale face and hair.

Despite the silver of his hair and beard, his skin was unlined, his eyes clear. When he smiled—which was rarely—his teeth were white enough to hurt. There was a joke, among the knights and courtiers who orbited the Eternal Queen, that her Spymaster was similarly timeless.

Vina had once referred to him as *an eternal pain in the arse*, and she was fairly sure he knew. There was something particularly vicious about the way he tapped his bejeweled fingers on the table in front of him as she approached and bowed.

"What does Her Majesty desire from me?" Vina asked.

"She desires nothing from you, Lavinia," said the Spymaster. "I, on the other hand, have questions."

"Sir," Vina acknowledged. She didn't bother to grab a chair. He would have told her to sit if he'd wanted her to.

"Your quest went well, I take it." His voice was neutral. "Was it worth disobeying orders?"

Vina tried not to wince. Well, she'd expected to be harangued.

"I apologize," said Vina. "I should not have left the grounds, but I wanted to assist Matthias and Edmund. They did try to stop me."

"Mm," said the Spymaster. "And how successful was their quest, with your assistance?"

"The ink made it to the Tower safely," said Vina.

"All of it, Lavinia?"

He already knew, then. No point in lying.

"We were waylaid," Vina admitted. "I committed a bit of a gaffe, I'm afraid."

"You do seem uniquely prone to them."

"A woman stole a vial," said Vina. "She trapped me in something like a fairy ring. It took a while to get me free, and by then there was no worth in chasing her." She gave him a sheepish grin. "It was quite clumsy of me, really."

"Tell me about this woman," he said.

"There isn't much to say," Vina said apologetically. "I don't remember much about her. She was young. Pretty."

"Edmund claimed you flirted with her," said the Spymaster.

"Ah," said Vina. "I did that, yes."

"And yet, in the midst of all your flirting, young Matthias informs me you ascertained that she was no fae, and worked out how to break the trap holding you," the Spymaster noted.

"Did I?" Vina frowned. "I'm sorry to say it, sir, but I'm sure that was Matthias, not me."

"One would almost believe that you're pretending to be a clumsy idiot," the Spymaster said dryly. "And yet I do have to wonder why you would *choose* humiliation at every turn."

"Believe me, sir, if I could be anything but what I am, I would be," Vina said with absolute sincerity.

The Spymaster gave her a thin-lipped smile.

"You went to see your father," he said. "What did you discuss?"

Somewhere between truth and lie, Vina said, "He told me a friend of mine is dead. Not a close friend, I admit. But Soren is—*was*—a fellow incarnate. It shook me."

"A sad business," said the Spymaster, his expression unchanged. "It is not news we wanted spread across all of Parliament, but I expect your father can be circumspect when he must be. But if I were you I'd be honest now. I don't believe you went to Westminster for a social call. You went for information. He told you about the terrorist, didn't he?"

"Terrorist, sir?"

"What else would you call someone who imperils the safety of the Isle?" the Spymaster asked coolly.

Vina adjusted subtly, one foot to the other.

"He didn't tell me himself," said Vina. No need to get her father into trouble with the Crown. "But I heard elsewhere, sir. The archivists were—overwrought. A tale died when we arrived. They can't be blamed."

"They can indeed be blamed," said the Spymaster. "But no matter. This is better. Come closer, Lavinia. No, closer than that," he ordered, when she took two steps toward him, the table still between them.

She walked to stand beside him, uncomfortably close in her eyes. It was strange to be so near to him, and to be towering above him.

He didn't look at all ill at ease.

"There are some who think the start of a tale imbues incarnates with a certain *luminescence*," said the Spymaster. "I do not mean light, in any prosaic sense. Theologians have called it a halo, a sanctity. A sign that your kind are imbued with power and purpose. An incarnate before their tale subsumes them is an empty vessel, only notable and worthy when their tale begins, marking them with the ink of meaning."

There was probably a point to this. Vina listened attentively, hands clasped neatly behind her.

"But I don't place trust in theologians and philosophers," the Spymaster continued. "If there is something that needs to be ascertained, then I make sure I find the facts. Place your hand here. Palm up."

The item he placed on her palm was some kind of compass, with a dial of feather and bone. It was cool on her skin—but the minute it touched her palm, its feathered needle began to glow, then hiss, as if the marrow inside it were cooking through. He lifted it from her palm and whisked it away.

"I see," he said.

There was no need to confess. Vina did not need to be a lord of spies or a theologian to understand she'd been found out. She took back her hand.

"When I inform Her Majesty and the rest of the privy council that your witch has been found and then immediately misplaced…" He drummed his knuckles against the table. "The Queen will not be happy. She expects newly discovered incarnates introduced to her promptly, as you well know. Parliament will be wroth. There are tales imperiled, Lavinia. Your tale cannot join them. Your witch must be found. If you could tell us where she is, that would be far better. Ideal, even."

"I don't know where my witch is, sir," said Vina. That was nothing but the truth. "If I could find her I would."

"You should have brought her in immediately."

"She used magic to escape."

"And you attempted to conceal her. Don't deny it," he said waspishly, when she opened her mouth to speak. "You've made plenty of errors in your time here, Lavinia, but this may be your most serious."

Vina bowed her head and said nothing.

"The archivists are seeking out all stray incarnates," said the Spymaster. "When I inform them the witch of your tale has been seen by you—and has met you—they will set out to find her. No doubt they'll take witch hunters with them." A slight derisive twitch to his mouth. He didn't think much of witch hunters. But then, who did? "They rightly fear she's a plum prize for a killer determined to destroy powerful tales. But this killer is quick, and I fear what will be lost with the witch's death."

The witch, not-Isadora, with her dark eyes and dark skin, her crown of fire—dead, murdered, by a hand that wasn't Vina's? What a strange thought.

It felt almost like...relief.

The Spymaster was still speaking, watching her as intently as a hawk.

"In the past, I might have given you a quest on Her Majesty's behalf and urged you to seek the girl out. You, after all, are far more likely to find the witch swiftly than any puerile witch hunter with silver needles in his belt. But these are perilous times.

"Her Majesty does not bid you to undertake this quest," said the Spymaster. "In fact, Her Majesty has ordered you to remain on State grounds. We cannot allow another incarnate to be placed at risk, of course."

"Of course," echoed Vina.

"But if the witch were to be returned to us without any fuss involving witch hunters, that would be...ideal." He gave her a significant look, then returned to his papers. "You may go," he said. "Remember your orders, Lavinia, or the Queen will be wroth."

"Sir," Vina acknowledged. She bowed and left the White Hall.

It was clear what she had to do.

Back to the barracks she went without detouring to the stables. She couldn't afford to draw attention to her officially unsanctioned, but unofficially vital quest, so she'd have to leave her horse behind.

She changed into plain clothing—a hooded cloak over her shirt and trousers, bracers at her wrists, and strong boots fit for walking on her feet. Her sword and her bow were the only knightly things she'd take with her. She had no desire to be without them.

She left her room, making her way down one winding corridor.

"Vina," said a voice.

Edmund was leaning against the door of his room, his sleep-shirt rumpled but his eyes alert. "Where are you going?"

Just her luck. Matthias would have been fine—he'd choose peace over any battle. Edmund was going to be pure piss and vinegar. Vina gestured at herself, encompassing her plain clothes, her hooded outer robe, and the pack at her shoulder. "On a quest."

"You haven't even got your armor."

"An adventure, then. What does it matter, Eddie?"

He crossed his arms.

"You got us in some trouble," said Edmund. "The Spymaster gave us so much shit for letting you out. How were we meant to know you're on house arrest?"

"I didn't think I was."

"Didn't you?"

"I thought it was more of a suggesti—never mind," said Vina. "Forget you saw me."

"Go back into your room," Edmund said. "I mean it. House arrest's got to mean something to you."

"Oh, come on, really, Eddie? I won't tell anyone I saw you. I promise you won't get in any trouble this time."

"That old goat Spymaster knows everything that happens here," Edmund said. "You think he won't know that I let you go?"

"I'll tell him you put up a valiant fight," Vina said, and started walking.

Edmund moved in front of her, barring her path.

"Seriously, Eddie, I need to go."

He didn't move.

"I swear, Vina. You're not going anywhere."

"Are you really going to stop me, Edmund Tallisker?" Vina asked softly. "You're welcome to try."

He was taller than Vina. But he quailed, just a little, at whatever he saw in Vina's face.

She held his gaze for a long moment. Then she smiled, clapped him on the shoulder, and kept on walking.

"Do you need someone to come with you?" Edmund said abruptly.

Vina stopped and turned to look back at him. He was staring sullenly at the ground.

"If it's an 'adventure,' then—fine. Go. But if this is something more than that, if you're in some trouble…" His jaw twitched. "Just tell me," he said finally.

"Don't worry about me," Vina said. "It's nothing like that."

"Fine," Edmund said. "Go. Fuck. Fine."

He slammed back into his room. Vina winced, lifted her pack higher on her shoulder, and kept on walking.

London was smog and cobblestones, tall buildings, squat houses. But London was also a park studded with trees, loamy-soiled and owl song-rich. For Vina, made of tales of chivalry and blood, it was the part of London that welcomed her most easily, and sure enough that was the land that met her as she left the Palace. It opened to her like an exhalation.

Where to go now?

The witch could have gone anywhere. It should have been impossible to find her. Even witch hunters struggled to find their maleficent prey. Most incarnates were like Vina—discovered as children, soon after their first encounter with a ghost of their last self. They were recorded in the royal archives, formally introduced to the Queen, and carefully molded toward their destinies.

The others turned up, inevitably, when their tales began. They just had to make do, stumbling into their tasks and roles at the calling of fate. They'd find each other when the tale demanded. That was natural.

But Vina couldn't afford to wait for the witch to begin cursing the Isle, and for the Queen to give Vina her quest, and so forth until she and the witch were dead. There was too much at stake.

There among the trees, with the wind rustling through her short hair, her body strangely light without her armor and her sword heavy at her hip, Vina closed her eyes and listened to her heart.

The tale wanted them to be together. Knight and Witch, as they had been for a hundred or more lifetimes. It wouldn't let her down. *Show her to me*, Vina said in her heart, *or there'll be no tale after this.*

There was a tug under her breastbone. A faint scent of apples and golden wheat in her nose. *There she is*, the tale whispered. *I'll show you the way.*

She heard sobbing.

Vina's eyes snapped open.

A man kneeled on the path. He was golden-haired and broad. When he raised his head she saw eyes of the bluest blue and skin freckled gold with sunshine. There was blood on his cheek.

"Isadora," he whispered. "Isadora, no, no."

The wind blew, rustling the trees. Vina blinked, and her past life was gone.

There was a path in front of her. Vina drew her hood over her hair, and went to find her witch.

# Chapter Five

## *Simran*

*Isadora Delaney was born with a silver spoon in her mouth. She should have had the world. If she hadn't been an incarnate, she really could have been somebody.*

Source: Transcription of speech at the funeral of Isadora Delaney, by Lara Atwater

**Archivist's Ruling:** For retention as evidence of treason. Interrogation advised.

**Senior Archivist's Ruling:** Atwater is a known incarnate (The Laidly Wyrm). No interrogation required at this time. Document earmarked for disposal, review in 12 months.

The wind was roaring, rain lashing down. The stagecoach carrying Simran and Hari to Gore stopped at a roadside inn, and thirteen passengers dressed in greatcoats and shawls and bonnets tumbled into the muggy heat of the dining room. They'd be back on the road as soon as the worst of the storm cleared, so Simran ordered some bread and cheese, which was the best she could afford.

She'd desperately needed the limni ink she'd stolen. Tattooing was an art and paid well—but Simran was not a traditional tattooist, with a gift for skin and art. She was a scribe through and through.

When she drew limni ink into her needles, it was her intent that tangled with the ink and made something useful out of it. "Shit at art, good at magic" was how she described herself, and it was no more or less than the truth. No limni ink meant no meaningful work.

Being far from her scriptorium meant no work too, but there was no avoiding that.

The stagecoach had jolted angrily through the rolling countryside like a bucking horse. Simran's lower back still ached, and Hari was perched on his barstool with his head in his hands, chewing an aniseed sweet to settle his stomach. "Bloody coaches," he muttered. "One day we're going to be rich and get better transport. A gilded carriage with ten white horses or something that never jolts."

"Sure," said Simran. "That sounds realistic. Eat your sandwich."

"I don't want to eat maggoty cheese."

"Then don't," Simran said, poking the back of his head with a fingertip. "Starve to death. I don't care."

The cheese *was* maggoty. Some people considered that a delicacy, but Simran liked her food dead before she ate it. She stole one of Hari's sweets from his pocket and sucked at it desultorily as she pondered the twinged muscles in her back and the stranger twinge in her chest.

There was a tug inside her, urging her back to London. There was nothing in the smoky inn to distract her from it. The tug was a tale, and the tug was the knight, with her sly, knowing smile.

The tug was going to be the death of her.

*Our tale hasn't begun yet*, Simran reminded herself. But it was cold comfort. It was going to, after all. Seeing the knight—the knight seeing her—had set the clock ticking.

"Will you go and see your parents?" Hari asked. "They'd like it."

Simran pointedly said nothing.

Hari sighed. "Uncle doesn't write to you every week because he hates you."

"No," said Simran. "I know he loves me. That isn't the point."

The door creaked open, bringing the storm in with it. The wind groaned, and the rain splattered on the rough wooden floorboards, heralding a line of figures who glided in. Simran saw their shadows first, and some bone-deep instinct made her body tense and her blood run cold. Slowly, she raised her head.

Witch hunters.

She watched them glide by, in their copatain hats polished to a keen shine, their doublets starched flat and stiff.

Simran sat about as stiffly on her stool, stomach curdling with more than nausea or hunger.

Oh, Simran knew the shape of a witch hunter. They were bruisers and opportunists. They didn't just hunt witches, no—any monster that required capturing or killing was their business. They were functional, a necessity for trolls under bridges and corpses rising from graves with overly sharp teeth.

They had to be here for her. She thought of her knight again; that sly, knowing smile turning to horror. That name on the knight's lips.

*Isadora.*

Of course there were witch hunters looking for her. She should have expected it. She was an incarnate, and her tale had begun. Someone would be seeking her out. Maybe the knight Vina had sent them. Why wouldn't she? She couldn't kill Simran if she couldn't find her.

When was the stagecoach driver going to call them all back? Simran looked out the window. The rain was still pouring. She couldn't use magic here without drawing the witch hunters like bloodhounds to a hare, and her pistol would do her little more good.

"I'm going," Simran said under her breath to Hari. She didn't wait for him to respond. Taking advantage of the milling crowd of travelers, she slid from the stool and headed toward the back of the inn. The tables were full, and it was hard to weave around them. Her hip knocked into one, and a man's ale spilled. He swore, and Simran muttered, "Sorry, sorry."

Someone was following her. There were footsteps behind her. Not Hari's footsteps; she knew those like her own. This was a heavy tread in heavy boots.

There was another door beyond some busy tables. She went through it out into a courtyard, green and hazy under heavily falling rain. There were low stone walls, cracked with age, and a few wooden tables moss-touched and damp. There was no cover in the courtyard, but beyond it were rolling green fields, patchy with bushes of gorse. She jumped the wall and crouched low in the bushes, belly to the muddy ground, mist cloying the air and giving her cover.

The door creaked open, and through a crack in the stone, Simran saw Hari.

Hari stumbled breathlessly out the door, straightened his greatcoat, and fished a hand-rolled cigarette from his pocket. He must have run to catch up with her. He didn't look at her as he fumbled into his pocket again for a match, cigarette caught between his lips. His hands trembled. He struck the match once, twice, cupping the lit flame in his palm to stop the rain and wind from putting it out. He lit the cigarette. A second later, the door slammed open and a witch hunter emerged.

"Oi," said the witch hunter. "Come over here."

"Can't a man smoke a cigarette in peace anymore?" Hari asked, affronted.

"I know what you are," the witch hunter said. He stomped across the muddy ground and grasped Hari roughly by the arm. Hari almost dropped his cigarette.

"Let me go!" Hari said, voice going high.

"You'll bloody wait, boy."

Simran lurched up to her knees, rage boiling up in her blood. As she looked over the wall, she saw Hari's free hand go behind his back abruptly. His hand behind him opened up, palm bare, fingers stretched out. *Hold.*

She froze. Slowly, she lowered herself back down.

Another figure emerged. A woman in a scholar's robe, high-collared, a chain hung with ink vials and a quill at her waist. An archivist.

"I've got him here, ma'am," the witch hunter called proudly.

She walked over unhurriedly and fished a monocle from her clothing, placing it over her right eye. The monocle was golden, but the lens over the eye was a prism, fracturing rain and light like a diamond. She peered at Hari.

"He isn't a witch, never mind an incarnate," the woman said. She didn't sound posh the way Simran had expected an archivist would. Her voice was all London, and oddly musical. "And we're looking for a woman, Jones. Honestly. Whatever made you think he was the one?"

"I smelled one, ma'am," the witch hunter said, eyes narrowed. "I followed my nose." Simran saw his nostrils flare, but the rain and the tobacco smoke seemed to be enough to block the scent of Simran's tale from reaching his nose.

A sigh. "Well, your nose has clearly led you astray."

He scowled. "There's other work I could be doing," he muttered. "Work where I'd be appreciated. Scads of witches running off into the ancient forest, each worth a good sack of silver, and here I am with you, being judged by a paper-pusher."

The woman's expression cooled, and her voice with it.

"Head inside, Jones. Test your nose again there."

As the witch hunter, grumbling, released Hari, the archivist turned to Hari and said cordially, "I'm sorry. For your troubles."

Simran realized with a start that the archivist was as brown as she and Hari were. Unusual for their kind. They were usually Isle stock through and through, white as paper.

There was a clink of coin. The witch hunter and the archivist turned and went back into the inn.

A pause.

"You can come out now, Sim. I don't think they're coming back."

Simran stood and met Hari's eyes.

"How did you know what to do?" Simran asked. "Distracting the witch hunter with smoke—I wouldn't have thought of it."

"You think I'd live this long with a witch and not make sure I knew how to scare off a witch hunter? Come on, Sim. I can't fight the way you can, but I can at least get us out of trouble," Hari remarked, stubbing the cigarette out with his boot. "What should we be doing?"

Simran thought of walking back through that inn to the front entrance. They could perhaps sneak around the inn to the stagecoach, but the rain was still pouring furiously and the witch hunters were inside, *looking* for her.

"Hiding," said Simran. "Or walking. We—I—can't risk them catching me."

"It sounded to me like they're not just looking for a witch. They're looking for an incarnate," Hari said carefully. "And that can't be you."

There was a way for Simran to wend to safety through this conversation. She could see it. She had a knack of traps and thread. *It's my bad luck to be here when they're looking for an incarnate. But witch hunters... it's in the name, isn't it? I can't risk them scenting me out. Let's wait here for now. Trust me, Hari.*

Instead, she looked away.

"If you go in you won't face any trouble," said Simran.

"As if I'd leave you," said Hari. "You sure we can't risk the stagecoach?"

Simran shook her head.

"Then let's start walking. It's only what—four, five hours from here?" A grim smile. "It'll give us lots of time to talk."

The rain stopped after two hours, and for those two hours Hari said nothing as they walked. They sat on a fallen tree trunk together to recover, damp and miserable. There were some sheep ambling around ahead of them, apparently impervious to the cold.

Hari finally spoke.

"I heard a little what the man said. The one who attacked you. Not much, but now..." He shook his head. "I thought he was talking nonsense. But he wasn't, was he? He was looking for you. He thinks you're an incarnate."

"He did say that," Simran said, throat tight. "He was right. I am."

"You're not," Hari said, as Simran stared fixedly at the sheep ambling on the road ahead of them. "You can't be."

"You had to be suspicious, at least. I'm a *witch*, Hari. Isn't that a clue?"

"The Isle does strange things to everyone," Hari said immediately. "And Lydia's as Elsewhere-made as we are, and *she's* a cunning woman."

"She's got the ink for it," said Simran. It was true. Like most folk not born to a tale, Lydia had gained her magic by having the gift written into her skin by a scribe. She'd told Simran once that she considered her magic worth the death price.

"Incarnates have to be born here," said Hari. "They're Isle blood and Isle bred. Maybe if you had a parent from here, but Sim... you're not from the Isle. You can't be part of their stories."

"I'm not making it up."

"I didn't think you were. I just think you're wrong about this." He sounded upset. "There has to be another reason."

"Sometimes I see her," Simran said, voice rough. "My old self. The last lifetime the witch was called Isadora, and she told me what I am. That I'd been her, once, and another person before her. Hundreds of lives, Hari, and I died in all of them." The wind rushed over them, tangling in Simran's hair, biting and cold. She shivered. "I wish it were just... a lie I told myself, or a curse on me. But I recognize other incarnates when I see them. I feel my tale. And now, witch hunters and archivists being after me is just more proof. I'm truly an incarnate, Hari. I can't lie anymore. I don't know how, or why, but I am."

Silence. One of the sheep bleated, and Hari rubbed a hand roughly over his own face.

"How long have you known?" Hari asked.

"I knew when we came to the Isle," said Simran. "Before that I was just—myself. And then, when I was on the ship, and the sea was stormy, I..." She trailed off. She couldn't explain what she'd felt then. How she'd been one person, one Simran before she'd entered the ship, and another when she'd left it. It was as if the tale had snatched her up and changed the nature of her soul.

It didn't matter anymore. Whatever she'd been before, she was the witch now, and Isadora was part of her.

"You've known the truth as long as you've known me? *Sim*. I've told you everything about me," said Hari. "Everything in my life. Why did you keep this from me?"

"What was the point talking about it?"

"That's such bullshit," Hari said, but he didn't sound angry, just disappointed. Of course that was infinitely worse. Simran felt two feet tall. "You know that. I *know* you know that. Things you don't bring into the light, that you stick into the dark—they hurt you, Sim. You told me that once."

"That doesn't sound like me," said Simran.

"A half bottle of whiskey turns you into a poet," said Hari. "The transformation's pretty impressive. Really. Be honest. Why didn't you tell me?"

*You would have loved me differently*, Simran thought. Hari would understand if she said so. Of course Hari would understand. He knew what it was like to fear what being known, seen, would do to the strange, fraying bonds that make up friendship and family.

"I wanted to forget about it," she said. "If you'd known, I wouldn't have been able to. One day, sooner than I'd like, my tale's going to kill me. I think about that every day. But around you, I don't. It's like it doesn't matter. And once you know it all, I won't be able to forget. I'll see it in your eyes."

"Kill you? Simran." His voice went urgent. "What's your tale? What is it called?"

"The Knight and the Witch," said Simran.

He was silent for a long moment. Then he placed an arm around her, so tight she could barely breathe.

"Oh, Sim," he said. "Oh, sweetheart. I'm sorry."

Her heart ached. She felt sick. This was exactly why she'd never told her parents the truth—to spare them this. To spare herself.

Gently, she pulled away. "See," she said, brushing her knuckles against his cheek. "What's the point of both of us being sad? Now we're miserable together." She looked out at the gray horizon. "Let's get moving again."

Hari stood up, boots squelching.

"You've got some terrible luck," he said.

"Absolutely awful," she agreed.

"It's, uh, not the same," he started. "But my luck isn't so good either."

"In what way?"

"I think I've walked into a cowpat," he said.

She looked back at him, and his defeated expression, and burst into laughter.

Gore was a lot of things, depending on who you asked. A hundred, a county, a part of London, absolutely *not* part of London. It was partly farmland, rolling fields and yellow carpets of wheat. It was also a set of factories snagged between the farms, tales of industry and nature messily entangled. And it was the town where her parents lived, of course.

Family came in so many shapes, and Simran had grown used to thinking of family as her folk in London. Her father sent her letters, and Simran sent money back when she could, but she didn't visit if she could avoid it. When she'd left at seventeen, she'd told herself to never look back.

She had, of course. And she'd seen what she saw now: a paved, quaint street lined with homes. Little shops with colorful canvas awnings, hanging baskets of flowers arranged over their large windows. The sweet shop her parents owned was shut, but the window display was still piled high with silver trays of treats. Above it was an apartment with sunlight reflecting on a single window.

Simran knew when you stood in that kitchen you could still smell the sugar-scent rising from below. Every time she came home—and somehow this was still home, and always would be—the smell struck her like a new thing, and she was a girl again: ten years old and still unsteady from their sea journey, salt on her cheeks, not even knowing her own name. Her hair in looped braids, a crown against her skull. She could vaguely remember feeling sick for a home that was slipping out of her skull like ink in water, smeared out of shape. What she could remember far more clearly was how tenderly her parents had tucked her in the first night in their new home, when she'd lain between them in an unfamiliar bed, the burnt toffee of sugar in her lungs. She remembered how glad she'd been to be safe together. A family.

She stared up at the kitchen window. The curtains were open.

"We could go in together," Hari said.

Simran shook her head.

"Something's after me. I can't risk them by going in."

Hari did her the kindness of not pointing out that she was just making excuses. She always made excuses.

Her father would welcome her. She could see him in her mind's eye, sitting at the kitchen table by the window under weak sunlight, laboriously writing a letter in a language that still didn't come easily to him. But traveling from Elsewhere had taken any other words from him. That was the price of crossing the silver sea.

Letters every week. He loved her.

Simran swallowed.

"I'm going to check on Bess. You... you can check on my parents. They'll be happy to see you."

"I should come with you to see Bess," Hari protested.

"If he's done something to her, I'll deal with it on my own," said Simran. "It's better that way."

Hari frowned.

"I know I've got no magic, that I'm not a fighter, but I did pretty good with the witch hunters, didn't I?"

"Bess is magic business," Simran said. "She always has been. We agreed. Magic and scribing's up to me."

He nodded slowly, but he didn't look convinced.

"Look, Hari, I'm really glad you're with me. These last two days have been supremely shit." Her voice cracked a little. *Hell*, what she'd give for a nap. She couldn't stand this level of emotional rawness. "I couldn't do much without you. You being here when I get back... That'll be a relief. Just—don't tell my parents I'm here. Say you've come for a visit without me."

Hari gave her a skeptical look. "Do you want me to say hello from you?"

"Of course. Give them my love."

She watched him walk up to the shop. She watched the window for a moment longer. Then she wrenched herself away, and turned and walked to the woods.

When Simran was twelve, she walked alone into the woods for the first time.

At school, other children had been gossiping about an evil witch hiding out there. *You know the tale! Old Mad Bess axes her husband to death, and his ghost haunts the woodland. If you creep into the wood you'll hear him screaming. And if you get too close—bam!— she'll get you with her axe too!*

They'd shrieked, all daring each other, all claiming they'd do it. Simran had said nothing to them. She hadn't even told Hari. She'd packed a cheese sandwich and walked toward the forest. She'd slipped between the trees and walked until she was thoroughly lost—walked until she found a dilapidated house in a clearing, and a woman in front of it, leaning against an axe embedded in the stump of a tree.

The woman smelled like wildflowers and herbs. Rosemary and sage infused the air as Simran walked closer, bold as brass. The woman's dress was white cotton and weeds. Roots were tangled in her knotted brown hair. To Simran's childish eyes she was terribly old—but adult Simran guessed that Bess had only been in her early twenties, freshly grasped by her tale and flung into the woods where she'd live, murder, turn to madness, and perish at its whims.

"You're Bess," Simran said.

"I am indeed," the woman said, watching Simran with beady eyes.

"You killed your husband and now you kill interlopers." Simran shifted on her feet and raised her chin. "You can *try* and kill me, but I run very fast and that axe is buried deep."

The woman laughed, a quavering sound.

"You cannot run faster than a tale," she said. "But it's no matter, dearie. I have no interest in axing *you*. The death of my husband is what my tale hungers for, and I haven't even wed him yet in this life. He still lives in Spellthorne, waiting in terror for our tale to bring him to my door. You're safe here."

"Are you a witch?" Simran asked.

"I am," said Bess. "And mad, by the crude standards of a tale. But for now I am just an incarnate waiting for her tale to begin. Just like you."

Simran took a step closer. This was what she'd been looking for. Someone who would see her.

"Am I?"

"Are you what?"

"An incarnate."

The woman threw her head back and laughed.

"Of course you are, child. I knew you'd come here eventually. I felt you. Didn't you feel me?"

"I don't want to be one," Simran said thinly. "Is there a way not to be?"

The woman drifted from the tree stump toward Simran.

"Oh, dearie," she said tenderly, taking Simran's hands in her own. "You need not be afraid. What you are is an honor. There are parts of the Isle that exist because of you."

"What exists because of me?" Simran asked.

"I don't know, do I? I know my tale is a small, sweet one. Just large enough to feed these woods, and keep the deer dancing." She knelt. "The woods shall eat me," said Bess. "I am the bone porridge that gives them life, aren't I? I shall be a haggard witch, terrorizing unwary travelers, and then I will die. And then I'll be reborn again, I suppose, to sharpen my axe and kill another poor man. That's the normal way of things. What else do you want to know?"

"Are you happy?" Simran asked. "To be an incarnate?"

A shadow passed across Bess's face. She smiled.

"Well," she said. "Of course. I'm as happy as you are. What else?"

Simran took a deep breath.

"I want to learn how to be a witch," she said.

The woodland around her, now, was silent.

She was dressed for a tale of fields and sheep, countryside inns and the gentle pleasures of a green and simple land. Dressing for the kind of tale you were walking into was *respectful*, everyone on the Isle knew it. The mud on her clothes was a start, but as she walked she unwound the bun of her hair, purposefully mussing it into tangles. Some witches were for cursing cities; for hooded cloaks under lamplight. And some were for the woods, where wildness shaped them.

For a little while, she had to be a witch of the woods.

Around her the blackthorn trees were white-blossomed and spindle sharp. That was their nature. There was a faint scent of sage and rosemary in the air. She walked to Bess's cottage. There were no lights in the windows. The birds were silent.

"I know you're here," she said, voice hoarse. "Show yourself. Bess! Answer me!"

No answer. She walked forward warily, each step measured. Her boot hit something solid in the ground.

An axe lay half-buried in the soil. Bess's axe.

The trees groaned, and Simran turned. A forked path lay ahead of her. One winding toward light, and one wending its way deep into the woodland darkness.

*Come*, the woodland beckoned. *Come to me.*

She hefted up the axe, in all its terrible weight. Gritted her teeth, and walked deeper into the woods.

# Chapter Six

## *Vina*

*The committee will note that Archivist Summers states that the archives maintain scrupulous records of minor incarnates. Should any local councillor or parliamentarian wish to consult the preserved records of their borough incarnates, responsible for local farmland, wildlife and vistas &c, they are directed to contact the reference team of the archives directly for assistance.*

Source: Ministerial Committee Notes,
Committee of Local Affairs

**Archivist's Ruling: Preserve. Publication permitted. No further action required.**

She followed the pull and gravity of the tale miles and miles out of London. When the rain came she was in a verdant field, and ran for the cover of the boughs of an old oak. Water lightly dashed her shoulders. She'd seen inns and small villages along the way—an occasional farmhouse with lamplight gleaming in the windows—but she didn't stop at any of them. The journey was pastoral, almost uncomfortably so. She saw no people—only occasional small shadows, shifting through fields of wheat and pale long grasses. Brownies, perhaps, industrious around their home farmsteads, doing small chores in return for bowls of milk and a warm fire. Or possibly just mice. Just in case, she dropped some torn fragments of fresh bread as an offering. Mice and brownies alike deserved to eat, and their goodwill couldn't hurt her.

It was only when she skirted a quaint brick town with smoke rising from—disturbingly cheery—factory chimneys, and reached the edge of a wood rising up a hill, that the tug of the tale finally loosened its grip. Vina took a deep breath.

This was the place.

These were witchy woods: blackthorns blossoming, and dark green trees thickly rising up the hillside. Vina walked slowly along the perimeter, and internally noted that some of the trees were witch-marked, scarred with circles of spellwork. Vina was no witch, with no magic in her but the weight of her incarnate tale, but she knew a witch's work when she saw it.

Vina drew her hood back and stepped into the woods. She started walking upward. The air pressed heavily on her, oddly cold.

There was something more than witchcraft wrong with the woods.

Of course knights rarely went to woods that were *not* wrong. Vina had been into the ancient primordial forest—far older than these small woods—that crossed the length and breadth of the Isle more times than she could count. That forest was nothing but danger, layers of festering magic that needed a knight's blade to quiet them. Quests had led her and her fellow knights of the Queen's order to enchanted towers and fairy rings, moss-drenched hags feeding on children, green-skinned wild men slinking through distant looming trees, and snake-tailed women in deep lakes, venomous and hungry. But this was something else, a new danger sharp as nettles prickling her skin, a gut instinct to get *out*.

It was almost a relief when Vina saw strange eyes glaring at her from among the black trees, lambent gold.

She began to reach for her sword, then forced her hand to pause.

"Come now," she said gently. "I won't hurt you. This blade isn't for you. We're friends, aren't we?"

The trees rustled, whistling with an ominous wind. But Vina kept her hands lax at her sides.

Not all strange things in the woods, she reminded herself, were dangerous. And even dangerous things did not deserve to die simply for obeying their own natures.

The trees quieted, slowly. And then the gold-eyed creature emerged.

The creature was a deer, but not quite. It was ghostly, its tawny limbs glowing, mist rising from its semitranslucent skin. It limped toward her, its ears twitching wildly, tail lashing.

"You're in pain," Vina murmured. She didn't approach it, but she looked over it carefully. There were no visible wounds on it, and its limping hind leg was golden and unmarred. "What's hurting you, little one?"

Its tail lashed again. It nudged its nose against one blackthorn.

Carefully, Vina reached a hand out and pressed her bare palm to the wood. The trunk was disturbingly soft under her palm. When she pressed harder, it turned to black mist, distorting, running into spidery rivulets. She felt sharp pain, like pressing her hand into boiling water. She swore and snapped her hand back. The skin was unmarked. The tree solidified.

Her heart was thudding painfully.

An illusion? A beast hidden in the guise of a tree, or a possessive dryad? No. This forest was real, or had been once.

"Something is killing your home, isn't it?" Vina said to the deer. "Will you show me the cause? I promise, I'll help if I can."

The deer's gold eyes were knowing. It shook its head and turned, light-footed between the trees.

Vina followed.

The trees grew thicker, gray and snarled and menacing. A leaden weight of fear sat in Vina's stomach. The tug was back, but this time it was like a scrabbling hand, dragging her frantically forward. She could not see the witch yet, *her* witch. But she felt her.

A strange itch filled her fingers, urging her to reach for the bow she carried, the arrows at her belt. She did not want to hunt the deer, but the urge to hunt was rising up in her, regardless. Her hands ached like they were being tugged by strings.

*The tale wants something from me,* she realized. The last time she'd felt anything like this had been under the shadow of the church, when she'd met the witch's blazing eyes. She ground her teeth, jaw tightening, and clenched her hands firmly at her sides.

*No. Not yet.*

The tale's grasp slipped once more, and the urge for the hunt left her.

As Vina rose up the wooded hill, she finally saw her. Trailing an axe behind her in the dirt, stumbling, was her witch.

She was no longer in her hooded cloak and cotehardie. There was no bonnet on her tangled hair, but her dress was a column under a short jacket; a dress from promenading and countryside ambles.

Her dress was slashed with dirt. The axe in her grip was splotched with lichen, bronze with rust but oddly shining and sharp at its edge. She turned and faced Vina, and her eyes—familiar, dark—flashed with fury.

"You," the witch spat out. "I do *not* have time for you."

She raised her left hand in one sharp motion and opened her fingers wide.

Before Vina had a chance to speak, to placate, to do *anything*, she felt her feet go out from under her. It was lucky she wasn't in her armor, which would have overbalanced her. Instead, she was able to twist as she fell and catch herself on her hands and knees, before leaping back to her feet. The soil beneath her was thrumming with magic, but as she straightened she realized the trees around her were spell-marked just like the tree line. They glowed even more brightly when Vina looked at the witch once more. The witch was scowling, her tangled hair a dark flag of warning in the wind eddying through the woods.

"If you come closer I swear I'll curse you," the witch said, voice low and fierce. "Do you like welts and boils? I can make sure you have some very *intimate* problems if you dare reach for that damn sword—"

"I vow not to touch my sword," Vina said quickly. She held her arms wide in front of her. "Peace, lady witch."

The soil trembled ominously.

"Peace," the witch spat. "There's no peace between us, knight. Go away. I'll face you when I must, but right now you'll leave me be."

"I'm not here to cause you harm," Vina said. She kept her voice soft. It was no different from handling the ghostly deer. Here was a woman that was perhaps predator or prey, who was dangerous to her. Here was a creature she did not want to raise a blade to.

A pity one day she'd have no other option.

The witch barked a laugh. "I'm sure."

"Perhaps I can assist you."

"And why would you assist me? You're hunting me like a hare, don't pretend."

A shiver ran through her, remembering the tug on her hands, the urging of the tale.

"I'm not," Vina said. "I can promise you that." *Not yet.*

The witch's hand clenched and loosened on the axe handle, full of anger and distrust. The trees began to smolder malevolently.

Vina bowed, neatly. A hand to the heart.

"My name is Lavinia Morgan," she said. "I am a knight in the Queen's service. Not of any traditional order: I am one of those the Queen keeps near for use in a tale. While my brethren hunt loathly ladies and women with the bodies of asps, I am an incarnate. Even though I am, I'm afraid, a disappointment of a knight, the Queen retains me because one day I am meant to be enthralled by you, and then I am meant to destroy you."

She thought about apologizing for it, then decided better of it. What could she say? *Sorry I'll kill you one day*? That would be absurd. Being sorry made no difference.

"For my duty," Vina said, "I am here to take you to our Queen. Before the witch hunters find you, ideally. But I would also be glad to help you first, if you allow it."

The witch's mouth thinned.

"How," the witch said flatly.

"I have a sword," Vina offered. "If you agree not to attack me for using it, then it's yours."

"You told me you're a disappointment of a knight. Why would I need your sword?"

"Knighthood is more than swordsmanship. Fighting, I can do ably enough. Direct me on what to hack and cut, lady witch, and I shall."

"As long as it isn't me, you may cut what you like," said the witch.

"Direct me, ma'am," said Vina. "And I'll do as you bid." Slowly, Vina grasped the hilt.

The witch weighed her options, visibly conflicted.

"I can't break through this wall of trees," the witch said finally. "I've given the trees my blood, and written spells into the soil. I've made a trap of my own hair. I have nothing left to give."

"You have your axe," Vina suggested. Then she paused for a breath, noting the tic of the witch's jaw. "The axe is too heavy for you," she said.

"It wasn't made for my hands," the witch said tightly.

"If I may?" Vina held out a hand.

"Take it, then," said the witch abruptly, angling the handle to her. "I need to reach the top of the hill." She hesitated. "I don't know what's waiting for us there."

That was warning enough. Vina took the axe by the handle. Her fingers brushed the witch's for a butterfly's breath—then the witch drew back. Vina hefted up the axe. It was heavy.

"This may take some time," Vina warned, then began to chop.

She hacked at the tree again; again, and again, and again. Ten dull thuds, and then the treelike thing shuddered and began to twist in front of her, wildly, the branches shaping into claws. Shit. Vina reared back, angling her weapon to meet them, and the witch snapped, "I can deal with the claws! Keep hitting the weak point you've made."

"Will that be enough?" Vina asked, lurching to avoid a branch slash aimed directly at her throat.

"Every monster has its weakness to be exploited," the witch said confidently.

That sounded reasonable enough, so Vina obeyed, hitting the same deep groove over and over.

Sweat ran down her body, but she hacked, and hacked, the reverberation thudding through her. The witch was muttering something—sharp, staccato words. Marks on the trees and in the soil began to blaze hotter still, smoldering and spitting as the witch poured magic into the webs and traps she'd already made. The trees contorted, ink oozing from them like blood. If Vina hadn't known better, she would have believed they were in pain.

The tree finally gave way, and a scream ran through the branches around them.

Silence.

A tree's-breadth of a path had opened in front of them. Darkness ahead of them. Vina breathed deeply, shoulders heaving, and wiped the sweat from her brow.

"What next, lady witch?" Vina asked.

She heard the whisper of the witch's footsteps. The witch moved to stand by Vina's side. From the corner of her vision, she watched the witch cross her arms, expression wary.

"My name is Simran," said the witch. "I am only telling you so you don't call me Isadora or 'lady witch' again."

"Simran," Vina said obediently.

"Follow me."

The witch—*Simran*—walked through the trees. And Vina, who'd promised to do what the witch told her to, followed.

Ahead of them, clad in briars, stood the ruins of some ancient temple to gods Vina could not name. Figures held up the broken remains of the roof. The figures were so eroded that their faces were not visible, their bodies devoid of fingers, mouths, hair. An old tale, tucked away among blackthorns, nearly forgotten.

But it was not the temple that made Vina's heart thud in warning, and her muscles coil. It was the smell. Some strange, discordant mix of herbs and metallic blood met her nose and her lungs.

The witch made a noise; a hiss between her teeth. She raised a hand barring Vina's path, forcing them both to stop.

Vina looked around Simran and saw it: a body lying on the ground. It was freshly dead, still intact, its chest unmoving, its skin pale and cold. It looked like a woman, older than both Vina and Simran.

A mark was carved into her forehead. A perfect circle, bloodless.

The witch lurched forward one step. Her hands were clenched. She made a noise, a little shudder of breath, and kneeled down. This was someone the witch knew. Vina's heart gave a sympathetic pang.

Vina almost spoke. But as she opened her mouth, she felt a coldness brush at the back of her neck—the wind, perhaps, or a warning. She carefully lowered the axe to steady soil. The sword at her belt was better fit for her hands, familiar and sharp. She turned her head slowly.

There was a figure behind her. Tall, and broad, and silver-haired.

"No traps for me, witch?" he said. The witch startled, turning where she kneeled. "I thought you'd be better prepared."

"You're the one who set a trap," Simran said. Her voice was thick with unspent tears and fury. "You baited it with my friend's corpse."

"She should have rotted by now," said the man, circling. Somehow, his feet made no sound.

Vina watched his footsteps. He threw no shadow, and the grass under him did not move out of shape.

"The woods are protecting her," said Simran. She watched him hawkishly, intent. "They're *her* woods after all, and they love her. Are you here to try and kill me again?"

"I did not try to kill you," he said. "I offered you a gift."

"There's no gift sweeter than a blade through my chest, I'm sure," the witch said tartly.

"Peace, witch. That is what I gave her. Doesn't she look peaceful? Death is kinder than the fate that was awaiting her."

"The forest is dying. She wouldn't have wanted that."

He shook his head.

"She told me," Simran insisted, voice shaking.

"You fall so easily for lies," the stranger said. His gaze cut, abruptly, to Vina. "You haven't tried to kill me yet, knight? Strange. The last time we met you gutted me from navel to neck."

He looked like a tall man, broad, fair-haired. Vina looked more closely. His murky eyes went from gray to blue to deep red as she watched him; as she breathed carefully and told herself, *Look, all magic is illusion, look under the veil and see him. Look!*

"I would gut you, stranger," said Vina. "I hate to disappoint. But there is no point trying to gut someone who isn't here."

The witch's eyes sharpened.

He quirked an eyebrow.

"What exposed me?"

"If you don't know, sir, I don't feel inclined to tell you," Vina said, tone amiable.

Simran had no questions. She was digging now through the soil by the corpse, long fingers scrabbling in the mud, nails stained with dirt.

"Keen hunter's eyes, you have," he said. Mildly said, but mocking. "And yet so easily bespelled."

"Do you know me, sir?" Vina asked. "I'm afraid I don't know you."

"No," he agreed. "You don't. I see that."

The witch drew a hank of hair from the ground, expression triumphant. Silvery fair, tied with twine.

"I see I'm not the only one with a gift for witchcraft," Simran said.

"I had a fair teacher," the stranger replied. He swept toward Simran, all his focus on her. He bowed over her, throwing no shadow, his voice low. "You have something of mine, now. Before you send me away, let me give you something of yours."

He held out his hand. On his palm lay a single coil of black hair. Simran stared at it, uncomprehending.

"Do you recognize it? No? Then perhaps these."

The lock of hair vanished. In its place... Vina peered closely. Cigarettes? Perplexing.

But the witch understood. She straightened, eyes flashing and wrathful.

"What have you done to him?" she demanded. Around them, the witch marks she'd set began to glow again, burning with her fury. "*Where is Hari?*"

"I've pondered you, witch," the man said, staring at Simran so intently it was as if Vina did not exist at all. "I often ponder you. You don't see the gift death is. Maybe you don't recognize your own chains. I could lay a thousand truths at your feet. And you would reject them all because they come from me... and because you are craven." His voice turned ugly. "You are worse than a dog, compared to what you were. But still, I'll give you a chance. If you want him back, you will have to find the truth yourself. The mountains of copper, witch. Come to your ancient tor. Meet me there, before the winter solstice. Tell me my name, and tell me why I cannot die, and you may have him back whole and alive."

The witch shook her head, lowering her face, squeezing her eyes shut. Her mouth moved, soundless, shaping words.

"You have until the winter solstice, witch," he continued. "Then your friend will die."

Simran twisted the lock of silver hair between her fingers, mouth still moving.

The man shuddered. Lines of gold appeared on his face, livid as scars. His eyes widened, then narrowed to slits.

"No more of this," said the stranger. "I know you're seeking me out. I can feel you trying to trap me."

"You gave me the tools," Simran said. "Give him back to me. Now."

"No. Find me, or he dies. You have your quest. Farewell."

He snapped his fingers, and Simran yelped as the silver hair burned to dust. Before the two of them, the stranger vanished in white smoke.

The witch was breathing hard, blinking back angry tears.

"I need to go," she said. "I need to go to Gore—the town, the houses beyond the woods. I need to go *now*."

It sounded like it was already too late for urgency.

"Who did he take?" Vina asked, low and gentle. A sibling? A lover?

The witch swore, shaking. She walked back to the gap in the trees, then stopped as rainfall brushed her head. She raised a hand to her forehead. The fingers came back black.

Vina raised her head quickly. Above them, the branches were beginning to crack and groan. Ink was pouring from them like blood. A burst of it touched her own face. It bloomed, painfully hot on her skin, then slithered lifelessly to the ground.

"We need to leave," Vina said urgently. "Go, Simran. I'll follow."

"The way is gone," Simran said, and Vina saw that their path had vanished, swallowed by the trees that were closing in, drawing together.

"Use the axe," Simran ordered then. Vina was already hefting it up. She threw the weight of her whole body behind the axe, but the trees were growing larger around them, filled with the screaming wails of dying birds.

"Your magic," Vina bit out.

"I can't feel it," Simran said. Her face was gray, her hands raised as if she was trying to seek her magic in the air, in her fingertips. Her voice wavered. "I can't feel my magic at all."

# Chapter Seven

## *Simran*

*They'll tell you the tales don't exist, but I assure you they do! Lost tales, secret tales, from Elsewhere lands, exotic and strange. For a price, you can find them. Make a deal with a cunning woman Dockside, and she'll tell you the way.*

*But I warn you—the archivists won't think much of you. Look out!*

Source: *Secret Tales of the Isle Revealed!!*, Pamphlet of unknown provenance, discovered at Leadenhall Market

**Archivist's Ruling:** For retention as evidence of treason. Review in 6 months. Further investigation required. Interrogation of local vendors recommended.

Where the hell had her magic gone? Her heart was pounding, blood roaring, and she couldn't feel any magic at all.

Maybe it was the shock of seeing Hari's carefully hand-rolled cigarettes in the palm of the stranger that had twisted her witchcraft from her grasp. The sight had hit her stomach with a cold gut-punch of dread that had nearly leveled her. Bess's death had been something she'd been braced for—nothing could have prepared her for the sight of Bess's corpse, waxen on a bed of leaves, but at least she'd known it was a *possibility*.

She hadn't been prepared for anything to happen to Hari. That wasn't how it was meant to be. She was the one who courted danger, who carved spells into bones and limni ink into flesh, who stole from knights and merchants to maintain the life she and Hari had cobbled together. It was Hari's role to run from danger; to be her heart and her home; to work tiring jobs and sleep like the dead, and still smile at her when she slunk in at twilight with ink under her fingernails. The stranger had rewritten that story she and Hari had written together, and it had left her with fury and grief churning inside her, and *no magic*.

"If you could find your magic swiftly," the knight gritted out, wrenching Bess's rusted axe from the trunk of the tree, "that would be—ideal!"

"Shut up," said Simran, crushing her panic. "I have to think."

From the axe wound that knight had made in the tree, ink oozed out, a mingling of black and ichor red. Simran could only think of real sap, the way it could smear like blood. Trees could be naturally cruel creatures, any tale could tell you so. To have a forest turn on you was a risk of life on the Isle. Cruel trees, cursed woods.

This was different from all of that. This was a tale collapsing.

Think. *Think!*

Witchcraft needed conduits. Earth, blood, trees, bones, guts, flowers. The best witchcraft took time to cultivate and grow.

Simran had left her marks here. Fresh marks: her own hair, plucked from her head and knotted into a charm; spells scuffed into soil with her own feet. Bird bones, taken from an abandoned nest, buried carefully to the sound of a song from her own lips.

But she'd also cultivated magic here for years. Her whole childhood had shaped this forest, and been shaped by it in turn. There was magic in the shape her footsteps had left in the soil on rainy days, when she'd been twelve, then thirteen, then fourteen, as the seasons turned. There was witch-strength and witch-knowledge in accidental blood from scuffed knees, and then later from deliberate blood, when Bess had told her the magic of flesh and a knife.

Her childhood magic had dug its claws into this place. She knew how to draw her strength from these woods. The fact she couldn't was more than strange, and no grief should have blotted that old magic out.

There. The answer. As the trees shuddered, creaking out of shape into spasms of ink, it came to her:

Her magic wasn't gone. In all the ways that mattered, the *forest* was.

"Stop cutting that tree," ordered Simran. "Put the axe down."

The knight gave her an incredulous look.

"I'm afraid if we don't have your magic, lady witch, we're certainly going to need the axe—"

"Simran. I told you my name is Simran."

"Simran, Simran," the knight parroted back, her voice timed with each furious thud of the axe as the ground shuddered and the trees screamed, and screamed, and screamed. The knight was sweating visibly, her face shining and her curling brown hair plastered to the shape of her skull. Her eyes, when they cut to Simran, were determined, and her full mouth unsmiling.

"Why do you want me to stop?"

"Because in a moment it isn't going to matter," said Simran. Her voice was grim. "Can't you see? The woods are dying. There's no saving them."

The knight paused, then flinched. Cursed. She flung the axe from her hands as if burned, and Simran watched it fracture, prismatic, then collapse into pigment and smoke. Bess's axe, she realized. Fading out of the world along with Bess's tale.

The trees in front of them snapped entirely out of shape, spidering into ink in the vague shape of trees. And then suddenly, simply, they were not even the suggestion of trees anymore—just ink, a mist of black, a darkness falling down. The knight hissed with obvious pain as the ink touched her.

Simran grasped the knight's wrist, and in the gap where the woods were dying and *nothingness* was growing, she ran.

The trees were snapping around them, twisting out of shape, turning to liquid and ether. They ran, and Simran tried not to consider what would become of them if they did not escape the woods before the woods died along with Bess, withering without her tale to nourish their bones. The darkness grew denser, and the knight was running with her, steady thudding footsteps and steadier breaths as she matched Simran step for step. If she was still in pain, she was hiding it well. They weren't going to make it. They had to try.

Around them, in the dark, lights were glowing. The lights were moving in closer, and as they did so, Simran began to discern glowing shapes.

Deer.

One careened in front of them, stopping in their path. A ghostly doe, ears flicking, its golden skin glowing like a lamp in the inky darkness.

"My friend!" the knight crowed, her mouth shaping into a grin as she stepped forward and out of Simran's grasp. She bowed to the deer, and the deer watched her back with what Simran would have called bemusement. "It's good to see you again. Have you come to lead us to freedom?"

The deer shook on those light, leaping legs. Uneasy.

The knight kneeled and held out her hand.

"We need to run," Simran began.

"No," the knight said, voice still level and gentle. Ink brushed her in a coiling wind. She flinched but didn't move. "Not yet. Wait." To the deer, she said, "You needn't fear me now. We are friends, aren't we? I wouldn't have found your lady Bess or the witch without your help, and I'm thankful for you. I know you're afraid, but you came to us for a reason. Please. Will you help, as I know you want to?"

Her voice was soft and deep. It made Simran's skin electrify strangely.

The deer, hesitantly, moved forward. And touched its soft nose to the knight's waiting palm. The knight's smile deepened.

She was so absurdly lovely, in that moment: the noble angles of her jaw, the softness of her dark-lashed eyes, the faint curl of her hair, her body limned in darkness. All of it could have been an oil painting, and if Simran had possessed any gift for art she would have wanted to paint her, preserve her.

Simran's admiration was quickly followed by a stab of envy. Surely the deer should have been Simran's friends? She was the one who'd watched them for years, drifting between the trees, always darting out of reach. Why did they come so easily to the knight's hand?

Simran had never been so... so open. So soft to anything, anyone. Only perhaps to Hari—and look where that had got him. Envy curdled in her blood as she looked at the knight's soft and noble face. Envy and fear, as if she were standing on a great precipice, and one gust of wind would send her hurtling into the unknown.

Some unspoken understanding had clearly passed between knight and deer, because the deer drew back its head. Unburdened by the trees, the ghost deer leapt. Its herd joined it, running forward, carving a path through the trees like a golden arrow dispelling the dark.

The knight grasped Simran's hand.

"*Now* we run," she said.

They raced forward. Simran's lungs burned. She stumbled, and the knight steadied her, practically lifting her from her feet with breathless strength. "A little farther," the knight urged, which was a lie—how could the knight know how much farther they had to go? But Simran found her feet, and suddenly they were free, blazing sunlight above them.

Simran wrenched free from the knight and fell to her knees on the grass. She had a second to breathe, inhale and exhale with relief—and then she heard a crash, and a helpless noise from the knight behind her.

The herd was crashing against the edge of the woods, beating their bodies against an invisible barrier. They were crying out, and Simran realized with horror that they could not cross the boundaries of the woodland.

The deer herd belonged to the woods. They belonged to the tale that had made them, as much as Bess. None of them could escape.

The knight was staring at them, naked horror on her face. Her jaw hardened. She took a step toward the woods, reaching out a hand. Simran lurched forward and caught her by the leg.

"Don't you *dare*," she said, tightening her grip.

"I can't just leave them," the knight protested.

"You have no choice," said Simran. "You can't help them. You can only save yourself."

The knight was breathing hard, hands flexing. But she didn't try to pull away again. Simran stared at her own hand like it was a traitor.

She should have let the knight go. What did she care, if the knight lived or died? The knight was going to kill *her*.

But the knight had helped her. The knight had reached out, gentle and open-hearted to the deer. The knight would show her true colors soon enough, but right now, Simran couldn't see the villain under that noble surface. Damn it all.

The darkness grew thicker. One of the deer—the one who had touched her nose to the knight's hand—lowered her head. The deer's light was blotted out entirely—and then with an exhale like a sigh, a last breath, the darkness vanished. And the woods with it.

There was a moment of trembling air, as if the entire Isle was shuddering around the wound of the lost woods. Then the seam closed. The landscape that had once surrounded the woods fused together, fields joining, the horizon meeting in one endless line of blue marked by the distant smoke of factories. It was like the woods had never existed at all.

Simran realized they were both trembling. She felt exhausted.

She saw the knight huff out a breath and brush her sweat-damp hair back from her face.

Unwanted, a pang of sympathy rang through her. And godsblood, she had no time for sympathy. She had time for none of this. Not grief, not horror, not sympathy for a knight meant to take her life. She had to go to her parents' home—to Hari. She rose to her feet, turned on her heel, and began to walk.

"Wait," the knight called out, after a beat. "Wait!"

Hurried footsteps behind her. The knight's voice was close to her left.

"The witch hunters will be close," the knight warned. And damn her, why was she pretending Simran's freedom mattered to her?

"I don't care," said Simran. Her voice shook. The anger and panic in her were wild as briars and thorns, growing as she thought of Hari and her parents and the stranger, and his cold, malevolent eyes. "What does it matter if they see me? What we are—what *I* am—I can't let that hurt my family. *I should never have come back.*" Her voice snapped, broke like kindling wood.

"Simran," the knight said gently. The pity in her voice was unbearable.

Simran couldn't look at the knight. Her heart was a drumbeat in her chest, thudding in her ears.

"If you try and stop me I swear I'll hurt you as badly as our tale allows," Simran vowed, voice low. Then she took a deep, ragged breath and started to run.

The ground turned from untended grass to muddy tracks to paved stone under her feet. They were on the cobbled road outside her parents' home when she saw a crowd ahead of her, local folk gathered together in a thick huddle of long coats and caps and muttering voices. Broken glass littered the ground in front of the shattered window of her parents' store. Among the gentle peace of those colorful shop awnings and redbrick buildings, the damage was as livid as a scar.

She paused, her stomach sinking. She was too late.

Her thoughts kept racing, parsing what must have happened as she elbowed through the crowd. Instead of shoving her way to the shop, she headed for the wide-open side door that led to the flat above the store. She paid no attention to the creak of the wood under her feet, or the voices behind her. She had no time to prepare herself—nothing but her hammering heart and her ragged breath as armor, as she came face-to-face with her parents for the first time in years.

And there they were: her mother, tired lines bracketing her mouth, her hair pinned in a bun. Her father, a slight man, throat scarred. The furniture was broken around them, the window to the right smashed. Hari was not there. But her parents, at least, were safe.

"Mama," she choked out. "Papa."

She didn't want to see the love in their eyes. *Don't look at me like that, don't love me, you don't see the knife at my throat—*

"Simran," her mother said, trembling. "Darling."

They reached for her, and she didn't step away. The warmth of her father's arm around her. Her mother's perfume.

She gripped her mother by the sleeve. Forced herself to breathe.

"Where is Hari?" Simran asked.

"Gone," said her mother. Her voice was sharp, brittle. Her eyes red. But she hadn't wept. Simran had never seen her parents cry. "A devil—a man—came and told Hari if he left with him he would not hurt us."

"Are you hurt?" Simran asked tightly.

"No," said her father. His voice was as warm and weighty as his hand, a balm. "We are safe."

"Hari said you had not come with him," said her mother. "He said it to us. He said it to the devil. But the devil said Hari lied, and then he took him. They vanished like mist." She waved a hand, as if to say *it was like this*. Sudden, swift as a breeze. "I understand Hari lying to him—but to us? Why, Simran?"

He'd lied for her. She met her mother's piercing eyes for one heartbeat, then two, and said nothing. She saw understanding dawn in her mother's eyes—and worse, resignation.

"I see," her mother said.

A clatter at the door. The knight stepped in through the entrance, alone. She ducked her head apologetically.

Simran's parents stiffened at the sight of the knight. In their usually cozy kitchen, with its net curtains, its faded but carefully tended-to rugs, the knight was an unnatural sight, a warning of violence, an interloper. Even without her armor, she reeked of what she was.

The knight paused, head still tilted. Her long fingers moved to her waist and swiftly removed her sword, then the bow at her back. She laid them on the ground. Her shoulders rounded; her posture changed. When she stood, Simran would have sworn the knight had somehow grown smaller.

"I'm sorry," the knight said, in that low, rich voice of hers. "I'm here to help, if I can."

"Wait outside," said Simran. Godsblood, she didn't want the knight here.

"Our friends are coming," said the knight. She moved to lean against the door—barring the way out, but also the way in. "Please allow me to help. At least I can keep watch."

Simran's parents were looking at her. Swallowing her instinctual bile, Simran said, "Fine. Stay if you want to." To her parents, she said, "She won't cause any harm."

"Who is she?" Simran's father asked. "What is happening, Simran?" His grip had tightened, his eyes dark. "Beti, if you're in danger..."

"I'm fine," she said shortly. Then, forcing herself to speak gently, respectfully, she said, "I'm really fine, Papa. Don't worry about me. Let me find Hari. Sir Lavinia will help me."

She tugged herself from his grip. He let her go.

The knight said something to her parents, but Simran couldn't hear it over the panicked buzzing in her own skull. Being here made her feel raw.

Simran walked over to the biggest mess: the broken kitchen table. Her parents' favorite teapot, flowered and ceramic, was broken into shards. It lay in a pool of spilled tea, a scattering of glittering white sugar. Simran kneeled down, examining it all. She mouthed a spell under her breath as her fingertips traced the remains.

The knight, as if drawn by gravity, came to loom over her.

"Will this help you find him? Your friend?" Her voice was a respectful whisper, but Simran took a moment to glare at her all the same. The knight didn't have the good sense to recoil.

As if it were that easy, Simran thought bitterly, despairingly. People without any touch of magic had a tendency to think it could do anything. But magic obeyed the rules of tales as much as anything did, and Simran couldn't find Hari from spilled tea and will alone.

The knight's voice lowered further.

"If your magic isn't back…"

"My magic was never the problem," hissed Simran. "I was wrong. It's still here."

She touched her fingers to the pottery. Her eyes snagged on something she hadn't seen before: a shard stained in bright blood.

She touched it. Rubbed the blood between her fingers. At the back of her throat, she didn't feel the telltale scent of a story marking the presence of an incarnate, the pale-eyed stranger with the circle on his brow. Instead, the blood buzzed at her touch, singing a familiar note.

"Hari's blood," she breathed. "That brilliant man."

The knight shifted next to her, forehead creased.

"He's hurt?"

"I think it was intentional." *I hope.* "Hari knows I can use blood," Simran said hoarsely. "He's never been a fighter. He knows he should leave the fighting to me. He did this *for* me." She raised her head. "I need a cloth. Something clean and dry."

Without hesitating, the knight ripped her sleeve and offered the cloth to her, eyes steady. Simran gave her an incredulous look.

"You call this clean? It's been against your skin. It's covered in—in dirt!"

"It's all I have," said the knight, mouth twisting into a lopsided, self-effacing smile.

"It won't do." She tucked it away anyway. If she ever needed some way to trap the knight, it would help.

"Here," her father said. He gave her a soft tea towel, clean. "This is... magic?"

She froze, the cloth tight in her fist. Then forced herself to move and breathe.

"Yes, Papa," she said thinly. Another thing, among so many, that she'd never shared with him in her brief letters.

There was no surprise in his face. The same resignation, the same familiar grief she'd seen in her mother's face, flitted across his own. He stepped back.

*No guilt*, she told herself firmly. *It's better this way.*

She dabbed up the spill of blood, whispering a thread of a spell as she did so, to preserve the blood and Hari's presence in it.

"Quickly," the knight said suddenly. She'd tilted her head, eyes as alert as a wary doe's. "I can hear someone coming." She moved to the entrance.

Now that Simran was also listening, she could hear footsteps like those at the roadside inn, heavy and brutish.

Simran looked up at her parents, panic welling up in her. Knowing about her magic was bad enough. She didn't want them to know what she truly was.

She straightened up fast. "I'll go down and meet them," she said tightly.

"You don't have to," the knight began, cautious. But Simran couldn't listen to this. She pushed past the knight and headed down the stairs.

Her vision tunneled as she walked down, brushing by locals milling in the street. On the road stood three witch hunters, black and ominous as ravens in their high hats. Between them stood the archivist, looking supremely irritated. One of the witch hunters was haranguing the baker, hissing something about *stray incarnates* and *hiding from the law*. The baker's face was splotchy red with anger.

Simran took a step forward. And a figure swept past her, blocking her path.

"You're looking for an incarnate, then?" The knight sounded bored, drawling. She straightened, rolling back her shoulders, holding her arms out expansively. "Well, you've found me."

A rustle of alarmed—and interested—noise ran through the crowd.

What was the knight *doing*? Simran couldn't see around the barrier of her body. Did she think she could protect Simran? And why for the Isle's sake would she want to?

"You're being noble," she said, acid in her tone. "But there's no need. I'm who you're here for."

The knight turned her head and gave Simran a sharp look. Simran ignored it.

The archivist stepped forward. In the clear light of day, without a wall and rain and panic and mud to separate them, Simran could see that she was older than Simran by perhaps a decade, and just as brown-skinned, with the look of Elsewhere all over her. The same Elsewhere as Simran, perhaps, though it was hard to know, when arriving at the Isle tended to blur the edges of memories of before and give the ones that remained a strange, tarnished patina.

"Stay still, miss," the archivist said. "Let's be done with this."

The monocular prism set over the archivist's eye shifted like clockwork, semitranslucent dials under the faceted surface shifting.

"This is the one." She sounded satisfied. "It is good to meet you, witch. We need to take you back to London. You deserve a formal introduction at court."

"Take me, then," Simran said. "Do I get handcuffs or a leash? Or, oh—chains, perhaps? How novel."

"You're not a prisoner. You're going to be celebrated."

"I don't want to be celebrated," Simran said. "So am I free to go?"

The archivist's mouth twisted. "We'll talk more, miss. For now—come."

Simran took a step forward. She looked back behind her.

Her blood ran cold.

Her mother was watching from the door, her mouth thin, her eyes unreadable.

She'd heard, but Simran had to believe she hadn't. She'd heard, but Simran couldn't allow herself to know it. A hand closed on her forearm.

"C'mon," a witch hunter said gruffly.

"She can walk on her own," the knight said mildly, from somewhere ahead of Simran. She was being led away, to wherever Simran was about to be led. Nobody was holding her. She looked calm.

"I'll write," Simran called out to her mother. Even though her mother knew well enough that Simran wrote only rarely, and then only the briefest, most meaningless letters. *I'm well. Here is some money. Love to you and Papa.* "I'll—I'll tell you when I've found Hari."

The witch hunter tugged her arm again, and if her mother said something in return, then Simran didn't hear it.

They dragged her into a sprung, horse-drawn carriage, waiting at the end of the road. The curtains were shut, and the interior dark. The knight was sitting across from Simran, silent and watching her.

The carriage jolted abruptly. And in a breath, they were moving. Heading back to London.

# Chapter Eight

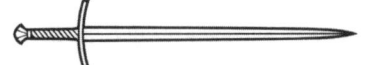

## *Vina*

*The Crown has always been one with the Eternal Queen. There were no rulers before her, and there shall be none after. To claim differently is to court death. When you next travel to Nonsuch at her pleasure, I advise you to hold your tongue.*

Source: Correspondence between Lord Arthur Wincroft and Lewis Spencer (deceased)

**Archivist's Ruling: Destroy. No further investigation required.**

Would the Spymaster forgive her for making a mess of her unspoken quest if she told him there had been extenuating circumstances?

A murderer in a forest; a dead incarnate; and the other half of her tale, the witch, threatened by a collapsing inky woodland and a pale-eyed man who watched her with malevolence and something else Vina couldn't place—a *knowing*, maybe. Vina could not have planned for any of it. Vina had been a victim of circumstance.

There had been no easy way to collect the witch—*Simran*, she corrected internally. No easy way to collect Simran. Simran had been angry and rightfully wary, and she'd shown no sign of softening in all the hours she'd been stifled in the carriage alongside

Vina. Simran had responded to every prodding question from the archivist with silence, her back ramrod straight, her lips as thin as a knife cut.

The carriage itself was dark with the curtains shut, gloomy and oppressively silent. In the thin facets of light that broke through the gaps in the curtain, Vina examined Simran's face, which was turned to the side, showing Vina her profile. A sharp jaw, sharp cheekbones, a strong nose. A lovely mouth, and dark brown eyes. Simran's expression was stony.

Vina couldn't help but look at her and remember how incandescent she'd been in the woods. She wondered what small spark would set Simran ablaze again. Vina couldn't help but wish for it—anything to break the brittle cold of her, that still face.

The archivist tentatively cleared her throat and said, "Sir Lavinia. I have some questions for you."

Vina wrenched her attention away from Simran.

"Of course, darling," Vina said, with a languid smile. "Ask me anything you like."

The archivist stared at her, mouth thinning with displeasure for a moment, before a veneer of politeness swept the contempt away.

Vina bit back her own laugh.

Laura and her father had tried to teach her how to charm and make polite conversation; *politician's wife conversation*, Laura had called it dryly. But Vina had taken those lessons and quickly learned how to irritate rather than soothe, anger rather than calm. Sometimes charm wasn't enough; sometimes Vina had to be an ornery little shit, for the good of all.

"No questions?" Vina said innocently. "I can tell you need to relax. Let your hair down a little more. I know an excellent pub in Waterloo—"

"No," the archivist cut in through gritted teeth. "We need not talk now. Later, perhaps."

Vina looked at the witch again. Simran was still sitting straight and tense, but her mouth had softened infinitesimally.

There was little time left to mull the fate awaiting them. They were almost back. Vina knew the jolt of those London cobblestones, as they crossed the London Wall into the ancient city proper; and she knew what it meant when the cobbles smoothed, the carriage moving onto the path that led to the royal Palace itself.

They came to a stop. Vina did not think of golden deer, as bright as phosphorus lamps, bounding through the trees. She did not think of the man who'd murdered incarnates and murdered a forest. Instead, she thought of the expression she'd need to wear when the carriage door was wrenched open—and ah, there the door went, flung open by a witch hunter's careless hands, letting the cool night air in. Vina schooled her expression into something suitably contrite, a crease between her brows and no smile on her lips—and offered Simran her hand.

Simran did not look at her. She slunk out of the carriage, landing lightly on her feet. Vina followed after her, all her bones aching as she unfolded from the cramped position she'd held all the way back home. She wasn't used to being still for so long.

Beyond the gloom of the carriage, the evening was somehow painfully bright, painted with torchlight. Awaiting them under the golden light of the courtyard stood a coterie of archivists, robed and solemn. At their head waited an austere man with blond hair that Vina did not recognize by face alone. But she recognized his clothing: the grand chains of knot-worked gold at his throat, and the chatelaine at the waist of his robe, weighed down by vials of ink and a feathered quill of beaded silver-gold.

A senior archivist. No, the *head* archivist, keeper of the great tomes of the Isle, Apollonius Roland himself.

If he was here, then finding the witch had been more vital than anyone had admitted to Vina. And Vina was, quite thoroughly, fucked.

The Spymaster stepped forward, face cold and forbidding.

"Knight," he said, voice pure frost. "You were forbidden from leaving State grounds, by royal orders."

Embarrassed men were dangerous men; but Vina was ready to be the Spymaster's scapegoat, and danger didn't frighten her as it should.

She bowed low, hand to her heart, and said, "I am sorry, sir. My past self came to weep at my door. I could not resist my tale. I had to obey." Her voice wavered appropriately. "I will take any punishment the State sees fit to lay upon me. In this I followed my heart, but I failed my duty."

She spoke with as much sincerity and feeling as she could press into her words—and heard the witch snort faintly, derisively behind her.

Archivist Roland gave a booming, indulgent laugh. "These incarnates," he said. "They can't be helped, they're always off gallivanting. At least these two are now accounted for." He patted the Spymaster on the shoulder. "No need to thank me, of course. We're here to support you, my friend, whenever the privy council falls short."

The Spymaster's face somehow grew even more pinched.

"Meera," Archivist Roland said. "Come here." He crooked a finger, and the archivist she and Simran had traveled with walked to his side.

"Sir Lavinia," said the Spymaster. His gaze flickered to Simran. "Witch," he said. "The Queen is expecting you both. Follow me."

The whole group of them—archivists and Spymaster, witch hunters and watching guards—swept toward the steps of the Palace. At the entrance, the witch hunters were barred. They protested loudly, but they were soon left behind.

This was going to be a formal audience, Vina realized. Simran's formal audience. They were walking along the main corridors of the Palace toward the White Hall, chandeliers twinkling above them, plush carpet beneath their feet.

"I can't see the Queen," Simran said, voice thin, looking for the first time not furious or stony but...nervous.

"Why not?" Vina asked gently.

Simran said nothing for a beat. No doubt Simran had heard all sort of stories about the Queen: of her hair blazing behind her like fire when she rode into battle; of the petty love games she played with her courtiers; of her luminous beauty, her terrifying temper, her joy in bear baiting and fox hunting, her love for good marchpane and glorious balls.

Of her power, Isle-wide and Isle-deep. The Queen was the most ancient incarnate tale of all, and her bones were the bones of the Isle, her heart its very life.

"I suppose she's just a woman," Simran said finally.

*No*, Vina thought. *Ah no, she's not just that.* But no warning could truly prepare Simran, and there was no time for it now anyway. They were at the White Hall.

Great doors were thrown open. At the circular table before the throne sat the privy council, robed and silent. On her unassuming throne, sat the entirely *assuming* Eternal Queen, surrounded by her flock of ladies-in-waiting, raven-haired and masked in vizards, ovals of concealing black velvet that only left their eyes bare. They were all utterly silent, which was no surprise: Their masks were held in place by a bead clenched between their teeth, maintaining their muteness.

At her side she saw Simran pause, blanching in shock, before steadying.

Vina felt a pang of sympathy. Even the hardiest folk were thrown the first time they saw the Eternal Queen.

The Queen's face was porcelain: inhumanly white, unlined, rosy-mouthed, and glassily blue-eyed. Her face would have been doll-like if it hadn't been so animated, mouth curving into an enigmatic smile as she beheld them, her winged eyebrows drawing together as she examined her visitors, then smoothing as she leaned back. Her hair was red—vibrant, a mingling of copper and rose, somewhere between blood and fire. Her gown was expansive, white, and her neck was surrounded by a ruff like a white halo, glittering with a frost of diamonds.

Even if she had not looked as she looked, her presence was overpowering: a cloying, warm fragrance of hazel and nutmeg that mingled with rosewater that scented the room. She smelled like the incarnate she was, the flesh that grew from an old, vast, and deep-rooted tale. She was so distracting that it was almost possible to miss her behemoth of a pet coiled loosely around her throne, her ladies-in-waiting, and the steps that led to the throne. Her beloved pet was a wyvern, two-legged and two-winged, its scales a burnished gold and its snout long, barely concealing serrated teeth. It would have looked like a frightening beast indeed, if it were not collared with a velvet black collar like a small dog, and if it were not snoring faintly, asleep with its snout at the Queen's feet.

Vina bowed, and after a moment Simran followed suit, as the entire hall rippled with genuflection. There was a long silence. Then the Queen leaned forward with a rustle of silks, a coo of delight.

"We have not seen you for decades, witch," the Queen murmured. Her voice was rich, musical. "To see you alongside my dear knight, to know your tale is safe in the cradle of our hand... it is glorious, truly! How well you suit one another!" Her gaze fixed on Simran. "We have seen this knight many times, and marveled at her womanliness and exotic blood—why not a witch of similar oddness?" She laughed, and her women rustled, clinking with teeth-gritting laughter along with her. "Strange. But incarnates are incarnates, are they not? They do not adhere to traditional morality, we understand."

She crooked a finger.

"Step closer," she commanded, and both Simran and Vina did so. "Closer," the Queen urged, and one of her ladies-in-waiting drifted down from beside her throne to guide them to the Queen's feet.

The Queen placed one pale finger beneath Simran's chin, raising her head to examine her. Simran stared back, transfixed.

"Has your tale begun? Has the knight hunted you yet, dear witch—bow in hand, arrow cocked?" Her eyes creased into a blue smile.

"I don't understand, Your Majesty," Simran said, voice tight.

"No, then," said the Queen. She released Simran abruptly, waving her hands about in an airy fashion. "You will stay with us. You will dine with us. A week of feasting! You will entertain me, regale me with tales—and then, a *ball.*"

The courtiers cheered, clapping merrily. The Queen smiled back at them, beatific.

"I—I can't," Simran said, but the sound of clapping courtiers had turned her voice small. "I need to leave. My friend—"

Vina touched Simran's arm. Simran's head whipped to face her.

"You can't question her," Vina whispered. "Not here."

The look Simran gave her was viperous—and betrayed. But Vina stared back, unflinching. Simran had to understand her. This was a warning. Vina had lived in this Palace since she was young. She knew what the Queen was capable of.

When Vina was first placed before the Queen as a child, and felt the Queen's rose-scented hands on her chin, she had been entranced. She'd wanted to love the Palace. Laura had told her to love her purpose, so she'd *tried.* That had lasted until the day a courtier had displeased the Queen—traitorous words written to a lover had been discovered by archivists who sifted through letters just as they examined coffeehouse papers and books. The courtier had been brought before the Queen, where he'd begged and groveled, and kissed her dainty slippers. And she had smiled at him, beautiful as ivory and rose, and told her wyvern to eat him feet first.

It had.

Vina did not often think of it. It had been horrible, to be sure. But there was no escape from it. Her tale was her cage. It was a nice cage, as they went. And the bars of her tale would follow her no matter where she tried to run.

The Queen clapped her hands before Simran could say anything more. The Queen stood, and her audience bowed as one as she and her women left the room in a rustle of silks and perfumes.

"Lavinia," said the Spymaster, when the Queen was gone, and their audience had risen from their bows. "With me."

Simran was being led away by a guard. She didn't look back at Vina.

Vina turned and followed the Spymaster. He took her to a small salon, decked in powder-blue settees. The windows were open onto the black night. He shut them officiously, then turned back to her.

"Now," he said. "Tell me what happened."

She told him everything—everything, apart from how she'd almost let Simran go. That had, indeed, been a foolishly noble impulse. Better to keep it secret.

"What did you tell the archivist?"

"Nothing, sir."

"Good, good. She'll report your every move to Roland, of course, but at least the damn man won't have your words."

"Sir," said Vina. "The killer of incarnates—what is to be done about him?"

"Nothing that concerns you."

"A woodland died because of him," said Vina. "Two tales I know of have been lost, but I know there must be more. This is an emergency, sir, a catastrophe for the Isle. If I can help—"

"You can help, Lavinia, by doing what the Queen wants, and keeping your thoughts to yourself," the Spymaster said coldly. "Do you understand?"

A beat. Vina inclined her head.

"Apologies," she murmured.

"Your father has sent you a message," he added. "It will be in your room. Head there directly. When you're not dining at the Queen's pleasure, that's where you'll remain."

"Understood," said Vina. She'd go mad being so inactive, but what could she do?

She was followed by a guard to her room. When she closed the door she waited a breath by the entrance until she heard the telltale click of a key. She was locked in.

The message from her father was on the table. It was on his official stationery, headed with the sigil of Parliament. The letter was a simple thing: an admonishment for how her behavior had harmed his standing. *A minister cannot have an incarnate child who strays from their duty.* It urged her to remain on State grounds.

*You could have come and told me yourself,* thought Vina. There was also a letter from Laura. This was neat, delicate script on flower-scented paper. Her letter was softer, cajoling. *Don't be hurt by your father, dear Lavinia. He was terribly frightened for you. Look after yourself. I'll keep him safe.*

She placed the letters back on the table.

She lay back down on her bed and thought of phosphorescent deer, and a pale-eyed man, and Soren, dead. What a curious and dreadful business. *Someone* had to find answers, if the Queen and Commons alike were unwilling.

She could bide her time. She was good at that.

The dinners were excruciating. Long mahogany tables were laden to the point of ludicrousness with lush feast after feast, honey apples and suckling pig, cockentrice sewn together with neat thread—but no less grotesque because of it—and roasted rabbit, garnished with apricots and pearly onions. Courtiers filled every available seat, elbowing one another for space in their ridiculous finery. No other knights or incarnates were invited so Vina and Simran were on their own, seated on opposite sides of the table where they could look but not speak.

Fantastic, truly. It left no way for Vina to explain herself. She was trapped staring at Simran, who refused to look back, and instead picked at her food in stony silence.

The Queen, in the largest seat with her wyvern curled about her, was the one who spoke the most, regaling them with tales of her nigh-on-immortal adventures. Simran sat to her far left in a stiff-necked borrowed gown, her hair bundled into a gable hood, pearls wreathed around her throat, and her expression a rictus of simmering rage. She had a lady-in-waiting on each side, guard dogs in black masks. She'd tried to run, then. Vina hadn't expected any less.

Vina, in her doublet, her resignation, could only stare at her and say, *Wait, wait, bide your time* with her eyes alone.

That night, the Queen was relating how she had crossed paths with the Laidly Wyrm, a small incarnate tale she had crashed into on a fox hunt. "It was Apollonius's predecessor who warned us the wyrm was no simple beast, but part of a tale that breathes life into an array of crags in the north. And to think we would have cut her down!" She laughed merrily. "Poor girl, ensorcelled into the form of a wyrm until her brother could break the curse upon her. Certainly our lance would have been no replacement for his brotherly kiss! What would we do without our dear archivists to advise us?"

"Her Majesty would have seen the truth a mere moment later, of this I'm sure," Apollonius protested, oily and smiling. "Her Majesty is, after all, the greatest of all incarnates—her vision and knowledge are unparalleled."

The Queen smiled graciously as if to say yes, this was indeed true, and Apollonius was correct to say it. A great tumult of compliments followed.

Buoyed up, the Queen continued boasting.

"Indeed, we have hunted far greater prey since. You cannot envisage what we were at the ritual of the royal hunt: garbed in armor that shone like moonlight, high upon our white horse." She sighed, reminiscing. "It was the winter solstice. The spirits were high—we sought a wild hunt," she said, naming a ritual hunt that fell at the liminal times of solstices and equinoxes, when the magic of spirits and fae was at its greatest, and renowned hunters sought out mythical prey in order to feed upon their power. "We hunted a whisper: of a great beast prowling the ancient primordial forest, a cockatrice perhaps, or another form of wyrm whose venom and wickedness filled the minds of all who gazed on it with ugly terrors. It is the duty of a monarch to hunt great beasts, and so we did. All night we chased... but we found only our dear wyvern, no venom in her, though her teeth are sharp indeed. We fought, but we chained her to our will soon enough. And now she is our dearest companion."

She petted its great head, nestled on her lap. Its eyes were dull, its scales glossless. It made no sound, and did not move at her touch.

Not for the first time, Vina felt pity well up in her heart. How trapped the creature looked. How sad, to see such a beast at the Queen's feet. She looked away, gaze sliding toward Simran once again.

With a start, a shock, she realized that this time Simran was looking back at her. They shared a moment of perfect understanding—the same pity, the same frustration, the same disgust. Then Simran's look hardened with judgment.

*Look at what happens right in front of you*, her expression said. *Why have you never done anything about it?*

Vina looked away first, shame in her belly.

The balls held at the royal Palace were lavish beyond all belief.

Vina had attended her first soon after being found out as an incarnate. She'd worn a stiff dress, flat at the bodice in the style the Queen favored, her hair piled on her head in plaits beneath a veil. She'd loathed that entire candlelit banquet and formal dance, as she'd stumbled through steps as the adults watched her with curious eyes, this child incarnate trussed in velvet and gold.

But now she was an adult, and although she couldn't avoid probing eyes, she had more control over some things than she'd once had. Her appearance, for one.

Her doublet was unadorned by ruffles, plain velvet stitched with silver, broad at the shoulders and whittled at the waist. In front of her small bathroom mirror, she wetted her short hair and combed it until the curls fell in a pleasing shape. She changed her earrings from gold to silver to match. It was enough.

The banqueting hall was warm, scented by the pine smoke of open hearth fires, the ceilings high and wooden floors polished to a gleaming shine. The walls were covered in tapestries of great incarnate tales: dragons with lustrous green scales, and women in coned hats; serpents and warlocks, great giants and wolves vaster than houses.

She avoided looking at them. Instead, she looked at the throng of nobility in the hall, the great lords and ladies all dressed for the

Queen's pleasure in her preferred clothing, ruffs and gowns, doublets and hose. The candlelight was warm on their milling figures; the air smelled like rosewater and cardamom.

Among them stood a few alien figures; gowns at a closer glance woven from rose petals; imps, dryads; figures with faces of exquisite beauty.

The fae were here.

She thought of Soren and all her unanswered questions, tracking one figure with her eyes as she did so: a dryad perhaps, her hair woven into a long braid of leaves, and her companion, a tall figure with a long fall of golden-blond hair, power radiating from their form like light. The beginnings of a plan began to form.

"Vinny," a voice said.

It was Matthias, concern and sympathy in his eyes.

"So," he said after a pause. "You're... Well. It begins. How do you feel?"

Vina smiled. "Have a wine for me," she said. "Get one for Edmund too, if he's here."

"He's here. He doesn't want to talk."

She didn't stop smiling. "That's fine," she said lightly. "I'll corner him another time, I'm sure."

She grabbed her own glass of spiced wine from a silver tray. One drink would do her no real damage, and would make this whole business more palatable.

She downed it. Lowered the glass back down. As she did so, a chorus of trumpets erupted, and the nobles bowed low and graceful as the Queen swept in and took her seat at the high banqueting table, raised above the room.

That was Vina's cue. She was moving even before a harried maid began to walk over to her, summoning her with flapping hands.

The floor before the banqueting table was bare of people. Waiting.

"The knight and the witch," a herald announced, and Vina stepped forward with a breath, a smile.

Vina knew keenly that a tapestry of the knight and the witch hung in this room. That golden-haired man and that palely blond woman swooning in his arms were stitched into cloth behind the Queen's seat, their bodies surrounded by a circle of blood.

The pale witch could not have been more different from Simran, who was being harried to the center of the hall by two ladies-in-waiting. Simran's brown skin glowed in the candlelight. Her expression was flat and unreadable, her bones sharp, her arms crossed. She was angry and beautiful—like a sharp blade, to be held with reverence, moved with skill. Vina's throat felt dry.

Simran wore her hair in a simple black braid. Her gown was stiff brocade but entirely black, copper embellished where Vina's was silver, as if they were twined together by the language of cloth, not just their shared tale.

Vina stepped forward and took Simran's hand in her own.

Simran stared back at her, defiant and cool, but under the surface Vina could see her panic. Either she had not been told what to do, or she had forgotten.

"First, bow to the Queen with me," Vina said in a low voice. She turned and bowed, Simran mirroring her.

The Queen smiled. Raised a hand. A lute began to play to a slow and mournful rhythm.

"...then we dance," said Vina.

"Dance," Simran repeated. "Is this necessary?" Her voice softened to a whisper. "This ball, this stupidity. All of this. What is the damn point?"

"Monarchy is a performance," Vina said, smiling, always smiling. Few would be able to read her lips—and after so long unable to speak to Simran, it seemed important to tell her this. "It needs balls and feasts and thrones and crowns to survive. We're food for her power. We dance to serve." She could feel the prickling heat of all those eyes on her, the wine in her belly. "Think of us as a dancing bear, here for entertainment. Have you ever danced the pavane?"

"Fuck no," Simran said under her breath.

"Follow my lead, then." She raised Simran's hand in her own, feeling the light, warm weight of it. "The pavane has been danced a thousand times here in this hall," she whispered, as she began to turn, a slow and stately motion. "The tale of it will guide you where I can't."

It was a solemn thing, this dance. Vina circled Simran. Simran moved with her whispers, and with the tug of the subtle tale threaded into the floor, the air.

When their hands touched again, she felt the absurd warmth of sunlight on her hair, so distinct from the hearth fire's warmth. She smelled rustling green leaves. She could see from the widening of Simran's eyes that she had too.

Others joined them, beginning the steps of the pavane, mingling on the waxed wooden floor.

Their hands were still joined. Vina forced herself to let go.

"Is it enough?" Simran asked. "Can we stop now?"

"It's enough," said Vina.

"Good." Her mouth firmed. "We should talk."

"I agree," said Vina, relieved. Finally.

Simran hesitated, moving to speak. Then paused, turning her head. "Damn," she said. The ladies-in-waiting were swiftly bearing down on them, now that the dance was done.

"They won't leave me alone," Simran muttered. "I've already tried to escape twice, but they won't look away."

"Twice?"

"Are you surprised? Truly?" Simran's eyes snapped to hers, full of familiar fire.

"No," said Vina ruefully. "It surprises me you didn't try more times."

"All the tools of my magic were taken."

"They'll be returned to you when our tale begins, I'm sure."

Simran's expression grew suddenly pinched. Vina knew her words had been no real comfort, and perhaps the opposite. She winced internally.

The ladies-in-waiting came over to take Simran each by an arm. They led her away.

Vina watched for a moment. Then, realizing how many eyes were on her, she loosened her posture.

She went to seek out another drink. She drank one mouthful for show, then carried the rest of the glass out with her into the gardens attached to the banqueting hall. There were a few figures already standing out in the moonlight, laughing quietly and kissing in the shadows. Vina sauntered past them into the maze that filled the garden, crafted out of roses and thorns.

Inside it, she kneeled and carefully poured her wine into the earth. She held her breath, the moon looming above her. A gift to the ground could summon any waiting fae. But Vina was sure there was only one that would seek her out.

"A libation to the soil, knight? How kind of you to summon us in the traditional manner."

She raised her head. A dryad and a fae stood suddenly before her. The dryad wore roses and green braids within her hair. The fae was beautiful beyond comprehension, radiating the same power they had when Vina had first spied them across the room. But that beauty was typical of their kind, and did nothing to move Vina's heart.

"My liege is Alder," said the dryad proudly. "They serve in the House of Lords, integral to the leadership of the Isle. You should be honored to have them answer your call."

You could tell, often, from looking at a fae whether they were ancient and worthy of respect. This one wore a diaphanous gown of blue beneath a cloak of silver, flowers in their golden hair, their authority undeniable.

"I am honored," Vina said, standing and bowing deeply.

"You're looking for one of my kindred," the fae said. Their eyes were as green as grass, lividly bright. "I feel the desire on you."

"I seek the Merciless Maiden," Vina admitted. "My friend—the knight of her tale—is dead. Murdered by a killer of incarnates. Something is rotten on the Isle, fair liege, and I must put it right. I hope she may have answers."

The fae hummed, a light and thoughtful noise.

"You are not the first, and will not be the last to seek out the Maiden. Your house of mortal ministers has been wroth at the fae courts keeping her from them." They cocked their head. "You have seen this killer?"

"I saw the man," Vina admitted. "I saw him kill another incarnate. If you cannot introduce me to the Merciless Maiden, then all I seek is...information. I fear my own tale is in danger too." She swallowed. "Tell me what the man is, Liege of the Fae. Tell me what I face, and how he can be killed."

Their eyes glittered, amused and curious.

"I cannot tell you *exactly* how to defeat him, or all that he is," they said. "But he is old and canny and known to us. We can tell you a secret we have not even told the Commons, the Queen, the ink-pushers in the Tower. We can tell you a secret that could lead to his destruction. Will that suffice?"

"Yes," Vina said.

"Come, then," they replied. "Follow me into this labyrinth, knight. I am a Liege of the House of Fae, and I can give you what I have no desire to share with your mortal ministers. We will bargain."

Vina hesitated.

"And what must I pay for the knowledge I seek?"

The fae's smile lengthened and deepened. And they answered.

# Chapter Nine

## *Simran*

*The dragon is a royal symbol, and a symbol of the Isle. A beast to be slain, an ancient strength to be quelled by the bravery of men.*

*It is a symbol of the Crown. When you see no great wingèd beast flying over London, only clear and starry skies, hold your hand to your heart, and thank the Queen for taming all dark beasts to her luminous will.*

Source: *Essays on Our Glorious Isle* by Samuel Tattersall

**Archivist's Ruling: Preserve. Publication permitted. No further action required.**

The knight had entirely abandoned her. She could no longer see the knight through the throng of dancing people, circling each other before the Queen's banqueting table. She craned her head as the two ladies-in-waiting led her away, but the knight was gone.

Fine. Simran didn't need her. They weren't friends. They weren't even allies. It was important to remind herself of that.

She'd never seen people dance so...mournfully. She'd danced plenty—outside ale-houses and inside molly-houses, to the thump of drums and guitars, or belted ribald songs. But she hadn't liked the pavane. She'd felt clumsy, exposed in front of an audience, reliant on the knight's gentle instruction and her guiding hands.

Hot, steady hands. Her stomach somersaulted, remembering them on her. She hated herself for that. Her body was an evil traitor.

A lady-in-waiting bid her with a gesture to stand by the wall. Simran wondered if those women had faces at all beneath those masks, or blank ovals of skin.

Although many nobles walked by her and looked at her, none stopped to talk. She didn't want to talk to them, mind—but it wasn't pleasant to be an ornament on display either. She gritted her teeth and resolutely did not smile.

Two figures broke from the crowd and wended toward her. They wore neat doublets and swords at their waists, their clothes not as fine as the lords around them—marked only with a little embellishment at the ruffed collars and the darted sleeves.

They bowed.

"I am Sir Matthias, and this is Sir Edmund," the first man said, gesturing at his companion. His eyes were gentle, his hair deep red, and his beard neatly trimmed, his voice distinctly familiar. These were the knights she'd stolen the limni ink from. "We are members of the Queen's knightly order, alongside Lavinia. Which you likely know." He smiled. "It's a pleasure to meet you again formally, lady witch."

She was silent. The hand on her left arm tightened in warning.

"It's a pleasure to meet you again too," she said, voice flat, unsmiling. It wasn't a fucking pleasure. "But I suppose we won't do so again, since your friend will soon kill me. Have you tried the wine? No one will let me have any, because they're afraid I'll throw it on someone or break a glass into a makeshift weapon, I suppose." She tapped her foot thoughtfully. "Or no. Maybe they're more worried that I'll cut myself and use my blood to curse someone. Who knows! Let me know if the wine is any good, regardless."

They stared at her, open-mouthed.

"Excuse me." The archivist—Meera—was behind the two knights, hands clasped in front of her. "I'm sorry to interrupt, but I've been tasked by Archivist Roland to take the witch away. He requires her."

She looked drab, in her archivist robes, against all the fluttering pomp around her. Without her prism lens on her eye she seemed... tired. Her mouth, painted plum, was pursed.

The ladies-in-waiting shared a look over Simran's head, then released her.

The archivist left the room. Simran trailed after her, shocked at how light she felt without figures at her shoulders.

They entered narrow, claustrophobic corridors. She was led to the left, to a quiet chamber, muffled from the noise of the lutes and conversation in the banquet. The room was lined with dark mahogany shelves crammed with books. Low lamps lit the space.

The Queen's wyvern lay across the room, somnolent as it always was. Simran paused at the door, wary of moving closer.

"Do not be disturbed by it," said the archivist. "The creature is well controlled."

Fine, then. Simran stepped farther into the room, skimming the shelves with her eyes. The writing on those bare spines was faded gold, barely legible, but Simran grasped words here and there: *Gloriana, Merrie England.* Her fingers itched to pull at one of those books, but she resisted.

"This is not the main Palace library," the archivist said helpfully, as Simran turned in a circle, taking the room in. "But it is close to the banqueting hall, which serves our need to speak privately—and, ah, interestingly, this library is concerned only with ancient texts focused on the Queen herself. I gather she likes to keep them close. The original editions are in the archives, of course."

"It doesn't look like your boss is here," observed Simran.

"I hoped you and I could talk alone. Archivist Roland asked me to do so." The archivist's smile was thin, polite, and strained. "He thought we might have more in common than you and, ah, other archivists."

"Your name's Meera?"

"Archivist Sharma is my formal title," she said. "I prefer it over my name when I am in my professional capacity, but with you—Meera is fine."

"Meera," Simran repeated. "Well, Meera, let's talk. How did you come here to the Isle? Where were you born—Elsewhere, or here? Elsewhere's obviously in your name and your face."

There was a pause. "I was born Elsewhere," she said, with audible reluctance. "But I do not remember it. I was lucky enough to come to the Isle as a small child. I could ask you the same, but I know the answer, of course."

"Do you?"

"You're an incarnate. Of course there's Isle blood in you," said Meera. She said it as if it were mere fact.

Simran said nothing. She'd been told all her life on the Isle that incarnates were Isle-born and Isle-blooded.

She wasn't going to tell the archivists—or anyone—the truth if she could avoid it. If she hadn't lived through the impossible, awful magic of Isadora on the ship's deck, the silver sea roiling beneath them, she wouldn't have believed it herself. And frankly, she wasn't going to bring more danger to her parents' door.

"Obviously," Simran said.

"It is hard to be an outsider," said Meera, tracing the edges of the books, removing a fine lace of dust from their surface; she lifted one book and moved it, as if she could not help but reorganize. "But you need not be. Look at me, witch. I was a scholarship apprentice—a rare archivist drawn from Elsewhere blood. I worked hard. I proved myself. My journey hasn't been easy. Still, I'm proud of myself and glad for what the Isle has given me."

"How lovely to hear," Simran said dryly. "Why tell me this now?"

"You weren't willing to speak to me on our journey to London."

"Your boss told you to," Simran surmised. "Do you value his opinion so highly that you're really willing to spill your guts to me? Do you have any sad childhood stories you think might win me over too?"

The archivist gave her a pitying look.

"I am trying to help you," said Meera. "I know it's hard to believe. But your position as an incarnate is clearly... difficult. The Queen has her own concerns and her own fears. Parliament desires to maintain peace and order—and public happiness. But we archivists value the tales above all else, and their survival. We value *you*. And we know you need our guidance. You're not exactly as you should be. You're—aberrant, Simran. I'll be frank—you're not pure Isle blood, as you should be. But we can help you to behave as you should. Without us, you could break your tale and doom more of the Isle. But with us the Isle will be safe." Her eyes were earnest. "I promise."

Simran frowned.

"Aberrant," she repeated. "And what does that make you? Should you be an archivist, with your Elsewhere blood?" She grabbed a book from the shelf, riffling through it idly, awkwardly. The pages were surprisingly crisp. "The Isle isn't a good place for our kind, is it? We're everywhere, and only a few of us get to have the kind of power that gets you into a place like this. I don't even know why the Isle takes us, do you?"

"Nonsense," Meera said, ignoring her question. "We're lucky to be here, witch. We should be grateful. If you stand by the values of the Isle, live by its values, you can find hope and glory here that you would never find Elsewhere." She spoke with absolute conviction.

Meera took a step closer to Simran.

"But never mind that. Listen to me," said Meera. "I'm afraid I can't keep you here for long. So I must tell you this now, a secret held by the archivists and the Queen alone. Someone is killing incarnates, and the Isle is dying. We believe an eighth of the land is gone."

Simran stared at her in shock. Meera nodded gravely.

"You won't know the places that are forgotten," Meera continued. "The villages and towns, the *people*. But we archivists keep the maps and protect the stories. We watch our maps erode, words fading to nothing. We see tales die as our maps wither and change. The Isle is scarred and broken, and all of us must work to save it. You *must* be good, and you must learn and you must serve, because you're more important than you have been in a thousand lifetimes."

Simran's thoughts were racing. They settled, arrow-swift, on a grim reality.

The archivists were desperate, and they were never going to let her leave.

But Hari needed her. And nothing mattered more than that.

Simran started riffling through pages again, idly.

"Why talk to me," she said after a beat. "Why not talk to my knight?"

She crumpled the pages a little, then thumped the book down. The noise of the book hitting wood made Meera wince—and concealed from her the paper cut Simran managed to scythe into her own thumb, drawing blood.

"Lavinia Morgan may seem like us, Elsewhere-blooded, but she's a different breed entirely," said Meera. "Her father is a government minister from an old bloodline. They have an estate in the countryside, and a house in Kensington with a *garden*. She was raised in the Palace. She may be brown-skinned and illegitimate, a scandal to her family name—but she has an old Isle name, and old Isle duty, and she knows what she must do. She doesn't need the guidance our kind do."

"Fine. Say I trust you, work with you, learn from you: What does that actually look like? I'm a prisoner either way," Simran said.

"Don't think of it as imprisonment," Meera urged. "You must understand. Every change to an incarnate tale is a ripple, an alteration, a torn seam in a tale, a step toward the tale becoming no tale at all, a stranger to itself. There are dangers to the Isle, everywhere. And in a way you're part of it, you see? But you're also part of the answer to putting it right." She placed a hand lightly on Simran's shoulder, as if she had the right. "You can be a hero. You can overcome your flaws and be the witch you must be."

"I think you'll find I'm meant to be a tragic villain," said Simran, and slammed the book into Meera's head.

"Ah!" Meera stumbled back, more from shock than pain. "What the hell? Did you think hitting me with a *book* would hurt me?"

"No," Simran said mildly.

Bloodred lines began to spider across Meera's skull from the point where the book had touched her. Her eyes widened, her fingers reaching for her own skin. Too late for that. Simran began to hum the first strains of a lullaby, and Meera's eyelids fluttered. Her eyes rolled. She crumpled.

Awkward magic, tied with just a little blood meeting paper, but enough.

Simran felt the hairs on the back of her neck rise. Slowly, she turned her head and looked at the wyvern.

It was awake, watching her. It hadn't moved, but its eyes tracked her.

She had to walk over its body to reach the window—and she wasn't going out the door, where the ladies-in-waiting would be. She took a step. The wyvern made a noise, its scales trembling. It craned its neck. The collar around its throat looked painfully tight, and Simran couldn't help but pause. If someone had stuck something so small on Maleficium's neck, she and Mal would have gutted them.

"Please don't bite me," she muttered, and, against her better judgment, leaned down. She brushed a hand against its collar and froze. The velvet was no velvet at all. It was liquid. Ink. She snatched her hand back, fronds of ink moving with her, leaving the collar frayed.

The wyvern's eyes widened, awareness seeping into the narrow slits of its pupils. Simran shook her hand clean and went for the window.

"I'm sorry," Simran muttered to the unconscious heap of Meera on the floor. She was, a little. "Don't you dare eat her," she said to the wyvern, for what good it would do.

She struggled with one stiff, creaky window latch.

The door behind her rattled. In the night-dark glass of the still-closed window she could see the reflection of the door as it creaked open. Cold, white fingers curled around the doorframe. The ladies-in-waiting had followed her after all.

She wrenched the latch. It shattered. She shoved the window wide and looked down at a wall of hedgerow, thick and ominous, in the moonlit garden. It would be a long jump down, but Simran wasn't afraid of that. She crawled out of the window, snagging her skirt momentarily on the frame, then leapt.

She landed with a thud, dragging what felt like half a bush down with her. She struggled to her feet.

Simran found herself in a maze made of dark, shining leaves embroidered with spindly thorns. There was a strong scent of blossoming roses, but no visible flowers. She looked up at the window—heard both windows rattle—and made the decision to keep on running deeper into the tessellated hedgerows.

She turned—left, right, right, left, left, right again—she was already losing track of where she'd been. She hit a dead end, a wall of green. Turned back, and took a left instead, and heard the hollow, rustling noise of the blank-faced ladies-in-waiting, somewhere in the distance behind her.

A hand grabbed her firmly. Her stomach plummeted. She tried to fight, but she was wrenched immediately into a gap in the bushes, a body-sized hollow, where she met the knight's deep brown eyes.

"Shh," the knight breathed, hushing her. "You're being chased."

"I know I'm being chased," snapped Simran. "Let me go so I can keep on running away, you fool!"

The knight shook her head. Simran was just about to kick her, when the knight swayed into her and then, with infuriating grace, crumpled to her knees in front of her. The knight was still clutching Simran's skirt in two fists. Her head was tipped forward, baring a golden-brown neck and her dark brown curls.

Simran looked at those strong hands on her skirt and felt a shivering, embarrassing flush of heat in her stomach.

"Let go," Simran ordered.

The knight did, slumping backward. Reflexively, Simran grabbed her to steady her. Lavinia Morgan's skin was blisteringly hot under her hands, kindled with fever.

Simran heard footsteps, close as a kiss. She froze, her body bowed over the knight, with the knight's neck hot against her palm.

She breathed shallowly. She could feel the knight's warm body, smell her hair, apple-sweet like sunlight.

From the corner of her eyes, through the gap in the hedgerow, she saw the ladies-in-waiting drift by, velvet masks turned forward. They didn't turn. In a blink, a breath, they were gone.

Simran exhaled with relief.

The knight was shaking in her grip. Simran, panicking, tilted the woman's head up... and realized the damnable knight was laughing.

"Stop it," whispered Simran, outraged. "This isn't funny."

"I'm afraid it's a little funny," said the knight, still laughing. "You—you can let go of me now."

"Will you fall?"

"Probably," the knight said lightly. "But I'm not afraid of a little dirt."

"What about of cracking your skull?"

"I have a hard head."

Simran clapped a firm hand against the knight's forehead.

"Right now it feels like your hard head is on fire," Simran said. "Are you sick?"

"No," the knight said. "I've just had a lot of wine."

Simran kneeled down until they were at eye level with one another, the ground soft beneath her feet, the maze prickling her spine. She held the knight steady by one hand to the back of the neck. The other, she used to trace a line from the knight's forehead down to her feverish cheek. The knight stopped laughing. She watched Simran, solemn, almost entranced.

"This isn't wine," Simran said. "I can feel the magic under your skin. What have you done?"

"Nothing we can discuss now," the knight said hoarsely. "You're trying to run again. You won't be able to do it in this maze. The Queen's women know the labyrinth too well."

"Not well enough to find us here, apparently," noted Simran.

"Oh, this hiding spot? This is a secret place. Sometimes the Queen comes here with her paramours when she wants privacy."

"And how do you know that if her own women don't?" Simran demanded.

The knight winked, then said, at the look on Simran's face, "I'm joking, I'm joking! I'm not her type. I've just got a good ear for gossip. But forget about me. We were discussing your newest escape attempt."

"Are you going to stop me?"

"Do I seem like I'm in any state to stop you?"

Under Simran's fingertips, the knight's skin was humming with magic, teeming like a river full of fish. It had to be painful. Simran had no desire to be kind to her knight, no—but it was against her professional decency to let this kind of magical malfeasance stand, when she wasn't the one who'd inflicted it.

"I can pull this magic from you," said Simran.

The knight's eyes widened in alarm.

"Don't!"

But Simran had already pressed one paper-cut thumb to the knight's cheek and tugged a thread of magic. A groan left the knight, and light flushed her skin. Simran gave a hiss.

What lay under the knight's skin wasn't a witch's curse, or even a cunning folk's blessing. It was complex, liquid light that spiraled and changed under the tug of Simran's own magic. It was a contract with language, a trickster's pledge, written in words instead of blood.

A fae geas.

"Don't," the knight repeated. She heaved a sigh of relief as Simran let the magic go. "I made a bargain."

"With a fae? You *fool*."

"Don't worry about it," the knight said earnestly.

"How can I not? What did you give up? What's been demanded of you?"

"Oh, Simran," the knight said. "I didn't know you cared."

Simran pushed her away. The knight landed with a thump.

"I'm not staying," Simran said. "I can't stay. I need to find Hari. And the answers the stranger wanted." His name and why he couldn't die, and godsblood, how was she going to do that?

"That makes sense. If you want to find your friend, you're going to need to do what the stranger says. That is how bargains in tales work."

Simran could sense a *but*.

"But he isn't playing by the rules of stories," the knight went on. "He's killed more than you can even know. For generations, he's been plucking incarnates up."

"The archivist told me that already," Simran said.

"Do you know how to kill him?"

"Do you?"

"The fae gave me the key," said the knight, face still flushed, eyes bright. "It's *you*."

"Me? How in the hell is it me?"

"I don't know," the knight said, and Simran resisted the desperate urge to throttle her.

"Then you made a bad bargain," Simran said instead.

"The fae were sure," the knight insisted. "You can end his immortality. But you can't kill him alone. Surely. Let me come. Let me help you."

"Why by the Isle would I let you come with me?" Simran laughed jaggedly, still reeling from the idea that she was the answer. She'd shot the stranger, and it hadn't been enough. What else was there? "Letting you near me is just a way of making sure I'll die before I can get Hari back. *No*."

"You need me if you want to escape. You don't know this maze.'"

"I know how to burn a path through it."

"Then let me come with you because *I* need your help," the knight said, voice low and earnest. "Let me come because I can't live in a world where that man is still alive. He killed a friend of mine. You must understand how I feel." The knight straightened, expression sharpening. "People are getting close," she said.

Simran heaved a deep breath. Her head was buzzing—with panic and anger, but most of all with determination.

"Fine," she said. "Get me out of here, and you can come with me." She could always abandon the knight later.

The knight laboriously climbed to her feet. She still looked feverish, but the golden flush was fading from her cheeks.

"There's an escape route used by the gardeners," she said softly. She stepped out of the gap in the hedgerow and crooked a finger. "Follow me."

Simran crept after her through the maze. She could see lights in the distance drawing closer; hear shouting voices and the distant strum of lutes from the banqueting hall. At one point she heard running; the knight drew her into a curving path to the left, and they stood there silently until the guards had run by, calling Simran's name.

The knight led her to a cleverly concealed exit: a path at the angle of two hedges. It was only broad enough for one person to walk through. "Let me go first," the knight whispered, and Simran gave a curt nod. Followed her.

Dark, cloying walls of green around them. In the shadows, Simran followed the knight's breath, and warmth, and her footsteps. Her heart was pounding in her ears. She could almost taste freedom. Then the knight stopped, and swore softly under her breath.

"What is it?" Simran demanded.

"The garden is changing," the knight said. "The Palace does this—it shifts and alters at its own whims. I just hoped it wouldn't do it now. We're trapped."

The voices were getting closer. Desperation clawed up in Simran. She had no tools of magic. She was almost powerless here.

"Will you fight when they find us?" Simran asked.

"If I must."

"Don't lie. Of course you won't. This is your home."

"It doesn't matter where my home is," the knight said. "Your friend Hari is what matters."

"And why does that matter to you?" Simran demanded. "Don't tell me about *vengeance for your friend* or whatever lies you want to spew at me—why did you try and spare me from the witch hunters in Gore? Why do you keep helping me? Why—why—?"

"Because it's *right*," said the knight sharply. "Because you don't deserve this and I...I want to help you while I have a choice. Soon, neither of us will."

Their eyes met. Held. Then finally, the knight's gaze slid away from her. A look of relief suddenly graced her face.

"The gardens have changed," she breathed.

"I know that," said Simran.

"No. *Look.*"

Behind them, the maze had withered. In its place lay a hollow in the soil—a door leading down into the darkness.

Simran didn't wait, and didn't question. The knight strode into the tunnel, and Simran dived in after. She paused, as the darkness swallowed her. A twist of magic, her hands to soil, and the way closed behind them.

# Chapter Ten

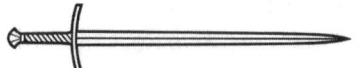

## *Vina*

*Sometimes I think of the tales that keep our Isle alive as a great wheel—like the sundial we saw at Oxford, when we studied together as boys. Do you recall? The sun rises and sets. The solstice returns. Tales end, and they begin, and end. And so forth.*

*Every day I grow more convinced that nothing can truly be immutable. Even incarnates perish. My vision fades, my skin wrinkles—and I wonder, my love, if we will renew too in the fullness of time. If we will return again as boys, and meet once more at that sundial, a story spun into new gold.*

Source: Letter from Dr. Felix Scott to<br>Mr. Cillian Ferrers

**Archivist's Ruling: Preserve. Review in 6 months. No interrogation currently required. Continued surveillance recommended.**

Fire was a drumbeat behind Vina's eyes and in her veins. But as they walked down the slope leading them deeper and deeper beneath the Palace grounds, the air grew colder and wetter. It felt blessedly cool against her skin.

Simran raised a hand in the air. Vina heard her click her

fingers—one crisp snap, followed by small flames rising luminously on the ends of her fingertips. The darkness around them eased, revealing a vast, cavernous space. The walls of the underpalace were white stone, rising to a vaulted ceiling.

"A crypt?" Simran asked, but even she sounded dubious. There were no graves visible—no tombs with sleeping figures in repose carved on their surfaces. Simran was striding forward without pausing, the lights of her fingertips throwing long shadows on the high walls. She wasn't slowing down.

"We're not being followed," Vina said. "You don't need to run anymore."

"You can't be sure of that."

"I'd hear them," said Vina. "I promise."

Simran didn't reply, but she did slow down a little.

The air smelled loamy. Vina could hear the rumble of running water.

"There's a river down here," said Vina. "The Tyburn. You'll never see it anywhere else in London. It's tangled with the royal Palace."

"A river passing through a crypt seems like a recipe for disease," Simran muttered.

"I haven't caught cholera yet," Vina said cheerily. "I told you, there are so many tales wound about the Palace that it can't always hold its shape. Sometimes the tales mingle together. Crypts, rivers, lost parts of the Palace gone to rot—whatever lies through there." She gestured at the tunnels leading off from the vaulted roof hall around them. "They cross paths, then they diverge as they like."

"You know this place," said Simran, looking around carefully, eyes narrowed.

"I've been here once before," said Vina.

"Is there another exit we can reach fast?"

"I didn't stay long enough to check," Vina admitted. "I turned back."

"I can't imagine you being frightened of the dark," said Simran. "You're a big fighter with a sword, what's a little gloom to you?" Her words were mocking, but the flames on her fingertips grew brighter, illuminating the cavern around them.

"How did you end up here, anyway?" Simran asked. "Does the Queen have you gardening or digging tunnels in your spare time?"

Vina laughed. "No. I, uh." What was the harm in saying it? "I tried to run away, early on. Sometimes the Palace responds to strong feeling, and I wanted to escape. It gave me a way down here." She gestured at the space around them—the grand, vaulted darkness. "I was very young, and very stupid. I didn't know how to control my feelings. Things got better when Eddie and Matthias joined me as royal squires. This is the first time I've seen it since."

A beat of silence.

"How long have you lived in the Palace?" Simran asked. Her voice was unreadable.

"Since I was ten."

"No wonder you were scared down here," Simran said, after a moment. Her voice was soft.

"I wasn't really," Vina admitted. "I just realized I had nowhere to run *to*. My father would have simply sent me back."

Something flickered at the edge of her vision. Dark as ink, and swift. Vina paused.

"What?" Simran asked urgently. Her face was painted in licks of gold, her eyes wary and vigilant. "What is it?"

"I saw something," said Vina.

"So we have been followed."

"No. I—" Vina hesitated. She pointed at one of the tunnels coming off the central underpalace—ominously dark, an unwelcoming circle of black. "I thought I saw movement. Something low to the ground. Rats, probably."

"If there's rats, there might be a way out." Simran turned to the tunnel.

"I don't think rats guarantee an exit! Simran—"

But Simran was already gone, swallowed by the dark. With a sigh, Vina strode in after her.

The dark gave way to a room half-flooded with running water: the Tyburn's work, no doubt.

Rats were scurrying across the ground. But it was the detritus that caught Vina's attention. A broken table—a circle like the one in the Queen's White Hall, but vaster, white as the moon, and broken in two. It looked as if it were fused with the wall—immovable, and deep-rooted.

*This was the first*, an old instinct whispered in her head.

Simran kneeled by the table, holding her fire-lit fingers up to reveal its surface.

There were images carved into the table, gouged deep and with grace by an artisan's hand. A sword, haloed in swirls of light. Knights, each helmed, faceless, lances in their hands. A woman with loose and trailing hair, sitting in a barge on water, holding a body in her arms—a crowned body, a man with a great wound at his heart. A ghost of emotion ran through Vina as she gazed at him, as if a tale had touched her, then drifted away. She felt the edges of awe—and fear too.

Beneath it all was an inscription.

" 'I live and live again,' " Simran read out. " 'Eternal.' "

Something at the corner of her vision again. This time, Vina could have sworn it was a chain, red-black as ink, worming its way through stone and soil. When she turned her head it was gone.

"There's no way out here," said Simran, sounding displeased. But her eyes were still fixed on the broken table.

"We'll follow the water," said Vina.

They did, following the black sluice of water until the ground began to turn soft.

Finally, they came to a grate. Vina managed to ram it open, and they emerged on the far edge of the gardens, no guards or courtiers around them. They were alone.

"I can see the walls," said Vina. "We won't go to the main gate. The other gates are manned but the guards move on a schedule—if we're lucky we can slip to freedom."

Simran nodded, jaw tense.

They strode forward. They were almost at the postern gate when Vina heard the silvery hiss of a blade ahead of them, and saw two figures emerge from the shadows of the fortified wall.

Vina sighed. "Ah, shit," she said. "Eddie, Matthias, lower your swords. Let's talk."

"We'll lower our swords when you come back into the hall," said Matthias. "Come on, Vina. We can sit and talk there."

Really, it would have been ideal to have a sit-down. Vina's skin was burning. She could feel the fae's magic moving under it.

She watched Matthias and Edmund through a thin golden haze. They were creeping hesitantly toward her and Simran. Matthias, usually the more sensible, was in front. He had one hand up, palm out in a calming gesture, which would have been more convincing without the sword.

She thought he'd be better at diplomacy.

She kept her hands lax at her sides. *Someone* had to remember how not to escalate a conflict.

"This seems silly," she protested. "The Queen won't be happy if you hurt us."

"Of course we won't hurt you," Matthias said, as Edmund simultaneously replied, "We were ordered to bring you in 'by any means,' you think we're waving these swords for fun?"

"Edmund," Matthias groaned.

"The Queen probably doesn't care if you've got all your limbs," Edmund went on doggedly. "You think the Queen really gives a shit if you lose a toe?"

"Probably not," Vina agreed.

"We don't have time to banter," Simran said frostily. "Let us pass, boys. You've exhausted my patience."

Edmund hissed between his teeth.

"I've got to say, Vina. I'm not sure even you deserve a shrew like her."

"Don't go around calling witches 'shrews,' Eddie," Vina said. "That's how you get cursed."

"Are you threatening me?"

"Of course not," she said. "We're friends. I'm *advising* you."

"I'm not friends with any of you," Simran said, impatience in her voice. "But one of *my* friends is in trouble, so I need you to get out of my way."

"You have a duty to the Isle," Matthias entreated. "Both of you do. You serve the Queen—please. Come back. All she wants is to ensure your safety."

Edmund muttered something under his breath, sword steady in his firm grip.

"Duty," Simran scoffed. "Is it my duty to dance? To wear gowns? I don't bloody think it is. You toffs may love your duty, but I have no time for it. It's not my business." She took a step back, her footsteps as light as her words were hard, one heel scuffing the ground in a neat line. Vina noted it, then looked away; shuffled on her own feet, letting her own hand brush her sword hilt, drawing Edmund's wary gaze to her.

If Simran had a plan, if Simran wanted a distraction, then Vina would provide it.

"I don't understand why the Queen wants to have me under her thumb," Simran was saying hotly. "I can feel the tale. I felt it the moment I saw Lavinia. It's going to drag us along no matter what we do. What's the fucking use of having us bow and dance in front of her? Why keep me here with *her*?" She gestured dramatically at Vina. Her heel dug into the earth. "The tale should just happen. She doesn't need to do this. None of you do."

Edmund and Matthias didn't know about incarnates being killed. They wouldn't understand the Queen's drive to keep Simran here alongside Vina, safe from a stranger's blade. But it wasn't their place to question the Queen, and Vina knew they would do as they were ordered to.

"The witch isn't wrong," said Vina.

"What are you saying?" Matthias asked, frowning.

"I'm saying the writing's on the wall. I'll die no matter what happens next, and so will she." A hum shivered through Vina's veins, and the fae magic in her sparked faintly in response to whatever Simran was doing with her feet. "Before that happens I need to do this. I need to—"

"—what, run off holding hands into the sunset?" Edmund sneered. "I don't know what fantasy you're living in, Vina—"

There was a sharp hiss, a whistle—and Matthias's sword was suddenly at Simran's throat.

"Stop what you're doing, witch. I see you."

All good humor fled Vina's heart like a wolf was on its heels. She felt entirely cold. Steady.

"Leave her," Vina said in a low voice. "Right now."

"If she won't put down her magic, I won't put down my sword," said Matthias.

"Fool," said Simran, implacable under the blade. "I carry my magic with me everywhere. I *can't* lay it aside."

"Step back, Matthias," Vina ordered again. She heard the scuff of footsteps; from the corner of her eye she saw Edmund approach.

Edmund grasped Vina's arm. That was enough. She was done.

She slammed her free arm up, smashing her fist into his eye socket. Before he could react—he'd never been quick with his reflexes—she threw a fist into his stomach, and then another into his jaw.

He raised his sword without any intent as he fell. But sharp-ended weapons didn't need intent to do damage, and Vina barely avoided a blow as she wrenched herself back.

No second-guessing. Her blood burned hot in her veins, half fae geas and half fury. She drew her blade and turned it in a sweeping arc that raised the hilt angled to the sky. She slammed the dull hilt into the side of Matthias's skull. Simran sensibly ran, moving out of reach of his sword.

Vina used her weight and momentum to throw Matthias off balance. He stumbled and fell with a thud, gravel crackling under him.

Her blade sang with her. She twisted her arm, turning the edge of the blade toward him. It would be easy to finish this—two clean blows would see them done. They'd always underestimated her. They wouldn't expect her sword.

There was ink in her, an old tale in her young bones, that knew a thousand ways to kill her fellow man.

"Lavinia."

Her own name was like a discordant twang of broken strings in Simran's mouth. There was no gentleness, no compassion. Simran's arms were crossed, her jaw tense.

But there was no fear either. That calmed some terrible, wing-beating shame in Vina's chest, and turned her rage hollow.

"Simran," Vina said hoarsely.

"Turn that strength of yours to getting me out of here," said Simran. Her voice was steady, her chin raised. "You promised."

"I did," Vina agreed. She exhaled steadily, violence still pounding hotly in her blood. She struggled, caught still in the grip of a deadly rage. She sheathed her blade as her friends groaned on the ground.

Matthias and Edmund were not dead. That would have to be enough. "Follow me," she said. "Quickly."

The exit she'd planned was likely no good now. But unless the Palace planned to helpfully spit them out across the borders of the Palace grounds, they had no choice but to try.

She moved to try the gate, when she heard a sound unlike anything she'd ever heard before. A howl, guttural and polyphonic, that echoed across the Palace grounds and turned her blood cold.

"Look up," Simran urged. Her hand was suddenly on Vina's arm—still hot from the flames no longer on her skin, her grip vise-like. "Knight, *look*."

Vina looked up. A huge shape loomed in the sky above them.

The Queen's wyvern was free—and flying high above the Palace. Its great golden wings were spread. Its mouth was wide. She realized the sound she'd heard was its screaming. She'd never heard the creature scream before, entirely unfettered, free in the open sky.

*Hell*, the damage a wyvern could do to London was incalculable.

Soldiers and knights were yelling. The beast was rising, against the velvet backdrop of the sky, when arrows reached it, fire-tipped. Some missed—one landed in the garden, burning a hedgerow in an instant conflagration. But others hit their mark with one flesh-cracking thud after another. The wing-beats slowed.

Then went still.

The wyvern fell in an arc. Its body crashed into the rose garden, the sound reverberating across the Palace grounds. Then, utter silence.

It was broken by a wail. Weeping. The sound echoed more loudly than any mortal voice had the right to. It was the Queen who grieved.

"I never thought I'd see her escape the Queen's control," Vina breathed. "How did it happen?"

Simran said nothing for a moment. Her expression was shuttered. Then finally she swallowed and said, "While they're distracted—let's go."

"Vina," a voice said. Thick with blood.

Edmund was up again, limping toward them. Vina's stomach dropped.

"Don't try and stop us again," said Vina. She felt exhausted. "Seriously, Eddie. It's enough."

"Enough, you say. Like I'm not the one with the busted face." Edmund stepped forward. "I used to think you were a coward. When we were children you'd never want to pick up a sword if you could avoid it. You'd only do it if you were punished. But now I know—you were hiding what you can do. Didn't want to humble us, is that it?"

"Being an incarnate changes you," Vina said. "It's not skill. It's a gift that lives in me." She didn't mention hours of practice, the calluses on her hands; didn't tell him that it wasn't a gift that being an incarnate had given her, but a compulsion. *You must learn to fight. You must be honorable. You must teach your hands to understand the weight of a sword, the way it feels to force a blade through a sternum. You must become strong.* The voice of her tale dogging her heels, demanding she become what it needed her to be.

"All I've got is the skill I've learned," he said. "But I'm in a tale too,

Vina. I may not be an incarnate, but I'm a Queen's knight. I've got a duty."

"Edmund Tallisker," she said. "I don't want to fight you. I never want to fight you. But if you try and stop me again, I'll have to draw my sword."

"You going to stab me this time?"

"I don't think either of us really wants to stab each other." Godsblood, even her veins hurt. The fire of the geas was dying, but the embers still burned. "But I will, Eddie. I will."

His expression flickered with betrayal. Then his jaw firmed, and he threw something to her. She caught it, and looked down.

A key to the postern gate.

"Go, then," said Edmund. His voice was rough; a quiet rasp in the screaming clamor of the night. The bruise around his right eye was a livid circle, already purpling. "Get lost, Vina. If you don't want to be here anymore, I won't keep you."

There was a lump in Vina's throat. Her chest ached strangely.

"Eddie," she said.

"*Go.*"

Simran snatched the key and went to the gate. If Vina didn't want to lose her, she had to follow her now. So she forced herself to turn— to grasp Simran by the hand as the gate creaked open to drag her through into the grounds beyond.

She looked back once, for a half second. Edmund was still standing there in the open gate, watching her go, a small and isolated figure in the dark.

# Chapter Eleven

## *Simran*

*The water keeps rising, but the knights will not let us leave. They say it's a tale—our town drowns, and a lake called Semerwater rises in its place. They say a woman called 'Mother' or some such foretold it. They say some of us escape, but they don't yet know who. But I cannot leave or the tale may shatter, and no good Isle folk would allow for that. They say this is the fifth time our town will drown. That a new town will appear when one day Semerwater dries up, and new folk will move in, and everything will happen again.*

*I want to be good. I am staying. I am staying.*

*~~I do not want to drown.~~*

Source: Diary of Jane Sheavers (deceased)

**Archivist's Ruling: Destroy. No further action required.**

They made it to Limehouse the unmagical way—on foot—which meant Simran arrived outside her home sweaty and exhausted, too hot in her ludicrous starch-stiff gown. Usually she would have stripped the damn thing off, propriety or watchers be damned. But this time, the knight was with her. She needed the armor of clothes around the knight.

The glow had faded from the knight's skin, and she looked human again; mild, disturbingly handsome, quick to smile when Simran met her eyes. But Simran couldn't forget the way the knight had moved when she'd attacked her friends—the look in her eyes, cold as flint, the angles of her face turned austere and ferocious.

The knight wore her easy smiles like a mask, like camouflage. What lay under the surface should have frightened Simran, but she found herself... intrigued. A dark, squirming curiosity was awake in her chest, a black flame she couldn't extinguish.

It was better to think of that, than think of the wyvern. Its neck under her hands. Its dead body, falling from the night-dark sky. When she'd somehow ripped the collar of ink, she'd caused its flight—and contributed to its death. Guilt ate at her.

*Don't think of it. Think of Hari. Think of saving him.*

*Think of breaking the stranger's throat with your own hands.*

The knight was silent when Simran stepped forward to the staircase that led to her flat and whistled. The lantern bird unfolded from the light hanging above the steps; it flapped frantically.

"Tell your mistress I need her urgently," said Simran.

The bird flew away, and Simran climbed the stairs. She heard the knight follow her.

"That was a beautiful creature," the knight said. "One of yours?"

"I didn't make it, no."

Her scriptorium was exactly as she'd left it—messy. The burn marks were as livid as scars on the floor. Simran walked straight into the room, leaving the knight hovering in the doorway.

"Is this your home?" Vina asked.

"You're welcome to come in and take a seat if you want," Simran muttered. "Have you seen a cat anywhere?"

"This is the first place anyone will search for you," the knight observed.

"I know that," said Simran. "But I have to speak to someone. This is the only place I can do it."

There was a knot of anxiety in her chest.

*Come soon, Lydia.*

The knight could move quietly when she wanted to. Simran went to her work desk, rifling through her supplies—her other needles, her scrawled notes on spellwork—and nearly jumped out of her skin when she heard the knight's voice to her left, by the narrow window.

"No cats here."

"Shit. Do you have to creep around like that?"

"Ah," the knight said, a smile twitching at her mouth. "Sorry about that."

The knight stepped away.

Simran took a deep breath. Her box of inks was still pristine. She hadn't knocked over anything in surprise, at least. She delicately lifted out her single vial of limni ink and held it in the palm of her hand. She'd take this with her.

She had a thin leather case for carrying her needles and her ink. She packed it now and tucked it into a satchel that she threw over her shoulder.

There was a thud, and another, outside the flat. Simran whirled, facing the door. Vina tensed, one hand moving perilously close to her sword hilt.

Simran raised her own hand. *Wait.*

It was Lydia who came up the stairs, and Simran's relief was like a deluge of rain on parched soil. But her relief quickly died at the look on Lydia's face.

Lydia crossed the room and grasped Simran by the arm.

"You were foolish to come back here," said Lydia. "But I'm glad you have. Is this your knight?"

Vina and Simran exchanged looks.

"How do you know about her?" Simran asked.

"You were in the papers, Simran," Lydia explained. "They did a nice likeness of you."

Damn. Of course the newspapers had written about her. A new incarnate, brought home, was a coup. Proof the government were doing what was needful. She ground her teeth.

"Something's wrong," Simran said. "Tell me what it is, please."

"Where's Hari?" Lydia asked.

Simran swallowed.

"We found trouble in Gore," she said thinly. "But he's going to be fine. I'm going to find him. Now, tell me what's wrong."

Lydia gave her a searching look, but didn't press her with further questions. That, more than anything, confirmed to Simran that something was seriously amiss. Lydia cared about Hari too much to let Simran's platitudes go unquestioned.

"We've been facing some trouble," Lydia said carefully. Her gaze flicked to the knight, then back to Simran. She wasn't sure if she could trust a stranger.

Simran couldn't reassure her. She didn't know if she could trust the knight either.

"Sounds like something we should talk about properly," said Simran. "Wait for me outside?"

"Gladly," said Lydia. "Be quick, Simran." She gave the knight a nod and left, closing the door softly behind her.

Simran inhaled slowly; exhaled.

Cracked her knuckles.

Her magic was a whip-crack of power, lashing out of the wall behind the knight. The knight was fast, there was no denying that. She leapt forward and ducked, avoiding the net of magic that was intended to snare her. One of her boots hit the edge of the scorch-marked floor.

There was enough magic left in those burns for Simran to tug the dregs out and snare the knight by the foot. The knight fell forward, almost smashing her face against the floor. She threw an arm out in front of her, taking her own weight on her right arm instead of her nose. That gave Simran enough time to trap her properly, lines of magic binding the knight in a bundle to the floor.

"Simran!"

"Knight," Simran said flatly. "I'm glad you helped me leave the Palace, but I can do the rest on my own."

"You can't fight the pale assassin alone," the knight snapped. "You don't know what he's capable of."

"Pale assassin, is it? I suppose the name suits him. You clearly know things about him that I don't. Care to share?"

"We have a lot to talk about," said the knight. "If you'll just let me go..."

"Why should I? Because you helped me when Bess died? Because you taught me a silly dance to please the Queen? That was very nice of you. You're certainly an expert at playing *nice*." She could feel the sneer in her voice, curling her lip, as she looked at the knight on the floor: her bared throat, her narrowed eyes. Simran's skin itched, electric, looking at the knight, and that just made her angrier. To want what was going to kill you—that was a shame she couldn't stand. "But I don't trust you. I've got no reason to trust you. If it hadn't been for our shared tale, we never would have given each other a second glance. Let's leave it at that."

"Simran, please," the knight begged. Her eyes were dark, fierce. "You don't understand what's at stake."

Simran didn't respond. She went into her bedroom—grabbed one of Hari's shirts, and her own trousers. She stripped off the awful gown, leaving it in a pile on the floor as she pulled on the shirt, the trousers, her satchel of needles and ink. Then she went back out to the knight, who wasn't struggling anymore. The knight was lying still on her side, gold squirming under her skin, the bonds of Simran's magic holding her body still.

Simran stopped beside her. The knight looked up.

"Don't worry," said Simran. "We'll meet again. When you put a sword through my ribs, obviously. I'll look forward to it."

"You're going to ensorcel me first," said the knight. "You seem to have conveniently forgotten that. Our story doesn't begin with me just flailing a sword at you."

"I have no interest in ensorcelling you."

"And I have no interest in killing you," Vina retorted. "But that is the point, isn't it? What we want doesn't matter. I've known it all my life." Her hands shook, straining against her bonds. Not so placid after all. "We aren't our tale. We just have to serve it."

"Is that what you tell yourself? That's sweet," Simran said, mockery curling her lips, her voice. "But I saw you with your friends. I saw your face when they made you angry. The knight of our tale was charismatic and beautiful... and a brute. Under that golden hair, he was a man who killed the woman he loved for honor and because he wasn't good for anything but killing. Isn't that all you are too?"

The knight flinched as if struck.

"I don't know what you think you saw," the knight said, "but I am a knight, not just *the* knight. A soldier of the Queen. I have to fight and I have to kill, but by my own choice—if there's an alternative, I'll take it."

The deer in the forest. The knight's gentle voice, her hand outstretched. Simran banished the thought.

"You could have gutted the both of them, and you wanted to," Simran snapped back. "I saw it in your face. You would have done it if I hadn't stopped you."

"You're no different from me, lady witch," said the knight. "And you know it. You're built for dark arts and cruel tricks. Do you even fight your nature?"

"I'm not arguing with you," Simran said. "The magic holding you will fade in a few hours. You can go back to the Palace then. Or go somewhere else, if you like. I don't care." She stormed off.

"Simran, wait—"

She slammed the door shut.

"Something strange is afoot," said Lydia, when Simran joined her at the bottom of the staircase. "Not out of any kind of tale I've seen. Nor any you've seen either, I expect." She hesitated. "My fellow cunning folk—we can't untangle it. We need someone with darker magic to intervene."

So this was work for a maleficent magic user. A witch like Simran, not a cunning woman like Lydia.

"You don't have any other witches you trust?"

"No, darling." Lydia's eyes were sad. "Truth be told, I wondered why you took up with it—dark business over the bright, when you could easily have inked yourself with useful gifts. But now I understand why you're like you are: The witching was your lot, your destiny. You had no more choice than any other incarnate on this ancient land."

Lydia led her through Limehouse, away from the docks. They walked together under drizzling rain, two unremarkable figures among a sea of other Londoners. The walk from the Palace had been long, and Simran's legs ached, but she ignored the discomfort.

Whitechapel greeted them in a cloud of smog. Lydia walked briskly through it, leading Simran to a familiar, discreet brick building. A molly-house. A laugh bubbled in Simran's throat. She knew this one.

"Muff's House? Really?"

"I usually prefer to pray closer to home, Simran, but needs must," Lydia said, sounding long-suffering. "Come, quickly."

Inside, the molly-house had the look of a coffeehouse, and smelled of a mix of mildew and roasted coffee, gin and juniper, bittersweet.

Lady Juliet was sitting in the entrance, desultorily unlacing her gown. She was eighteen, gangly and tall, in a dress already too small for her at the shoulders. Under the light of the lamps, her deep brown cheekbones glittered with pearl-dust.

She was usually laughing, smiling—Simran had seen her at other molly-houses, and at salons, and had never seen her without a grin on her face—but today she looked solemn.

"Auntie," she greeted. "Simran. They're in the chapel. But I'm warning you, it's not pretty. You'd best brace yourself."

"Thank you," murmured Lydia. She gestured at Simran to follow, and went up the stairs.

"The chapel" was the name everyone used for the room in the molly-house that people went to if they wanted a little privacy. Simran had always called it the sex room, because she liked to be factual, and Hari had always called her crass for doing it.

That said, Simran could admit there was something a little sacred about that space. The windows were covered with thick curtains; the floor was polished smooth, the walls undecorated around a single bed at the room's center. But there was love too, in the lit brazier, which smelled of honeyed warmth, and the roses always set in a vase above the fireplace, replaced whenever they dared wilt.

In the room was a circle of ten people, all but one of them regular visitors. The tenth stranger was an older man, gray-haired, white-skinned, and ruddy-cheeked, with his cap clutched tight in his hand. He looked like he'd been weeping.

On the bed was the body of an Elsewhere-blooded girl with the legs of a bird, a splash of feathers spread out around her waist. Simran stumbled in shock at the sight of her, then forced herself steady.

The girl's torso was covered with a cloth, but her hair was splayed out—ink on white. Each feather fanning from her body was like flame, saffron mingled with gold. Alive, she must have been a beautiful thing.

Simran took a deep breath. The air carried the scent of what the girl had once been. A cry of birds, the scent of light. Good fortune. A sweet tale of lovers, perhaps.

An incarnate.

"Lydia," she said. "Who is she? *What* is she?"

"Her name is Mary," Lydia said heavily. "She lived near St. Anne's Church. I know her mother and father—they arrived alongside me on the Isle, when we were young." Lydia's voice shook. "Not from my Elsewhere, but somewhere close. For a month, maybe more, before we forgot them, we had languages in common. I don't know how she ended up here. But she had normal legs when I last saw her, and she's got no limni tattoo on her that would have changed her. We can't make sense of it."

"We don't know who did this," said a woman called Ella. She was a cunning woman like Lydia, hair coiled into braids threaded with charms, magic inked into her brown throat and collarbone, revealed by her low-cut dress. Her face was troubled. "Her spirit won't answer, her body won't speak. We know she'd come into her own as an incarnate, but no more. We've never heard of a tale like it. Have you?"

"No," Simran murmured, shaking her head.

"James here found her—he thinks she ran from the one who tried to kill her, then succumbed to her injuries."

"She was badly hurt," James, the gray-haired man, said gruffly. "Very badly hurt, young miss. I did all I could. Didn't know where else to bring her."

Simran could use blood, or the girl's bones to seek answers. Her stomach roiled, but she kept her face calm. This was ugly business, but she was fit for it.

She drew back the shroud on the girl's face. She was tanned, her Elsewhere features similar to Lydia's own. Thick black hair, a rosebud mouth. And her face—

Simran didn't need to use any dark arts after all.

There was a circle carved into the girl's forehead.

"I know who did this," Simran said softly. Him. The stranger with his pale eyes, his hair like silver. He'd killed this strange, feathered incarnate, just like he'd killed Bess.

She wasn't even going to use magic to kill him. She was going to gut him with her own two hands.

*Let's see him come back to life without his heart in his chest. I'll rip it out myself.*

She closed the girl's eyes with her fingertips.

"The man is hunting incarnates," said Simran. "He came after me, Lydia. He was the one in my flat. He murdered another friend of mine. He took Hari. He's murdered many others. I failed once, but I still mean to find him and kill him."

She thought suddenly of Vina. Vina, whom she'd left alone and magically bound, unable to protect herself from the stranger and his knife. Fear curdled in Simran's stomach.

Shit. She was going to have to go back for Vina. She had no choice.

"You think you can?" Lydia asked.

Simran focused on her, forcing thoughts of Vina away.

"What's the point of being a witch if I can't take a life that deserves to be taken?" She wasn't going to tell them what the knight had told her. Let them think she was just driven by confidence.

If the fae thought she could end the stranger's life, then she'd do it.

"What holds you back?" Ella asked, eyes sharp. "Why have you not disposed of him yet, if you have the means?"

"He's strong and wily and old," Simran said. "He doesn't believe he can die, and since I shot him and his body spat the bullet back out, I expect he's right."

A hiss from her watchers.

"That can't be."

"I've never heard the like."

"Doesn't sound…"

"Believe what you like," said Simran. "But it's true. I know where to find him." He'd told her himself. *The mountains of copper, witch. Come to your ancient tor. Meet me there, before the winter solstice. Tell me my name, and tell me why I cannot die, and you may have him back whole and alive.*

Even without the archivists, she'd wend her way to the Copper Mountains eventually. Her tale would demand it. They were the place she was destined to die. "But there's knowledge I need to fight him, and I've no way of getting it yet." She looked from Lydia to Ella, to the other thoughtful, wary faces of cunning folk and queer folk lining the room. "Perhaps," she said carefully, "you can help me. Everyone says you know all there is worth knowing in London, Lydia. I bet you other cunning folk are no different."

They exchanged looks. One of the younger folk slipped from the room, giving Simran a look as they went.

Simran waited for their judgment.

She'd been welcomed by Lydia, but there had always been an—edge—to other cunning folk. They liked her limni ink well enough; they paid decently for their tattoos, scribed on the cheap but with all the care Simran could give them. She was no Harley Street scribe, but she knew magic. But a witch was a witch, and not welcome among kindlier magic users.

Now something had turned. One of Lydia's own people had died—an Elsewhere girl, Limehouse-raised, murdered. And cunning folk protected their own.

"Tell her," an older gent said eventually. His voice quavered. He adjusted his lavender cravat with shaking fingers. "Tell the witch about the library."

"That doesn't seem wise," said Ella. "She's a *witch*."

"She's trustworthy," said Lydia firmly. "But I'll defer to the group when it comes to this."

There was a knock at the door, and another figure entered.

Lady Juliet was gone, carefully wiped away—there was just Oliver, in his crisp shirt and breeches, a little faded lip stain still at his mouth. "Auntie Lydia," he said, with a respectful nod. "I'll take Mary to the embalmers. Me and some of the girls. We'll see her safely put to rest, quiet like. No one will know."

"You're a good boy, Oliver," Lydia said gently.

"I'll help," Simran said. It sounded like the cunning folk needed to talk, and corpses didn't frighten her.

Carefully, she and Oliver transported the body down the stairs on a cot. A few girls were waiting at the bottom of the stairs. "We can manage from here," Oliver said. Hesitated. "I heard your rotten news, Simran. I'm sorry you're going to die."

No one had said it so simply before. It was almost a relief to hear it. She *was* going to die, after all.

"I am too," she said. She looked at the dead girl. So young. Her voice trembled. "But it hasn't been a bad life."

Oliver and the girls left.

Simran stood in the coffee-scented room, and breathed deep, and felt the tug of her tale beneath her breastbone. The knight was near.

Relief, guilt, and irritation rushed through Simran in a nauseating tide. That trap hadn't held the knight for long. The knight was safe. The knight was here, and Simran hadn't inadvertently left her to die.

At least now Simran wouldn't have to go and find her.

The creak of stairs behind. Simran turned, and Lydia was there. Waddling affably beside her was a ball of fluff. The fluff, spying Simran, chirped and raced toward her.

Simran blinked.

"You brought my cat to a murder scene?"

"I brought her to a house where she'd be spoiled rotten, my love. Besides, I could hardly leave her alone," Lydia said, as Maleficium purred and wended her way unhelpfully around Simran's ankles. "Look at her, she gets lonely."

Simran did look at her. Maleficium blinked back balefully, then settled in the approximate shape of a loaf on Simran's foot, pinning her where she stood.

"Foul creature." She leaned down and scritched behind Mal's left ear. Maleficium began to purr malevolently. It was, Simran could admit in the quiet of her own head, a relief to see her cat safe. "I missed you too."

"What do you need to know about the man who did this?" Lydia asked as Simran reluctantly straightened.

"He set me a quest," said Simran. "I have to learn his true name. I have to find out why he can't die. Then I'll get Hari back safe, and I'll be free to murder him. He won't have a hostage anymore."

Lydia nodded.

"We talked, the other cunning folk and I," said Lydia. "I have something you can use, Simran. Something to kill this bastard and bring our Hari back safe. The greatest weapon of all: knowledge the archivists don't have."

Afterward, Simran went outside and pressed her back against the wall. Muff's House wasn't her usual haunt, but it was a sanctuary for queer folk, *her* people, and seeing that poor dead Elsewhere incarnate girl inside it had sent her head spinning like she'd drunk too much liquor. Her eyes ached. She was not going to weep—she hated crying. But she did slide down to the ground, back to the wall, the rest of her sprawled on a dirty London street with the gray sky thickening with clouds above her.

Bess. Mary. Two incarnates dead at the stranger's hands.

It could be Hari next. He was no incarnate, but his life was at risk because he knew an incarnate. Knew *her*. She couldn't allow it to be Hari next.

She rubbed her face with the back of her hand, then raised her head.

The knight was waiting for her on the other side of the street. She'd changed into a plain shirt and trousers, a sweeping greatcoat thrown over them. Hari's clothes didn't fit her as well as they fit Simran—the knight was too broad—but they served well enough.

The knight approached slowly. She didn't look angry. The gaze she fixed on Simran was gentle and knowing—worse than a knife, worse than pain. To have her grief viewed, seen, handled with such gentleness...

Simran exhaled sharply and leaned forward, elbows on her knees. She forced her face into a scowl.

"How did you escape?" Simran asked.

"Your trap didn't care for the fae magic in me," said the knight, tone annoyingly apologetic. "And I always carry good iron and good silver." She tilted her head to the side. The earrings adorning her ears gleamed.

"I thought you wore gold."

"Gold paint over iron," the knight said. Her face was expressionless. Without her smile, it was hard to look at her. "I know you don't want me here. You can go alone if you really wish to. But I'd like to help."

She must have walked through the rain. The knight's hair was dark with water. Her skin glowed with it.

"You called the stranger the pale assassin," said Simran, finding her voice.

"I asked the fae to tell me about him," said the knight. "The fae told me his moniker, and that he's older than we guessed. Ancient. There are incarnate tales younger than him, and he's been killing incarnates just as long as he's been alive. The fae told me the stories have been going wrong for centuries, Simran. Because of the deaths. Because of *him*. The way the Isle is dying is just...a culmination of his work."

An Elsewhere-blooded incarnate from an unfamiliar tale, dead in the molly-house behind her. Blood pounded behind Simran's eyes. He'd done this.

"And no one's stopped him?"

"No one can catch him, and the archivists and government alike try and cover up his presence. But you might. The fae was right about that. He wants to see you." The knight took a step toward Simran in turn. "He needs to die so that the stories can be saved."

"I can't worry about fixing stories," said Simran. "I need to save Hari. And then I need to kill the stranger. That's all."

"The whole Isle relies on stories," the knight said. "When a village is lost because the story that sustained it has perished, everyone and everything that lived within it is lost too. Saving stories means saving people. *All* the Isle's people. I know that matters to you. Our goals align. Killing the pale assassin—that will help put the stories right."

"I can't think of them," said Simran. But her voice wavered as she said it. "Maybe I'm just more bloody selfish than you are."

A brief silence, as the knight looked at her with that steady, awful tenderness.

"I have a more selfish desire driving me too," the knight said. "Beyond what the Isle needs, I want him dead because he's the cause of so much of our suffering. Yours and mine. Don't you see, Simran? He's the reason we exist." A shadow crossed her face; a single chink in that armor of affability. "We're a mistake—a story gone wrong. We shouldn't *be*. We've got Elsewhere blood. Incarnates are meant to be Isle-blooded. We should be—free."

How sweet of the knight, to believe there was any inherent justice in the world, beyond the justice that sometimes cropped up in tales—rewarding the demure, the meek, the palely beautiful girls who had never touched dark magic, who were not queerly wrought or Elsewhere-born.

"There's no escaping our fates," Simran said.

"I'm not sure I believe that," the knight said earnestly. That impassivity faded from her face and what Simran saw under it wasn't the cold sharpness of the woman who'd turned a blade on her fellow knights, but something much worse—naked, blazing idealism. The knight *cared*. "I have to believe there's hope for us," the knight continued. "This Isle is a wild, tale-wrought place—if tales can live on its shores, then I have to believe miracles can too."

*That one was born to throw herself on a sword*, said an old, knowing voice in Simran's skull. It sounded like Isadora. *All for a hope or a dream. Poor thing.*

The hope was foolish but there was something contagious about the light pouring from her. Looking into the knight's face, Simran felt a little less like tears were going to take her. She felt like she could stand. Maybe she could even face what came next.

"Archivists hoard knowledge like gold," said Simran. "They say they preserve and care for it—but they also *control* it. They decide what we get to learn, what tales we know, what books and papers we read. If they don't want us to know how to chase down the pale assassin, we won't."

"You've found another way," said the knight. She said it with sureness.

Simran nodded.

"There's a library in the ancient forest," Simran said, remembering Lydia's words to her, feeling their echo in her own mouth. "Deep in its heart there's a green library, which holds forbidden knowledge— rejected by the archivists, and saved by cunning folk. Some cunning folk believe there's a hidden relic there, that can reveal secrets and bare truths. I know that knights and enchanted woods go together hand in hand. If you promise to protect me in the forest, I can do the rest."

"That knowledge could be a risk to the Isle," the knight said reluctantly, as if she were loath to say it. "Forbidden knowledge, forbidden tales... They could rip the fabric of the Isle further."

Simran snorted. "You sound like an archivist."

"You wound me," the knight said, touching her fingertips to her chest. Her hand lowered; her expression settled to graveness. "They do what's needful."

"Do you really believe that?" Simran shook her head. "It doesn't matter. What matters is this: The green library might give us answers. The archivists can't. Even if they know the truth, the minute we speak to them they'll lock us up in the Palace until we're ready to love and stab and so forth, and then Hari will be dead. So will you come with me into the ancient forest? Will you help me find the library?"

She saw the knight hesitate again, and saw her come to a decision. "I will," the knight said. "But in return I'm going to ask a favor. Call me my name. I'm not just the knight, and you're not just the witch. Not anymore."

"And what name shall I use? You told me your name is Lavinia, but I've heard so many names for you. Vinny, Vina—"

"Vina," the knight repeated. "Call me Vina."

"Is that the name you let your enemies use, or your friends?"

"It's the name my mother gave me," said the knight, her gaze direct, her mouth unsmiling. "My father never much cared for it, but it is mine."

"Fine," Simran said. "Let's go, Vina. We have an assassin to kill."

# Chapter Twelve

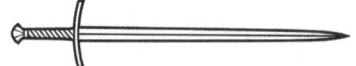

## *Vina*

*I promise you I had a wife. I know I wed her. I remember, she was going to visit her mother. She said she would be home in a week. It's been three months.*
*I cannot recall her face or her name.*
*Something is wrong, Amina. Her mother's village is gone. I went there and found nothing but fields. I searched for her name and her face in my heart and I could not recall them. I wake weeping, but I don't know who I weep for, or where she died.*
*Please, Amina. Dear sister. I had a wife, didn't I? What was her name?*

Source: Confiscated correspondence between
Ibrahim Saddiq (deceased) and Amina Khan

**Archivist's Ruling: Destroy. No further action required.**

The ancient forest. Vina couldn't help but feel unease about traveling through its depths.
There were so many tales about forests—haunted, enchanted, wondrous, and eldritch—that all those dreamt-up woodlands had melded together, making the forest as chimeric as the Palace, a changeable roiling sea of green. But beneath the magic, the shifting

trees and twining tales, lay a deeper truth. The forest was the oldest of tales. Before mortals knew how to name love or hate, lust or anger, they knew the woods, and they knew how to fear what lived in their darkness.

What had mattered to Vina, when she'd still been green to her knightly training, and the calluses on her hands had been fresh, was that the forest was dangerous.

She and the boys had been taught by Sir Maraid—a grizzled, broad knight with a scar over her left eye and cropped brown hair. Vina had been more than half in love with her, and that had made her inclined to listen attentively, in the hope their mentor would notice her. Alas, it was not to be.

"The woods'll be full of temptations," said Maraid. "Comely beauties, rich fruit that'll poison you, gold that belongs rightly to forest wights. You want to be canny and careful when you're on a mission. Trust none of it." She'd walked back and forth in front of her squires, all of them standing to attention. "They're also home to things that belong to deep, old tales. The kind people no longer speak of in polite society. And they're home to other kinds too. Undesirables."

"Undesirables?" Matthias had piped up, softly baffled. "What does that mean?"

"People unwelcome in our fair cities and towns, lad," she said. "You'll see. Besides, nothing I say will rightly prepare you. Knowing is different from knowing."

And that was all Maraid had ever said about the ancient forest.

"Tell me," Vina said to Simran, as they walked through the gloomy streets. "Have you been into the forest before?"

They'd left the streets lined with gas lamps and moved onto lightless roads. They'd walked for hours—on Vina's insistence. Buses and hansom cabs would be watched. People on foot were more likely to go unnoticed. It helped that Simran had dragged some kind of magic around them that drew the shadows close and made them stick.

"I've never had a reason." Simran was looking straight ahead. The moonlight reflected in her eyes, liquid silver on black. That was the mark of the magic in her—it made her strange even in the darkness she'd cloaked herself in. "I prefer cities."

"You mean you prefer London."

"What other cities matter?" Simran shrugged. "I had my fill of woods with Bess. I don't need aught else."

"The home of your friend Bess—that was a copse of woodland, conjured from a small local tale. This forest is…" Vina searched for the words. Made of ancient tales? A sentient, cunning creature? She couldn't be sure of that. "Older," she settled on. "It's older."

"I know it's dangerous."

"You don't understand," said Vina. "This woodland, this forest, it's not like any forest you've seen before. It's ancient. Primeval. You know that, but you don't truly feel it in your bones. It's…I don't know what it is, but it feels like one of the oldest stories, half dead. Every wood that has come into existence since looks like an echo of it, once you've seen it. That's how it feels."

"That doesn't frighten me. I've seen worse."

"Until you've experienced it, it's…" Vina sighed. "Knowing is different from knowing," she said finally, echoing her old mentor.

"I suppose I'll learn soon enough."

Simran looked pensive.

Vina hesitated. They'd fought so recently. Simran didn't even like her. But eventually, she said, carefully, "What happened to you? After you left me in your flat?"

"Your pale assassin's been busy in London," Simran said. "He's killed other Elsewhere-born incarnates. I saw one. She was—young." Her jaw tightened. "I'd guess he doesn't like our kind particularly, but he killed Bess too, and she was old Isle blood through and through."

"He killed Soren as well," Vina said. "A friend of mine. He was Isle-blooded. I don't think a hatred of Elsewhere is what guides him." After a breath, Vina said, more gently, "I'm sorry you had to see the young girl he killed."

"Me too. I'm sorrier she's dead, and the assassin isn't. But we'll fix that."

Simran hefted the pack her friends had given her higher on her shoulder. Her expression was determined.

Highgate Wood loomed in front of them. From the outside the trees were simply trees—glossy brown and green, with golden leaves carpeting the soil beneath them. Vina could hear the distant hooting of an owl. It was a pleasant scene.

She knew better than to trust it.

Simran was already striding ahead. She was beyond the tree line when she turned back and raised an eyebrow. "Are you coming?" she asked.

Vina gave a playful bow, then followed.

Mist bloomed under their feet as they walked farther into the woodland.

"So," said Vina. "How will we find this library?"

Simran drew out a compass—it was strange, made of wood with a faint green burr of lichen on its surface, its needle a brassy gold.

"The cunning folk gave it to me," said Simran. "They told me to head to the darkest part of the forest."

"Of course," said Vina brightly. "The safest part."

Simran snorted and tucked the compass away in a quick gesture, almost a sleight-of-hand trick. Vina would have missed it, if she hadn't been watching closely. Simran had deft hands. She'd proved that when she'd stolen the limni ink.

The deeper they walked, the more the landscape changed, deepening into ancient strangeness. Moss and bluebells covered the ground, in a carpet so thick it swallowed Vina's boots up to the ankle. She could hear distant rustling—animals in the undergrowth, and wind pressing cold hands to the trees.

A shiver ran through her, all animal warning. Wherever they were, they were no longer in Highgate Wood. That wood had acted as their portal into this deep forested land, this ancient tale woven into the Isle.

Night surrounded them, but even without a torch in hand Vina could see through the shadows. It wasn't her vision she had to thank for that: There were lights floating through the trees. Will-o'-the-wisps, fae things sent to guide travelers astray. Vina watched them warily as Simran steered them through the trees, in a looping, winding motion, following the trembling needle of the compass. The darkness was already growing more oppressive. The silence too.

It was broken by a yawn. Simran covered her mouth, glaring at Vina, as if daring her to say anything.

"We should rest," said Vina.

"We should keep moving."

"I'm afraid I'm absolutely exhausted," Vina replied, giving an exaggerated yawn that made Simran narrow her eyes to slits. "I can't possibly go on. We'll have to rest here and move at first light."

Simran's nostrils flared as she huffed, but she didn't argue. She had to be tired. The circles under her eyes were like licks of black paint.

"You think it's wise to sleep here?" Simran asked.

"I've slept in this forest before. As long as we have light and someone to keep watch there's nothing to fear." Probably. "I'll stay awake and start a fire."

"You'll need wood for that," Simran said, after a pause. "I'll find some for you."

Vina almost cautioned Simran not to walk away, but she bit her tongue. Simran was a witch. She could take care of herself.

Simran returned with wood, and they started the fire.

They were silent for a while, sinking into the peace of the forest after the chaos of the last few days. The warmth of the fire was unbearably good. They hadn't packed for the winter cold, no bedding or extra woolens, and Vina hadn't realized how deeply the cold had already wormed its way into her bones. Simran sat with her chin tucked against her knees, staring into the darkness. The compass sat at her feet.

Vina leaned forward and adjusted the logs in the fire. The heat warmed her face.

"Do you truly believe killing the pale assassin will free us from our tale?" Simran asked.

Vina paused, hands stilling. "No," she admitted. "It's just a hope."

"That hope is very foolish, and it's going to hurt you when we've gutted him and our tale's still in us. Not as much as it's going to hurt me to get stabbed, of course."

"It'll hurt me too," Vina said. "Alas. We truly are tragic figures. Do you think there's food in the pack your friends gave you?"

"When I trapped you and argued with you earlier, you were a great deal sharper," said Simran, sounding displeased that Vina had dulled herself into more blunted company. "Don't you care that we're going to die?"

"Of course I care," said Vina. "But now that I'm not tied up, I don't see much point in yelling. Do you?" One look at Simran's face confirmed that she probably would prefer yelling, so Vina relented, and turned finally to honesty. "If it helps, I truly don't want to stab you, Simran. Or stab myself. I like being alive."

Simran looked away from her again, head angled to the darkness, concealing her features.

"Doesn't it leach the joy from your life?" Simran asked, her voice so empty it surely had to be hiding a symphony of emotion. "Knowing your death is written, and that it's cruel, young, unavoidable—doesn't it make it harder to do more than survive?"

"I think you've been doing well," Vina said gently. "I saw your flat. You've got friends. Work."

"Illegal work."

"Work you're good at," said Vina. "Work you value. Those tattoos on your arms—they're beautiful." She gestured her fingertips at the black roses winding down Simran's arms, thorny and lush-petaled, visible where Simran's sleeves were rolled up to bare her forearms. "You love so many things. You have a good life. Maybe your death is fixed—and I hope it isn't—but what you've built in the time you've won is meaningful."

"I didn't ask about me," Simran said, after a beat. "I asked about you."

Vina didn't know what made her be honest then.

"My father is a government minister. High up. Very important—he's damnably proud of it. He's old money, blue blood, so perhaps it all should have come to him easily—and it did, truly—but he thought he'd lost his chance. When he was younger, you see, he had a 'misalliance' with a dancer from Elsewhere. She got in the family way. But it wouldn't have been a scandal, I think, if he hadn't wanted to marry her." She looked at the way the flames danced their lights on Simran's skin, making her tattoos shimmer. "Anyway, his family convinced him not to go through with it. He stayed with her until she…" Vina shrugged. "Went missing. Or left. Who knows? I was two years old. I don't remember, and my father doesn't speak of it. But he kept me, loved me, raised me. When he married, he made sure his new wife would be kind to me. When he realized what I was, how I'd die…I think it made it hard. To, well. Keep loving me.

"I find he somewhat set the pattern of my life. I've spent a great deal of my life training to become the knight I must be. And all the people who've known me, met me, have known the shape of my death. I understand that makes it difficult for them."

"Vina," said Simran. "I asked about *you*."

Vina gave her a blank look. "I've told you about me."

Simran stared back, just as unblinking, then heaved out a sigh and turned her head away.

"I'm not hungry," she said. "Let's just try and sleep."

Vina knew she'd said something that had angered—or upset?—Simran. But she was prickly, and apologizing was likely to only make her angrier. So when Simran lay down, Vina crossed her arms and sat on the ground to keep watch.

It took only a moment for Vina to rise to a crouch.

"Simran," she said. "Do you see them?"

Simran sat up. "See wh—?" She stopped, head raised. "Oh."

The will-o'-the-wisps were gathering into a spool of light, one rope of fae light twisting between the trees. They were a shining thread, pulsing in the air above both Simran and Vina. Their light was cold, lovely—as remote and pale as starlight.

Simran was on her feet. Vina quickly followed suit, as Simran hefted up her pack and began to walk.

"You shouldn't follow them," said Vina. "Their whole purpose is to lead travelers away from the path."

"That's good," said Simran, "since we're not trying to find the path. We're looking for darkness. That means we're looking to get lost." She continued to walk, following the light of the wisps.

She didn't check if Vina was behind her, but of course Vina was. She strode forward, following the lights and the silhouette of her witch.

She felt a—twinge. Looked down.

The light of the fae geas was blinking in and out under her skin. As if it were struggling against something. Simran came to a dead stop in front of her. Vina moved to stand beside her.

The will-o'-the-wisps had settled in a cloud of foaming light above a clearing, studded with bushes of holly. The air smelled overpoweringly of the scents of all seasons—summer's wheat and spring's bright narcissi; autumn's golden decay and winter's evergreen.

Gold eyes flashed, lamp-like, across Vina's vision.

*The doe,* a voice called. It was deep, susurrating. *Give us the doe, tale-born.*

Vina took a step forward. Simran grasped her arm.

"Maybe we shouldn't be here," Simran said.

"I think it's a little too late," Vina said faintly in return. She could not resist the tug of her own feet. "If I—if something is wrong—"

"If you're getting yourself killed, I'm going to run and save my own hide, I swear it," Simran hissed.

"Good girl," Vina managed, then found herself jerking forward into the clearing, under a halo of light.

The scent of seasons grew stronger still, and Vina felt ancient fingers rummaging in her skull. It was the deer she saw then in her mind's eye—the herd in Gore, darting through the trees. The shadows consuming them.

She felt Simran's hands grasp her sleeve.

Simran was murmuring some terrible magic under her breath, but her witch-gift of blood and bone and earth was nothing to this ancient power. There was a wrench, and suddenly Vina was in Simran's arms, the two of them stumbling back. And before them was a pale will-o'-the-wisp in the sparkling, faded shape of a lambent-eyed deer.

The deer from Gore. She knew it. She'd seen it die.

"Come on, you fool," Simran muttered, dragging Vina farther back. They were at the edge of the clearing again when a figure emerged.

A man, in a great cloak of oak leaves. A crown of mistletoe haloed his forehead, which was fleshly—ruddy-skinned, with thick eyebrows, set over brown eyes.

"Wild-man," whispered Vina, awed. Now there was an old tale, and a powerful incarnate. Was he the source of all these great, mist-flecked woods?

The wild-man—the wodwos—bowed his head to her, giving a blink of his brown eyes. He reached out a hand and placed it on the deer's muzzle. It lowered its head. And then, with the ponderous weight of his own magic and the green mantle at his shoulders, he vanished back into the trees, the deer alongside him. The clearing closed behind him, swallowed by trees.

Abruptly, the will-o'-the-wisps were gone too. They were alone in the moonlight.

Simran looked just as awed as Vina felt. For once, Simran's face was oddly vulnerable—her eyes wide, her mouth a little parted.

"I felt that," Simran whispered. "He saved the deer. Or some little speck of their magic that was in you. How did I not feel it? How did I not know—?"

"You were hardly checking me for magic," said Vina.

"The fae geas must have concealed it," Simran muttered. She brushed her hair back with one restless hand. "Lydia and her like won't believe it," she said. "Some cunning folk have a soft spot for the men of the woods. They'll be so jealous."

She spoke lightly, as if she felt nothing but a kind of crowing satisfaction. But Vina could still see her wide eyes—and the hand she'd splayed over her heart, like she could clasp a fragile fluttering feeling, a new-formed joy, and hold it close forever.

It wasn't the sharp words she should trust. It was Simran's actions.

They went back to their fire. Simran stoked the flames this time, as Vina looked through Simran's pack. Simran looked distant, a little elated. It had been an overwhelming experience for Vina, who had no magic. She couldn't imagine how it had felt to the witch.

Vina paused in her rummaging.

"Have you even looked in this pack, Simran?"

"No. It's bloody heavy, though."

Vina pulled out two cloaks first—both thinly woven, but oddly warm under her hands. Bespelled, surely, with the kind magic of cunning folk. Then, like a prince holding aloft a fabled sword, Vina raised up the true spoils she'd unearthed from the pack: two bottles of wine.

Finally, Simran's lost wonder cracked into laughter.

"Godsblood, we deserve a drink," she exclaimed. "Pass it here."

"You'll never get the cork out."

"I've spent most of my life in molly-houses, Sir Vina. I know how to uncork a bottle of wine."

In the end, it was Vina who got the cork out, using a little knife while Simran directed her. They wrapped themselves in the cloaks, then passed the bottle back and forth. The wine was cheap and strong enough to knock down an ox.

They drank together. Maybe they drank too fast and too deep, but these were strange and perilous times, and they deserved it.

Vina was leaning back against one tree, Simran another. Under the moonlight Simran looked flushed and hazy-eyed, more relaxed than Vina had ever seen her.

"Tell me," Vina said.

"What?"

"What you're thinking." She meant it. If she could have plucked the thoughts from Simran's head and laid them out, tender under her fingers, she would have done it.

"I think... I'm glad," said Simran. "I grew up around those deer. They were sweet. Sometimes I'd cut up apples into half moons with Bess and we'd feed them together. I'm glad a little bit of them can survive now, even if Bess is gone."

Her smile was soft, a little lopsided. It made Vina's heart tip like a ship on high seas. God, the witch was beautiful. But that had never been in doubt, and Vina would be a fool to do more than notice it. She had to wrap all that noticing, that nascent want blooming in her belly, away. *Godsblood, Lavinia Morgan, don't be a fool—*

"And are you glad I'm here with you?"

"Why would I be glad of that?" Simran asked tartly. Then she shook her head, and said, "I am. I—it's a damn shame you are what you are, and I'm what I am. You're not so bad, Vina." She sighed, tilting her head back. "It's been a strange night. It feels like we're outside of time."

Simran was smiling, a little, her sharpness folded away. It made Vina *want*.

What does it hurt to offer something? If it wasn't wanted—there was no harm in that. Vina expected nothing, generally. She expected nothing now. But it was sweet and easy to stand, and cross the ground, and move to kneel on the cool soil in front of Simran's bent legs.

Simran looked back at her—something expectant in those dark eyes.

Vina reached a hand out. Not quite touching.

"If you want, I could..."

"You could what?" Simran whispered.

"There's a sorry business waiting for us in the morning," Vina said, with the softness of a fingertip on skin—the touch she hadn't given, the touch she yearned to give. "It wouldn't mean anything," Vina said gently. "You wouldn't be misleading me, or making promises you didn't intend to make. But you are beautiful, and I like you very much." She leaned a little closer; an inch, a breath. "Let me kiss you, Simran."

Simran looked back, lashes half lowered.

"You think I trust you enough for that?"

"I don't know," said Vina. "But I'm asking."

Simran grasped her wrist. She was stronger than she looked. Her narrow fingers were like iron.

"What do you want, Vina?" Her eyes were searching, her mouth firm. "Tell me what *you* want."

That was simple. Easy.

"I want to make you happy," said Vina.

Simran's expression shuttered.

"Get lost," she said flatly. She let Vina go.

"Ah, well," Vina said lightly. "You can't blame me for trying." She winked, and with a laugh went to seek out the last dregs in the wine bottle. Simran rose to her feet behind her, fury in her eyes.

"Must you always laugh, and smile, and play the fool?" Simran seethed. "I know that's not what you are. Do you?" Her hands clenched into fists, then abruptly lowered to her sides. "I'm going for a walk. Don't follow me. I mean it."

She stormed away. Vina watched her go, laughter dying in her throat. She lowered the wine. She didn't want it anymore.

She waited. The night was full of the whisper of trees, the hoot of owls. Simran didn't come back.

Vina scrubbed a hand roughly over her eyes, then walked off in the opposite direction.

She thought of the fae lord. Fire burned under her skin, half wine, half fae magic.

"You're lucky," they had said, "that your mortal overlords have not yet realized your witch was born beyond the Isle. But they will, and then I ask you to consider what is more dangerous: the pale assassin who lies beyond these walls, or the dangers that lie within them?"

"What do you mean?" Vina had asked.

"Our bargain is done, fair knight," they'd replied. "And there is no more I want from you. I shall tell my kindred of your interest in the Merciless Maiden. I'm sure she'll be very glad such a thoughtful knight keeps her in her heart." Their fingers had brushed her cheek. "Thank you for your payment," they'd murmured. "It was very sweet."

A shudder ran through her. There was water ahead; a true babbling brook, dancing under moonlight with silver fish.

*Why did I try and kiss her?* Vina thought deliriously, kneeling by the water. Mud on her knees. *Why did I offer to please her?* There was no world where Simran would have said yes.

In the black water of the river she saw her reflection waver, liquid. Her own face flickered, for a moment, growing harsher angles—a broader jaw, and blond hair, and eyes a burning summer's day. Blood across the bridge of a nose, flecked against a cheek. Then her face returned, golden brown, unstained and water-fragile, angles unforgiving without a necessary smile to soften them.

Vina let her mouth uptick into a more comforting shape. There she was again: mild, charming, soft-eyed. The bloodied monster under the surface, the knight who'd killed their love and would do it again, and again, and again, was gone. For now.

There was no easy path to love from here. Not for her and Simran. That was good.

She started to rise unsteadily to her feet when she felt something cold and sharp at her back.

"Well, well," a woman's voice said softly. "What are you?"

# Chapter Thirteen

## *Simran*

*You may chastise me all you like, you may speak of duty until the sky falls, but it changes nothing. I don't want to kill her. What do you say to that? I. Do. Not. Want. To. Kill. Her.*

*God help me, but if I can stay my hand, I shall.*

Source: Letter from Tristram Thorne to the Spymaster

**Archivist's Ruling: Preserve. Tristram Thorne (deceased) was a known incarnate (The Knight and the Witch). No further action required.**

*I* have to go to the Copper Mountains. The witch's tor.
I have to learn the stranger's name.
I have to tell him why he can't die. All by the solstice.

She held her mission, all three parts of it, steady in her mind. Three golden coins that had to be paid, the promise of them weighing heavy on her tongue.

She needed to find answers. She needed to find the words.

Once she'd paid the price, she could take the pale assassin's life.

She kept trudging forward, as the undergrowth grew thicker and thicker, bluebells circling her up to the knees. She was shivering, hot with anger but also...not with anger, which made the anger sharper.

It was awful of the knight, to want Simran just because Simran wanted her. How embarrassing, how uncomfortable—how thoroughly fucked-up of both of them.

It was easier to hate the knight than it was to face the enormous absurdity of all the things she'd seen over—hell, was it less than a week?—and Simran knew she wasn't being entirely reasonable. But fuck being reasonable.

She stopped among the trees. Leaned back against one.

A wind blew through the trees. Her chest ached. It had to be her tale, she told herself. Growing stronger, tugging her toward her purpose.

*I'm not going to love or die until I save Hari*, she thought angrily, in its general direction. *You and the knight can wait.*

"Your tale won't wait for you patiently," a voice called out. A woman's voice, rounded at the vowels—ghostly as the wind. "It's a clever, cunning thing. It will find you, darling. Don't doubt it."

Simran angled her body toward the darkness between the trees. There, half shadow, stood her past self.

"It's been a while since I've seen you," said Simran.

"Did you miss me?"

"I didn't say that."

"I knew you missed me," Isadora said smugly. She moved through the trees, fading and returning. "You've found your knight—or your knight found you. Don't you have questions, Simran? Ooh, do you want me to share the juicy parts of your tale ahead of you?"

"Unless you can tell me how not to die, no," said Simran.

"Oh, I'm afraid not!" Isadora tutted. "You're so focused on death, aren't you? You never ask me how to avoid falling in love."

Images flashed through Simran's mind. Vina kneeling before her, tracing tenderness through the air, a promise. Her soft mouth, an offer. *I want to make you happy.* Simran's stomach swooped.

"That's not going to be a problem," she said.

Isadora sighed. Her breath was a song, rustling through the leaves. Simran knew she'd disappointed her.

"I could tell you how your tale begins," Isadora wheedled. "That isn't in the version the archivists like to dole out in pretty story books."

"But you won't," Simran said. "You've always liked to mock me."

"Ah, pot and kettle, darling."

"I don't like mocking people."

"Don't you?" Her mouth curled. "What a curious thing for you to believe. What did you do to that poor chivalrous knight, then? You fair broke her heart."

"Shut up," Simran said flatly.

A tinkling laugh, both pretty and cruel, came from Isadora.

"Fine, you've amused me, so I'll tell you."

Isadora drew nearer. Her chest was bloodied, her skin corpse-pale.

"I met Sir Tristram in the woods adjoining his family property to my aunt's," said Isadora. "He was on a hunt. He was an old-fashioned man, I'll say—nothing so modern as a rifle for him. He had a bow and he was hunting deer and hares. He turned his bow upon me—the handsome fool thought I was a deer! I was wroth with him. I told him he was lucky I hadn't hexed him. If he kneeled and apologized I would allow him to go free. A witch—and a debutante, mind—must have her pride."

She tossed her blond curls, a coquettish gesture that made Simran visibly roll her eyes.

"Oh, you don't like that?" Isadora said. A ladylike huff. "Well, I know your taste doesn't run to femmes."

"Finish your story, if you must," Simran said impatiently. The sooner Isadora stopped, the sooner she'd vanish.

"Oh, no one likes backstory," said Isadora. "But you asked. I thought you should know. I kissed him there, the first time. We *always* meet the knight over a hunt, a bow, a kiss. Isn't that terrible? The knight knows us, wants us—even before they agree to find us and kill us." She tutted. "My Tristram was just like your Lavinia: charming as glitter, and so nakedly hungry to beat the world into a better shape. I was the one thing he couldn't fix—and because he couldn't fix me, he couldn't fix himself. The best thing we could do for the world was die for it. Or so he believed."

Simran stared at her. "Did you believe it?"

Isadora opened her mouth.

There was a crunch in the undergrowth. Simran turned her gaze toward the sound. She didn't need to look back to know that Isadora had vanished.

It was probably Vina. She almost called out to her—then paused. Those footsteps were light, whispering—marked by the rustle of long skirts.

That was not her knight.

There was no time to run. She plucked a strand of her own hair and tangled it over her fingers. Whispered a curse into it, a brief, soft thing.

The figure that emerged from the trees wore a long, serviceable gown in plain blue, laced at the bodice. Their cloak was black, and long enough to trail through the dirt. Their hood was thrown back, revealing a white face, blue-black eyes—and a suspicious curl to the mouth.

Ah. Simran knew a fellow witch when she saw one.

She did not often meet with fellow witches. She knew that their tales often set them together—in vast covens or in threes—but there were also those known for keeping their distance from one another, and those were Simran's true ilk.

This one did not have the scent of an incarnate. Still, it paid to be cautious.

"I was not expecting to see a sister," said Simran. "If I've walked where I'm not welcome, I'll be on my way."

"No need to make your apologies," said the other witch. "How did you make your way here?"

There was a light in her eyes, a cautious and searching thing. There was a right answer to this question, and it was surely not *I'm chasing an assassin of incarnates*. If she gave the wrong answer, this could end very badly.

Simran thought carefully, feeling the latent magic of the ancient, primeval forest around her, trembling in the golden fallen leaves, in the trees, and the curling mist seeping along the soil. She thought of the will-o'-the-wisps, who were spirits under the hand of the fae, used for trickery. She thought of the golden deer, and the wodwos who'd been waiting to welcome it.

"There are many spirits moving here," she replied confidently. "Spirits all over the forest. I may be a witch of smog and city folk, but I couldn't resist that call."

The blue-eyed witch smiled, and Simran knew she'd given the right answer.

"Then it is your good fortune that we've met," proclaimed the witch. "Come with me. There are many of us here already, and a feast awaits us."

There was no sense in trying to run or fight, now that Simran had at least temporarily ensured her own safety. So she smiled tightly back and followed the other witch through the trees, on a winding route that finally opened to a clearing beneath a rock face. There, surrounding a blue-flamed fire, were more than twenty figures. They turned to look curiously as Simran and her new companion approached. Simran took in a breath through her nose, her mouth, tasting the air. There was only the smell and scent of forests the Isle over: petrichor, green, rot.

They weren't incarnates, but they *were* witches.

"Sister," said another witch. "You're welcome among us."

"I usually prefer solitary work," said Simran, looking at each person carefully in turn. "But it seems like something is afoot."

"A special convergence of spirits and magic," said the blue-eyed witch, excitement threaded through her voice. "A chance for us all to strengthen our craft and bind more spirits to our service. There will be plenty for all of us. You'll see soon enough!"

Hands touched Simran's arms and her back, urging her forward. They let her into their grotto, a concealed mound in the rise of a cliff, with a low, broad entrance curtained by shadows. The shadows in the grotto were deep, and Simran had a moment to think of the compass tucked away into her pocket, before a few women urged her to sit by the fire, which had a pot atop it. Simran sat. A red-haired witch was stirring the pot, her face glowing from the heat.

Simran shivered, despite the heat of the flames. The grotto was full of spirits: ghosts of the dead, and the elemental sprites of the seasons. Spirits of vengeance and old, amorphous sentiences were parading through the air and clinging to women's skirts.

"It isn't the solstice, and All Hallows' Eve neither," Simran observed. "Why are the spirits moving?"

"They've been summoned here by a great power," the red-haired witch said, pouring another bowlful of herbs into the stew pot. It was only food, Simran was fairly sure, not something more occult. It did look appetizing. "The first witches who arrived called them, and when other spirits felt them converge, they came too. Like calls to like, and strong magic is like flies to honey."

"No witch has the magic to call so many spirits herself."

"We didn't use our magic," said the blue-eyed witch. Simran turned away from the fire to look at her. She stood at the entrance of the grotto, cross-armed, radiating smugness. She clearly thought she was the master of this place, or close enough to it. "We had a great lady to grant us the power to summon them, and her ritual will give us more power still. I know that other witches you may have met in the past prefer to hoard their power, but that isn't the way of us here. It's a pleasure to get to be generous. You'll see."

She was implying that Simran was exactly the sort of witch to hoard magic for herself. Maybe that was fair. But Bess was the one who'd taught Simran long ago that too many witches meant trouble.

*They'll say they're helpers, siblings, family,* Bess had told her. *But family can be dangerous, and no person hungering for magic is kin to you. Put too many hungry witches together, and they'll eat the world.*

*But you're a witch*, Simran had replied. *You help me.*

*No*, Bess had said. *I'm not helping because we're witches. I'm helping you incarnate to incarnate. It's different.*

"I'm interested," Simran said. "What does this 'great lady' want in return?"

"Gifts," said another witch. She gestured at the far end of the grotto, where the darkness was thickest. Simran looked toward it—and realized the darkness was not dark alone, but a shroud hung from hooks in the stone.

She rose without thinking, and crossed the grotto. Here, the spirits were even thicker. She pulled back the shroud, and found the bars of a prison.

Behind them huddled a group of people. Living humans, some young, some old, dirt on their faces, their expressions terrified. Simran's stomach dropped. They'd clearly been taken from the forest and imprisoned here—as Simran would have been, if she hadn't been a witch.

"What fine gifts," she said casually, letting the curtain drop back into place. "Is your great lady some kind of human-eater, then? A vampire?"

Nervous titters of laughter. The blue-eyed witch frowned. "Nothing so crass as that," she said shortly. "You dare—"

"Oh, let her see, Sarah," the red-haired one said. "I like their natural reactions when they see the lady, don't tell her. She'll be properly contrite once she understands, I'm sure."

Sarah's frown deepened. "Fine," she said grudgingly. "You're a wet pudding, Cora. But fine."

"I didn't mean to upset anyone," Simran said, frowning in return. She wasn't going to simper at them and apologize. If they were smart, and had the measure of her, they'd read that as false. And then she'd be in real trouble. "I guess I'll see your lady when I see her."

Was there any way she could warn Vina? It was only a matter of time until Vina followed her, and then they'd both be in trouble. Simran, at least, could be *a* witch, and conceal herself in the general hum of eldritch magic swimming around her. But Vina would shine like a sword in this hubbub: obnoxiously bright and unmistakable as a threat to be put down.

"We have fresh prey," an older witch said merrily. "Come out, come! The lady will be here soon."

Simran drifted outside.

One witch was dragging forward a corpse—she dropped it unceremoniously, disgust in the twist of her lips. Even from a distance, Simran could see the black clothes, the unmistakable hat. A witch hunter.

A faint memory came to her—of the witch hunter outside the roadside inn speaking about his kind converging in the forest. Had the witches been gathering here for weeks? More?

There was no helping the corpse. Simran looked beyond it to the other new arrivals.

Five people were being dragged forward, hands in chains. The fact that the witches had found five people in one night, in this vast and strange forest, was impressive. Perhaps the ancient forest was a little like London—so tale-rich that it drew mortals inexorably into its grasp. Stories, after all, needed people to feed upon.

At first the people were too far for Simran to easily discern their features. But as soon as they drew closer, being dragged toward the grotto, she bit back a curse.

Vina was among them. There was no mistaking her. Her sword was gone. Her head was lowered. But as Simran sucked in a breath, Vina turned her head, and their eyes met for one electric second before Vina deliberately looked forward, as if she hadn't seen anything at all.

All the witches gathered, jostling together. Someone elbowed Simran sharply in the back. Simran turned, ready to blister the witch's ear with curses—and realized she was being faced with the witch who'd defended her from blue-eyed, brown-haired Sarah. Freckled skin, curly red hair tied into a bun it was violently trying to escape from. There was a dab of blue ink, barely discernible on her hairline.

She shoved a charm roughly into Simran's hands. Woven wood, and pansies, and the faint, cloying smell of magic drawn from deep waters—maybe a well, or a river deep within a cave.

"A charm of heartsease," hissed the woman. She crushed Simran's palm around it. "Place it in your clothes. In your shoes works, or in your hair if you can't do better. Quickly now! You've got a handful of heartbeats, and then she'll be upon us. It'll hide your scent from her for six nights and no more, you understand?"

Her blood ran cold. How had the other witch realized what she was? Before Simran could even think to threaten or ask questions, the redhead was gone, stomping back to her stew pot, her shoulders hunched.

Simran held the charm tighter. It hummed in her grip—soft-smelling, sweet. It didn't feel cursed. And anything that could keep her incarnate nature hidden was worth having.

She hurried away to a corner. Unlaced her boot just enough to make a gap, and placed the charm inside it.

Just in time. The sound of bells, silvery and high, filled the air.

A fae woman rode into the clearing on a white horse. Her hair was long and black, liquid ink pouring in ripples down her back, long enough to pool on the ground around her. The fact it didn't trip up her horse was more proof than her beauty that she wasn't human, Simran noted, with some grim amusement. Nymphs walked along the ground alongside her horse, their hair braided with narcissi, their eyes wide and wet. Around her stood a retinue of ghostly horses, glowing like moonlight, their riders spectral.

*The wild hunt*, a voice whispered in her head. Maybe it was Isadora's. In a way that made it her own.

"Such lovely gifts I have!" The fae's voice was crooning, as she examined the five who were her "fresh prey" from her high perch. "I will dine tonight under moonlight, little sisters," said the fae, a merry smile on her luminous face. "And I will examine my new foxes. You've done well."

Her words were infused with the weight of her fae magic, all glittering enchantment. They settled like gentle, healing hands on Simran's heart. *Be glad. You've pleased me.* Contentment and elation threatened to wash over her.

Simran shook the feeling away. She and false, soft contentment had never been good friends. Her ankle was pulsing where it touched her new heartsease charm.

It occurred to her that she could slip away from the coven and the spirits. She had a charm of protection. And she had her compass to the green library. She could go now, as she'd wanted to all along, and save Hari without the knight's help.

She looked at Vina's face under moonlight. How calm Vina looked; how utterly unafraid. What would she do without Simran to save her? Die, surely, in some ludicrous and noble manner. That couldn't be allowed.

She wasn't going anywhere until she'd gotten Vina back.

# Chapter Fourteen

## *Vina*

*If you fall into the grasp of the fae, you must not eat or drink. Seek cold iron. Show them respect. They are our elders on the Isle, and will no doubt outlive us all, save our fair and just Eternal Queen.*

*And finally, make peace with your death. The fae obey their own laws beyond our ken, and take pleasure in mortal suffering. You may obey every rule set before you and still lose your life.*

Source: *Parables for the Elfshot* by Dr. Felix Scott

**Archivist's Ruling: Preserve. Publication permitted. No further action required.**

Around Vina, the other people were shivering with fear. The air was oddly heavy and cold—colder than it had been when she'd been found by a witch (not *her* witch; and how shameful it was, to be captured by someone else).

Vina wasn't shivering. Under her skin, the fae geas was running hot. Her skin wasn't shining this time—which was certainly a relief, considering the situation she was in—but the fire was awake. It must have sensed the fae maiden.

The fae maiden did not look familiar to Vina, but there was

something about her that made a deep instinct twang in Vina like an untuned lute. The maiden was riding away now, her horse's cantering sharp and light, the sound of raindrops on stone. Surrounded by her nymphs, she looked like a royal holding court.

They came to a deep valley that arrived so suddenly, Vina was sure the latent magic of the ancient forest had carved it out for the fae maiden's pleasure. The fae maiden held out a hand; her nymph took it, holding the fae maiden steady so that she could slither elegantly from horseback to the ground.

The maiden turned. Her eyes lit on Vina.

"Ah," the fae maiden breathed. A smile stretched her beautiful mouth, the bloodred lips, the pearly white teeth. "My gift has truly arrived." Her gaze slid away, starry and cold. "The rest of you may sit at my table. Feast. Be merry."

It was like the Eternal Queen's balls, seen through a dark looking glass. The feasting table was wizened wood, a living tree sculpted to the fae maiden's pleasure. It lay in the basin of the valley, on grass turned silvery by moonlight. Music began—strains from a violin, the high call of a flute. No nymphs were playing.

Spirits and ghosts, Vina realized. It explained the coldness—and the way Simran's eyes had shifted, cataloging things Vina certainly couldn't see. Ruefully, Vina considered—not for the first time—how useful it would be to have magic.

A pale figure, fish-eyed, grasped Vina's arm.

"Sit," the nymph said cordially. Her white fingers clasped the back of the chair, drawing it out. Vina sat.

She'd been seated opposite a thronelike wooden chair. The fae maiden swept into the seat, settling in a cloud of black hair and scent like violets. Vina gripped the arms of her own chair.

The scent was unmistakable. The fae was an incarnate.

No wonder she'd taken special notice of Vina. It was a stroke of good luck, at least, that the fae maiden had not sensed Simran. Vina had, of course. Vina couldn't help but notice Simran, no matter where they were.

The maiden smiled, and gestured at the feast before them. Purple, fat grapes, and tureens of miniature birds in a rich gravy; bowls of trembling jellies, and sliced fruit that fair glowed with its own richness.

She grasped a silvery jug and raised it over the glass set by Vina's empty plate.

"Will you drink, Sir Lavinia?"

So. She knew Vina's name.

"I'm afraid I've had my fill of wine."

"Yes." Her nose wrinkled. "You do smell like you have. But mortal wine is nothing compared to the sweet ambrosia of the fae court."

The lady poured the wine. It was the color of rubies, and swirled of its own accord in the glass, sparkling and unnatural. Vina's mouth ached with the desire to drink it.

That was the problem with fae food. It made you hunger for it; it wanted you to want it. But once consumed, it placed you in the thrall of the fae who'd offered it. All children on the Isle were taught to avoid and abhor it, but that was easier said than done. Around her, she could see the four other people who'd been hunted down by witches. They were eating, their eyes feverish.

She took a slow breath. The scent of violets reminded her that this was not a feast she could afford to partake in.

"I am grateful for your hospitality," she said slowly, carefully. "But I'm afraid I must refuse for now."

The fae woman laughed and poured her own goblet of wine.

"My name," she said, "is Tristesse. I believe you were friends with my dear knight. I did not have the pleasure to meet him in this lifetime, so I am very glad to meet you."

"You mean—Soren? Soren was your...?"

"My knight," she said. "Yes. Born to love me and perish lovelorn. He should have been mine again, and he was stolen from me. And now I am alone. Our story is broken. He will never return."

"I'm sorry for your loss," Vina said gently. "Soren was a good person."

"My loss? I did not know him, Sir Lavinia. Had we met, I would have destroyed him. His fate was to wither from loving me, and mine was to enchant him and take his heart and his strength with me. I cannot grieve him. I would never have known him. No, I grieve my tale. That, and no more. Are you sure you won't drink?"

Vina felt parched, so thirsty that her throat ached.

"I'm sure," she said.

The others were gorging themselves now, caught in a magical frenzy. The violin was screeching. Vina grappled for words, for any distraction, as the fae looked at her and the food beckoned.

"I met Liege Alder," said Vina. "They said they're kin to you."

The fae's mouth curved with pleasure.

"Alder is wise, are they not? I can sense their magic in you. What bargain did they strike with you? No—don't tell me," she urged, leaning forward. "Let me see."

Vina could say nothing before she felt the fae's magic stretch its fingers into her blood, seeking out the geas still webbed inside her. Fire raced through her skin again as Tristesse examined the geas.

"Oh, I knew you were a gift," Tristesse said, beaming. "They told me you were—but I did not realize! What a fine surprise. You will do nicely."

Abruptly, she released Vina.

"Where were you going before I claimed you?" Tristesse asked, cocking her head. "What quest has led you to this forest, that blankets the land and breathes in the oldest tales? Were you searching for *him*?"

Vina did not know who she meant. The pale assassin, perhaps?

"It matters not," Tristesse proclaimed. "Your old quest is over, and a new one begins. I am in need of a knight."

"Well, that's what I am," Vina said agreeably, her veins still aching. "Do you need me to slay a monster? Seek out a lost treasure?"

"No." A laugh. "No. I need a knight to love me and lose me; to wither to death, feverish with love for me. I need my tale to survive. That means I need *you*."

For a moment Vina didn't understand. It simply wasn't possible.

"You can't simply take me," said Vina. "I'm not Soren. I don't belong to the tale of the Merciless Maiden."

"You're a knight," Tristesse said dismissively. "That's good enough."

"One incarnate knight can't simply replace another." Vina leaned forward. "Lady Tristesse, I am desperately sorry your tale has died—and all of the Isle that relied upon it. But I must serve my purpose and my own tale. I cannot simply enter yours. Such a thing isn't possible. It can't be done."

"How do you know? I am afraid you're an ignorant creature, with barely any knowledge of what you are or how you came to be."

"I know that I am the newest knight in an unbroken line," Vina said evenly, trying to remain calm. "I know that I've lived and died for centuries. As a fellow incarnate, you must know you cannot change that."

"Do you think you were always destined for this?" The fae laughed, a trilling sound of silvery bells. "You were a mortal child once—shaped only by your blood and birth and the folk who raised you. But you had an open heart, a seeking and curious mind—and the tale found the keyhole into your soul, and took you. The tale claimed you. Wrote upon you, like ink on vellum, and remade you entirely. But *I* am not like you." She leaned forward. "I am not a wide-eyed child, snared and changed by the needs of a tale. I am tale-born and tale-made—a being of enchantment and eldritch might, born from the ink of the Isle itself. Without my tale, I cannot return to flesh alone. I must fade away—back to what made me."

Tristesse reached for the long, flowing silver sleeve of her gown and drew it back. Her hand was pale, elegant, talon-nailed—but the arm was scarred with ink, peeling to reveal bubbling darkness. Vina recoiled, viscerally recalling the trees in Gore that melted away.

"Lady," Vina whispered, horror-struck. "You are dying."

"No," snapped the fae, tugging her sleeve back into place. Her voice was suddenly as sharp as a knife, her eyes just as cutting. The humans around them went still, their faces smeared, their eyes wide—horror seeping in, as they realized what they had done, and what they had bound themselves to. "My tale and I have bargained. It understands I am going to save it. I have promised it a knight, a mortal with an open, tale-seeking heart. A knight to love me and die for me. You'll do. I'll write my tale over your own."

Vina shook her head, cold and horrified. "No," she said, aghast. "It isn't possible. You'll destroy two tales instead of one."

And yet disquiet filled her. Was it possible? She hadn't thought you could reason with a tale. But she thought suddenly again of Gore, where she'd felt the tale tug and pull at her, and she'd firmly refused it.

And the tale had let her. She had bargained with it, just as Tristesse had claimed to bargain with her own.

"The wild hunt's power will help me use you," the fae maiden confided, smiling again, the knife blade of her desperation tucked away. She swirled the wine in her glass with her fingertip. "I've gathered spirits and ghosts and witches to my service—forced them to bloodlust and hunger, without even the solstice to compel them. The wild hunt is an old ritual and an old tale—it will feed the witches who have served me very well indeed, and feed my strength also. When I am glutted, I will consume you—all your glistening lust, your carefully cultivated desire. And you will perish—lovelorn, for my sake. You will have played your role in my tale, and the Merciless Maiden will continue." She leaned closer. "It does not matter what ink runs in your heart," she murmured, "if I have stolen your heart with magic."

"I won't agree to this," said Vina. "I cannot agree to this."

"You will, darling," said Tristesse. She reached a hand out, and touched a fingertip to Vina's lower lip.

Vina tried to wrench away—but found some kind of magic was holding her still.

"Remember what you promised Alder?" asked Tristesse. "Tell it to me."

"I promised a debt to their blood," Vina gritted out against the taste of ink, cold skin, understanding already filtering coldly through her.

"I am calling in my debt," said Tristesse. Her eyes glowed golden, and in response, the geas in Vina's blood flared to horrible life. "Love me. Adore me. Yearn for me. Be my lovelorn knight."

The words were like hammer blows to Vina's skull. They were already beginning to reshape her.

Vina could barely breathe. She strained against the fire, but she could not resist. She'd made a vow, after all, a fae contract. She'd made her own noose. Fool, always a fool—

Something bloodied, ink-deep, flared in her chest. She saw Simran, hood falling back, motes of fire haloing her forehead. Blond-haired, laughing Isadora, smiling as hands—Vina's hands—turned an arrow toward her chest. Rowan, the witch who came before Isadora, with his braid like golden autumn unraveling at his bloodied throat, his mouth twisting into a smile. *Kill me now, my love. Let's end it again. I've done all I can.*

In her pounding skull, Vina turned wildly to her tale—to the ink flowing through her veins, her spirit, her nature.

*Help me escape*, she begged it. *You want to live, don't you? You want me to love and kill for your sake, don't you? Then help me!*

It gave her the strength to wrench up from her seat, her chair falling back. She bolted.

She heard Tristesse shriek her name behind her, but it wasn't enough to stop her. She ran across the valley, the silvery tread of nymphs behind her, the spirits wailing in her ears. She ran into the trees and ran straight as an arrow, her heart roaring in her chest. *Turn back, turn back, you love her, beautiful Tristesse, turn back.*

She pushed the voice away. Her knees buckled, and she dropped to the ground. The forest was silent now, the trees looming large. Even the birds were not singing, hushed and expectant. It was as if everything was waiting for her to yield.

She was resisting with all she had. Her stomach was roiling. But it was only a matter of time before the compulsion Tristesse had set on her won.

"It would have been quicker if you'd drunk the wine," a voice said. "Painless, even. You'd already doomed yourself at the Queen's ball, when you bargained with that fae. What good does it do you, knight, fighting now?"

She knew that voice.

"Assassin," she said.

"That is only my title, not my name," he said. "Your witch hasn't found my answers yet, I take it."

She turned to look at him. He was as silver as the sea. In his right hand, he held an axe. It was similar to the one Vina had hefted in the woods at Gore, cutting through trees to escape the impact of tale-death. Lichen edged its hilt. But the blade was the same color as moonlight, and sharp as Simran's temper.

But Vina wasn't afraid. His footsteps had made no sound. He had no shadow.

"You're not really here again," Vina observed, breathing coming short. Either she'd run faster than she was used to—unlikely—or the geas was testing her limits. "Did you bury a lock of hair in every corner of the forest, in the hope you'd be able to find incarnates?"

"I often find incarnates," said the stranger. "But there is only one I actively hunt."

She looked again at his axe. "I'm flattered," she said. "I didn't know we had that kind of relationship."

"Not you," he said. "You are only of consequence because you belong to her tale."

He kneeled down. His blade moved with him, solid and menacing.

"A shame you've only found me, then. Simran will be so furious that she missed you," said Vina. She was losing focus—it was growing harder to taunt him, to prod information from his unsmiling mouth.

"The witch is often furious," said the assassin. "And her heart is more fracture than flesh."

"You know her," Vina guessed, leaning toward him, curiosity cutting through her pain.

"I've known many versions of her."

"How many times have you met her? Have you tried to murder her before?"

"So many questions." His lips quirked. "You always begin with a gentle, curious heart. But it hardens—calcifies. The worst of you becomes diamond hard in its brilliance: your morality, your idealism. Your belief that she cannot be enough, and you are worse for loving her. Better to die, than live so broken. Isn't that so, knight?"

"Well—that isn't going to matter in a moment," Vina forced out. "It seems as if I'm going to belong to a different tale soon enough."

"I could release you from the fae's grasp. Save you. For a price." He straightened fluidly, then began to walk around her. The axe sang where it touched the ground; a slow, whining cry as the pale assassin circled her. It should have made no noise. It wasn't here. He wasn't here.

Vina blinked, and blinked again. Her head felt a little clearer. The pain was a muffled roar. Somehow, the sound of the axe was disrupting it.

"How kind," Vina said, smiling—well, grimacing—through her pain. "But you're not here. You're a shadow. There's little you can do."

"Is your clear mind not proof enough of my power?"

"It's a very fine trick," Vina said politely. "Thank you."

The assassin sighed. If Vina had felt a little better, she would have laughed. She could really irritate anyone if she tried.

"The fae maiden's ritual has made the forest stranger than it is by nature," the assassin said finally. "It is not the solstice, but the forest behaves as if it is. It has opened a door for the living and the dead—and the ever-living, like myself—to walk without barriers. Already, the forest stretches across the Isle. With the fae's hunt feeding more power into it, I can move wherever the forest grows. I can do as I have offered."

"And what would I need to pay for your help, my ever-living, murderous friend?"

"I want the witch," the pale assassin said simply. "I want her placed in my grasp. Vow to bring her to me, on your honor as a knight, and I will help you escape the geas you chose to bind yourself into."

"Impossible."

"All tales—and all laws of the Isle—can be broken."

"No. That isn't why it's impossible." Anger was a fine knife in Vina's belly, stirring her. She looked the assassin square in the eyes. "There is no world where I betray her to you. None."

"You love her already?"

"Of course not," said Vina, even as her heart tugged at the thought of Simran's frown, her dark hair, her bared arms. What she felt— that small ember of affection that, carefully tended, with hot breath and tender hands, could bloom miraculously into love—wasn't yet love. So her words were not a lie. "I barely know her. But it would be wrong to betray her to you. She has a good heart. She deserves better. Even if she were coldhearted, she'd deserve her life."

"Such idealism," said the assassin. "What an excellent rock to break yourself against. Fine. I will leave you to your fate, knight."

"Stop," Vina said forcefully. She grabbed for his leg as he moved away, and watched her fingers pass through skin and bone as if nothing were before her at all. Still, the assassin stopped, staring down at her with his pale eyes.

"Speak," he said.

"Is her friend, Hari, alive?"

"I made a vow," said the assassin. "So he is."

"Is he well?" Vina asked. Simran would want to know. When— if—Vina was able to tell her.

The assassin...paused.

"Well enough," he said finally, a strange note to his voice. "He misses her. He misses London."

Relief rushed through her, quickly put to rest when he said, "But my axe is sharp, knight. And it is hungry. Her friend, however beloved of her, is not my beloved. Tell her to move swiftly, if you can.

Though I am not sure how much of your free will shall survive the pact you've made."

He gave her a contemplative look.

"My great hope is that Lady Tristesse will accomplish what she desires to. If you become her knight, then the tale of The Knight and the Witch is dead. And my work will be done."

She'd known he had no real desire to help her. She'd been right.

"You were testing me."

A thin smile was his response.

"What do you gain by killing incarnates?" Vina asked, as the geas began clamoring and clanging in her head once more. "What can you possibly achieve by it?"

"The Isle must fall, knight," said the pale assassin. "And your tale ending will lead it closer to its death." He drew back, the night turning his moonlit form to gossamer. "Goodbye, knight. I do not wish you well; only what you deserve."

Vina watched him go, breathing through her nose, her jaw clenched. Two tales warred inside her. She saw Simran; felt Simran's fingers beneath her chin, and Simran's magic at her wrists. She saw Tristesse, grief and fae strangeness turning her eyes to liquid pools of hunger. *Love me, love me, love.* How could she not love Tristesse? Loving the maiden was all she had ever known, and all she had ever been.

The pain—had she been in pain?—was quite gone. She straightened up, standing, and brushed the dirt from her trousers. She could hear her love calling for her from the valley. Her voice was like the song of the wind through trees, more beautiful than any music. Vina would have crawled to her on broken glass, if the maiden had asked it of her. She'd known the minute, nay, the very second she saw her.

"Tristesse," she called into the night. "I am coming!"

As she walked, a small voice clamored angrily at the back of her skull. But her skull and her whole body were full of a song in gold, a fae thing—and she could hear nothing beyond it. Why would she want to?

# Chapter Fifteen

## *Simran*

*The Merciless Maiden has been told in many forms, from poetry to song, but it is this author's humble opinion that art is the form that does it the most justice. Inquire cordially with the conservator at the Dulwich Picture Gallery, and he will show you a painting wrought with exquisite care. The knight weeps and weeps eternally, forever discarded, and forever in love. The Merciless Maiden, flushed with power, smiles at his suffering.*

*There are claims, titillating but likely spurious, that the artist was the past incarnation of the knight himself, Daniel Hawker. As Sir Daniel has been dead some two decades, we shall never know.*

Source: *Art of the Isle* by James Belafonte

**Archivist's Ruling: Preserve. Publication permitted.
No further action required.**

Golden hair stained in blood. That was all Simran saw at first, until her muddy vision sharpened. Then she saw more than she would have liked to: Isadora crawling on the ground, alive despite the wound in her heart, the sword through her chest. Her hair was golden, but her skin was pale and bloodless, marked lividly with her own spilled blood.

In front of Simran's eyes, her blood turned to ink.

"Can't you feel it?" said Isadora, laughing, laughing, even as she wept. "Something is trying to break our tale. Something is very wrong—"

Simran woke.

Why had Isadora come to her? Simran didn't need a warning. Of course something was wrong. Vina was imprisoned by a damn fae.

It wasn't light yet, and Simran was surrounded on all sides by sleeping witches, curled up together under blankets to ward off the cold. Her own head ached. Her eyes were gritty with exhaustion.

Simran had waited all night for the witches to sleep, or for their focus on her to waver, so that she could seek out that fae maiden and her "foxes." But the witches had reveled all night long, feasting and drinking. None of them had left, and the fae maiden never returned. So Simran had been forced to exercise patience. It wasn't her strong suit.

She sat up, cracking her shoulders. It was cold, and her joints felt stiff. There was a twinge in her ankle. She turned her ankle back and forth—then remembered that the pain was from the charm still tucked in her boot.

She looked around. There was no sign of Cora. Everyone else was slumbering. She had to take advantage while she could.

One witch, brown-haired, woke up when Simran walked past him, and hastily shoved on his spectacles. He squinted up at Simran.

"Where are you going?"

"For a piss," said Simran. "Why? Are you worried I'll run off and find a gaggle of witch hunters to kill us all?"

The man quailed, letting Simran stalk off.

She didn't have to go far to find the place where she and Vina had camped last night. Their fire had burned out, guttered to nothing but sad ashes. Their pack had been gnawed at by something—probably by animals trying to get at the food inside. But they hadn't managed it.

Simran opened her pack and took out exactly what she needed, sighing with relief when she realized her scribing tools and ink were unharmed. Food, she could afford to lose. These, she'd happily give up a limb for.

She returned to the witching grotto. There were more witches awake now, but no one seemed to have noticed Simran's absence. Sarah was holding court, sitting cross-legged on a tree stump. She was combing out her hair, her blue eyes bright, her voice gleeful.

"Tonight is the night, sisters," she was saying. "Can you feel it? The air is sweet and heady with magic. We could be walking in the fae court itself, that's how sweet it is, to be sure. Tonight our foxes will run through the woods, and we will hunt them for the lady. Our hunt will feed her, and it will feed us. The tale will empower us." She spread her arms wide. "No more fearing witch hunters. We'll be strong enough to hold our own demesnes in the great forest, where they cannot touch us!"

Simran had mulled it over in the night, before uneasy sleep and bad dreams had knocked their way through her skull. Not all tales were incarnates' tales, enacted by mortal players who returned, lifetime after lifetime, to play their roles. Some could be ritual—performed with purpose. The pouring of cider over apple tree roots, to summon a good harvest, or wassailing—songs sung in the orchards to bless trees with good health. Beating the bounds, when a town could be protected and magicked to full strength by branches beaten against its borders.

That was what Sarah spoke of; that was the game the fae maiden was playing. She wanted to feed on the power of the ritual tale of the wild hunt.

A foolish game. Tales were liable to consume masters who weren't fit to hold them. But the witches were clearly desperate, which was understandable. They were hunted, drowned, burned. If Simran had been a witch by choice instead of by her incarnate nature, and had not had Bess's mentorship, and Hari's unwavering support, and even Lydia's kind guidance, she could have gone the same way.

From the corner of her eye, she saw Cora dragging a fly-clouded, foul-smelling bucket out from the grotto.

"What is Cora doing?" Simran asked the witch next to her.

"Her? The ginger?" The other witch's nose wrinkled. "She's slopping out the foxes. They smell, and they shit in buckets in their cell—it's vile. Someone has to look after them, and it's Cora who does it."

Simran cursed inwardly. Somehow she'd missed the moment when the prisoners were brought back.

"What did she do to deserve getting stuck with that job?" Simran asked.

"She volunteered. Same as with the cooking. Some people just like mothering, the good and the bad of it." She shrugged, and ambled off.

Simran had a half plan, a little snare of wild ideas and hopes. She strode over to Cora, wrinkling her nose a little at the smell. Cora glared back.

"Let me help," said Simran.

"I don't need any help."

"A job shared is always faster," said Simran, trying to sound diplomatic. When Cora only glared at her again, Simran internally gave up, leaned forward, and hissed, "I need your help. If emptying shit buckets is going to help me get it, then I'm happy to do it."

Cora also lowered her voice, jaw bullish.

"I think I've helped you enough."

"You care about one of the prisoners," said Simran. She saw Cora stiffen, and knew she was correct. "I need to get into their cell. If I can, I can help them."

Cora frowned.

"No matter what story you're part of, I doubt you've got the kind of magic it takes to save them," she said. "Everyone here is drenched in magic—the lady's been generous to the witches. There's nothing you can do—"

"Hell, I'm not just an incarnate. I've got other skills." Simran fumbled open her bag, revealing the edge of the tools inside—the needles, shining. She covered them swiftly.

Cora's eyes were wide. She clearly knew a scribe's tools when she saw them.

"The prisoners may not want—"

"—the power to escape? I think it's unlikely." They were starting to attract attention, so Simran said, even lower, "I can tell you care about them. Give them a chance."

Cora's mouth thinned. She took keys from her waist, and shoved them into Simran's own.

"Let's stop talking over a shit bucket," Cora said. "Go and talk to them. I'll say one of them had an accident and I've set you on cleaning it up. Try and look unhappy about it."

Looking unhappy was Simran's forte, so she scowled and stomped into the grotto. The pot over the fireplace was empty, and the fire was dying. She pushed back the curtain, and went up to the bars. The smell, without fire and smoke to conceal it, was overpoweringly of sweat and piss and fear. Eyes, white and wide, stared at her again from the dark.

You could hardly blame people for shitting in their cell if you locked them in there and gave them no alternative. Simran thought it was bloody obvious. She wasn't going to make the prisoners feel bad about it. She kept her face neutral as she kneeled down, eye level with the man nearest the bars.

Someone hiccuped with terror. She touched a fingertip to her lips, urging them to be quiet.

"I'm here to help," she said quietly. "First, tell me. The knight who was brought in with you all. The woman with the short hair. Where is she?"

"The lady took special interest in her," the nearest man said. "I'm sorry, young miss. I'm not sure there's going to be much of her to save. No good comes of a fae lady's attention."

"There's always a way to overcome a fae." True love, usually, or some rot like that. But Simran didn't need true love. She had an incarnate tale to protect her and Vina both.

The people here didn't have that.

"I'm a scribe," said Simran. "I'm going to come in and those of you who're old enough and unmarked—if you're willing, I'll give you ink that makes you strong enough to break spell-marked bars.

It'll make you fleet-footed and built for stealth. It may not save you from the witches and the fae lady, but it might. You understand the price of ink?"

Most of them stared at her uncomprehending, but the man, grizzled and bearded and broad, said, "I do. But you don't understand, lady witch. We supped on fairy food. We're enthralled."

"I expected you would be. But there's still a chance you'll be able to flee the forest before the fae comes to claim you." She moved to unlock the bars. She could feel the magic—blood and spit and secrets—worked into the steel. It gave way at the key in the lock, and the iron of her witching will, urging it open. "Fae magic's an old tale, and strong for it. But there are older and stronger. Scribing isn't one of them—but a plucky mortal tricking the tricksters *is*."

The man looked dubious. She gave him a clinical once-over. He was strong, to be sure. His body would be able to handle a feral tale; something built for brutes at war, for the weight of an animal's rage. And they'd need strength to escape this place.

"You'd protect them?" Simran asked.

He met her eyes and nodded, determined.

"I would," he said.

Good. It helped, when the magic of the ink matched the nature of its would-be bearer.

"Do you have any farmer's sons here?" Simran asked. "Young, idealistic, good-natured?"

There was some shuffling. Finally, a gangly, acne-marked boy raised his hand. "Me? Maybe?" he said. "I'm not a farmer's son, but I am sixteen. And my nature's all right, I suppose."

"Have some confidence," said Simran. "You're going to need it. Now, we'll need to mark you somewhere the others won't see it, and fast. Lift your shirt."

She couldn't rely on her witching. Not here, surrounded by a shark bath of other witches, many of them cannier, cleverer, and more powerful than she was. But her scribe work wasn't witchcraft. It was tale-magic, and it would serve her well now.

The boy lifted his shirt, and Simran wetted her needle. She worked fast, without loveliness, the limni ink pearling like the pupil of an eye on the tip of her needle. It met the boy's skin—and his blood— with a crackle of pure energy, the kind that lay in the very marrow of the Isle. Simran bit her tongue and focused as she inked a deer. In her scriptorium, she would have made it a lovely thing—wide-eyed, graceful-limbed. Here, brutal, economic swiftness was paramount.

The boy was breathing raggedly by the time she was done, crushing the hand of the person next to him—but he was firm-jawed, and his tears hadn't spilled. Good.

She turned to the man.

"You next," she said. "He's got the swiftness. You're going to need the strength to protect them."

The man had already rolled up his sleeves. "One of my arms," he said grimly. "Feels fitting for strength."

He had a missing ring finger on his left hand, so that was the arm she chose. It took strength to recover from wounds, after all, to be harmed, and to scar, and to survive. A bear was the first thing that came to her needles. She created it with scrolling, looping movements of her needle. Its head was upraised, its eyes oddly soft. Sometimes the ink-wearer changed the design by their nature. That had to be what was at play.

She could hear footsteps outside, approaching. Two voices arguing. She clenched her jaw. She was almost done, so close.

"I told you, I got her to help me!" Cora's voice. "She's a silly fool, you should be glad I'm putting her to use."

*No time*, she thought. Her needle slipped, panic leading her astray. She hissed, biting back a curse as the needle rolled to the ground. In a few seconds, the witches would be upon them. No time, no time.

It would be crude work, but damn professional pride. She pressed her fingertip to the ink on the man's arm and drew it into the shape of the bear's furred belly.

She could see the prisoners breathing fast, hands over their mouths, urging her to go faster with their eyes. But she wiped her hand on the ground, scrambling for the needle, and tucked it into her sleeve.

The ink was done. Simran felt the limni ink settle and flare into place, filtering magic violently through the man's blood. Then she shot to her feet and strode to the edge of the room, where there were still two stinking buckets.

"What are you doing?" one of the prisoners asked, voice thin and alarmed.

"If you survive, you'll thank me," she muttered, then tipped over a little of the shit bucket onto the floor. She aimed for the corner, but it still made everyone scramble to the other side of the cell, gagging.

The cell door slammed open. Sarah strode in—then propelled herself out so fast she almost knocked herself to the floor.

"Oh, wonderful," said Simran. "Have you come to help, Sarah? That is so generous of you! Truly, we *are* sisters in magic—"

"You can stop," sighed Cora. Sarah was already speeding for the exit, making retching sounds as she went. "Is it done?"

"Yes," said Simran. "I'd help you more, but I've got someone else to save."

"Not until you're finished here, you don't." Cora shoved a mop into Simran's hands. "You're lucky Sarah was too distracted to see you don't have anything to clean with. But I'm not cleaning shit, so get on with it."

"Fine," said Simran. "You stay and keep watch."

Cora crossed her arms, eyes narrowed.

"Trust me," she said. "I will."

After Simran was done, Cora directed her to a place to bathe—a clearing, equipped with buckets and ewers of water, heated by gentle magic or small, carefully stoked fires. She washed out in the open, scrubbing her hair with lavender-flecked soap, trying not to feel ridiculous for keeping her boots on. She wasn't going to risk the damn charm leaving her side. That was just inviting trouble.

Then, when she was done, she went to find her clothing—and found another witch waiting for her.

The witch was young, soft-faced—clutching a bundle in her arms.

"Simran? Cora told me you need some clothes. We have some spares to share between us. I thought these might fit you."

"Oh, thank you," Simran said, relieved. She scrounged through the pile, wrapped in a towel—also borrowed, thank you, dear coven kin—and found a skirt of deep blue, the color of midnight. Next she found a white shirt, more gray than white-white, and slightly too big, but nice enough. She knotted it at her waist to give it shape, and combed her hair with her fingers. Easy enough—her hair had always been pin straight, stubbornly uninterested in both knots and curls.

She returned to the others, walking with the girl. The younger witch needed no encouragement to start talking. She told Simran her name was Diana. She'd come from a small town on the edge of the forest that was, in her words, uncomfortable with magic. "It's not a bad place, but it's no place for cunning folk, never mind a witch. But I chose my path, and I've never looked back." She puffed up with pride. "When Sarah found me she told me I could have a better future if I came here. Growing my magic—that's going to mean I can be *more*. There won't be a fire or dunking for me. I'll be a legendary witch."

Unlikely. No one seemed to have considered that legends were few and far between. Most folk—even witches—were fodder for tales. But Simran bit her tongue, and tried to pretend she was a sympathetic ear instead of a bundle of furious nerves.

"The lady's been so good to us," Diana was saying happily. "I hope she will let us stay with her when the hunt is done."

"And where is the lady now?" Simran asked. "I haven't seen her anywhere."

"She doesn't visit us in daylight," Diana said. "I don't know where she goes when she's not with us."

Excellent. Simran ground her teeth. She had no choice, then, but to wait until dusk.

* * *

Dusk fell.

There were bows being prepared. Courtly weapons. Fae were not much for axes or rifles, though she'd seen them carry a sword or two, wrought out of wood.

Someone offered her a glass of wine in a silver cup. She tipped it back and drank none of it. Lowered the glass carelessly, letting it spill. She needed a clear head.

Finally the scent of violets hit her nose, and the chill in the air became oppressive. Her skin rose in goose bumps. The spirits were swarming, haloes of white in the trees, their mouths and eyes stretched in anticipation.

The white horse approached through the trees, its footsteps rainfall and chimes in the wind—light, airy, and nothing like the clopping of hooves should have been. Nymphs moved around her, dancing, fish-eyed, and singing with bloodlust. But Simran's eyes were drawn immediately to the figure walking at the fae maiden's side. On foot, shoulders squared, face serene, was Vina. Vina's gaze passed over Simran dismissively, unseeing. Then she raised her head and looked at the fae maiden, and finally her gaze blazed, hot with want.

Simran's stomach twisted. Her skin felt cold. Even if the tale in her hadn't been screaming, she would have known something was wrong. It was only in that moment, watching Vina, that she realized Vina always looked at her. Always, with soft and clever eyes, that guarded smile. To not be looked at like that—

She cut the thought as sharply as if she'd taken a blade to it.

If something was wrong with Vina, getting her back was going to be harder than Simran had expected. Something had happened to their tale. No wonder Isadora had come to her in a nightmare. Some part of Simran was wounded.

*I should have noticed*, Simran thought. Maybe this was the price of the charm in her boot—a muffling of not just her incarnate scent but her incarnate magic.

"Our hunt begins, sisters," the fae said, in a low and beautiful voice. She raised a hand. "Bring out the foxes, and we will glut on magic."

The ghosts began to sing—high and wailing and celebratory. The witches raised their hands, crying out with the ghosts. But their joy was cut short when a witch emerged from the grotto, panicked.

"The bars are—broken," the witch heaved. "They're gone, the foxes are gone!"

"They can't be gone," snapped Cora, and Sarah said, hotly, "We've been watching them all this time! How could they creep by us? Don't be absurd."

"Is this true?" the fae asked. Her voice had turned cold, her expression so remote it had to be hiding intense fury.

"One of them is still here." Her face was blanched with terror. "He—he's—"

Heavy footsteps echoed from the grotto behind her. The man she'd marked emerged, sleeves still rolled up. He looked bigger than he had before—grim-faced, and ready for battle. He held a broken bar from the cell in his hands, bending the metal in his powerful grip.

"You will not run, fox," the fae maiden said coldly. Fae magic infused her voice. "You ate at my table. You belong to me."

"I'm no plucky young hero, built to trick the fae," he agreed. "But I will not be yours, Lady. I will fight to the death. I will not remain here. I was a woodcutter before your witches stole me. I know what it takes to fell a great and ancient thing." He curled his hands into fists. "Let us see who wins."

One of the witches loosed an arrow with a panicked shriek. That began a battle of arrows and magic—and the man using a rod of the prison gates to beat his way through the crowd, teeth bared.

This was the best distraction she was going to get. She shoved through the crowd, using her elbows viciously, until she was at Vina's side. She grabbed her by the biceps. Vina was dressed in new clothing, part silver cloth, part filigree silver armor, and it was cold and strange under Simran's hand. A bow the color of moonlight was strapped to her back, a matching sword at her belt.

"Vina," she said. "Sir Lavinia. Knight. Come with me."

Vina stared at her uncomprehending. Of course it wasn't going to be that simple.

"Vina, you're better than this," Simran said sharply. "She's enthralled you—clearly she has—but you're an incarnate. You should be able to resist. You were built to resist her! You belong to your tale, which means you—you belong to me." If her voice went a little high and her face flushed as she said that, well, clearly not even Vina was in any state to notice. "You—oh, godsblood, you're not even hearing me, are you?"

It had to be the charm, blocking even Vina from feeling the pull of their tale. It was a risk to remove it, but Simran had no choice. An arrow whistled over her head, and Simran kneeled down and unbuckled her boot. She pulled the charm free and laid it on the ground. When she did so, she felt the pull of her tale rush over her. There it was, the familiar tug of the tale at her breastbone, strong and firm, drawing her toward Vina and toward their fate. But now, as she focused upon it, she felt how strangely frayed it was—torn and twisted, as if someone or something was trying to pull the knight from her.

That could be... good, surely? The tale dying, freeing them both? Hope kindled in her chest—then sputtered and died when she realized that she couldn't leave Vina in the mire she'd found herself in.

"Vina—"

"Hush," said Vina. Her voice was deeper than Simran had ever heard it—not softened to make her seem smaller or less significant. The angles of her face were harsh with love and hunger; her voice was a rasp. "My lady acts. Watch her."

Simran turned her head, and watched as the fae conjured a lance of light in her hand. She raced forward on her white horse, the witches parting around her. She threw her spear forward.

The man stumbled. Blood was pouring from his chest. But he was smiling.

"The others—got away," he heaved. "Bought them—time. You've got. No hunt."

He fell forward. He crashed to the ground. Birds screamed, rising and flying away from the trees.

He was dead.

She'd carved strength into him with limni ink. But it was his own strength that had killed him—made him too slow to run, too brave to flee. The inevitable price of limni ink, this time taken swiftly. Guilt shot her.

Maybe he'd known the risks, as he'd said. But what he'd known, or hadn't, was beyond her now. She just hoped his soul wouldn't remain here, a ghost among dozens of other writhing specters.

"Lavinia," the fae maiden said. "I want her."

Simran let out a shuddering breath—which meant there was no breath in her to scream when she felt Vina's fist meet her stomach. She flew back, falling with a thud.

Simran was on the ground, arms abraded, winded. When she looked up, she saw Vina above her, cold-eyed and unsmiling, sleeves rolled up to bare her arms. Her right hand flexed—a beautiful, menacing display of tendon and muscle. Those hands were truly made for murder.

Well, there was some hope in this fucking mess. She knew Vina was perfectly capable of killing her in a blow, if she wanted to. And she hadn't. Instead, Simran was painfully alive.

"Ah, witch," the fae was saying, her sweet voice traveling sinuously to Simran's ears. "I see you now. I have your scent. Don't try and run now. Wait a moment, as my witches prepare." The maiden was no longer on her horse. Her footsteps whispered against the ground. Ghosts were wings of light and shadow at her back. "We need a fox, after all."

Oh hell.

Vina hadn't left Simran alive for the sake of their tale, or because she was still aware beneath the weight of the enthrallment on her.

She'd left her alive as prey.

Simran rose laboriously to her feet. She sucked in a breath, then another. She touched her fingertips to her abdomen. She ached, but nothing felt broken.

"You'd kill an incarnate? You'd end a tale the Isle needs to survive?"

"Your tale is not as important as my life," the fae maiden said tranquilly. "These witches rely upon me."

"These witches are just tools you're using," Simran said harshly. "You'll glut them with magic, give them a taste for something they'll never get again. It's no different from fae food: When you're gone they'll starve, pining for you and the gifts you gave them. You'll use them up and leave them with nothing. Don't deny it!"

The fae laughed, tossing her head back.

"You say that as if you think I am evil for what I am, and what I do! But I am not. Mortal lives are fleeting, and I have ensured they will taste unparalleled sweetness in their short lives. What does your Queen give you, in return for all she's taken? Do you even know what she thieves from you? I think you don't." Her smile was smug. "Besides," she continued. "They cannot hear you. They do not care."

Simran looked around, breath short. There was no doubt at all reflected in the eyes of the witches around her. They were already too well-fed on magic; already owned.

Simran was on her own.

"Will you hunt this fox for me, knight? Will you skewer her and bring her back to me, a prize for my love?" The fae's voice was triumphant, her eyes brilliant as diamonds.

"I would do anything for you, Lady Tristesse," said Vina. Her voice still did not sound like her own.

Simran didn't bother to look for humanity in Vina's eyes. She was lacing her boots tight, fast, breath already short. She was going to have to run, after all. And she had no plans to be caught.

Fuck dying for this fae.

"The hunt begins," said a voice. Cora, of all people. She looked over Simran's shoulder, as if she couldn't stand to meet her eyes.

"The foxes—the fox—will be allowed to run unimpeded until the song of the ghosts ends. But when it does, we witches and our lady will follow."

"My knight will have the pleasure of killing my prey," said the fae woman. She held out a pale hand, a single finger pointed to the trees. "Go, fox."

"I'm not a fox," Simran muttered. "I'm a witch."

The ghosts began to sing—a song like a scream, a heraldic call with macabre trumpets. Simran turned on her heel and ran.

Trees around her. Her lungs aching. Her boots thudded hard against the ground, blood pounding in her ears. *Think. Think.* What could she do before the song ended? No doubt she didn't have long.

If she'd known this was coming, she would have left her own magic in the trees—hexes of hair and blood, spit and secrets.

Unfortunately, the other witches knew everything she knew about magic, and they'd had time to leave their mark. There were traps in the trees, spellwork hidden under the golden fallen leaves. If she hadn't been a witch herself, they would have been able to snare her. Hopefully the boy she'd marked had used his deer-swift gifts to escape more easily than she could.

*If only incarnate skin could hold limni ink*, she thought, not for the first time.

The song ended abruptly. Her skin prickled, hot and cold. She was running as fast as she could, but she could hear the neighing of the white horse, and the sudden shrieks of the witches.

And worse still, she heard familiar footsteps: a tread so light it was almost inaudible. Whisper-soft, thoughtful, quick. The knight was catching up with her fast.

Isadora, speared through, flashed through her mind. Simran didn't want to die at all, but certainly not like this—murdered out of sync with her tale, pointlessly, the tale dead along with her.

*Think.* She breathed hard, ragged. *Think, think, think, think, think!*

There was no magic she could draw upon. No way she could outrun Vina.

She stopped. Caught her breath, straightened her spine, and turned.

Vina was staring back at her, a bow in her hands. Angling her body perfectly, she nocked an arrow. It was aimed at Simran's heart. She didn't even have a hair out of place, the beautiful bitch that she was.

Their shared incarnate tale sang in Simran's chest. Isadora, bloodied, warning her. The key was there, in the past Vina and Simran shared.

Their tale had begun like this. The knight hunting the witch. The witch had—she had—

"Fool," Simran said. Her voice was thin, wavering. She swallowed. She raised her head. *Be the witch*, she told herself. *Not the witch you are now. Be the cruel, laughing thing Isadora was. Be her.*

*Be yourself.*

She took a step toward Vina. Another. She'd never walked like this—a sinuous movement, as if she wanted to be looked at and admired; as if her body were a beautiful weapon to be displayed.

"I would have your apology, knight," she said, and her voice left her low and velvet in a way her voice had never been before. The tale brought the words to her lips; the tale moved her like a puppet on strings. Under her skirt, her legs were shaking. But she placed her fingertip under Vina's chin, and Vina did not shoot her with an arrow nor reach for the fae silver-sword at her hip. Instead she watched Simran with eyes blown wide, more black than brown. "You could have shot me. Can't you see I'm not prey?"

A shadow rippled across Vina's face. Her expression changed as the tale caught her in its web. Amusement curled her mouth. Curiosity—and want—lit her eyes. She looked down at Simran with the confidence of someone born to a charmed life, someone who had never wanted without getting.

"A creature like you should not be out in the woods when a hunt is on," said Vina. "You shouldn't be surprised to be mistaken for a fox or a hare. You should apologize to me, sweet maiden—you are the one who should not be wandering the woods, leading innocent hunters astray."

"Leading you astray, am I? The pile of insults grows and grows," Simran declared, her mouth shaping words of its own accord, her lips curving into a smile that wasn't her own. There was amusement in her face, and anger in her heart, and a fire in her belly, and all of these things were her own and not her own.

"Is it an insult to mark your strangeness?" The knight quirked an eyebrow. "You appear from the mist of the woods, unbidden. You look at me without fear. And you demand apologies. I think, sweet lady, that you are not a simple maiden gone far from the safe woodland path, nor even a poacher's daughter trespassing on the land of her betters."

"Shall I weep for you, sir knight?" the witch asked, tossing back her hair. "Cower? Simper? Would that put your fears at ease?"

"I would not have you weep from fear," said the knight, low and brazen. Bold, indeed. "And I do not think you would have me fear you either, lady witch."

She laughed. "You think me a witch?"

"I know it," the knight said. "Lesser knights would slay you now for the crime of your nature. But I have never killed any monster for its nature alone."

"Nature, nature," she echoed. "And what is my witchly nature?"

"To hunger," the knight said, gaze flicking to her mouth, then—slowly—back to her eyes. "To trick. To take from the world, no matter how Queen and Isle may deny you."

She could bed the knight here, she thought. It would be a feast—all those strong limbs, that fine neck, the strength whip-corded through that body, set upon the purpose of her pleasure. Oh yes.

The distant sound of yelling and hounds. (There were no hounds, Simran thought, and yet there had been, and so in this hallowed moment where an incarnate tale breathed deep into its lungs, there were.)

The witch felt a tingling in her belly—a kenning. Sometimes the future touched her. It was the kind of curse often lashed down upon witches who played foolishly with mirrors; and oh, the witch had meddled more foolishly than most.

"One day you will be sent to my abode," said the witch, sharing the sweet curse of her knowledge, and her desire. "Your foolish Queen will ask you to hunt me down. Know this: Everything I will do, I will do to draw you to me. I do it so you will lay your heart willingly in my hands. Bare your throat to me, my darling." She ran a fingertip along the line of the knight's throat. The soft skin flushed deeply under her touch. "I can collar you now, if you like. A circlet of gold, perhaps. Or the marks of my teeth. Perhaps I'll let you decide."

It was like the pavane. A slow, steady dance, written so long ago that the steps could only be followed, unchanging. The knight tipped her head back, baring the sinews of her throat in relief. But she was not mastered.

"Why place a collar on me, when I will follow you gladly? The Queen will not need to send me. I will offer myself to the quest. What knight would not follow a beautiful maiden across the breadth of the Isle?"

The knight grasped the witch by the waist; drew her closer. For all the strength of her hands, the touch that followed was feather-light, and all fire—a thumb to the witch's bared clavicles and the swell of her breasts at her shirt. The knight's fingertips, circling the shape of a breast, a tender promise of sword-calloused fingers on flesh, of *more*. The knight's head tipped forward as the witch gave a ragged, soundless breath, baring her own throat.

"Is this penitence enough, lady witch?" The knight's voice was husky in her ear. "Shall I go to my knees before you and show you due worship?"

"Worship my lips, first," Simran whispered. Maybe it was her voice, her want. Maybe it was the tale. She did not know. But she knew it was her belly that was somersaulting; her skin that was electric. The knight's—Vina's—hands moved to her hair, tracing tingling fire into her skull.

Vina drew her face up and kissed her—and all was flame.

# Chapter Sixteen

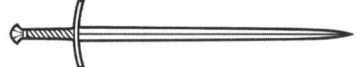

## *Vina*

*Incarnate tales linger over the power of kisses. A parent kissing their child good night, or a sibling placing a kiss-wrought blessing on their kin's brow, are familiar tale-matter. A kiss to the cheek can break a spell just as well as any ardor-fueled kiss to the lips between lovers. But the kisses of true love, of desire—these kisses are the ones with the greatest tale-born strength. None of us, after all, can resist the allure of a love story.*

Source: Transcription of lecture by Mr. Cillian Ferrers, Corpus Christi College, Oxford

**Archivist's Ruling: Preserve. Publication permitted. No further action required.**

She'd been in a haze of yearning. Loving Tristesse had been all-consuming. Everything in her had yearned for the fae maiden, for her approval and her touch. The fact that Tristesse had barely touched her had only made the desire sharper. She had seen nothing but Tristesse, and thought of nothing but Tristesse. When the fae had told her to kill Simran, it had been so easy to agree. Necessary even. Tristesse's wants had been far more important to her than her own.

Loving Tristesse had been false.

Kissing Simran was sharply, achingly real.

Simran was warm in her arms, her lips soft. Her hair under Vina's hands was silk. She smelled of smoke and sweat and of herself—of skin, heat, the promise of velvet under Vina's mouth. Simran gasped against her mouth as their lips parted for a brief heartbeat. They met again like the tide touching the shore.

Vina wrenched herself back with a ragged gasp of her own. They both stepped back. Stared at one another.

"I'm me," Vina blurted out. "And—I am sorry."

All she wanted was to lean forward, press their mouths together again, to kiss Simran and taste Simran and kiss her some more until time was worn smooth, obliterated. The want was vast, but it had no place here. Simran had drawn on their shared tale. That had been their first fated meeting, the first steps of their story. And now Vina felt like *herself* again. Tired, and furious, her head clear and her thoughts a swarm. Inside her chest, the blood-ink tale of The Knight and the Witch held steady. Vina was the knight again, and the woman in front of her was her destined other half, the only one she'd love and the only one she'd kill.

Tristesse's thrall on her was broken. The tale of the Merciless Maiden was shattered once more. In Simran's arms, Vina had been the knight, and she had kissed Simran as the knight.

As Simran had kissed her as the witch.

Vina resisted the urge to touch a hand to her own mouth. Her lips were sore. Simran had turned a little, face in profile. She had a hand over her lower face, knuckles against her own mouth.

"You're free," said Simran. "You're free."

Those weren't questions, but Vina still felt compelled to reassure her.

"I am," she said. "You saved me."

"We need to get away from here." Simran's face was half concealed by her own hand, but Vina could see her guarded eyes and the wings of her black hair. A dizzy fondness rushed through her at the sight, bigger than she had any right to feel. "I can hear the witches coming. If any of them catch us we don't stand a chance."

"I don't know," said Vina. "I certainly wouldn't bet against you. Thank you for helping me, Simran. I won't forget it."

Simran's eyes flashed, meeting Vina's. "I wish you would," she said.

"Witch," a voice whispered. "Witch, come here!"

Simran was turning, looking for the source of that voice. Vina had been in the ancient forest often enough to know how voices could come from all directions, impossible to follow. You couldn't easily hunt through these woods by sight and sound alone. On early quests, when she'd still been a stripling girl, she'd been taught to navigate the woods, to ignore the illusory and focus on the real.

She'd been using those skills to hunt down Simran, only moments ago. She shuddered at the realization. It was blessedly lucky that Simran had found a way to break the fae's hold on her.

"I know that voice," Simran said. Her eyes had brightened. "I gave some of your fellow prisoners limni ink. I gave one of them a deer so he'd have the fleet-footedness and stealth to get himself and the others free. I think he's here."

"Call to him, then," urged Vina.

Simran hesitated. "I never learned his name."

Vina stared at her.

"You tattooed him with magical ink in a prison," she said slowly. "But you didn't learn his name?"

"Survival and escape first, niceties second," said Simran with a scowl—which, at least, did explain why she'd insisted on calling Vina nothing but *knight* for so long.

There was no chance to say anything more. A figure appeared from the shadows to the right of them. The boy was ruddy-faced, brown-haired, and wide-eyed. The boy also had nascent antlers growing from his skull. Going by Simran's expression, giving him the "fleet-footedness and stealth" of a deer had changed him in ways she hadn't expected. But she'd been right to say there was little time for niceties.

"I'm no threat," Vina said quickly. "I was thralled, just like you."

"I know," he said, staring at a particularly fascinating tree over

Vina's shoulder, instead of meeting her eyes. "We arrived just in time to see you kissing." He gestured at the trees behind him, and Vina saw the other freed prisoners huddled in the shadows.

Vina heard a strangled sound come from Simran. Despite herself, she grinned.

"Oh good," Vina said brightly. "My name is Vina. And yours, friend?"

"Vaughan," said the boy.

"You were made for the ink I gave you," Simran said approvingly. The boy gave her a startled look, face lighting with tentative pleasure at her words.

"I'll try and be worthy of it," he said earnestly. "Shall we go?"

"Yes," said Vina. "Let's go. Fast."

They ran. Raced, feet pounding the soil, but utterly silent. Vaughan was wielding the gift the limni ink had given him to cloak them in a prey animal's learned stealth.

The footsteps behind them were growing louder. Vina couldn't see the ghosts, but she could hear them drawing in, cold voices rending the air.

"She's determined to find us," gasped out one of the freed prisoners. "We've been going—so long—but there are still more ghosts and more witches, and always the strange sound of that damn horse!"

"She won't catch us," Vina said, her breath faintly ragged. If she was feeling the strain, trained as she was, the people around her were certainly on their last nerve. She tried to make sense of the landscape, to remember where she'd been before she was snapped up. "There's a brook near here," she said to Vaughan. "Can you lead us to it?"

He veered, and they followed, an arc through woodland. They were wheezing, stumbling around her. Their energy was running short. But there was the brook, broader here, but still a paltry stream of silvery water. They waded through it, slipping and crawling through silt, and then heaved themselves onto the other side.

"Summon the wodwos," Vina said to Simran.

Simran stared at her, breath heaving, face aglow with sweat.

"How do you expect me to do that?" Simran demanded.

"You have magic, don't you?"

"Witchcraft doesn't mean I can do anything magical at any time! If it did I bloody promise you we wouldn't have been trapped with that rotted fae!"

"Witches can summon spirit familiars, can't they? Isn't that why you were looking for a cat when you went home?"

"My cat is not an imp," Simran said, sounding enraged. "And that witching skill isn't one I have. My magic relies on physical things that belong to me—ideally of my own body. Blood, carvings by my own hand, hair…"

She stopped. Her gaze went focused and still.

"The deer came from Bess's woods," Simran said, more to herself than Vina. "Those woods knew me. I left my blood and magic in them."

"So it may be possible?"

"It may. But the wodwos called you to its side, remember. Not me."

"Be that as it may, my first job is to distract the fae maiden," said Vina. "We'll see what comes after that."

She urged the others to get back and hide in the tree cover if they could. None of them had strength left to run. They crawled under cover, terror in their eyes.

Vina stood steady at the thin water's edge.

Four or five witches emerged, panting. The white horse followed them, Tristesse on its back. Her long black hair was no longer sleek, but in wild tendrils around her. Her eyes were blacker still, her face coldly furious.

"I feel a wound in me, knight," said Tristesse. "My tale is broken once more. Your love for me is gone. You have betrayed the debt to my kin. You have stolen knowledge from the fae. They will hate you forevermore; no fae shall welcome you, no matter where you go." She held out a pale hand. "Unless you serve me once more, and make things right. My tale agrees; we wait for your answer."

Vina had wondered if any part of the geas on her remained. She could feel the frayed gold in her blood, and the wound where Tristesse's enthrallment had once entangled her like a strangling vine. The pain would be with her for a lifetime, and the consequences too.

"I'm afraid I can't," said Vina. "As I told you, I already have a tale I belong to."

Tristesse cantered forward. Paused, lovely mouth thinning.

"You think one of my ilk cannot cross water?"

"There are many beings of tale who can't," said Vina. "I hoped you were one of them. Alack, I am mistaken!" She held her arms wide, her fae-wrought armor glittering in the fractured moonlight. "Come and take me, Lady."

"I do not need to cross the water to kill you," said Tristesse. "If you cannot save me, then I cannot countenance allowing your ugly tale to continue. Let all our tales die together."

Tristesse raised her bow and arrow. Unlike the wooden bows of the witches, her bow was as white and pearly as polished bone. She raised it high.

"Wodwos," Simran called into the woods, her voice carrying high as a kestrel on the wing. "Wild-man. You and all your green brothers, your dryads and your greenteeth! I summon you!" Her voice echoed. She yelled again, "I summon you!"

The arrow was unleashed. Vina leapt out of the way. She heard a high whistle, a thud, and Simran's voice calling her name. "Vina!"

On the ground, weight on an elbow, Vina exhaled a shaky breath. "Deer of the woods," she whispered. "I carried your souls here. I saw you in the fae's feast. Bring the great spirits of the woods with you, the oldest incarnates, the green man and green children, the wodwos, the adders that speak riddles. Bring them here, and spare the foxes from the hunt. Foxes are your children. Hunters are interlopers. Please."

At first there was nothing, as Tristesse drew another arrow, and it sang as it was nocked into place. Vina rose up to her feet, ready to leap again. And then she felt a wind brush her cheek; rustle her hair. She raised her head.

The wild-man was not the only creature in the forest wroth with the unseasonal wild hunt. Perhaps others of his ilk had heard them, because the brook began to bubble and swell, growing into a full-blown river. The water was green, rich with leaves and the suggestion of teeth and eyes, spitting in waves that barred the passage of arrows. And Tristesse stared at Vina over it, eyes furious.

So Tristesse couldn't cross water after all. Or at least, not *this* water, made from creatures like her, of ink and myth.

"Your tale is broken," Vina called out, voice carrying over the rush of the leaf-strewn river. "Go, Lady Tristesse! There will be no wild hunt, no more Tale of the Merciless Maiden. Go, and be free, and say farewell to your kin!"

Tristesse stared back at her, face suddenly as sorrowful as her name. "I told you," she said in return. "I am not a mortal incarnate. Without my tale, without the hunt, my tale will know I cannot save it. And I am nothing but my tale. I will die. I—"

Her voice cut off abruptly. She released a shuddering breath, hands rising to clutch her own throat.

"It comes," she forced out, voice thin as frayed silk. "Hold vigil, knight. See what you have done to me."

Ink bubbled and coiled up her wrists, her hands. It turned to mist, rising in the air. It seemed to happen both so slowly and suddenly, this ending. Before Vina's eyes, Tristesse began to fade and distort, like ink shot through with water. The Isle shuddered beneath them. The trees, the soil, even the water seemed to exhale. Tristesse closed her eyes.

Tristesse vanished.

Vina fell to her knees, relief and horror shearing her strength. She craned her head, seeking Simran. Simran was walking toward her, shaky on her legs. Behind her were the freed prisoners, all of them trembling with relief.

Simran came next to her. They collapsed onto the bank. The freed prisoners lay or kneeled around them, dazed. The water was high and churning, and Tristesse was gone—nothing but black, rolling and fading to nothing on the far riverbank. Distantly, over the water, Vina could hear the crying and wailing of witches.

"There's no helping those witches," Simran said, after a moment. Her voice was firm. "They've doomed themselves. It's not our problem."

"I am sorry for them, Simran," Vina said softly, reading the tension in Simran's shoulders, the tightness of her jaw.

"It could have been me," Simran said abruptly. "If I hadn't been an incarnate—if I'd stumbled on witchcraft without a fate, and a friend who'd do anything to care for me—I could have become like them."

"The friend—that's your Hari?"

"It is."

"I had an...experience, when Lady Tristesse was trying to enthrall me," said Vina. "I can't be sure if it was real, but I must share it with you."

She told Simran about the pale assassin, and his offer, and his obsession with Simran alone. Simran listened, tense.

"I suppose at least I have more reason to believe Hari is alive now," Simran said. "If the assassin wants me, he'll keep to the bargain he forced on me."

It was possible the assassin had been lying, but from what little Vina could recall of that hazy, fever-fueled meeting, he'd seemed oddly...sincere.

"The fae woman mentioned your geas," Simran said after a beat, voice frighteningly neutral. "Care to share?"

"My fae geas compelled me to serve her," said Vina. "I know. I was a fool. It's done."

"You should have known fae can't be trusted." Simran leaned forward, pressing her forehead to her knees. "I don't even have the strength to be angry with you. You really got us into shit, Vina. You were meant to help me."

Real guilt twisted in Vina's chest.

"I promise I will do better," said Vina softly.

After that, as they found their strength, the freed prisoners discussed what to do next.

"We'll take you to a village bordering the forest," said Vina, not looking at Simran. She knew Simran would agree, but she was aware they'd lost precious time in their search for the answers that would save Hari.

"Finding the way out won't be easy," said Simran.

"Do you have your compass?" Vina asked. "If it points to the darkest depths of the forest, we'll simply go exactly where it tells us not to."

"That's utterly mad," Simran said flatly, but she did fish out the compass. Then she cursed. "The damn thing broke at some point when we were running away." Simran moved as if to fling it away—then braced herself, paused, and put it back into her pack. Vina could see the tightness in Simran's jaw and shoulders. Her path toward the library—and the information that could save Hari—was gone.

"I can lead us out," said a woman. "I know this part of the woods. My town isn't far from here."

"Thank you, ma'am," Vina said, with all the gratitude her weary heart could muster. "If you could lead the way, I'm sure we'll all be forever thankful."

It took a week of travel. Another precious week wasted. Vina hunted to feed them, using the bow Tristesse had left with her, the oddly light armor that whispered instead of clanging, imbued with fae magic. Simran made traps from her magic, and placed defenses around the places where they slept. Vaughan, for all that he was young, was helpful and good at starting a campfire. They kept moving.

She and Simran didn't talk about their kiss. But they did begin to talk—just talk. Vina told her what the fae had said, about being born from the Isle itself, and Simran smiled, a bitter and wistful thing, and said, "Wouldn't it be nice, to be born from ink, and not have to worry about the people you'll leave behind?" She shook her head. "Never mind."

She didn't talk about it again. But Vina didn't forget.

It was a relief when the light finally changed, and the trees thinned, and they broke from the boundary of the ancient forest onto the margins of a village. It was a quiet place, with thatched-roof cottages and wary locals in doublets and gowns, warding symbols from cunning folk daubed onto the perimeter walls. The only significant landmark was a bell tower in the center of the village, marked with protective symbols, daisy-petaled hexafoils and stars alike.

The villagers welcomed the prisoners.

"We've seen people taken by the forest before," the mayor said, her voice steady and knowing. "It's a blessing to see them free."

When the goodbyes were done, only the boy Vaughan was left.

"You're going back into the woods?" he asked.

"We are," said Simran. She was already fair vibrating, desperate to leave.

But Vaughan's face was firming with determination.

"I won't let you travel alone," said Vaughan.

"It's not up to you," Simran said immediately, with typical tact.

"It's safe in this town," Vina said. "You should stay here and recover, and live a good life." She placed a hand firmly on his shoulder, meeting his eyes. "You've been brave. But your quest is done."

The boy hesitated. His gaze flicked to Simran, settling on her even as he spoke to Vina.

"My home isn't here," he said. "My home is in the forest. I need to go there."

"You've got good limni ink in you," said Simran, obviously trying to hide her desperation to get moving. "You don't need us to protect you as much as they did. I'm sorry, Vaughan, but there's someone else I need to save, and his life is in far more danger than yours will be."

"I know you're looking for a special place, a hidden place," said Vaughan quickly. "I saw your compass—the broken one." He looked around, then lowered his voice. "I know you're looking for the green library."

Simran tensed. "What do you know about the library?" she demanded.

"I know how to get there," he said. "I can't say anything else. It's not allowed. But if you keep me safe, I'll make sure you find your way."

Vina tried to meet Simran's eyes—could Vaughan be trusted? What did they truly know about him?—but Simran was already nodding.

"It's a deal," she said.

They should have stayed in the town to rest before continuing their journey. Vina wanted to. But Simran was on edge, and refused to do so.

"I can handle any witches who catch up," she said. "I can sense their craft, and I'll make charms to keep them at bay. I just need a little wood and blood, and both are easy to get hold of."

Vaughan looked a little alarmed, so Vina said mildly, "You can't keep bleeding yourself, Simran. Blood's best kept in the body where it belongs."

Simran clucked her tongue dismissively.

"We'll also need to sleep," Vina pointed out. "And neither of us have the strength left to keep watch."

"I can keep watch," said Vaughan.

Both of them ignored him.

"When we're ready to rest, I'll set traps in the ground," said Simran. "Those have worked for us so far."

Vina watched, when night fell again, as Simran traced a wide circle with the branch of a yew tree into the ground. She'd soaked its edge in ash from a short-lived fire—and as expected, a speck of her own blood. As she worked, Vina kneeled in the center of the circle and watched her. And built a proper campfire.

"I've done my best," said Simran. She sounded exhausted. The magic had clearly drained something from her. "We'll be fine."

All three of them lay on the ground, the fire crackling. As the sky darkened further, Vaughan quietly began to snore.

Vina was lying flat on her back. She turned her head. Simran was looking back at her. In the firelight, her skin was warm honey, her hair bronze-flecked and black, a dark halo around her face. This was the most alone they'd been in days.

"You're looking at me," said Vina.

"No," said Simran, even though she absolutely was. "You're the one looking at me."

"How can I not?" Vina whispered back. "We kissed."

Reckless, to say it. Simran had rejected her when they'd both been themselves, without enthrallment or their tale driving them to kiss. Simran hadn't spoken of it since. And yet she saw Simran's gaze flick to her mouth, then back to her eyes again, a slow, inexorable look. She knew Simran was thinking of it too.

Her stomach ached with warmth.

"I kissed you for a purpose," said Simran.

"I know you did. And I'm thankful."

"I wish you'd stop talking about it," said Simran. "And stop looking at me."

"As you desire," said Vina, who'd perfected the art of being a little shit while also obeying orders long ago. She rolled onto her back, stretching as she did so, arching her back, then lowering it. She stared up at the tree canopy.

One heartbeat. Two. Three.

Four.

"I can feel you thinking about me," Simran whispered, viperous. "Stop it."

"I'm not thinking of anything," lied Vina.

A huff of breath. She heard the rustle of Simran's skirts. Then suddenly her vision was full of the sight of Simran. Simran threw one leg over her, straddling her, hands pressing to each side of Vina's head. Vina's heart started pounding.

Simran leaned down—and gave Vina a brief, dry kiss. Simran raised her head back up. Vina's lips tingled.

"See," said Simran. "The kiss before was an aberration. There's no need to think of it anymore."

Vina craned her neck up and pressed her mouth to Simran's. This time the kiss was no quick brush of mouths. It was shallow, still; a slow brush of lips, deliberate and teasing. Vina let her lips part; an invitation. *Take me, darling*, she urged. *Go on.*

Simran pressed Vina down, kissing her intently, deeply. Simran knew how to kiss, and she did it as she did everything else—with impatient, nearly violent intensity. Vina breathed with the kiss, reaching up, brushing her knuckles along Simran's earlobe, the angle of her jaw, the sleek sharpness of her face. She felt Simran shiver—then wrench back with a gasp. Simran's eyes were blown dark, her lips red.

Vina smiled.

"Consider the old kiss forgotten," she said breathlessly. "This is the one I'll remember."

Simran rose up abruptly onto her knees, then stood and strode back over to the dry patch of ground where she'd been sleeping. She lay back down with a thump.

Vina closed her eyes, still smiling, and slept.

They kept walking toward the deepest shadows of the wood.

When they weren't sure of themselves, Vaughan led the way, lightly moving ahead of them. He had a canny ability to sense where the darkness was deepest and move toward it. Vina tried to wheedle information from him, but he always avoided answering, scampering ahead of them.

Vina and Simran moved after him, walking side by side.

"Leave him be," murmured Simran. "If you scare him and he runs off, we'll have no chance of finding the library."

"Scare him? Me? When you're here?"

"I'm not frightening," Simran said after a beat, but she sounded more pleased than enraged.

Simran's shoulder brushed her own—one small butterfly wing of contact. Vina hadn't considered how closely they were walking together until that moment. They'd done it as naturally as breathing.

The trees began to grow sparser. The air was cool, but not with the weight of ghosts—instead, with darkness, untouched by the heat of sunlight.

"Stop," a voice said. "No farther."

"Listen to them," said Simran, voice low and tense at her side.

"I can feel witchcraft." She shifted her foot, drawing it back—and exposing a gouged line in the wet dirt, hidden beneath a cover of leaves.

A figure appeared. Red hair, in curls, clasped in a bun at the nape of a neck. Freckled skin, a scowling and wary face.

One of the witches from the hunt. Vina tensed.

"Cora," said Vaughan, smiling.

"Vaughan," she said back. Relief in her voice. "You're finally here."

"You were there to save *him*?" said Simran.

"I was," said Cora. "He's my family."

"She's also a librarian," said Vaughan quickly. "We both are."

Vina's mental image of a librarian was quite at odds with the scowling red-haired witch and lanky antlered boy in front of her, but she sensibly held her tongue.

"Sharing what you are is forbidden, Vaughan," Cora said sharply. "You can't just bring strangers here."

"Simran has a compass," Vaughan said earnestly to her. "I saw it. And she's an incarnate, and she saved me, even though she didn't know it would do her any good. Please, Cora. We have to help her."

Simran stepped forward, expression suddenly blazing with hope.

"Cora. We're looking for a library. Your library." She held out the broken compass. "I was sent by cunning folk from London. One of their own was killed. I need answers the library might be able to give. Can you help?"

Cora was silent. Her mouth was thin, her eyes wary.

"I helped you once," Cora said. "And you got Vaughan free, though you marked him. That's worth something, and I thank you. It doesn't mean I have to help you again."

"Please," said Vaughan. "Cora. We do owe them. *I* owe them. I'd like to pay my debt."

Cora hesitated. Then spoke.

"I can't promise you entry into the library. That will be up to powers greater than me. But I suppose you can follow me."

# Chapter Seventeen

## *Simran*

*The hunt is sacred to the Eternal Queen. When the solstice comes, let all wyrms and wyverns, beasts and chimeras, flee into the darkest reaches of the forest. Let the hounds howl and the goodly knights take up their arms. The Queen will find the enemies of her Isle and skewer them through.*

Source: Parliamentary speech by
Rt. Hon. Harold Harper

**Archivist's Ruling: Preserve. Publication permitted. No further action required.**

Cora led them farther into the dark with Vaughan at her side. She wrapped her arm around him. He made an embarrassed noise but didn't shrug her off. The relief both of them felt was obvious. They were a family, and they were whole again.

Looking at them made her think of Hari. Not that she ever really stopped thinking of Hari.

If there weren't answers here, she didn't know what she'd do.

No, she did. She'd stop playing the pale assassin's game. She'd go to the Copper Mountains and rip him apart.

Simran looked away from Cora and Vaughan and tried to look for the green library instead. But there was nothing—only mist thickening into smoke, leeching the color from everything and everyone. Simran's own hands, when she glanced down, looked gray, her boots black on the blacker soil.

She looked up and saw a gray cliff ahead of them, opening into a narrow chasm. The chasm appeared so suddenly, it made her pause.

"In here," Cora urged, and she and Vaughan stepped into the chasm confidently. The mist swallowed them.

She and Vina followed. Simran sucked in an immediate breath. In the chasm, color reappeared, green and lush all around them. The chasm was covered in ferns, the walls of rock on either side glowing and feathered with emerald light.

Vina looked just as awed. She raised her head, all the color spilling jewel-like over her gold-brown face. "It's beautiful," she murmured.

*Yes*, Simran thought, looking at the light on her, the curls at her ears. She turned away.

They walked for a long time, the ferns a susurration of greeting around them in a faint forest breeze. Finally, Cora and Vaughan stopped.

A winding circle of stones lay on the ground before them, looping in on itself in a crude spiral. The path ahead was cloaked in mist.

Cora kneeled down and knocked a hand thrice against the earth.

"I come seeking knowledge," Cora called out. Her voice echoed back on them in dozens of whispery echoes. "I come seeking truth. May I drink of knowledge? May I enter?"

Ritual words. They waited, together, for the ritual answer.

The ground shuddered—groaned, like an old beast. Then ahead of them stood a door. The chasm ended, suddenly, with its ancient oak surface, pitted with moss, and the knocker of dulled brass. Vaughan pressed his hands to the door and laboriously pushed it open.

Stairs met them, made of dark stone, covered in moss, surrounded by sloping walls. Cora and Vaughan walked in. Vina and Simran looked at each other. Then Simran stepped forward, and Vina followed.

They entered a circular room, its floors stone, its walls the pitted sap-sweet wood of living trees. Six figures awaited them, dressed in plain robes as if they were archivists—but they were not, Simran was sure of that. She knew cunning folk when she saw them, and at least three of these were cunning folk indeed—clear-eyed, glowing with benevolent magic, limni ink written in their skin. They all wore chatelaines, the tools of an archivist's trade at their waists—quills, scissors, ribbon. These were the librarians of the green library.

One of them had their arms open, eyes teary.

"My apprentices!" they cried, striding over to grasp Cora and Vaughan both into an awkward embrace. "Where have you been? Vaughan, why do you have antlers?"

Vaughan was stammering out an explanation, but Cora cut in calmly.

"We'll speak later, Roslin," said Cora. "We have petitioners for you. They came with a compass—and they saved Vaughan and me from danger."

Simran immediately drew out her broken compass again, presenting it. The eyes of the librarians turned on her.

"Who sent you here?" Roslin asked. "And for what purpose?"

"We were sent by cunning folk in London," said Simran. "Lydia Chen and her circle. An Elsewhere girl was murdered in Limehouse—an incarnate from a tale none of us have seen before and can't name. She was killed by the pale assassin, and I must find him. I need your help."

"So you come here to learn to kill?" another librarian murmured, eyes narrowed with displeasure. "An easy enough task. Your companion has a sword—bid her to use it."

"He can't be killed. I shot him and he lived—healed, immediately. I'd like to kill him," she said bluntly. "But more than his death, I need answers. He kidnapped my friend. If I cannot tell him his name and why he cannot die, then my friend's life is forfeit."

Roslin clicked their tongue. "An old bargaining tale," they said, thoughtful.

"Please," said Simran. "The pale assassin is dangerous. He's killed many incarnates. If he isn't stopped, we fear the Isle may perish."

The librarians exchanged looks.

"If cunning folk have sent you to us, then you have the right of entry. That is the old bargain we hold to with their kind," one said reluctantly. "But the Beast will decide if you are worthy." From the corner of her eye, Simran saw Vina raise an eyebrow.

Roslin said, "Cora, if you're willing…"

"I'll show them the way," said Cora. She inclined her head to the other librarians, then untangled herself from Vaughan and walked across the room to another brass-limned door. "Follow me," she said.

They were led down a bark-lined corridor that seemed to stretch endlessly in front of them. A wind crept down it, whistling hollowly. Simran felt the urge to hesitate, and forced herself not to. She was a witch; no magic had the right to concern her. She should have been comfortable here.

"This place seems… large," Vina murmured, her voice reflecting the awe Simran felt but didn't want to express.

"It has to be," said Vaughan. "All the stories and tales the archivists reject, all the ones that threaten the 'correct order'—we collect and save those. In some ways we're more an archive than the royal archives are."

"We're two sides of the same coin," said Cora. "We're called to it, archivist and librarian alike—protecting stories, preserving them, keeping them safe in their books. But the archivists want to control stories—destroy the ones that don't suit them, and shape the others the way they like. They only care about bloody propaganda. We save everything. We save what they try to kill."

The rooms they moved past had wooden shelves crammed with books. There were labels on the shelves—some in gilt, some scrawled in black ink that had dyed the wood blue. The interior of the library wasn't damp like the outside, which seemed sensible, but also suggested some kind of magic was at work. When Simran breathed in she smelled dry air, dusty books, sweet ink. It was like ash to her. She forced her feet to keep moving. There was an impatient knot in her chest. She needed to save Hari. That was all that mattered.

It was Vina who lingered, peering into one room.

Simran paused, waiting for her. There was wonder in Vina's eyes—a slight parting to her mouth that made Simran think of how Vina had looked, before they'd kissed, all soft expectation. Any desire to snap at Vina died before it reached her own lips. When Vina realized Simran and the others were waiting, she gave a sheepish smile. "Terribly sorry," she said. "Let's keep moving."

"We can take our time," Vaughan said earnestly, but Cora was already striding industriously ahead of them.

Simran walked by Vina's side, through gray stone corridors, lit by lamps with pale flames that flickered under covers of glass.

"You like libraries?" Simran asked.

"I like books," said Vina. "I grew up surrounded by them. My father was never much of a reader, but my stepmother—she was a writer. Archivist approved, of course. They read all her drafts long before publication. She liked to read with me. At least when I was little. She had some beautiful tomes. When I visit my father's home I still like to look at them." Another smile, quick; a carefully, swiftly placed mask.

*My father's home*, Simran noted. Not *mine*. Not Vina's own. She had a sense of what Vina's childhood had been like, and she didn't care for it at all.

Her own childhood, at least, would have been decent—if Simran hadn't been herself. That was her own fault, and no one else's. Her parents had loved her, and loved her still.

She pushed her guilt away.

Whispers touched her ears again. They became sharper, clearer. This time it was Simran who stopped. She couldn't help herself.

The room they were walking by now had no books within it. Instead the room was filled with misty shadows that flitted back and forth, carrying whispers with them. Entranced, Simran stared as the shadows drew together, forming little animals—sparrows and goshawks, loping hares, and scurrying dormice; foxes with smiling maws, pointed ears. They made flowers—little daisies and snowdrops that bloomed in a carpet of shadow, then flickered away. She heard whispers sing together: a woman's creaking voice, a child's babbling laughter; and other voices, words she couldn't understand, and words she shouldn't have, but could.

"What does this room hold?" Simran asked. She sounded as breathless and awed as she felt.

It was Vaughan who replied.

"A room of stories," he said. "Just, not ones that are in books. Stories that were never written down."

"It's called oral storytelling, Vaughan," said Cora.

"You can store that?" Vina said. "I didn't know such a thing was possible."

"Lots of things are possible that the archivists won't admit to," Cora said with a faint curl of derision to her lip. "People bring their stories to us and breathe them out in whispers to the library. They don't come out like books—they come out like this. Making gardens, making animals to frolic in them. We think it's because they're so new. They're finding their shape." She hesitated. "Maybe I've talked enough," she said flatly. But there was a look in her eyes that said she wanted to continue. She loved the library and its tales.

"I thought tales could only be written," said Vina, voice coaxing. "It's fascinating."

Cora pursed her lips.

"My stepmother, Laura, transcribes important tales," said Vina. "And I've heard of plenty of writers—academics, mostly—who comment on tales. But to create new ones, when the balance of the Isle is so delicate…" Vina shook her head. "I've always been told that new tales are dangerous. Isle-destroying. But these…"

"They couldn't hurt anyone," Vaughan said, with gentle conviction. When he looked into the room, his gaze was tender. "They're good. You can see it. They want to *make* things, not tear them down. They were born here. They love the Isle."

"There's plenty of tales from across the sea that the archivists don't like either," said Cora dryly. "Those get destroyed too if we don't save them."

Simran thought, in a flash, of the girl with the body of a bird. And then strangely, rising on the back of that memory was one of her mother. Her mother, brushing her hair with a white-toothed comb, as the ship "on a sea of magic," as her mother had called it then, rocked beneath them. Simran remembered oil in her hair, and her mother lowering the comb so she could firmly massage the oil into Simran's scalp with her work-calloused hands.

Her mother had been comforting her. She'd been telling Simran a tale. It had been soothing—Simran remembered how it had made her feel. It was a tale she'd heard many, many times before, old enough to be an incarnate tale for the land where she'd been raised. In that Elsewhere place, the tale had possessed power.

Now it was gone. In its place was...nothing. A gap.

*Our tales are not safe for us*, her mother had told her, in a language Simran could no longer remember. That too had been scrubbed clean. *On this foreign Isle of stories, we will be safe. Now, shh. No more questions.*

Something about this place was changing her—needling at old memories long buried. She'd never recalled that memory in so much detail before.

One of the whispers sounded...familiar. The words. The cadence. The language.

"These stories," she said abruptly, making Vaughan and Cora and Vina turn toward her. "Some are in Elsewhere languages. Aren't they?"

"Some are Elsewhere tongues," Cora agreed. "And some are from here, in lost languages of the Isle." She was frowning, anger simmering under the surface. Her gaze fixed on Simran, and suddenly the anger was turned on her. "Some of you," she said. "*Most* of you think the Isle is one thing—one single land, one place built of one set of stories. But that's not what this land is. Languages get erased. Stories get taken, shifted. Lands change—stolen, leeched from, remade. So yes, some languages are Elsewhere, but some are from this thing we now call the 'Isle,' carved into the narrow shape the Queen and archivists allow it." She stopped. The door at the end of the corridor was shut—its handle carved into the shape of a dragon's maw. "Go in there," said Cora.

"And good luck," Vaughan said.

"Should we be worried?" Vina asked lightly. Her gaze turned to Simran.

Simran refused to meet her eyes, and the question that was in them. Whatever was beyond the door, she was ready to face it.

"Thank you," she said shortly. Then she wrenched the door open, the handle's teeth sharp against her fingers, and walked in.

The room was also stone. It was a hall, with only one librarian within, who was already walking toward them. She was a Black woman, slight of stature, her arms crossed. There were an alarming number of writing implements adorning her—a feathered quill in the chatelaine at her waist, next to a vial of stoppered ink; a pen tucked behind her ear. The most alarming thing she carried was a shortsword at her waist, bare and wickedly sharp.

"Ophelia Dindrane," she said, shaking Simran's hand firmly, then Vina's. Her gaze was direct, her expression flat and businesslike. Vina murmured some kind of syrupy greeting in return—Ophelia softened minutely in response, unsurprisingly—but Simran was distracted by the tingle of her hand.

Ophelia turned back to her, eyebrow raised. "What's wrong?"

"There's magic in you," said Simran. "That's all. It's none I've felt before, though."

"Of course." Ophelia nodded. "I'm no cunning woman or witch, but the stories have left their mark on me. It's why the archivists are strange too, you know—the magic they hang around, day in and day out. But never mind that. You need some ancient knowledge." A smile finally curved her mouth. She looked...excited. "I haven't had a penitent in a long time. And certainly not incarnates."

Vina cocked her head. "How did you know we're incarnates?"

"The stones talk," said Ophelia. "This library is an old creature. It speaks, if you listen. But I'll tell you this now, knight and witch: What you search for isn't knowledge we have readily to hand. *Ah*," she went on, raising a hand when Simran moved to speak, already panicked. "Listen! We may not have it, but we have a way to seek it. In the room beyond this hall lies an ancient item of knowledge. Some call it a cauldron; others a tray, or a plate, or a living creature. But most gaze upon it and see a chalice. To reach the chalice, you must be allowed to pass by the Beast."

"This seems rather complicated," said Vina.

Ophelia shrugged. "Tales are," she said. "And this is an old tale, told many times, with many shapes."

"What can you tell us about the Beast?" Simran asked, determined.

"The Beast deserves your respect," said the librarian Ophelia. "The green library grew here. It wanted to be a sanctuary. It wanted to be a gentle cradle for tales. But it grew around the Beast. Do you understand? The Beast is older than this library, this chasm, this forest." She touched light fingers to the hilt of her shortsword. "And I am the Beast's ally," she continued. "Its friend. I'm here to keep it safe. So the last thing I'll say is—leave your weapons with me, knight. And try to walk in with an open heart."

Vina reached for her sword, handing it over.

"No," said Simran, even as Vina placed the sword in Ophelia's waiting hands. "I have my magic. What do you have, Vina? Don't give her your bow too."

Vina, obviously ignoring her, removed her bow.

"I'm ready, Simran," Vina said. "I'm a knight, after all. What else am I for, than facing beasts?"

She was still wearing her fae-wrought armor, silver filigree, luminous against her honeyed brown skin. She looked every inch the knight, even without a weapon at hand, and Simran could do nothing but nod tightly, and swallow whatever it was that was rising in her chest—this butterfly feeling, like hanging on a precipice, fragile wings behind her that could not hold her weight.

"Thank you," she said, turning to Ophelia. "We'll be back."

"Good luck," Ophelia said. If she muttered something about "wanting to avoid the cleanup," Simran pretended not to notice.

The next room had a simple wooden door. Simran pushed it open and entered, Vina warm at her back.

The door closed with a soft thud.

There was mist again. The room was quiet, apart from a rhythmic noise—a hushed thump, like a heartbeat. It took a moment for Simran to realize the sound was breathing. The Beast was near, its breaths deep and guttural in the silence. There was no animal smell in the air, no sweat or blood, only the rain-sweetness of petrichor. The mist rising from the ground was thick, so thick that Simran could not see the breadth of the room or the ceiling above her.

But the Beast's eyes gave off a dim light. It was waiting for them directly ahead, its eyes yellow and blue, glowing. Simran could only see parts of its body through the shifting mist: a reptilian skull, quilled with feathers; a strong, bestial body, furred and panting; cloven feet that slowly, before her eyes, rippled into claws. As she drew closer, she realized its breathing was rasping, unceasing, like the tide on a rocky shore.

It was oozing magic, the force of it so strong it stole Simran's breath and made her knees threaten to buckle. Vina was breathing slowly, shallowly next to her. She didn't seem conscious of it, but her arm was slightly in front of Simran, her body angled to shield her. In a way, Simran was glad Vina didn't have a sword with her. Neither of them would have a hope in hell of beating this creature with mortal weapons or mortal magic.

Its magic tugged at her, oddly familiar.

*Ink*, she thought. *It feels like limni ink.* But more powerful, somehow. *Alive.*

She felt like Isadora was behind her eyes, under her skin; so close that for a moment they were almost utterly the same person. Their knowledge mingled.

*What does a tale seek, darling? Sometimes it hungers for a sword, but often the sword is a means to an end. I'll tell you. It hungers for a pure heart.*

Well, that Simran did not have. But her love for Hari was purer than the rest of her, and that would have to be enough.

She took Vina's arm and pushed it—and Vina—to the side. Vina resisted for half a second, then mustered some deep faith Simran wasn't sure she deserved, and stepped aside.

*Courage*, Simran urged herself. Then she took a slow step forward.

The Beast rippled, its eyes turning to slits. If it had been Maleficium, its ears would have flattened with displeasure.

Simran lowered her eyes.

"Peace," she said. "Beast, I come for knowledge—not to cause any good folk of the Isle harm. I come for love, and for friendship. I come to save a life."

She peeked at the Beast. It watched her unblinking. She realized it was slowly moving closer to her, undulating with the click and stretch of sinew and bones.

Her legs had turned to water. She kneeled.

She swallowed. What did this Beast require? Respect, Ophelia had said. Truth? Perhaps.

She took a leap of faith.

"I also hunger for vengeance," she said. "But vengeance is a desire for justice our Isle cannot provide us. This man has killed again and again, and no one has punished him. I want to do it. I burn to do it. That is my truth, all of it."

She held out a hand and closed her eyes.

After a moment she felt something brush her hand. First scales, oddly warm; then soft fur, animal and stinking; then a puff of hot breath against her cheek.

Then nothing.

"It's gone," Vina said after a moment. Her voice was full of relief. "It vanished. I think you passed."

Simran shakily lowered her hand. She rose to her feet and turned to look at Vina.

"I'm sorry you didn't have a chance to face it, knight to Beast."

"Don't be sorry," said Vina. "Any journey that ends without me drawing my sword—or, well, my fists—is a success in my book." Fingers touched her spine, urging her forward. "Your chalice awaits, Simran."

"It may be my tray," she muttered. "Or, who knows? I've heard of a salmon of knowledge. It might be a fish."

Vina gave a husky laugh. She hadn't stopped touching Simran. But then, Simran hadn't moved.

Simran took a deliberate step forward, then another. The mist parted, and there on an altar of dove-gray stone lay—

A chalice.

The chalice was plain and unassuming. It was pale, a stone so white it might have been chalk, but it was too smooth for that. The water in it sparkled. The water in it was not truly water. She picked it up.

She swirled the chalice a little. The liquid in it shimmered like the Thames, like the silver sea. Like a tale.

"What do you do with a magical chalice?" Simran murmured. The stone was cold, but not eerily so. It felt like the shock of putting your feet in an icy brook on a summer's day.

"Drink it, I suppose," said Vina. She'd drawn in close to Simran's side, and was looking down at the water with her. "How else can you take knowledge from it?"

"Drink with me," said Simran. She held the chalice toward Vina, who looked at her, startled.

"You passed the test," Vina protested. "You're the one seeking knowledge. You're the one the assassin knew."

"He knew me, yes," said Simran. "But he clearly knew you too. Why else would he have come to you when you were fighting the fae's thrall? If he knows both of us, then he must be connected to our incarnate tale. And if he's connected to both of us, then we both need to seek the truth about him. Together."

Vina hesitated. Then she reached out two hands, carefully placing her hands over Simran's own around the chalice's stem. Even through her gloves, her hands were warm—large enough to cover Simran's entirely.

"If you're afraid, Simran, you need only say so."

"Fuck you," Simran said, without missing a beat. She couldn't look away from Vina's eyes. There was no heat in her voice. Somehow her anger at Vina had stopped being anger. Now it was a prickling feeling that ran over her skin whenever she looked at her, and whenever she thought of Vina. It was infuriating, infuriating. "You're incorrigible. Just do as you're told."

"As my lady witch desires," Vina said with a wink. Then her face smoothed to seriousness again, and she looked down at the chalice cupped between their joined palms. "How would you like to do this? Shall I drink first, then you?"

"No. We drink together."

"It's going to be awkward," Vina remarked. "It's not a big chalice. Maybe we would have been better off with a tray."

"Too much spillage."

"A punch bowl, then. A decently sized punch bowl of knowledge."

"Oh, shut up and drink."

They both raised the glass and moved their heads down to meet. It was awkward. They angled their heads, careful not to knock skulls or spill the chalice. Their faces still brushed, breath mingling. So close, and not quite a kiss.

Simran closed her eyes, and drank.

And.

Fell.

She was the first witch.

She was the second.

She was the third.

She clung to Vina as she fell, as Vina fell with her. Ink ran by them in trailing sparks like falling stars.

Fourth—

And then abruptly it changed.

She was no witch.

She was surrounded by figures. A huddle of bodies. They wore clothes she had not seen in years, long cloth draped into saris, jackets over tunics and trousers, and other clothing more familiar to the Isle: long dresses and hats; suits, sleeves rolled up to the elbow. The air was humid, and panic was clawing at Simran's throat. Her father was lifting her up, arms strong. Her father was saying something. *I'll tell you a story. Don't cry, beta. Don't cry.*

She felt a cry in her own skull.

*Don't follow those tales*, Isadora urged. She sounded desperate. Frightened. *The answers you seek aren't there!*

It was not Isadora who frightened her away, but the fact that Vina had faded to mist at her side, impossible to touch. Wherever Simran had strayed, Vina could not follow.

Simran hurled herself back into The Knight and the Witch, her own tale wrapping around her in sheaves of parchment, ribbons of ink. She fell back into a memory of her fourth life, and despite her efforts, Vina was not in her grip anymore. Vina was gone.

It was raining above her. She lay in a heap on green sod, under a gray umbral sky. The air was singing wildly with magic. The rain splattered on her splayed arms, her dress. She groaned and turned onto her side. The rain drummed against her, black and red on her lily-white skin. It was not water. It was ink.

The knight was not with her. There was no lance through her belly, nor sword through her chest. No loving hands on her. She was wounded, but not mortally. Lacerations ran all over her body, thin and stinging like paper cuts, but deeper, weightier.

There was someone else with her. She forced herself to sit up.

"Vina?" she tried to croak out. But her voice wouldn't come. Her mouth wasn't her own, in that moment. Instead, her lips parted, and she said, "Is it done?"

The other figure rose. Bulky, hair as pale as winter. Pale, pale eyes.

"Well," he said, voice trembling. Blood was pouring from his forehead, and tears from his eyes. "What now?"

Her body rose to its feet, wavering, weak. Her vision swam, the sight fading in and out, in and out. Her body reached for her waist, and drew a dagger from her belt. She felt his clammy hand close over her own. He was trying to stop her, surely. How could he not be? Her body, thousands of years dead, leaned over the pale assassin and stabbed him through the throat.

Images hit her like shards: a child in her arms, hair like winter. *Be good, ▮▮▮▮, and quiet.*

Another life. An adult man, turned away from her child self as she looked up at him. *I'll teach you your craft*, he said, voice stiff. *Though it isn't my own.*

Another life. A figure picked her up, jostling the lance through her chest as she struggled to gasp her last breaths. He was haloed in light. She asked him, soundless, if he was an angel. *Sleep now*, he said. *Rest, Rowan. It won't always be like this. You'll manage it next time.*

A hundred lifetimes raced past her eyes and there he was, there he was, there he was.

The world blurred, water and ink, and faded again.

# Chapter Eighteen

## *Vina*

*Be wary of tales that offer you the truth. Truth is a cruel mistress. A lie, woven carefully into the fabric of a tale, is a kinder lover. Allow yourself to believe in happy endings, and gentle lives.*
   *Let truth rot in the dark.*

Source: Pamphlet on "Tales and Falsehoods" by Dr. Angharad Walsh

**Archivist's Ruling: Destroy. Publication barred. Unable to locate Dr. Walsh for further interrogation.**

She was falling through her own lifetimes, Simran's hand in her grip.

The memories came to her blurred. Water-stained splashes of the first knight and witch, the second, the third. She found herself hurtling, suddenly alone, no hand in her own.

Fourth life. She was on her feet in woodland, birdsong overhead. The air was muggy, thick. Her body was broad, flat-chested, her center of gravity changed.

A woman standing before her in the woods. Vina stood with a bow in her hands—but Vina was Perrin, the fourth knight. So often she was Tristram, her last life looming large, but she knew this version of herself too: his blond hair, his braided beard. The scar that curled his lip. The woman was the witch, Elayne, in a guise of beauty—her hair a golden braid, her mouth a lush curve, sweet as a heart.

The bow, the almost-shooting—this was their first incarnate meeting.

Words left her mouth. Familiar, honeyed words in a deep burr of a voice. Vina's mind raced, even as her mouth moved. Why had the chalice brought her here? She and Simran were not looking for their own story. They were seeking information about the assassin. Perrin had eyes for nothing but the witch, glowing as she was with magic and the beauty that came with it. The witch was close, her hand on Perrin's chin, her mouth curled into a smile. But it was Vina, under his skin, who looked over the witch's shoulder and saw a figure hiding behind a tree. Wide, frightened eyes. A short stature.

The witch was hiding a child. Tricking and flirting with the knight to stop him from seeing the figure behind the tree. The boy was pale-skinned and pale-eyed. Vina knew immediately, with a twist of shock, who he was.

Was Simran behind the witch's eyes, seeing this too? Did she know?

The memory blurred again, streaming into rivulets of ink. She saw lifetimes of the witch, dozens of them: Elayne with a child, his hand in her own; the witch Ismene drawing a blood circle in the dirt, a man watching over them. The male witch Rowan, bleeding, dying, as the pale assassin lifted him, sorrow in the assassin's mercurial eyes. Rowan's shaky voice.

*Who are you, angel?*

The pale assassin's lips parted.

Finally, she heard it. A name.

The images were gone. She began to rise up, up through the memories, a ladder of lives falling into the abyss beneath her.

Why could he not die? Why?

Simran was the one who knew the pale assassin. He'd always

been dismissive of Vina, never quite taking note of her in the same way. Vina was a means to an end to him. Simran was the end.

In another life, the witch had cared for him when he was a child. She'd *loved* him. And then he'd lived—through hundreds of Simran's lifetimes, he'd followed her.

He really was some kind of immortal.

And it was the witch who'd made him what he was. Vina felt that in her bones.

But why?

Her eyes snapped open, and her gaze met Simran's. They were still standing upright, the chalice in their shared grip. Vina felt terribly, unnaturally cold. They'd traveled very far. They'd not moved at all.

She watched Simran swallow, face gray. Simran said, "Put the chalice down. Now. I think I'm going to be sick."

Vina hurriedly put it down on the altar. Simran turned away and crumpled to the ground. She wasn't sick, but she was breathing unsteadily, deep and heaving breaths.

"What do you need, Simran?" Vina asked. She didn't touch her; just watched her shoulders rise and fall, rise and fall.

"Nothing. I'm fine. Fine. I just." Simran squeezed her eyes shut, as if she were in pain. "I've spoken to Isadora before, but I've never dived into my older lives like this. It's… it's shaken me."

Vina looked at her sharply.

"You've spoken to Isadora? You've had—conversations?"

"Yes." Simran hesitated, expression vulnerable, lips blue with cold. "Is that strange?"

"It's unusual," said Vina, carefully. "I know that what incarnates experience isn't talked about widely beyond our own circles"—and those circles were under the thumb of the Queen, a fate Simran had avoided—"but we… we see our past selves, but they're echoes. All I see is Tristram weeping. He cannot speak to me. He's—not a whole person, any longer."

Simran didn't appear as if she were listening. She'd turned her head away.

Vina took a risk and leaned down. She said, "Simran." Gentle, ever so gentle. She placed a hand against Simran's back. "Simran," she said again.

"Stop saying my name," Simran said, but her breathing was easing.

"You're not Elayne," said Vina. "Not Rowan. Not Isadora."

A choked laugh. "You know more of my names than I do."

Vina said nothing. She could feel Simran's back, warm under her hand.

"It's something I did," Simran whispered. "Some past version of me, lifetimes ago. Hundreds, I think. Maybe thousands. I did this to him. I just don't know how or why."

"Maybe it's enough to know that."

"I can't risk Hari's life on *maybe*." She stood up abruptly. "The assassin's angry with me," said Simran. "Or with the witch. And the witch is me, whether I like it or not. I need to face him and—I don't know. Apologize. Beg. Grovel. At least he may show mercy to Hari, even if he won't show it to me."

Vina recalled the assassin holding the witch Rowan. His grief-stricken eyes. "I'm not convinced he hates you," she said.

She snorted.

"He wants me dead," she said. "Of course he hates me."

Simran walked forward through the mist. Then she stopped, and said, "I need your help, Vina."

"What do you need of me?"

"Hold some of my hair. Like this."

"Anything you need," Vina said, obediently gathering the glossy weight steady in her hand, keeping it taut. Simran flicked her fingers, calling a flame. She severed a hank away with a hot stench of burning. It left her hair uneven, jagged in a way that oddly suited Simran's own lovely sharpness.

Simran took the shorn hair, then turned back to the rolling mist.

"Beast," Simran called. "Thank you for letting us pass." She bowed forward. "A gift."

There was silence. Then, a rustle of movement; a guttural noise.

Vina thought of the assassin, his buried lock of hair and the magic in it. She understood, in her magicless way, how much that tangle of black hair in Simran's palm mattered. And so, somehow, did the Beast. Its reptilian snout appeared through the dark and the mist; its eyes narrowed to slits, not with anger, but a kind of heavy-lidded gentleness. It sniffed at Simran's palm again. Its maw opened, taking the offering from her. Then it vanished back into the misty darkness.

Simran balled her hand into a fist.

"Let's go," she said.

Ophelia was waiting for them in the outer hall.

"You're alive!" Ophelia said, with disturbing cheer. Then her voice smoothed back into no-nonsense practicality again. "Did you find what you were looking for?"

"Not all of it," said Simran tightly. "What happens if I attempt to drink again?"

Vina wanted to caution her not to do it. Simran was already gray-faced, already trembling. The vision had not hit Vina as hard and she still felt terribly cold, uneasy in her skin. But Ophelia was already shaking her head.

"Once, and only once," she said. "All tales have rules, and that's one for the chalice. Was it a chalice this time?"

"It was," Vina confirmed. "Pity, really. I was hoping for something more novel."

Ophelia smiled weakly, more for pity than because she'd found Vina actually amusing—or so Vina guessed. There was a faint crackle of magic about her—a strangeness like the mist that surrounded the Beast.

"The library has one last gift of knowledge for you, witch," said Ophelia. "It's an old fragment of a tale—I don't know what it means, but perhaps you will."

She gestured at the bookshelves behind her. The books had fallen to the floor, as if swept down in a rage or a storm. One torn page lay apart from them, glowing with its own whiteness. There was an illustration on the center of the page. Vina caught a brief glimpse of water before Simran took the page from Ophelia's hand, looked at it, then tucked it into her skirt.

"The magic will stay in you for a while," Ophelia said. "Chin up. You may have some more revelations yet. Now—your way out is down the corridor you entered by."

They walked down the long empty corridor. At the entrance, there was no sign of the other librarians, but Vaughan was waiting for them alone. Relief rushed over his face.

"You're alive," he said. "I'm so glad."

"Where is Cora?" Vina asked, when Simran made no sound.

"She didn't think you'd come back," said Vaughan. "The Beast isn't always—forgiving. But you did, so it's all fine." His voice was bright. "Where will you go now?"

"On our quest," said Simran, voice returning. She sounded rough, hoarse. "Thank you for your help, Vaughan. Give our thanks to Cora too."

She swept out. Vina gave her own goodbyes, then followed her.

"Will I see you again?" Vaughan called.

Vina turned back at the door, and smiled, and said, "I hope so."

Simran didn't stop until the chasm was behind them, the library beyond their reach. Vina wasn't sure she'd be able to find it again.

"Simran," she said gently. She wanted to tell Simran she had the assassin's name—that she had a little more knowledge Simran could use. But Simran was already speaking, quick and sharp.

"I'll face him alone. I have to. I'll go to my old tor on the mountains before the solstice falls and I'll beg him—I'll fight him if I have to—I'll do whatever it takes—"

"The pale assassin? Alone?"

"Alone," Simran confirmed.

"I don't think that's terribly wise," said Vina. "Simran, what we saw in the chalice—"

"You're not coming with me," cut in Simran.

Vina wanted to argue. But Simran, for all her sharpness, was... trembling.

Vina hooked a hand into her belt and said, with forced calm, "Tell me why."

"Do I really need to explain? You've always known you can't come with me. It isn't what our story says you do. It's started now. We're done."

"You'll do what the tale desires now? Of your own free will?"

"I've got to do it," said Simran. "We both have to. What choice is there?"

What had Simran seen in the visions from the chalice that Vina hadn't? Why had it made her want to see their tale faithfully through?

"Simran," she said. "Didn't we hope for more? To—to find out why the tales are so broken? To face the pale assassin and put it *right*—"

"There is no putting it right." Simran's voice was cold. "There's just saving Hari, and then—well. We both know what comes next." She kept walking. "Don't follow me."

"If he kills you?" Vina asked. "What then?"

"Then I die, and I suppose you're free."

Free. The idea of it was too sharp to hold. Vina reached for Simran instead and grasped her wrist. Simran froze, turned away from Vina, ready to flee. But she didn't pull away.

"Simran, please," Vina said. "I don't want to see you hurt. Let's come up with a plan of how to face him? Together?"

"Don't pretend you care about me. It's the tale that makes you care," said Simran. "It's the tale that makes you want me. Don't you see? What you want doesn't matter, what I want doesn't matter. No matter what we've made or how we've lived, we're just the knight and the witch, again, and again, and again!"

Simran's back was still turned, but Vina could hear the tears in her angry, shaky voice.

"I do care about you, Simran," Vina said quietly. "*I* care. Not the knight."

"But you are the knight," said Simran.

"I'm not just the knight," Vina corrected. She felt like she could shatter Simran with a word—turn her to nothing but mirror-shards of grief and rage. It was an awful feeling, a power Vina abjectly did not want. "I've carried the weight of the knight my whole life, just as you've carried the witch. I know the knight's desires and fears and grief. I've always known the knight matters more than I ever could. But I do have my own desires. And I desi—I *care* about you."

"You're lying to yourself," said Simran harshly. "I've felt the weight of all our lifetimes. We're *nothing* compared to the tale we're cursed by."

"There are tales about tragic lovers under curses," said Vina. The power of the chalice, maybe, talking through her. "Who live day after day, year after year, lifetime after lifetime fighting a curse they may one day overcome. When I think of me, my own heart...those tales feel more true than a mirror enthralling me, and a sword in my hand, and both of us dead for my honor."

"We're not lovers," hissed Simran. "We're not even friends. You don't know me, Lavinia Morgan, don't pretend you do."

"I know you love your family deeply. Your parents. You tried to protect them when the witch hunters came," said Vina.

"I never see my parents," Simran said stiffly, through her tears. "I try to never—"

"You love them so much that you run from them, trying to save them from what we are," Vina continued. She could feel Simran's pulse race, the heat of her shaking wrist. "Even though it hurts you, you do it. You've traveled across the Isle to save Hari. You're not charming the way the witch has always been. You're sharp and you're blunt and you've got a shitty temper. You don't want to love people, but you keep doing it anyway. Deeply. And you're brave—brave without being a hero with a white steed, brave when no one watches, when it matters most." A step closer. "And you know me too, Simran. You know I make bad bargains. That I like books and hate to draw my sword, and that I'm a right fool, without a decent thought in my head, but I try."

"I know you pretend to be a fool," said Simran, voice thick. "All this talk of who I am—do you really know yourself, Vina? I don't think you do. You make yourself smaller, you make yourself less, because you think you're worth less than everyone else and—and it's not true. You're not a fool. All this… It would be easier if you were." Her voice firmed. "But I'm still going."

"Simran, don't—"

"If you really like me as much as you say you do, you'll trust me," said Simran. "You'll let me go."

Vina swallowed.

"Fine," she said. "Go. I'll see you again soon."

She released Simran's hand.

"I know you will," said Simran. She reached into her skirt's pocket, drew out the ripped page, and pressed it into Vina's still-open palm. "Here," she said thinly. "Maybe you'll understand what the green library wants. It's not my business anymore."

She watched Simran go. The mist swallowed her.

The tether in her chest tugged at her. The tale, calling her to the Queen—calling her to a quest. The Knight and the Witch wanted to exist. Time was running out.

Vina gritted her teeth. Resisted. She had hope now—a child, a man, she'd never known existed within their tale, who'd reshaped it little by little, increment by increment. If one part of their tale had changed, lifetime upon lifetime, what else could they alter? Could they survive?

She lowered her head and looked at the crumpled page. The art on it was faded, but still unmistakable: two images, side by side. On the left, a man in a woman's arms, being carried across shining seawater. A crown on his skull, a sword through his chest. On the right, the same man with a sword in his hand, a halo of fire at his brow—and a crown wreathed in roses beneath his foot.

There was writing beneath it.

*I live and live again. Eternal.*

A chill ran through her. The pale assassin, the ruins they'd found beneath the palace, the dying Isle. Somehow it was all tangled together. Somehow, Vina had to unknot this skein of thread.

Simran had left footsteps in the soil, and Vina was a good hunter when she needed to be. Lifetime upon lifetime had given her that. She followed.

# Chapter Nineteen

## *Simran*

*The Parys Mountain is in mining country, rich in lucrative seams of tin and copper. Its survival is supported by the incarnate tale The Knight and the Witch.*

*Cyclical presence of the witch may briefly hamper the efficacy of your investments. Inquire further in our offices for full details.*

Source: Advertisement for investment opportunities in the Copper Mountains

**Archivist's Ruling: Destroy. Publication barred. Refer to region as "Copper Mountains" only, as per the tale.**

The tale was burning in her, leading her through the ancient forest. It dragged her forward with eager hands. She didn't need to try to find the Copper Mountains. The tale would get her there, urging her to the place where the witch was destined to live, to bewitch, and to die.

That left her free to remember what the chalice had shown and feel hot-and-cold all at once with sickness.

She'd stabbed him. The pale assassin. The boy she—*Elayne*—had raised. She could still remember his trusting eyes. She could feel the blade in her hands. She'd chosen to hurt him, and she didn't even know why.

Drinking from the chalice had shown her so much, but not enough. She still didn't have the assassin's name. She still didn't know why he couldn't die.

*It's all my fault.*

That, at least, felt true.

Her heart was aching.

The forest was bitterly cold with the coming solstice, and she could still feel the heat of Vina's fingers around her wrist. The entreaty in her voice.

She cared for Vina too. It was awful, caring for her.

Could it happen so fast—liking someone? Caring about someone? It felt cruel, for something sweet to grow in her heart, all full of possibility, when she was carrying broken knowledge to her own doom, hoping against hope that at least she'd be able to save her best friend from death.

She traveled for days until finally the tale's demand became urgent, a hand to the throat. The tale urged her. *This way.* She looked to her left. There were stone slabs set along the hillside, surrounded by ferns that swathed the soil like shrouds. Beneath the ferns, the stones were more red than gray, ruddy with ocher dust. She raised her skirt to her knees and walked up, until the trees began to thin around her, opening to an undulating rocky countryside of autumnal stone, burnished green and purple with moss and heather, beneath looming mountains. The mountains were green, like velvet under the feathered shadows and light of the cloud-flecked sun. But their zeniths were bright as knives—bronze-tipped beneath snow.

In her chest, her tale twisted and settled like a satisfied cat. It knew this land: these mountains, this copper dust and copper-laced stone. This land lived and breathed because of her tale, and her tale alone. That sudden knowledge held Simran frozen for a long moment, alone on the windswept copper landscape, cold wind tangling her hair.

She clenched her teeth and forced herself to move.

She passed a few mining towns—dimly lit buildings, surrounded by low walls. She thought of going into them. But she knew what the witch did to the villages surrounding the Copper Mountains; knew she bewitched and enthralled their people, and had done it lifetime after lifetime, generation after generation. She kept on walking.

The sky was gray, dismal.

The Copper Mountains were all around her, rising and falling in stone the same color as the mountains' namesake. She walked high, the air growing cold. Finally, she came to the base of a tower—an old, soaring thing. The witch's tor. At its base lay a door carved into stone. It was filigreed in copper—a rose-golden, embellished arch of metal hewn into the rock. She hesitated in front of it. The assassin had told her to meet him here. For Hari's sake, she had to do it.

She pushed the door wide. It swung open at her touch, greeting her like an old friend. She supposed she was.

Inside the air smelled of dust. No one had been here in at least two decades, of course. She walked farther in, exploring. She found an abandoned room, with wide windows, no glass in their stone frames. There were broken pots on the ground, and ivy climbing the walls. Some witch had clearly been green-fingered, and built her own garden here. It was gone now, just like her.

There was a bedroom: a large bed, curtained, dusty, and spangled with cobwebs. A witch gone by had left a dress on the bed. She touched it—the dust rose as she pressed her fingers to the sequins embroidered into the cloth. It was rotting, moth-eaten, but it was utterly Isadora's taste.

She kept on moving.

A new room. A bathing room, with a recessed pool of water that rippled, still full to the brim. She kneeled down and dipped her fingers into it. It was cold but fresh. The waters beneath the mountains must have been feeding it constantly. She traced her fingers around the edge. A hum of magic etched into the gold around the rim of the broad, shallow bath explained its existence.

Then, finally, she went to the hall of mirrors.

She'd not been entirely truthful to Vina, when she'd told her witchcraft came from blood and bone, and hexes carved in soil. There were as many types of witchcraft as there were tales of witchcraft, which were almost innumerable. She'd avoided the magic of mirrors all her life.

The room was full of mirrors of beaten bronze. Dozens of mirrors, taller than her, suspended around the circular room. She pressed her fingers to the edge of one; dust rose under her touch. When she pressed harder, the mirror moved—shifting to catch the light from the windows. Its surface glowed.

Her reflection in the reflective bronze was distorted, softened and blurred. Her eyes were dark, her sharpness turned a haze. She looked...sad.

She turned the mirror to the wall and left the room.

She searched the rest of the tor and found no sign of the pale assassin or Hari. She was no judge of the skies, but she was *sure* the solstice was almost here. Panic was an itch under her skin. Who was the pale assassin to her? Why were they connected? What had she done to him? The questions whirled in her head and heart.

Finally, as the sun fell, she accepted there wasn't going to be any sign of him yet. She felt the tale tug at her, urging her to move.

There was nothing she could do. The tale had snared her.

The moon was moving across the sky. Her body carried her back into the witch's bedroom, even as dread pooled in her stomach. She stripped off her forest-stained clothing, without controlling her limbs; without any intention to do so. She opened a trunk of clothes—drew out a witch's gown, rich velvet, bloodred. She dressed.

She went back to the hall of mirrors, and moved those vast discs of bronze with her hands. The tale tugged at her hands, inexorable. The magic sang.

It was good she hadn't gone to those villages before coming here. If she had, she'd feel even more guilty than she did, as her magic poured from her, through the conduit of the mirrors—spilling onto the serrated edges of the mountains, where any villagers who raised their eyes to the mountains would be snared into her enchantment.

"Serve me," the tale whispered through her. "Love me."

Finally, the tale released her again. She gave a gasp. She wasn't just the witch. She was Simran in a ridiculous, musty gown, moth-eaten at the hems. She drew her hands back as if they'd been burned.

She fell asleep in the huge bed, then woke in the morning, and found food set out for her. It would have been nice to have a magical home that produced its own meals, but she was sure it was the bespelled villagers that had left it. The food was simple: bread, a little cheese, some pickles and thin slices of pork pie. There was wine too.

"Thank fuck for wine," she muttered, and knocked the bottle back.

"Is there any for me?"

Vina's voice echoed, low and warm and achingly welcome. Simran turned.

Vina was there, watching her.

Simran's mouth was dry. Joy at seeing Vina and terror at seeing the knight warred in her.

"Are you here to kill me?" Simran's voice was thin.

"The tale wants me to go to the Eternal Queen, and kneel at her feet, and take up a quest to destroy a wicked witch," said Vina. "But I resisted. I came here instead."

"Why?" Simran asked. "Why—why would you follow me?"

"Simran," Vina said, voice velvet. Tender. "I think you know why."

"I told you not to. I told you to leave me."

"I'm not sorry I came." Vina's voice was strained, her eyes bright. "You can't push me away, Simran. Until our tale compels me to leave, I'll stay by your side."

Simran looked at her, her heart like a bird rattling in her chest.

"Does it hurt?" Simran asked. "Fighting the tale?"

"Of course," said Vina. Her smile was faint. Hopeful. "But it's worth it."

That threw Simran out of her shock. She walked over and grabbed Vina's hand. Their fingers entangled.

"Come with me."

They went to the hall of mirrors. In the sunshine it was glorious. Light shifting and refracting, sunlight radiating into new shapes. She breathed her own magic through the mirrors and the moving light, letting it expand.

She couldn't leave the mountains, but she could do this at least. She heard Vina exhale. Heard her voice, full of wonder. "What just happened?"

"The mirrors are easing your pain," said Simran. "It's...it's a magic I used to do in other lives. I suppose now that I'm here, and the tale has me, I can do it too. The magic in you won't last long—the turn of the moon, at most—but it will buy you time before you have to return to the Queen."

"I've never seen magic like this," said Vina.

"You've seen it hundreds of times."

"I haven't," Vina said. "I'm not playing my role yet. I'm still me."

The golden light reflected in her dark eyes, flushed her skin.

Only a few hours here, and the loneliness and the power of their tale had cracked Simran in two. She couldn't even be angry at Vina for not listening to her, for following her here, defying her will and their tale. Instead she felt reluctant relief.

"The pale assassin," Vina said. "You haven't seen him yet?"

"I'm trapped here by our tale now," said Simran. "Maybe that was his plan all along—to make me come here, so I wouldn't be able to do anything but what our tale wants me to do." Her head pounded as she thought of the assassin, the child, the man she'd stabbed through the throat as he'd wept, kneeling in front of her.

"He'll come," Vina said, firm and sure. Now that her pain had faded she looked at ease again. Her gaze was fixed on Simran. "Give him time."

Time.

Soon the assassin would be here. But even if he didn't come, soon Simran and Vina would both be dead. The sun rose and fell, and the tides drew in and out, and the knight and witch loved and died. It was simple.

She wanted to hold this moment, this stolen thing where fate didn't have them, for as long as she could.

"Explore this place with me?" Simran asked.

"Of course," Vina said immediately.

She showed Vina the rooms of the witch's mountain. Vina followed silently, almost solemn.

Finally, Simran guided her to a door she hadn't yet used, which led to a narrow staircase rising through rock. She felt Vina at her back, trailing her as they moved up the narrow stairs.

They walked out onto the zenith of the tower. It was cold, but whatever discomfort Simran felt was washed away by the sight before them both: copper-colored landscape stretched out as far as the eye could see, beneath a gray sky. Mist roiled in the distance. Through it they could see the shadows of primordial giants, moving across distant planes of the Isle, their bodies black candle flames, wavering their vanishing.

"It looks beautiful here," Simran said, awed. It almost brought tears to her eyes. She'd been here before, but it was all new. And one day it would be all new again.

"It does," said Vina. She was looking at Simran, a smile curling her mouth; mirth and something darker, sweeter, in her eyes.

"You're ridiculous," Simran said flatly, but she couldn't help the smile that tugged at her own mouth in return.

The wind caught Vina's hair, those deep brown curls falling into disarray.

"Simran, I don't know what you saw in that vision from the chalice. But I know what I saw." Vina's gaze was searching. "Do you really believe there's no hope left?"

"I didn't see hope," said Simran. "And I still don't. But I've always tried to build a life that was mine—that mattered to me—no matter what my fate was. Hari, my scribing, my chosen family in London—all of that belongs to me, not our tale. I've lived a good life despite it." *And I wish I could keep doing it*, she thought; a foolish hope with teeth. *I wish, I wish, I wish.*

She hesitated, then forced any caution away. She wasn't a coward, and if Vina rejected her, Simran was a fucking adult—she could accept the blow of it. She'd done no less to Vina, when she'd thought Vina didn't want her. She knew better than that now. Just the look in Vina's eyes was enough. And even if Vina said no...

At least she would have tried stealing one last pleasurable thing.

She placed a hand against Vina's cheek, her jaw. She let her thumb brush the shape of her jawline—and watched Vina's eyes darken, molten.

"I can't promise this will mean anything," said Simran. "I...In a way, I can promise it won't."

"It'll mean something to us," said Vina, voice low and earnest.

Simran huffed a laugh; it was either that or do something awful, like cry. She couldn't stand that idea.

"Stop talking," she said. "Kiss me."

Vina leaned in and circled Simran's waist. She kissed her.

Simran hadn't expected the kiss to make her burn. The first time they'd kissed had surely been some kind of tale-driven magic, and the second an echo of that. But oh, it did burn. The touch of Vina's mouth on her own made every part of her sing. She felt the warmth of Vina's arms around her, and the points of her gloved fingertips against her spine. She tasted the soft lushness of her lips, the swipe of her tongue and teeth demanding entrance, urging her to kiss back, to demand in return.

She tangled her own fingers into Vina's hair, drawing her closer.

They kissed more, hungry. Vina's hands ran over her, drew her closer still. The gown, loose at Simran's shoulders, slipped a little; Simran shrugged it off, baring skin, drawing Vina down to her neck. Vina, obligingly, broke their kiss and fastened her teeth to skin. *Sucked.*

Simran's knees buckled. She heard Vina's husky laughter; felt the warm heat of breath, a sharp contrast to the cold air.

"Let's go inside," said Simran. "I'm freezing my tits off."

"You could put your dress back on," Vina pointed out, tracing the curve of Simran's shoulder with the brush of her moving lips.

"I'd rather take your clothes off."

"Maybe later," said Vina, and there was a promise in that. "But first, I want to see you."

She meant it. They made their way toward the bedroom—kissing as they went, once finding themselves against a helpful wall, where Vina pressed Simran to cold stone, cradling her head with one hand, her mouth at Simran's throat. Simran was tempted to stay there, but somehow, strength of will got them to the bed.

By the bedside, Vina unlaced Simran's gown; the hiss and slither of fabric, as it slowly unspooled, was loud in Simran's ears, louder even than her own breath. She removed her own underwear, unsure of how she made her fingers work. In a matter of moments, she was bare, skin prickling under Vina's heady gaze.

"You're beautiful," said Vina. When Simran scoffed, Vina said, "You know you are. Don't pretend it isn't nice to hear it."

"Shall I call you beautiful, then?"

"It would be nice to hear it," Vina said, laughter in her voice. She reached her gloved hands out and tenderly, carefully, brushed Simran's hair back from her shoulders. Her hands moved, featherlight, to Simran's clavicles, then her shoulders, then her arms, in nonsense patterns that sent sparks drifting through her. It took Simran a moment to realize Vina was following the lines of her tattoos.

"Beautiful," Vina said again.

"Touch me properly," demanded Simran.

"And what is proper?" Vina asked. She ducked her head, kissing a line of fire along Simran's throat. "Touch you here?" Her hands cupped Simran's breasts, cold metal and leather on her palms, and Simran arched into it, the relief and pleasure of the touch. "Or here?"

"I want your hands all over me," Simran said roughly. "I want your mouth on me. Taste me to your fill, Vina. I'm yours."

Vina groaned and shoved her down onto the bed.

Vina was still in her fae-wrought armor. She pressed her gloved hands to Simran's thighs, parting them. Inexorable, wanted. "Let me see you," Vina said, voice low. Simran let her legs fall open. She watched as Vina looked at her, Vina's eyes dark, her mouth a pleased curve.

*My knight,* Simran thought. *My Vina.* She reached for Vina's head, curling a hand in her dark hair. Urging her closer to the apex of Simran's thighs, where Simran ached, wanting her.

"Go on," Simran ordered. "Please me."

Vina didn't seem to need any more urging. She lowered her head, and Simran watched her for one long, blazing moment—snared by the sight of Vina's closed eyes, lashes dark against her gold-brown skin; the slow, graceful slide of her mouth. Simran felt the satin of it against her core, a slow, confident electric ribbon of pleasure unfurling through her.

Her head fell back. She closed her eyes. She could feel Vina's lips, her tongue, the sweet heat of her breath, the cold of her gloves at Simran's thighs. Her own heartbeat was thudding in her ears. She undulated her hips and Vina groaned.

"That's it," Vina whispered. "Move. I've got you."

"Stop talking," Simran said, and felt Vina laugh. It felt—strangely good, spiraling through her.

Vina's hands slipped from her thighs up to cradle her at the hips, holding her up to Vina's mouth. Heat, there was so much heat in her, rising to a blaze. When she thought it couldn't get any higher, she felt Vina's gloved fingers against her, between her legs—a teasing touch, a hint of pressure, the slide of cool leather inside her.

Her body exploded, pleasure a starlit arrow shooting through her. She must have cried out, but she couldn't hear herself. Her mind was white-hot. Then, slowly, she returned to herself.

She was trembling, throat sore—and then Vina was above her, cradling her face.

"How do you feel?"

"Great," Simran said, speech a little slurred. "We need to get your armor off you."

Vina gave a husky laugh and said, "I'll need your help."

Simran sat up, with some effort—her legs felt like jelly—and said, "Tell me what to do."

She followed Vina's instructions, removing her gauntlets first—baring those elegant, sword-calloused hands. Then buckle after buckle, each one releasing to reveal a little more of Vina beneath it. Her clothes followed, and this Vina helped with—their hands brushing, entangling. Vina's bared skin was brown, her hips narrow, her shoulders pleasingly broad. Her skin was scarred, her body strong. It made Simran's throat dry with wanting.

"You're beautiful," said Simran.

Vina grinned. There was a confident swagger to her steps as she climbed onto the bed, then crawled forward on hands and knees, bracketing Simran with her body. Simran reached up, palms sweeping against Vina's shoulders.

"How do you want to be touched?" Simran asked.

"If I had my strap to wear, you could ride me," Vina said huskily.

"I'd like that."

"We have your hands," said Simran.

She took Vina's hand in her own, circling her wrists; trailing her fingers against Vina's own. Vina's eyes darkened. She understood.

Vina leaned back against the headboard, her hands between them as Simran straddled her.

She pinned Vina with her weight, pressing herself against the whipcord strength of Vina's body: her breasts, paler than the rest of her, her toned arms, thighs thicker and stronger than Simran's had ever been. She rocked her hips, resisting the urge to close her eyes as Vina's long, lean fingers slid inside her, filling her.

Simran moved, as Vina murmured encouragements; leaned forward and kissed Vina again. They moved, rocking together, slick skin and rising hunger. Then Simran said, "More." And Vina made a wrenching noise, deep.

Vina withdrew, then rolled Simran onto her back. Simran moved with her, hooking her legs around Vina, welcoming her in. Vina made a sound of approval. Her eyes were almost black with pleasure as she filled Simran again.

When Simran came this time it rolled through her, a wave that lifted her with pleasure, then let her fall.

"Let me—touch you," Simran gasped.

"You are touching me."

"Come here," whispered Simran. "Come—here."

She guided Vina up the bed, to straddle her, thighs around Simran's head. Simran raised her head, and pressed her mouth between Vina's thighs, where she was hot and wet with wanting. Simran allowed herself the luxury of closing her eyes again—of feeling and tasting nothing but Vina, and listening to her breaths as they grew steadily more ragged, frayed velvet. She only opened her eyes at the end, as Vina gave a cry and tipped her head back, her body all taut lines, her hips pressing Simran down to the bed, pinning her, using her.

Later they bathed and Simran laid Vina out at the water's edge, tasting her, luxuriating in her one last time—mouth between her legs, the cold of the water a sharp contrast to the heat of Vina, the silk of her skin.

Then they wrapped themselves up in old clothes, taken from the bedroom, and returned to the bed, which looked a little worse for wear. They tried to neaten it, then gave up, collapsing on its surface with breathless laughs.

"That wasn't bad at all, was it?" Vina said.

Simran slapped her arm, more playful than stinging. "You know it was better than 'not bad at all.'"

"I do, I do." Vina's grin faded as she looked at Simran, melting into something smaller, sweeter.

Simran's chest ached in response. Old disquiet was threatening to rise again, breaking through the small sanctuary they'd carved out.

"What is it?" Vina asked, soft.

"Isadora told me once her knight knew we both weren't fit for the world. That we were broken. That the only good thing we could do for the Isle is die." Simran's gaze was searching. "That isn't how you feel, is it?"

"I'd rather break the world to fit you," said Vina.

"What about to fit you?"

"What about me?" Vina looked genuinely uninterested in the question of what the world owed her. No surprise there. "How can the world be any good if it doesn't give you a soft place to land?"

"Don't be sweet to me," Simran whispered. "I can't stand it."

Simran rolled onto her back. Above her, the ceiling was a dome, painted with faint white stars, faded from years of neglect.

"We're still alone here," she said, shivering a little as the cold air touched her bare shoulders. "The pale assassin said he'd come. He hasn't."

"He'll get a shock if he finds us now," Vina said. Despite herself, Simran laughed. The mood lightened again.

"What would you have done if you hadn't been an incarnate?" Vina asked.

"Why even think of it?"

"Go on, Simran. Humor me."

"I like to think I've built the life I would have chosen," said Simran. "But I'd be—I don't know. Maybe a cunning woman, though I've got little patience for their gentle magic. I'd like to think I'd still be an illegal scribe, stealing limni ink from unwary knights. And you?"

"I have no idea," Vina said, cheerfully enough. "But I'm glad that I'm here now, with you." A pause, then she said, "Are you happy, Simran?"

Simran turned her head to look at her.

*You shouldn't care only about other people*, Simran wanted to say. *You should care about yourself. Why can't you care about yourself, Vina?*

But Vina was lying there, bare-chested, loose-limbed. Her smile wasn't the fixed thing she used as a shield; it was lopsided, her eyes crinkled with joy. She looked like she didn't have a care in the world.

Simran placed a hand over Vina's own. She felt like she was holding the world in her palm.

"Yes," Simran said softly. "I'm happy."

\* \* \*

She woke in the dark, and knew he'd arrived. There was no evidence of it. Just the knowing in her heart.

She dressed and left the room. The broken garden was the closest, and she would have passed it, if she hadn't seen a shadow move—and then heard a voice call her name.

"Simran."

She stopped dead. There, among the broken pots, the lacework of dried thorns, stood Hari.

Her heart stuttered, losing a beat. Hari's eyes were wet, his mouth shaped into a trembling smile.

"Sim," he said. "I'm here. God, you're here."

She didn't care if this was a trap. She ran into the room and gripped his shoulders, then his face, then his arms—reassuring herself he was real, that he was unhurt. He felt broader than he had when she'd last seen him, like he'd had a proper meal or two. There were no visible wounds on him, and his skin was sun-darkened, a deeper brown. But she was trembling still, so relieved she could have flown, she felt sure of it.

"I'm fine," said Hari, crushing her tight. "I'm safe."

"Did he hurt you?" Her voice was savage. "I'm going to fucking kill him, Hari, I swear it."

"He didn't hurt me," Hari assured her. "I've got to admit, Sim, I was fucking terrified but he was—he was decent to me, for a murderous kidnapper. He..." Something flickered across Hari's face—an emotion she couldn't read. "He was all right."

"That doesn't really put my mind at ease."

"He was decent," Hari affirmed. There was a conflicted twist to his mouth; something tucked in his eyes. His grip on her was still firm, like he was afraid to let her go. "It's you he's after. I don't get why, but it's the truth."

"He told me he'd kill you if I didn't come here and find him."

"He told me he's trying to save you from being an incarnate," said Hari. "I told him if he kills you I'd kill him myself. He said I'd have to learn how to use a knife properly before I tried to kill anyone." Hari shook his head. "He—it doesn't matter. I'm alive. I'm safe. I wasn't even as afraid as I should have been. But he is here, Sim, and however decent he was to me, I'm not trusting him with you. You should leave now, while you still can."

Simran almost agreed. She and Hari and Vina—they could leave now, run to the woods. There were spells Simran could carve to hide Hari, at least. She could get him to Lydia, and once he was there, she'd know he was safe. That would be enough.

But something about this wasn't right.

"He let you leave his side?"

Hari nodded.

Simran thought of the boy—the man—she'd seen in her chalice-fall into her own past. She thought of the man who'd deceived her and entered her home. She took Hari's hands in her own and lowered his arms. She rolled up his right sleeve, then his left. He let her, frowning but silent.

There was a mark on his left arm, hidden out of his line of sight at the back bend of his elbow. He probably hadn't even noticed. It was not burned or inked in—it was a dye, carefully made from berries, sung over under a full moon, traced into the shape of a hook.

She hissed under her breath. The pale assassin really had been raised by a witch, once.

"What? What's wrong?" Hari asked, sounding alarmed.

"He's tethered you," said Simran. "It's an old magic—crude. It doesn't hold long without being reapplied. But if you leave he'll draw on the poison in this ink, and place you into a magical sickness." It probably wasn't enough to kill Hari, but it *could* be. It was certainly enough to prove that the assassin wasn't simply going to allow Simran to leave. "You'll be fine," Simran said brusquely. "Wait here."

"Simran—"

She strode back to the bedroom, calling Vina's name. Stopped dead. The room was empty. Vina wasn't in the bedroom.

Vina was gone.

# Chapter Twenty

## *Vina*

*In the opera of* Hecate's Daughters, *the witch's aria is a uniquely fiendish piece to perform. The witch, after all, must be both powerful and vulnerable, as guttural as any hag and as pure-toned as any tragic heroine.*

*Her dying lament, performed by an able performer, should bring its audience to tears. By the end, the witch is no loathly creature. She is a pure soul, transformed and dragged from the midden by the alchemization of pain. The lesson of the opera is straightforward: There is no greater joy than sacrifice for Queen and country. It can save even the worst of us.*

Source: Theater review by James Belafonte,
*The Times of London*

**Archivist's Ruling: Preserve. Publication permitted. No further action required.**

Simran was speaking in the other room with Hari. Through the gap in the door, through shadow, she saw them both—the embrace, the joy, the light of the moon on them. She knew what it meant.

The pale assassin was here. And this was Vina's chance.

Hope was a funny thing. It didn't die easily once it was ignited, but it could take a new shape. Vina had found hers.

Vina had never felt more sure of anything in her life. Her heart was beating steadily, an even and strong rhythm in her chest, as she walked toward the hall of mirrors. She felt calm.

Someone had scrounged up beeswax candles and set them around the room. The mirrors were reflecting the candlelight, making it shine brighter, mirror-strange.

There he was, haloed by that reflected light—a corona around his skull, making his pale skin blaze.

"Knight," he said.

"Galath," she replied.

He looked at her, unmoved. But she knew it was his name.

"You've let your prisoner wander freely," said Vina. "That seems rather silly of you, I must admit. You've lost your leverage over Simran now."

"He only appears free," the pale assassin—Galath—said expressionlessly. "I made a bargain with the witch. She will fulfill it, or Hari will die."

"You should have made a bargain with me instead," said Vina. "I make notoriously awful deals." She smiled, walking toward Galath fearlessly. "I'd like to make one more with you. But first, I have questions."

"Ask them," Galath said.

"How did Bess of Gore die?" Vina asked.

"At my hand. By my blade."

Vina nodded slowly.

"Galath," she said. "Did Bess ask you to kill her?"

Candlelight flickered in the assassin's pale eyes, which swam strangely like the silver sea. "Yes," he replied.

Simple questions, simple answers.

"Why?"

"She did not want to be an incarnate any longer. The only escape was death. But she could not give herself that gift." He also approached her, his tread light—made for hunting. "You have not attempted it this lifetime, perhaps. But many an incarnate has tried to escape their tale by ending their life—and all to no avail. The tale does not allow it." His gaze flickered. "Try and place a blade in your chest now, and you will see."

"I'd rather not, but thank you," said Vina. "Why did you scar her forehead with your mark?"

"So the witch would know it was me," he said. "And, perhaps, to wish a life for Bess beyond this one."

An endless circle. Immortality. Vina could see a strange, ritual sorrow in that act.

"You could have told Simran all this. She would have listened to you. Maybe she would have understood."

"I have told her many times," said Galath. "So many that I can no longer recall all the lifetimes I begged her in, entreated her in. But the witch never trusts my words. The witch trusts no one but herself. She will do a great deal to save a loved one. Things she will not do for her own sake." His gaze darkened. "And even when she understood—after grief and tribulations—she refused her own death. She always hoped for an alternate path to freedom. And I could not…" A spasm of feeling crossed his face, until it smoothed to coldness again. "In the past, I could not steal her choice from her."

He'd loved her, once. Maybe he still did.

"This is my offer, Galath. Let Hari go, and Simran depart freely. And you can take my life. You would have been happy with my death at the hands of Lady Tristesse. You can have it now—here, by my own free will. You want the end of our tale. You'll have it."

A cold, searching look.

"You'd truly risk the Isle for her sake?" Galath asked.

Vina thought, in a flash, of Simran in the bed beside her.

*I'd rather break the world to fit you*, she'd told Simran. Not just sweet nothings. She'd been telling the truth.

"I would," she said simply.

"This is unlike you," said Galath, voice oddly rough. Feeling hiding under the surface.

"Is it really that much of a surprise?" She held her arms wide, an expansive gesture. "Our witch has never been much for dying. But me—I've always had a taste for death."

"For murder," Galath corrected. Finally, for the first time in this awful, hopeful tangle of a lifetime, his expression of knowing cracked, and Vina saw the grief and rage that had lain underneath it all along. "This won't absolve you of all the times you've killed her," said the witch's son, and mentor, and angel—all of them Galath, the man cursed with immortality. "But it will be a beginning."

Galath had worn no visible weapon—but he raised a hand and the rust-lacquered axe appeared in his grip, as if it had swelled out of the mirror-light itself.

Vina stared at him, calm and ready. Of course she did not want to die—of course she wanted to live in the moment, forever, where Simran had smiled at her in that bed, tangled in sheets and beautiful and happy. But she'd known since she was a child that she'd die a villain, and now she wouldn't have to.

She couldn't kill Simran. This was better.

"Stop!"

The mirrors sharpened, their light blazing to bright points. Simran was striding into the room. She moved in front of Vina and held her arms wide, a barrier against the axe. Hari raced in after her, skidding to a stop.

"Stranger," Hari gasped, eyes fixed on Galath. "Don't do this. Any of this."

"I'm sparing your friend, Hari," Galath said. "I thought you would be happy."

"When I said she deserves to live I didn't mean for you to cut someone else's throat instead!"

"I offered my life to him, Simran," Vina said, not looking at the assassin or Hari. Just looking at *her*. "You need to let this happen."

"I bloody don't," Simran snapped. "No one is dying here."

"You'd rather die tomorrow, witch?" Galath said. "Die by this knight's hands, as you have so many times before?"

"My quest is nearly done," Simran announced—eyes blazing, hands balled to fists. "I have your name now. I've come to meet you, here at the Copper Mountains. And I know you were raised by me—by Elayne, in my fourth lifetime. That you came to find me again and again." She swallowed, visibly. "And I know," she said, "that Elayne killed you. On a small island on the silver sea, she put a knife through your throat. But somehow you didn't die."

"All true, but not enough," Galath said, voice cold, face empty. "Why can I not die? Answer me that."

"Some kind of magic," said Simran. "Some magic, written in the limni ink at your brow. It was something my past self did to you—that *I* did to you."

"Why can I not die?"

"Because of me."

"Why?"

"I don't *know*." She was still standing in front of Vina, arms outstretched. Vina could see that Simran's arms were trembling.

"I'm begging you," Simran said, chin upraised, jaw firm with determination. "To let Hari go. Stop this."

"I'll release your friend," said Galath. He drew closer, scraping the axe against the ground—an agonizing noise, sharp and high-pitched. "But I will have the knight."

"No."

"I won't claim a life that I'm not asked to take," he said. "But she has offered, and I have accepted."

"You really want me to believe Bess asked you?" Simran was viperously angry. Vina could hear it in her voice, see it in every line of her body. "That Mary in Limehouse wanted to die?"

"Bess chose her death, yes," said Galath. "But I know no Mary. I've killed incarnates in London, but none with that name."

"She had the body of a bird. Golden feathers." Simran sounded furious. "And you murdered her."

"I did not take her life," said Galath. "I told you the death I offer is a gift. I meant it. You should be thankful to your knight." Galath's eyes briefly met Vina's, winter-cold. "She seeks to spare you from your tale. To free you and allow you to live."

"Well, she can't." Without turning, Simran said, "You can't, Vina."

"Simran," Vina said softly, gently. "There's no other way."

"You keep doing this," Simran said, louder, voice rising with anger. "You keep throwing yourself away, erasing yourself, being what people need you to be even if it kills you, and I won't allow it. You're not dying for me. I don't want you to."

"Maybe I'm dying for myself, then."

"Oh, don't pretend."

"I'm not pretending. Maybe I don't want my whole life to be defined by murdering you." Vina's voice was steady. "I know what the knight was and is, Simran. It's an old evil, the business of killing the person you love. Our tale may try and make something beautiful out of it, but I know what it is. Power, control, destruction for the sake of honor. But that isn't what I want. I want *this*."

Vina stepped forward, moving around Simran. Galath stepped forward to meet her.

She heard Simran curse and felt her magic—explode.

Vina felt momentarily dazzled, lights sparking in her eyes. But the enchantment wasn't aimed at her. Galath was doubled in half, clutching the axe. Gold light was webbed across his body.

"You can't enchant me with your mirrors," Galath said, voice tense with pain. "I'm beyond such trickery."

"Then it's good I'm not trying to enchant you, isn't it? I'm binding you."

A ragged laugh left Galath.

"You think you can? I know all your traps and tricks, witch. I taught you most of them."

"And yet I tricked you once, and I've done it again. Curious."

"You've grown too used to the magic of flesh." His arms flexed, muscles cording. "You don't know how to finesse your mirrors like you used to."

"Simran!" Hari yelled.

An arrow whistled through the air and lodged in Galath's arm. The next in his chest. The third in his throat. They came in swift succession, too fast to avoid.

But Simran wasn't the one who'd shot him, this time. Neither was Vina.

Two familiar knights were standing at the entrance of the hall. Matthias was lowering his bow. And behind them stood a group of archivists, solemn in their sweeping dark robes. One stepped forward. A monocle was over their eye—that strange, prismatic device, golden around the glittering prism at its center.

"You are an aberration, assassin," said Meera, removing a stoppered vial of ink from the chatelaine. She was wearing white gloves, and even touching the ink made their fingertips bleed black with it. "You have the look of a tale—but you're not a tale codified in the archives, and you're not welcome on the Isle. This is a glorious and storied land, and it has no place for you. Once you're destroyed, the Isle will be safe."

Galath laughed, low and deep.

"Is that what you archivists claim? That I'm destroying the Isle? I would, and gladly. I wish I could claim the glory of the Isle's death." His grin was a rictus. Blood poured from his wounds. "You know the truth, ink-binder," he said. "You know what you do, and what your Queen does. All those lost places, those people erased, their blood lies upon your hands, not mine—"

The ink shot from her hands like a weapon, arcing toward Galath without care for the people it would hit on its path toward him. Hari stared frozen, eyes wide as it raced toward him. Ink would surely not harm him as it harmed incarnates, but the whip was knife-edged, gleaming with its own sharpness—it would still *hurt*. Simran screamed. But it was Galath who was leaping—Galath who stopped suddenly, body curving. There were burns hissing lividly on his arm. She realized he'd shielded Hari with his body, and paid the price for it. Simran's eyes were wide as coins, furious.

"Leave the man alone, lads," Vina called out, aiming for casual. Hard, when you were yelling over the eldritch hiss of limni ink, wielded in a way she'd never bloody seen before. "I'm more important, surely? Don't tell me I'm not, I'll be hurt."

Another whip of ink headed to Galath, Hari still under him. Vina ran toward them, but Simran was closer.

Simran's hand rose. The mirrors shone bright.

And the ink—froze.

Simran grasped it, teeth bared—held the ink fast in her own bare hand and flung the whip of it back at Meera, who was staring at her gray-faced and horrified. The whip shattered, a thousand diamonds of ink spilling across the floor like glass.

"Simran!" Vina cried out. It had to have hurt her, to touch so much ink with nothing but her bare hand. Simran was an incarnate, after all—the ink was inimical to her. But there was no pain in Simran's face.

Vina's thoughts raced. The woods in Gore. When the ink had fallen it had hurt Vina, of course. But Simran hadn't cried out in pain.

Simran hadn't been hurt.

"You fool," said the archivist, voice trembling. "Incarnates should not touch that. *Cannot.* You, you—"

"Get out of here, Hari," said Simran. "Please, please. *Go.*"

Galath grabbed Hari and slung him over his shoulder, and with athleticism Vina hadn't seen before, he leapt across the room, winding between the mirrors, and raced away.

Edmund moved to follow them, and Vina—without even pausing to think—drew her sword. It was the memory of the child in her head that made her do it, Elayne's boy.

"Vinny, what the hell are you doing?" Edmund asked.

"If he isn't the true cause of the Isle's death, you don't need him," she said. Her gaze fixed on Meera—on the archivist with her tight jaw, her ink-stained, gloved fists. "I'm much more useful to you. Take me from here instead. Set the story of The Knight and the Witch back on its path. Go on."

"You believe him?" Meera asked, incredulous. "A murderer, the killer of your kind? The killer of your own friend?"

Soren. She thought of him again, an awful lump in her throat. Soren, terrified of his fate. Soren, who did not want to die for love, for a fae maiden he didn't know.

She could well imagine him choosing the mercy of a clean death.

"I believe you have a choice, ma'am," said Vina. "You can fight me, kill me, to claim the assassin—I'd be a worthwhile sacrifice, tale and all, if he's the cause of all our suffering. But if he's not the Isle's blight, then keeping me alive and in your power serves the Isle far better than chasing him down."

"No one is taking you," Simran said, voice deadly. The mirrors began to rattle. The ink shards on the ground turned liquid, trembling.

"Sir Matthias," Meera said. "Do it. As I told you."

Matthias sucked in a shaky breath. He wasn't looking at Vina. He lifted his helm and placed it over his skull, concealing his face.

"Witch," he said, voice emerging hollow. "We see your craven magics. If you do not bow to the Queen's authority, her finest knights will be sent to challenge you. You will perish, witch. Will you not repent?"

What was this? This was no part of the tale of The Knight and the Witch that Vina had ever heard. But she could feel the tale roaring through the room, and roaring through her. Vina knew, instinctually, that she wasn't part of this moment. The knight was not needed here. If Vina hadn't been determined to remain with Simran, she would have been able to run.

But Simran was caught in the tale's snare.

All nonincarnates knew how to live inside tales; to speak and dress for them, to move through them. That was what life on the Isle required. Matthias was deliberately playing a part.

The mirrors dimmed. Simran threw her head back, drawn by the compulsion of their shared tale, eyes wide with fury and panic, even as her mouth moved, playing her role.

"Send your most honorable knight," she proclaimed, with a toss of her hair. "I assure you, they will fall to my eldritch magics, as all your kind do."

A hand clamped on Vina's arm. Her sword was taken from her lax hands.

"Come on," Edmund said gruffly. He wouldn't meet her eyes. "We're going. Don't fight, Vinny."

"You're not taking me?" Simran demanded, voice thin and strained as she struggled against her tale.

"Why would we?" Meera asked. "You're exactly where you're meant to be. The tale will hold you here better than any fetters of iron ever could."

Vina stumbled as she was dragged.

"Galath!" Vina called out. His name rang through the cavernous mountain, ringing songlike against the walls. "Keep her safe!"

There was no sign of the pale assassin, and no sign of Hari. Just Simran standing alone, face all harsh angles and shadows and burning eyes, lantern-bright with helpless fury.

"Vina," Simran said. "*Vina.*"

Edmund wrenched Vina out of the door. It clanged shut.

# Chapter Twenty-One

## *Simran*

*Incarnates aren't like you and me. They are special people, with special gifts. They can do things that normal folk can barely imagine. What a privilege it must be, to be an incarnate!*

Source: Introduction to *Incarnate Tales for Children* by Laura Beaufort-Morgan

**Archivist's Ruling: Preserve. Publication permitted. No further action required.**

She was frozen, heaving for breath. Her tale had rooted her feet to the floor.

The tale wanted her to stay.

"Run," whispered Isadora in her ear. "Run, Simran."

Simran couldn't run. She was bound to the tor by her tale. There was no escaping it. She could feel it holding her, pinning her in place.

"Run," Isadora urged again.

"I can't," Simran gritted out. "I can't run. I'm trapped here."

"Darling," Isadora murmured, voice dripping with pity. "Are you really going to let those archivists win? Are you going to roll over and show them your belly? Have a little pride."

She gathered all her strength and threw herself against the tale's grip. Agony speared her. *Let me go*, she urged her tale. *Let me go. I'll fight you until my bitter end, I swear it. Let me go!*

The tale did not care, but Simran thought of Vina's face, oh her face—those warm eyes, the farewell written into the way she'd looked at Simran. She'd burn this damn tor down before letting Vina suffer beyond her reach.

*I'll return*, she told her tale. *I vow it. I'll come back. But right now I must go.*

She flung all her magic, all her strength, all her fury and her want outward once more.

She felt the tale hesitate. It was enough.

She wrenched out of the grip of her own tale, pain needle-sharp in her lungs and her bones. It felt a little like when she'd held that whip of limni ink—a hot, bright power, a wrongness she could twist and mold to her own purpose. Why hadn't she been able to run earlier, when she'd really needed to? Damn her tale. Damn everything.

It didn't matter now. She had to *go*.

She ran out of the tor, down the steps onto pale grass. She looked around, frantic. But there was no one. Nothing.

The archivists were long gone. They'd probably arrived on horseback, or with carriages. On foot, she'd have no chance of catching up with them.

She heard a crash of noise behind her, as Hari ran after her. Galath was following more slowly on his heels, blood streaked across him. He pulled the last arrow from his torso as if he didn't feel it, tossing it to the ground.

Hari stopped in front of her, catching his breath. She put her hand on his shoulder, holding him steady or holding herself steady, she wasn't sure.

"Sim, shit, shit," he gasped out. "Are you okay? Are you hurt?"

"I'm fine," she lied. It wasn't even a good lie. How could she be fine? "I should be asking you."

"Sim," he said again. He pressed his hand to her cheek. "Darling. You're crying."

Ah. She was.

He wiped her tears with his knuckles.

"I need to get her back," Simran said. "I can't let her go."

"Then we'll get her back," Hari said. "I promise."

Hari turned to look back at the pale assassin—at Galath, in his blood-soaked and ink-lashed clothing. She couldn't see Hari's face at this angle, but she could see Galath's—the strange, sudden softening of his jaw.

"I hear I'm tethered," said Hari. "Funny how you got that past me."

Galath said nothing. The wind ran coarse fingers through his pale hair.

"Take the mark from him," Simran said. "Please, I'm begging you. Fuck you, damn you. Please. Let Hari go." She was crying earnestly now, whole body hot with miserable fury. "*Please.*"

"Even your begging is more a demand and an order than a plea," said Galath.

"Simran," said Hari. "Let me."

Hari stepped toward him; looked up and met his eyes.

No words passed between the two of them. But Galath's head lowered.

He touched his knuckles lightly to Hari's cheek. She felt the magic burn and blow away like ash, the mark erased, leaving Hari free.

"Go," said Galath. "But I will be waiting for your return."

She didn't know if he was speaking to her or Hari. She didn't care. She grasped Hari's hand, relieved. Ran.

There was no chance she'd catch up with Vina. Vina's face swam in her mind. Her own fingers itched with ink, magic.

"What are we going to do, Simran?" Hari asked, between panting breaths.

"I don't know," she gasped out. "I don't—"

And then she saw it.

A golden, ghostly deer was waiting for her at the edge of the woods, in the long shadows thrown by the trees. It changed before her eyes, growing larger, no longer the spindle-limbed creature it had been but a big beast, wrought from magic to the size of a carthorse.

"It looks familiar," Hari said. He was watching it move, eyes round as coins. "Bess's woods—Bess's deer?" Hari had never been interested in exploring Bess's woods with her when they were children, but sometimes she'd managed to coax him in. He'd watched the deer a handful of times in hushed, awed silence as they'd drifted between the sun-dappled trees. She saw the same awe in him now.

Simran nodded. She moved cautiously to the deer. It lowered its head.

"I suppose you are my friend after all," Simran whispered to it, curling her fingers against the long, velvet line of its neck. She clambered onto its back.

"You can't ride a deer," Hari said, strangled.

"It looks like I can. Come on, Hari. We're both getting on."

His mouth firmed, and he climbed on after her.

The deer glided through the forest as liquidly as a ghost. The trees shifted around it. She didn't know, for long, breathless moments, where they were—until suddenly the forest settled back into the shape of deep darkness.

They were near the green library.

The deer lowered its body, allowing them to slip down from its back. As soon as Hari's feet thudded against soil, the deer fled.

"This isn't where I wanted to go!" Simran called after it. But the deer was gone.

"Simran," Hari said in a low voice, eyes white in the dark. "I can smell smoke."

She inhaled and smelled it too.

Ashes, black and orange, rose around her as if caught in a breeze. Her stomach dropped.

"Don't follow me," Simran said. "Hari—I'll take a quick look and I'll come back. Just wait."

Hari protested, but Simran was already running ahead, into the cloud of smoke. The chasm lay ahead of her. She entered it. The ferns and moss that veiled the stone walls were dead, or burned; some had been torn viciously at the roots. In the soil were imprints of boots, still fresh.

Simran strode faster, holding her sleeve to her nose, trying not to choke. She saw the circle of stones and fell to her knees, bashing her fist to the stone, searching for the right ritual words—but a wind caught the smog of darkness and smoke, parting it in a wave, and Simran's hand stopped nervelessly midknock.

She could see the door of the library in front of her. It was cracked in two. Smoldering.

"No," she whispered. "No, no."

She rose to her feet and heedless of the danger strode into the library, forcing the broken door open with her body.

She saw no one. She ran farther and saw only rooms of smoke, torn and burned books, nothing and no one.

The room of stories—ghostly little stories, shaped like frolicking animals, all those gently tended to tales—was empty.

Everything was burned. Every book, carefully smuggled here. Every tale carried as a secret, a whisper, on loving lips. She stumbled forward, farther and farther, pushing open the door to the room where she'd met Ophelia, and then seen the Beast.

Ophelia was gone. Her sword was all that remained—a scar of silver on a bruise of charred books, smoldering still on the earth. Simran went into the room that had housed the Beast, that room of mist where the chalice waited, heart in her throat. *Please, please.*

The room was...empty. There was no sign of the Beast. No sign of the chalice, and no mist either. The air was dim and dank, thick with the smell of charred paper. She could feel none of the Beast's weighty magic.

Whatever had happened to it, the green library itself was dead.

Simran went to her knees, staring at the ground beneath her. Her legs couldn't hold her.

"It was the archivists, of course," a voice said breezily.

"I don't need you now, Isadora," Simran said hoarsely, smoke in her throat, eyes stinging.

A sigh.

"You're so convinced I'm Isadora," her past self said. "A few feathers on my hair and garnets at my throat, a few merry laughs and a tale or two—is that all it takes?"

Simran raised her head and stared at her numbly. "I don't know what you mean."

"I shouldn't blame you. You're no different from any of them. Well, any version of me." She waved a dismissive hand. "We're a little gullible, I'm afraid. But here. Let me show you the truth."

Before her eyes, Isadora transformed. Her body rippled, moving between hundreds of faces. She saw Morgaine, Ismene, Rowan—faces of the witch, reshaped, reworn, a hundred times, a thousand times over. And then finally the face settled.

Elayne. The fourth witch. The one who'd put a knife through Galath's throat.

"You should have spoken to your fellow incarnates," said Elayne. "Past lives are just echoes. They weep, they wail, they scream. They have no substance. Your knight will know all her past names and faces, but all they will do is cry at her feet. She does not speak to them the way you speak to me. No incarnates do. You're special, Simran," Elayne said with a smile. "Well. *I* am."

"I don't know what the hell you mean," Simran whispered.

"Well, that's your fault, not mine. Galath urged you to seek the truth, didn't he? The chalice offered you the knowledge, and you rejected it."

"I didn't," Simran said numbly. "I saw everything."

"You saw the edges of him, our poor boy, and you turned away. It was your knight who found his name, not you! But we've always been a little cowardly when it comes to him. A soft heart, and cruel hands—that's what we have." She sighed. "But now here you are, in the ashes of sacred tales, with the chalice's waters still swimming in your veins. You can have all the answers you seek. A second chance, if you're willing." She trailed her ghostly fingers through the dust of the library. "If you're not, we'll die again. And I'll live in the heart of a new young incarnate witch and wear your face in her dreams instead of Isadora's. But I promise you, Simran: It will be me under your ghostly face. You will be dead as any mortal girl born and raised beyond the Isle, where stories don't seep into the heart and puppet you."

The ash was swirling around her—tales burned and tales destroyed, their haunting cries filling the air. She had no choice. Elayne was raising her hands, calling the ash down, and it swallowed them both.

Her third life—

"We don't need to do this," said Morgaine, to her knight. "Twice, we've done this." His blade was to her neck.

But she knew how pointless her plea was. She had ensorcelled him through no desire of her own—simply because the tale tugged her limbs, her magic. Made use of her.

"The Queen demands it," he whispered. His hands were trembling. He was not strong and clear-eyed as he'd been the first time, or even the second, when they hadn't understood this would go on endlessly, a cycle they could not escape. He was wide-eyed, softhearted; a farmer's son stripped from a life he'd better loved. He'd told her once, when he'd been deep under her enchantment, when his hands had been awash in blood, that all he desired was a cottage in the woods. A handful of animals. Not to hunt or feast upon—to shelter and love.

She felt it, as their tale snared them tight. As his hand, without his say-so, pushed the sword through her flesh, and killed her.

"I'm sorry," he whispered, tears streaming from his eyes. And then there was darkness.

By the time she was Elayne—by the time she felt the first tug of her tale, and saw her past self bloodied and weeping upon the ground, and felt the ink of it rewrite her—she knew she could not allow this to continue. She was going to end her tale, and set herself free. Death frightened her. It was not an old friend but an old enemy, familiar with its sharp blade, its agony. She would not allow it to have her.

*I will live to be an old woman*, she vowed, thinking with horror and disgust of the women who came before her, who died violently and young. *I will be happy, and I will be free.*

She left her childhood home and searched for other incarnates. Surely there was at least one upon the Isle who had escaped their tale. She traveled far, through the ancient primordial forest, in the watchful company of dryads, and journeyed to the quiet backwaters of the coast where a selkie observed her from the rocky shore, eyes lambent in the gray light. She formed a strange friendship with an imp—a familiar with sharp teeth, bright eyes, a penchant for turning into small animals. She strangled a Jenny Greenteeth in her own waters. She met green children in the forest—eyes red as apples, their languages unfamiliar. They showed her where to hide safely from witch hunters. In a fern-laced chasm, she slept on cool soil, in darkness as gentle as a cradle.

On the outskirts of a paltry little village, on a breathless autumn morning, she found an overturned cart. Blood. The bodies of three adults. And a child—alive, breathing, frightened. He was only a few years younger than her but after her years of independence and her many lifetimes, he seemed like an infant in her eyes.

She was still young herself—near enough to be his sister, not his mother. But she took him in for the sake of pity. She taught him to survive. At first, she thought she would leave him at the next village she passed. But it was a poor place, unfit for his curiosity, his cleverness. The next, then.

Days and weeks vanished, and the boy grew stronger, cannier. His presence eased the sharp edge of her loneliness. He learned to scribe to make them coin. She, as an incarnate, could not touch limni ink without agony, but he could give mortals ink in the shape of luminous gifts, in exchange for coin. His name was Galath.

And then one day, as he slept curled on her bedding, by the

fireside in deep woods, she realized she loved him. He was her family, now.

That only made what she did to him later more heinous.

Her tale was closing in on her. She'd met her knight—Perrin, with his scarred face, his lust, none of his last life's lamblike softness. Her tale was drawing her to the Copper Mountains. The end was coming for her.

She took herself to the forest to be alone, despite Galath's protests. But it was her right to grieve on her own. "Your right to sulk, you mean," he muttered, but he let her go, once she made a solemn promise to return.

It was the winter solstice, and the spirits were thick between the trees. Their whispers warned her that a hunting party was on the move: a woman in white armor on a white horse, her hair blazing red, and a rose pennant upon her cloak.

The Eternal Queen was hunting. It would be sensible to leave. Elayne was turning to go when a sound crashed through the trees, echoing on the fallen snow. A great beast emerged from the shadows. It was monstrous, quilled and scaled simultaneously, its breath chuffing from its body. It was bleeding from multiple arrows. Elayne could hear the braying of hounds and ghosts, and knew it would not be able to run for long.

"Follow me," she said. "I'll show you where you can hide from her."

The beast seemed to understand. It followed her, eyes wary, ears flattened. She led it to the dark chasm. Its great body brushed the ferns, which seemed to grasp at it, seeking it out in return.

All night they waited in the dark, as spirits screamed and horses trampled across the forest. Finally, the brief night ended, and pale sunlight began to seep even into the dark of the chasm.

In the morning when she opened her eyes, the beast was gone. In its place lay nothing but a bowl. It was white, shallow, and filled with strange water that sparkled in the faint light.

Oddly entranced, she gazed down at it.

*Drink*, the water seemed to urge. Her mouth watered. *Drink, and learn the truth.*

She lifted the bowl in her two palms. And though it was foolish, surely foolish, she drank.

She fell.

In her mind she saw a man asleep in a broken abbey. There was a wound through his chest. On his head he wore a crown. Chains of ink held him fast. He looked like nothing but a boy, pure as fallen snow; he was as ancient as the sea, with a beard as gray as stone; he was a brute with blood on his knuckles, a glory of corpses at his booted feet. He was a horror, and he was death, and he was hope. He was a tale of kings.

When Elayne woke, she knew the name the Eternal Prince. And she knew, though she could not say why, that if she freed him, she would also free herself.

*"Simran? Sim? Answer me!"*

What did she pay to find where the Prince slept?

There was an incarnate who wanted to be free as much as she did.

"I turned a knife to my own throat," the woman whispered, trembling. "I tried to jump from a great height. I did many things, lady witch, and none of them would free me. But my tale's gift is to speak truth, so if you promise to free me from my life, then I shall help you."

"I promise," said Elayne.

Elayne broke the woman's neck herself. It was the least she could do. It was Galath who buried her. He planted bluebells over her grave. "It was a mercy," Galath told her gently, eyes haunted. "You were kind."

*"Simran, please. Just say something—"*

\* \* \*

Chains of ink held the Prince in place.

The prison that held him was a broken abbey on an islet accessible only on foot at low tide, when the sea receded. A rain of ink was lashing wildly down upon its surface. It was surrounded by a thin patina of water—the silver sea, slick and steady as glass, so shallow now that the witch could walk laboriously across shining sand to the islet's rocky shores, and the abbey awaiting her. Apple trees grew strangely around the abbey, wizened and twined with one another, the apples green and blushing red.

She approached him with Galath at her side. She gazed upon the Eternal Prince, solemn in sleep, a sword clutched to his chest. He was veiled in ink like smoke. Chains rose from his skin. The air around him thrummed with the weight of his caged tale. On her tongue, Elayne tasted blood and steel, the might and monstrosity of a king's crown.

She could not concern herself with what the Eternal Prince was: what he would do, once she unchained him. She had a task. Instead, she kneeled by his chains. They were made of limni ink, the pure magic that all tales rose from. Those chains were long and strong. Someone had very much wanted to trap him, and keep him trapped for eternity.

She looked upon him, this incarnate of carnage and mythic might, and did not allow herself to care for what he would do to the Isle. The beast had shown her a true vision. Setting him free would begin setting her free. It was all she wanted.

She touched his chains.

It hurt her. The tale in her screamed as the ink met her skin. Limni ink was the stuff she was made of, as an incarnate. She could not hold it. She snatched her hands back.

"Let me," said Galath. He kneeled beside her. "I'm not an incarnate," he pointed out, when she protested. "I can touch ink, even if you cannot."

He tried to break the chains. But whatever had made them was too strong for his mortal hands. They were harder than steel or stone, and would not be moved.

"It must be me," said Elayne. Why else had the beast shown her? She ignored Galath's warnings. She held the chains tight.

It was agony. It burned and slithered from her hands. It made her scream. Her own tale was constricting her, clawing wildly at her.

*That will destroy us*, the tale cried. *Let go, let go!*

She tightened her grip and held on.

*"Okay, shit. Okay. I've got you. Can you hear me?"*

She lay on the sand, gasping, eyes streaming. She'd never experienced such pain. Hours of pain. Hours, and around her were dozens of chains, untouched, unharmed. She felt changed inside—fundamentally altered.

A single link had broken. The ink of it had spilled, useless, onto the sand. She had done as much damage to the chains as an ant could inflict on a mountain.

"It would take me lifetimes to break all these chains link by link," she said to Galath, tears on her cheeks. "And I have lifetimes, but I will not remember this task. I will not remember what I must do. I will be nothing but a screaming and weeping ghost in some fool witch child's skull. I will forget the chance I had here. All is lost."

Galath was staring at the ink, his eyes thoughtful.

"I know what to do," he said.

*"Simran. Simran, please."*

"This is the purest limni ink I've ever seen," Galath told her, as he drew out his scribe needles. "There are limits to what you can write with tale-magic out on the Isle. But here..." His hand was trembling around his needle. He held on tighter.

"I cannot free the Eternal Prince, and I cannot scribe a tattoo on you to give you the magic you need," he said slowly. "But I can mark myself. I can make sure I'll be here in your next life, and the ones that come after it. I can be there to help you, and guide you back here. I can protect you like you've protected me." He met her eyes. "Limni ink can't give people immortality. But I think here, where its power is so great—perhaps it can."

She should have said no. It was wrong, and cruel. But oh, she wanted to be free. She wanted it so much.

"Do it," she said. "For me."

Ink in his hand, a needle in his grip, his eyes closed. He carved the symbol into his forehead. A circle, endless. A tale that would never end. A serpent eating its own tail.

*Be as immortal as the Isle.*

It was the very deepest limni ink, the stuff of the Isle, that burned its starry way into Galath's skull.

"Is it done?" Elayne whispered, skin burning, lips parched from her trials.

Blood pouring from his forehead. Tears in his eyes. His voice trembled. "Well?" Galath asked. "What now?"

She said nothing, frozen. He stared at her, blood-drenched and shaking. Then he smiled, and grasped her hand. He placed her knife in her palm; closed her fingers around the hilt.

"Trust me," he said. "Elayne, trust me. We can cheat death together, you and I."

They pressed the blade in together.

She withdrew the blade and watched the wound close. The light did not leave his eyes. He lived.

The knife dropped from her hand.

"It's done," she said, and wept.

She recovered, sick and shaking, in a hut by the sea until her tale dragged her back to the mountains.

Galath was not with her when she returned to the mountains; when she strung folk to her will; when Perrin came, and kneeled before her, and loved her, and killed her.

He found her in her next life.

\* \* \*

*"Please, Sim. Wake up."*

Lives passed.

Lifetime after lifetime, Galath sought her out and told her earnestly what she needed to do. *You must free the Eternal Prince. You must break his chains.* But the witch did not know him. The witch was willful. The witch trusted no one but herself. She never *listened*. Not until time had run short. It took lifetimes for her to break a single link of chain.

Time passed, and passed, and eroded the hope in Galath's eyes like water inexorably carving a path through stone. He stopped guiding the witch. Instead, he took up his axe and offered her a different kind of mercy. Death, after all, was another kind of freedom.

The witch refused this too. Lifetime after lifetime. But other incarnates did not. And Galath's hands grew bloodied, and the love that had once shone on his face turned to something that looked almost like hatred.

Almost.

It was a bitter irony, then, that Elayne was not gone. Touching the ink of those chains had preserved her so that she was no simple, wailing ghost. But when she tried to urge each young witch to the broken abbey, to those chains of ink, her mouth sealed itself. Tales are fickle, and rule-bound. Galath had bound himself to the task of guiding the witch, and just as only the witch could free the Eternal Prince, only Galath could show her the way to the truth.

Every life, the witch found her way back to the abbey. Every life, the witch battled with the chains that held the Eternal Prince fast. And the witch came to learn, over those many lives, that all incarnate tales were bound like her own. To free the Eternal Prince was to free them all, for he was an ancient tale, the foundation of the sea, the soil, the sky, as sure as the Eternal Queen was the Isle's bones. He was meant to rise and rule and die. As long as he could not change, the Isle's incarnates were held in a kind of living slumber with him.

All the witch desired was change, so that the end of her tale could be made anew. So that she could live.

There were lives when she drew the knight into her confidences. Lives, when they stood in the woods together, and the knight lowered their bow, and the witch said to him, *Please. Help me. Help us.*

She loved the knight in every life. Perhaps it was the tale—hurtling, inevitable. But her heart couldn't avoid it.

Galath, her Galath, grew ever more bitter and cold—striving to free her in the only way he could, in every life. Striving to free incarnates, any incarnates, while he remained trapped by the magic carved into him. Her kind boy.

She lived, and died, and lived, and died, and died, and died.

*"Simran."*

The voice was a shimmer in the ash, in her heart. She was herself again, caught in a storm of dark dust and fire. She turned her head and looked at the shadow of Elayne.

"Every life I returned to the place he sleeps, and unraveled another link in those chains. Every life. And now there's you," said Elayne. Ink ran, liquid and pearly black, over her limbs. "You, arriving on the Isle's shores with your heart so open, so ready to dream—and we became one person." Elayne smiled. "You were so small—so wide-eyed! Do you remember?"

Simran felt the echo of it in their shared memories. The moment when the tale had seen her, and Simran had seen the tale—and suddenly Elayne had seen her, known her. Simran's seeking and curious heart filled with the magic of a story.

"And then I came to the Isle," said Simran. "And I—became part of you."

"You did. You are the culmination of all my work," said Elayne tenderly. "A witch who can wield limni ink. One who can free the Eternal Prince, and free us all."

"Why didn't you tell me what I need to do? Why did you put me through all of this?" Simran asked.

"What do you think Galath is?" Elayne demanded. "He is the truth I seeded into the world for you to find."

"He didn't tell me *anything*."

"Galath has lost hope. All he has the strength left to offer you is cruel words and the mercy of death," said Elayne. Sorrow flitted over her face, a bird in swift flight. "Besides, a tale cannot be a simple answer placed neatly into the palm of your hand. Truth must be earned and wrestled with and fought for. Tales are ritual. You had to walk this path."

Elayne's hand touched her cheek. It was a shock, to be touched— to both be real for a moment, as dying tales swirled around them.

"Find the Eternal Prince," said Elayne. "Awaken him. Set us free."

She woke with a hacking cough, a gasp. Hari was holding her.

"I thought—smoke inhalation," he stuttered. His face was ashen. He'd clearly dragged her away from the still-burning library, and the ash and fumes of all those tales. There were black smudges on his face.

She needed to see Galath.

"We need to go back," she said. "Back to the mountains."

# Chapter Twenty-Two

## *Vina*

As the father of an incarnate, I understand your fears intimately. When incarnates falter, we all suffer. But I've seen the mettle of today's incarnates through my daughter, and I assure you we have nothing to fear. My Lavinia is willing to lay down her life for Queen and country. She, like every incarnate, places the Isle before her own wellbeing. I only strive to humbly follow her example.

Source: Transcription of speech by Minister Morgan

**Archivist's Ruling: Preserve. Publication permitted. No further action required.**

They held her in the Tower. Before it was an archive, it was a prison, of course. There was no place better fit to hold Vina.

There were guards on her room every day and night. She had windows at least—nothing large enough to squeeze through, or she would have tried to. She was haunted by the usual horrors of the Tower—the wails and cries of ghosts; the itch of being so close to so many incarnate tomes. She dreamt of that illustration of a wounded king, and the broken table beneath the Palace, oozing chains. She dreamt that those chains were roots, worming their way deep under the Palace itself.

She was kept alone for days.

She kept thinking of Simran, alone and stricken, on that mountain. The idea of returning to her wasn't even a comfort. Their reunion was going to be death for both of them.

There were carvings on the walls, old graffiti from prisoners long gone. Vina added her own marks with the edge of a spoon: a tower, rising above a mountain. A sky of stars. One good memory, crudely preserved in stone.

One evening the door clanged open. An archivist entered.

"Come," said the man at the door. It was the young archivist she'd met the first time she came to the Tower. He'd fixed his glasses. He wasn't looking at her, shame in the shape of his mouth. "Minister Morgan has come to speak with you."

She was led along the battlements from her tower to another. This tower was far more lavishly appointed, with a great burning fireplace, light pouring in the windows, and a vase of flowers on the table beside the chairs where her father and his wife sat. A much more pleasant environment than her cell, to be sure.

Her father looked tired and anxious, his hair somehow grayer. Laura was next to him, her hand on his arm in silent comfort. They both stood when Vina walked in.

"Father? Laura?"

"Lavinia," said her father. He didn't reach for her. His fists spasmed, then closed. His gaze fixing briefly on the archivist who followed Vina in, and the guard who remained by the door. "Are they treating you properly? Tell me if there's anything you need, and I'll arrange it."

"I have what I need," said Vina. "Don't worry." Everything she'd eaten had tasted like ashes, but nothing was going to taste good to her now. "Sit, Father. Laura. See, I'll join you."

They all sat. The archivist placed himself in a chair at a distance, by the wall.

"They didn't want me to see you," said her father. "Thank God, I have some clout yet. The Queen couldn't refuse me an audience with my own daughter. Vinny, God help you. Why did you run? What did you think you'd achieve?"

"You can't outrun your tale, sweet girl," Laura murmured. *Nor,* her gentle yet judgmental mien seemed to say, *should you want to.*

Vina couldn't feel foolish after what she'd seen and done. She'd met an ancient Beast, drunk from a chalice of knowledge, kissed Simran on a mist-limned mountain tor.

"I had to," she said simply. "Why have you come?"

Her father blinked at her.

"Why? Vinny, you're imprisoned."

"Have you come to get me released?"

"That won't be possible," Laura said gently. "Darling girl, we must trust the archivists. But we do want to do anything we can to make sure you're comfortable."

Vina shook her head. This was where she was meant to comfort them—put their fears at ease. This was where she was meant to smile or laugh, slouch back in her chair, say how much she'd enjoy a tea right now, or better yet, a really good glass of wine. *Tell me, Father, do you still have that excellent port in the cellar? Do you think you could sneak me a bottle in? Yes, yes, Father, I know I'm foolish, I never take anything seriously, but I'll be fine, fine—*

Simran's voice flashed through her mind, sharp as a good knife.

*You keep doing this. You keep throwing yourself away, erasing yourself, being what people need you to be even if it kills you, and I won't allow it.*

*I won't allow it.*

"I didn't think you'd come," Vina said dully.

Her father stared back at her. His throat worked.

"Why not?" he asked. He sounded baffled.

She didn't know what to say. Her mind was filled with the quiet grief she'd felt, the burning loneliness, all those childhood years in the Palace. He in Westminster, she under the Queen's aegis, never in the same orbit.

Her father leaned forward and covered her hand with his own.

"Lavinia," her father said. "You're my daughter."

She looked down at his hand over her own. His skin was

paper-thin—under his signet ring, his heavy gold watch, his skin was old. Her father was growing old.

"Stay," she heard herself say. Her voice cracked.

"What?"

"Stay with me," she said. "I've never asked you for anything, Father. But stay with me before the end."

Her father cleared his throat.

"The archivists won't allow it, dear girl."

"You told me you have clout," said Vina. "I know you do. Use it for me, Father. Please. I..." It wrenched her to say it. "I don't want to be alone."

"Vinny—"

"Please."

"Vinny." His hand lifted, leaving her own cold. "You must see it isn't possible, dear girl."

Laura and her father were looking at her with pity. It was as if they were a thousand miles away from her. She could not reach them.

*Would you have loved me if I were not an incarnate?* She wanted to say it. Her mouth almost shaped the words. But it was as if there was no air in her.

She thought she remembered times before—with her father, when he'd walked with her on the golden autumn leaves outside his countryside estate, when he'd pointed out leverets and songbirds alike, when he'd loved her. But sometimes it felt like she hadn't really existed before the moment in the orangery when Tristram had wept at her feet. Sometimes she was not sure if those golden memories were anything more than a child's wistful hope.

Her heart wasn't breaking. This was an old wound, an old pain.

"All will be well, darling," said Laura. "You'll see."

It was time to smile. It was time to smooth the sadness from her father's brow. Vina could not make her face move.

"I'm tired," she said thinly. She was not tired.

There was a creak of wood; the archivist standing, and the guard stepping forward from their watch at the door.

"Escort the minister beyond the Tower's walls," said the archivist.

The guard ushered her father and Laura out. The door was locked behind them. Vina, alone with the archivist, slumped back in her chair.

"I never asked your name when we first met," Vina said.

"Percy Archer," he said. She heard the rustle of his robes. He'd walked over to her. "I'm sorry you're suffering, sir knight," said Archer, his voice subdued. "But if it's any assurance, this will be over soon."

Now she found her habitual smile—a tug at her lips, something to set him at ease even if her own heart was a dull thud in her chest.

"Tell me, Archivist Archer," she said. "I'm curious about your work. You keep all the tales of the Isle, don't you?"

His shoulders relaxed. An easy question.

"Of course we do," he said.

"I'm curious about a tale I heard once, half told," she said. "I know only a little of it, but I would dearly love to know the whole. Can you help me?"

He nodded, eyes alight.

"Of course I can," he said. "Sharing tales, instructing—these are an archivist's greatest joy."

"Here is what I know of the story. There is a man," she said, "on a barge, being carried over silver water. He wears the crown of a king. He's mortally wounded, but he slumbers and he rises again. When people tell his tale they say, *I live and live again. Eternal.*" She cocked her head. "Who is he, Archer?"

The archivist stared at her silently, the color draining from his face.

"A guard will collect you in a moment," he said stiffly, and walked out of the room. The door clanged shut behind him, lock and all.

They came for her in the darkest hours of the night. Her sleep had been uneasy, uneven, but they still caught her unawares, dragging her out of bed, one guard grasping each arm roughly. Two guards, three young archivists—no sign of Archer. The candles they carried flickered in the blackness, turning their faces ghoulish.

They dragged her to a new room. Inside was a reclining operating chair, and one precious bottle of limni ink, still stoppered. Apollonius Roland was seated on an armchair, watching as Archivist Sharma—Meera—arranged scribe needles of various sizes on a table. Dozens of candles were lit, bathing the room in a warm glow.

"I would have preferred daylight for this," said Apollonius. "But the minister's interference delayed our work."

"Are you chiding me, sir, or apologizing?" Vina asked. She was slammed down onto the reclining chair—her sleeves were forcibly rolled up. Her arms were strapped down with bands of leather, buckles of brass. As soon as the guards strapped her into place, Apollonius waved them off. They left the room.

Only she, Apollonius, and Meera were left.

"How," Apollonius said into the silence, "did you learn of the Eternal Prince?"

Vina said nothing.

Apollonius rose from his seat. He rolled up his own sleeves.

"If it was from the library," he said mildly, "then you'll be glad to know we burned it to the ground."

The shock of that lanced through her. She tried to jerk up off the chair—failed.

"You—how?"

"Witch hunters are a blessing, for all the trouble they cause. It wasn't hard to follow your witch's scent." He drew white gloves from his pocket and began to roll them neatly onto his hands. "You will not live much longer, Sir Lavinia, so we may speak freely. And I do like to educate my lessers," he said, with that same awful mildness. "We archivists are an ancient order. We have studied and collected—sheltered and shaped—stories as long as the Isle has lived. We have had other names, in our past. But we remember him, the tale of the Eternal Prince, who always returns to rule, then die, then rule again."

Vina bit her tongue until it bled. Listened, as scribe needles were moved, clinking like pointed teeth—as Meera lit more candles, the room growing hotter, brighter.

"He is an old tale of a warlord," said Apollonius. "He is a murderous, powerful king—beloved and monstrous. Glorious, but destructive. He rules, until he is grievously wounded in tragedy, when he is carried away to an abbey of healing by a lady of great power. There, he sleeps to rise again—and bring tumultuous change with him." A sneer shaped his mouth. "In his absence, the Isle falls always to the Queen—eternal as him, but prosperous, luminous. A beacon of goodness.

"Long ago, the Queen sought out the ancient ancestors of us archivists," Apollonius said, examining the bare skin of her arm. She would have flinched, if she could. "In those days, we cared for tales in many forms: as whispers, birds, dances, song. Changeable, chaotic. She put an end to that. She wanted a peaceful Isle—steady, prosperous. A nation with an identity to be proud of, instead of a shifting sea of tales, never steady enough to have worth. A blessed stone in a silver sea."

Vina could not imagine a king upon the throne, at the first. The Queen was, after all, meant to be eternal. But even as the thought struck her, she felt the shape of a tale scratch at the edges of her mind: a bloodied throne, a sword, a man.

She heard the vial of ink being unstoppered.

"What are you going to do?" Vina asked.

He tutted. "Let me finish first," he replied. "It took us generations, but we chained the sleeping Prince with limni ink. Chain upon chain, binding him to his long sleep. As long as he is bound, he cannot awaken, and the Isle will have peace. It took almost all the ink upon the Isle," Apollonius said. "But we still have enough for our work. Including for you."

He placed a hand on her cheek. As if she were a book to be handled, to be *repaired*.

"You cannot be allowed to change your tale—to run, to hide, to resist. You must help us maintain order. You must be perfect."

She jerked her head to the side, knocking his hand away.

"I can't be perfect," Vina said. "I've never been capable of it, terribly sorry. I'm Elsewhere-blooded, a woman. I'm not fit to be the knight. I'm already changed. Why not cull me? End this tale?" She rolled back her head, baring her neck in a challenge. "I'm offering. Let another bit of the Isle die. Go on."

Apollonius sighed, already seeking another lecture, when Vina heard a hand slam down on a table. Furious.

"It's your kind who ruin the Isle," said Meera angrily, voice raised. "You—you don't love it as you should. You let false ideas about your blood and Elsewhere control you. You're *traitors*."

"Why let Elsewhere folk in at all?" Vina challenged. "If we're all traitors, aberrant—apart from you of course—why allow them on the Isle?"

"If we had a choice do you think we—"

"Meera," snapped Apollonius. "Be silent."

Meera fell silent, nostrils flaring, chest heaving with rage. But Vina's mind was aflame. She began to laugh.

"You can't stop it, can you? No matter what you try, the Isle welcomes Elsewhere folk in. It needs people like us." She grinned at Apollonius, at the shadow of Meera at the scribing table. "You'd never let us in if you had a choice. People like my mother. Like *you*, Meera. And you *hate* it."

"Enough, Sir Lavinia," said Apollonius.

"No, no, let me finish! If the Isle needs Elsewhere folk, then the Isle must need new tales," she said, with remarkable cheer, considering she was still strapped down. "It needs change to survive, and you're starving it, withering it, for a vision of a nation that was never meant to last." She strained harder, harder. She had to break free. "You're killing the Isle, and you know you are, don't you? But you won't stop, you or the Queen."

"The gag, Meera," said Apollonius. "She'll need it anyway."

He gripped Vina's chin, holding her still.

"You say a great many foolish things, sir knight," Apollonius said, voice hushed. "All we care about is the Isle's survival. People from Elsewhere may crawl onto the Isle's shores *now*, but we will heal her. We hold to our ideals. When you, and all incarnates like you, serve gratefully and correctly, she will live and flourish—and no new Elsewhere blood will touch her blessed shores. We know it. Do not blame us for your failures."

Vina, with a rage she didn't think she was capable of, tried to bite him. Something was wedged between her teeth.

"Now the needle, Meera," said Apollonius. "And the ink. I will need to work delicately."

The clink of instruments. Vina struggled harder.

"Hush, hush now. It will be done soon."

He stood over her, ink in hand. But now that Meera had moved, Vina could see what she hadn't before—what lay on the table apart from ink, needles, gloves.

A book. A book of plum-dark leather, writing gold-bronze upon its surface, entangled with briars. *The Knight and the Witch.*

Her book. Her tale, bound in ink and paper. Ink, like a shadow, like a chain, was rising from its surface, twined to the scribing needle.

"You may resist your tale," said Apollonius. "But we cannot allow it. We must bind you tighter."

The ink rose like a snake, like a noose, and wrapped around her wrists. It touched her skin. She remembered, distantly, how it had hurt to be scribed as a child, as a test of what she was.

It hurt more now.

Vina gritted her teeth, trying to hold the scream in.

Her vision whited in and out.

Eventually her head was released. She saw the book on a table, ink rising in coils from it to wrap around her, shape to her, burrowing beneath her skin.

All her life, these chains had lived inside her. She'd never known. The archivists controlled her tale. They had her. They had her.

There was pain for a long time.

\* \* \*

A cold cloth, infused with magic, was placed on her forehead, soothing the flaying echoes of ink in her skin.

"Apollonius did not tell you about your mother," said Meera, as the perfume of magic, cloying and strange, filled the air.

"Don't," Vina managed to whisper out. She could see the malevolence in Meera's eyes. There was nothing the archivist could say that would help Vina—only things that could hurt.

"She was an incarnate too," said the archivist, when Vina was silent, her blood beating in her ears, heart pounding. "Late discovered. Her story was foreign. *Elsewhere*. She must have carried it over like a disease." Her hand was cool on Vina's forehead. "I was only an apprentice when they removed her, but I remember. It was all properly hidden, of course. It's archivist business. It's lucky we don't have to be so careful anymore, now we have the pale assassin to blame."

"My father," Vina croaked out. She felt like she was going to be sick.

"What about him? I don't think he knew," Meera said with a calculated shrug. "Your father requested that you be kept at home, that you be raised under his care. But Head Archivist Roland and the Spymaster and the Queen all agreed—there was too much danger in not carefully managing you, with your blood."

Meera stepped back.

"I've spent my whole life, my youth, my apprenticeship, proving I am not like your witch, or your mother," said Meera, viperous soft. "That I am not simply an ugly, necessary thing that the Isle requires. I am a woman of the Isle—I have shaped myself for love of it, and because it's the right thing to do."

"They'll never—think you're like them," Vina rasped. Grinned, baring her teeth. "Never. You can destroy all of us. Any of us. You'll still be *other*."

Meera stared at her, stony-faced.

"Your witch is an abomination," said Meera. "And so are you. But in your next life, I'm sure you'll both be right. A golden man, a blond-haired maiden witch. I'll be proud and happy, when you return changed for the better."

She woke hours later to the Spymaster standing at her side, his hand on her book. His gaze was solemn. She was lying bound still, unable to move, the agony of ink and her tale settling around her.

"I'm sorry, Sir Lavinia," said the Spymaster. "There's nothing that can be done. You must do your duty, as you have all your lives."

She thought she could feel his hand on that plum-colored leather, that tome full of her fate. His fingers drummed gently on the surface.

"I understand you more than you know," he murmured. "All kings and queens need men like me. They have all needed *me*. The Queen has my loyalty. And my tale neatly under her thumb."

"I think you're too clever, truly, to think this can continue as it has," said Vina, finding her clumsy voice, raspy with thirst and pain. "The Isle will die if you don't let the tales—us—be free." Vina was shaking, clammy, cold and hot all at once.

"I've often theorized such," said the Spymaster. "And I will do what is needful. But you must do the same." He lifted his lamp—was it still night? Or had a whole day passed, and a new night fallen? "Dress, Sir Lavinia," he said. "The Queen has a task for you."

He unbuckled the straps around her, and she sat up without any plan to do so. She did not plan to stand either, or straighten, or follow him obediently when the door opened—but the tale tugged her forward, and she had no say in where it led her. She returned to her prison.

"Here," he said. "Allow me. I will be your squire."

With his help, she donned her armor—fresh Palace armor that had been laid out for her use. A new sword, sharpened and ready.

As he secured the last buckle, he paused.

"Tell me, Lavinia. In your study of the Eternal Prince, did you learn of the one who carries him to his resting place? Did you come upon the Lady, in her blue cloak, her eyes of midnight?"

Vina searched for her voice.

"I saw an image," she said thinly. "No more. I do not know her."

"She is the Lady of the Lake," he said. "Or simply the Lady. She is bound to my tale, in her own way. I was merely curious."

But his voice was not merely curious. There was grief in it.

That was when she knew with bone-deep certainty that she was going to her death. The Spymaster would not have risked being vulnerable to her if there was any hope left.

On horseback, on an unfamiliar destrier, she traveled to the Palace. She dismounted, and her legs carried her to the White Hall, where the Queen sat on her throne, with an animal-skin rug set beneath her bejeweled and slippered feet. A rug of scales, burnished gold. Her women in black vizards surrounded her, faceless.

Vina kneeled.

"Majesty," her mouth said. "You summoned me, and I am here."

The Queen looked down at her and smiled. In her hand she held a rose-red cloth—a favor, and a blessing, for a knight readying for a great and glorious journey.

"My dear knight," she said. "we have a sacred quest for you."

The tale snapped entirely into place. A key in a lock.

"My Queen," said the knight. "Anything you ask of me is yours."

# Chapter Twenty-Three

## *Simran*

*If it ends in death, it cannot be love. A tale that tells you otherwise is a sick thing, an evil thing, sent to lead naïve girls astray. Take The Knight and the Witch, for example. We're encouraged to swoon over the tragedy of the love story, the honor of the knight. But when you cut all the magic and armor away, what's left?*

*A man murdering a woman. That's all. It's not a love story. The love is a lie.*

Source: Pamphlet titled "Death of the Tale"

**Archivist's Ruling: For retention as evidence of treason. Review in 6 months. Provenance unknown. Investigation and interrogation strongly recommended.**

She walked toward Galath. Her footsteps echoed, singing against every hollowed wall.

He was staring out of the window carved into stone, *not* looking at her with such intensity that she knew he could hear her every breath. He probably knew she'd been crying.

"I remember," she said hoarsely. "I remember everything. But it's too late."

His smile was bitter.

"You always remember too late."

"You could have told me."

"I gave up long ago," he said. "You never believed me. You've always trusted no one but yourself."

He finally turned to her. She'd only seen an enemy the first time she'd looked at him. Now she saw the boy she'd raised, lifetimes ago. The boy she'd betrayed, and the man who'd mentored her, and the angel who'd protected her, and the limni-marked stranger who'd offered her a clean death of her own will, again and again and again.

The knight had been chosen for her, but for at least a handful of lifetimes Galath had been the family she'd chosen.

"Vina is gone," she said softly. "The archivists have her."

He shrugged. "It makes no difference. They would have compelled you eventually. Use your time wisely, witch. Break a little more of your tale. Maybe in your next life you'll be free."

"There won't be many more chances," said Simran. "The Isle is dying. Is that your doing? Because you've been killing—freeing—incarnates?"

"The Isle has been dying for a long time," said Galath. "It is not my doing. Nor is it yours. The archivists, their Queen, have whittled stories so small that they have begun to wither to nothing, parched for the power that gives them life."

"You don't truly believe I'll ever free the Eternal Prince," said Simran.

"I believed once," he said. "But that was hundreds of lifetimes ago. Time has eroded my faith to dust. So it goes." He did not move, but she saw tension coil his muscles, as he prepared himself for what came next.

"I will offer you the choice I offer you every lifetime," said Galath. "Let me take your life. Let me free you from your tale. You hold no real love for the Isle, nor anything upon it. Soon you'll be gone again, and this version of you will be placed in Elayne's hands. There will be no you."

Simran hesitated.

"I want an end. But not the way you're offering it."

"As you always say," he replied.

"Maybe I do," she said. "But I want to live. I want..." Her voice trailed off. She scrambled to find it again, her heart a hummingbird in her chest. "I want to live a full life. Just once." She took a deep breath. "I'm going to the Eternal Prince. I'm going to do what Elayne couldn't. I'm going to set him free."

"You always believe you will," he said.

Time to go to the Eternal Prince. Time to finally awaken him.

She could understand Galath having no hope, but Elayne had looked at Simran with light in her eyes. Simran could wield limni ink. She'd wielded it through her needles for years as a scribe. But when she'd faced the archivists in the Copper Mountains, she'd wielded it with her hands.

Incarnates could not touch limni ink. But over lifetimes, the witch—Simran—had made herself into exactly the kind of creature who could place her hands on the Eternal Prince's chains of ink and set him free.

"You can't go where I'm going, Hari," she said.

"You're always leaving me behind." He didn't sound angry. Only tired.

"You can't stay here with Galath," said Simran. "I...I can..."

He touched a hand to her arm, silencing her.

"I'll get home safe," he said. "I'm not a child. And I'm not in danger anymore. I'll be okay."

She shook her head.

"I can't leave you here. It's not a safe place. The forest—all of it. After spending all this time trying to save you, do you really think I'm going to abandon you here to die?"

"Simran. You worry and worry," he said. "If you're really going to be such a mother hen...well. Give me the strength to survive on my own, instead."

"What do you mean?"

"Magic has always been your business, not mine," said Hari. "And

I was fine with that. But if you're going, I want one last gift from you."

She understood, in a flash of awareness.

"It'll hurt," she said. "Getting limni ink put in your skin. And it'll demand a price."

"I've been through pain to get the life and the body that belonged to me," Hari said, quiet and sincere. "I'm not afraid of a little more. And I know all about the price. You think I haven't heard you tell your customers a thousand times?"

She unrolled her needles, for what was possibly the last time. She laid them out perfectly.

"I want witchcraft," Hari said, before her needle could meet skin.

She paused.

"I thought you'd want to be a cunning man," said Simran. "Like Lydia."

He smiled and shook his head.

"I want to carry you with me," he said. "I know what witchcraft is, Simran. It's you."

How long had Vina been gone? How long until the tale called her back?

Time was slipping through Simran's fingers like sand.

She'd walked this path so many times before, treading the boards of the Isle's stage lifetime after lifetime: from the Copper Mountains across the breadth of the Isle. There was no deer to carry her now. Just her own two feet.

She arrived at rolling green hills and felt Elayne's whisper in her skull.

"Light a fire, Simran," Elayne whispered. "Here on this field. Light a fire."

"It's not even dark," Simran told her.

"Isadora's magic is here," Elayne replied. "Can't you feel it? It's been waiting, all this time. For Isadora's sake—do it."

Simran kneeled and pressed her hand to the earth. She could feel an old echo of magic there—something a witch had written into the soil long ago. It was nothing but a little illusory magic; a faint and unmalicious trick.

Simran lit a fire. The flames drew on the magic, turning from orange to silver. Simran kneeled by them, entranced for so long that the sky began to dim with evening.

"Look up," Elayne whispered, something soft in her voice.

She looked.

A great wyrm flew down, swift as an arrow. It landed with a crash against the ground before her, and transformed fluidly into the shape of an older woman, a lamp clutched in her left hand. The air smelled of petrichor and iron around her.

"You're a fellow incarnate," Simran said. "But you know me. Don't you?"

The woman nodded gravely.

"I performed my tale when I was a girl," she said. "They called me the Laidly Wyrm. But I am a small tale; perhaps you will not know me." Her skin was delicate with age, her eyes pale as her sight had faded. Her lantern glowed, deep and silver. "I promised you a lifetime ago I would carry you to the abbey, if you needed me. Now that you're here, I will settle my debt." Her lamp creaked in her grip. "But I should not say 'you.' You are not Isadora any longer."

"What did I do to help you?" Simran asked.

"It does not matter, little witch," said the woman. "Even if you do not remember, I do. Isadora was a good friend, once." Sorrow lay in her eyes.

It faded as she transformed, her limbs stretching, flecks of scales clawing their way from her face down her body. In moments, liquid with magic, she was a wyrm—a whip-thin dragon-creature, its claws in the earth, a silver lamp clenched in its maw.

The wyrm lowered her head, welcoming Simran close.

Simran touched a hand to the wyrm's head. "Thank you," she said.

She clambered onto the wyrm's back. Even if the woman was

old and frail, the wyrm was hale—its scales a shimmering luster, its spine powerful. She grasped its back and hoped she would not fall.

There was a powerful beating of wings. The wyrm rose into the air.

The wyrm carried her across black water, green fields, gray beaches of rock and sand. In the distance, across the roiling water, Simran could see a black ruin, spires broken and reaching for the sky. It stood on an islet—a small formation of sand and rock, caught in the clasp of the sea.

Finally, the wyrm landed on the coast. When Simran looked at her, she flapped her wings, turning away.

She could not speak, but Simran understood. The wyrm could travel no farther. There was some dread power emanating from the distant ruin, on an islet enclosed by the silver sea. The power felt like the strength of a thousand incarnate tales, the charisma of the Eternal Queen, the pulsing cold of the archivists.

"Your debt is paid," said Simran. "I'm sorry you lost Isadora. She was lucky to have a good friend."

The wyrm rose into the air, flying off with powerful beats of her wings. If the woman within the wyrm felt anything about what Simran had said, there was no way for her to know.

It was night, but morning was coming. Simran kneeled on the rocks at the edge of the Isle as the tide began to recede. It drew back, creeping with silvery fingers, until there was nothing in front of her but sand shimmering with a patina of water, mirror-glass beckoning her forward. She stepped onto it.

At first the sand swallowed her feet. She stopped and removed her boots.

It was so far away. The walk was endless. She wouldn't make it before the tide returned and she was swallowed whole. That was her fear. But exhausted, she kept walking forward.

She had to see Elayne's work done.

The tale of The Knight and the Witch was clawing painfully at her skull, her heart, urging her back to the mountains. But she wouldn't go yet. She had to believe—had to hope—this was the lifetime when she could win.

She swayed on her feet, tears in her eyes. She couldn't go on.

She heard a meow. It shocked her right out of her self-pity.

What the hell was a cat doing here? She turned her head, and there was Maleficium, abysmally wet and forlorn, sitting on the wet sand. The cat mewed again, and Simran leaned down, picking her up.

"Oh hell," Simran said. "You are a familiar spirit, aren't you? Vina was right."

Maleficium, a ball of fluff in her arms, and also a demon, began to purr.

"Why do I have to feed you, then? Shouldn't you be able to live off the ether?" Simran asked. She began walking again. It was easier, oddly, with Mal's company. At least she wasn't doing this alone.

She made it to the islet. The abbey was ahead of her, jagged and black-toothed against the endless horizon. The apple trees were twisted, their fruit glossy and waxen. There was no birdsong here; nothing but the howling wind.

She walked through the ruin, its black and broken walls, studded with flowering apple trees, to the grave that lay at its center. On a raised plinth, on gray stone, lay a man. Barely a man—a boy, seeming healthy and tanned, his brown hair loose and long around his face. He was veiled by a gossamer of ink, as if under a shroud. On his wrists, his throat, his ankles, sat chains of ink. Many were broken. The work of lifetimes.

One still stood strong. The greatest chain of all—a great, long knot of smoke, of ink, that looked stronger than iron.

Simran took a deep breath.

"It's time for me to begin," she said. Maleficium, loafing on the floor at her side, responded to the nudge of her foot by padding to the entrance of the ruin. She settled back down, watching Simran with wide, reflective eyes.

Hundreds of witches, over hundreds of lifetimes, had torn at these chains with their desperate, determined hands, pouring all their magic into the task. And still they remained unbroken. But Simran had to be the best of them. She had to break these chains, so the tale of the Eternal Prince could rise again. He would awaken, and take up his crown, and do whatever bloody, ugly work came naturally to an incarnate whose presence thudded with the drumbeat of war. But his awakening would let her tale grow and change—let *all* tales grow and change.

When her knight came, blindfolded with sword in hand, they would be able to forge themselves a different ending.

Simran drew on all her courage. Without pausing to think, she grabbed the first chain link.

The agony flung her back.

Godsblood, how had all the witches before her done this? Grasped the ink, and torn at it, forcing it to slowly yield out of shape? She was near immune to the pain limni ink could inflict. But this—this was worse than she had ever imagined.

How had she held, controlled, the ink in the past? What had happened with the archivist, and that whip of ink, had been all impulse. This had to be controlled. Purposeful.

She clenched her still-burning hand. She lowered her satchel to the floor and pulled her scribing needles free.

She wasn't the witches who'd come before her. She was everything they'd worked for, each one returning here and building their magic in the hope that the next would survive. And she was also herself.

She pressed a needle to the ink.

It followed her needle, compelled. But it wasn't like drawing ink—it was like pulling a wave with nothing but her fingers, a single needle, the strength in her body and her bones. She gritted her teeth as her tendons screamed, her fingers trembled—and kept on moving.

Scribing required intent. If this was anything like it, then she had intent in spades. She poured it into the frayed link. *Break, break, I demand you break. Break for me.*

The chain snapped.

There was a frozen moment of silence, utter silence. Then she heard the sound of breaking glass as, one by one, the chains broke from his body. Scattered around him. They shattered with a howl—all that ink, all that pure potential of tales converging into a mass of darkness.

She collapsed, breathing raggedly, her magic spent. Lying on her side, as the ink snarled and shimmered in the air, near alive.

The Eternal Prince remained still.

She sucked a deep breath. She had no strength to move.

"Won't you wake now and end this?" Simran called weakly.

Still, he slept, unmoving.

Her heart plummeted.

She lay, face pressed to the cold ground, for a long time. Maleficium came to curl up by her face, grooming her hair.

"Horrible creature," Simran rasped. She touched Mal's little nose, and got a lick in return.

She could still feel the pulsing, inexorable call of The Knight and the Witch. Her tale was summoning her back to the mountains.

"Why aren't we free?" Simran asked. "*Elayne.* Why are we still trapped?"

"We can't be free until he awakens," said Elayne calmly. "We'll be free when he changes the Isle in tumult and war, takes up his crown, and destroys the Queen's archives, which imprison our tale in the cage of a book. And he will not awaken until he is ready."

"You never told me about tumult or war or the bloody archives," Simran said angrily, tears of fury starry in her eyes. "You never told me I wasn't saving myself." Coldness spread through Simran, icy rage. She knew. "You expect me to die," she said. "You expect me to let Vina die. So someone else—some other damn witch—can be free, and change her tale, and live and do all the things I can't."

"There's nothing else for it," said Elayne. "It's a cruel business."

"I want to live," Simran said, voice ragged. "I want to live. I deserve to live."

"There's nothing to be done."

As she lay on her side, the waters looked endless. The seething ink was a scar tearing the horizon.

"This ink," she murmured, "can turn a mortal man into an immortal one." She met Elayne's ghostly eyes. "I can do what you could never do," said Simran. "I can scribe. I can write my own story—or rewrite the one I'm in."

"It can't be done, Simran," Elayne said pityingly.

"It can be, because you did it. We did it, lifetime over lifetime." She dragged herself up and kneeled, looking down at her hands—burned by limni ink, but still strong, still her own. "We made me into someone who can touch ink. We made me into an incarnate who can write tale-magic into other people. We changed me. I'll never have so much powerful limni ink like this again. I have to *try*."

She thought of Vina calling them cursed lovers, forever under a spell that condemned them. She thought of the knight and the witch, always the knight and the witch, falling into a love that couldn't save them from destroying each other.

She stumbled onto glowing sand, toward the mass of ink. It was pure potential—the stuff tales were made of, written from, *reshaped* from, or so she could hope.

She pressed her needle into the ink. It hurt again. But she didn't stop. She tried to write it. *A tale of two lovers. Vina and Simran, and then we found a way to free ourselves. We were free and the sword never came, the bloody dying—*

The tale sputtered out. It was too weak. There was no strength in it. She didn't believe it. Not enough.

She collapsed to the ground.

She lay there on the mirror-sand, exhausted beyond repair, and thought of having done all she had and losing herself, and Vina losing herself; as if this life wasn't precious. As if this life wasn't hers. As if what she felt for Vina—this fragile thing, somewhere between hunger and the way it felt to watch the sunrise—wasn't hers, and worth saving. Unfit for an Isle-feeding tale.

She lay there and thought of the first time she'd seen Isadora—Elayne, truly—and how empty her head had been, Elsewhere scrubbed from it by the binding ink of the Isle. Her father, rubbing his scar, already forgetting how a man had held a knife to his throat when they'd run from their village, one bag with all their belongings, all her mother's dowry jewelry lost.

Her heart was suddenly in her throat.

A moment ago, she had not known why he had his scar.

Her father didn't remember, but she did. Right now, she did. Something about this place allowed it.

The chains on the Eternal Prince were broken. She was surrounded by the ink that made the Isle, the power of tales. And now an Elsewhere tale was creeping into her skull. There was *hope*.

Memories and tales rushed through her, now that she was grasping for them: a rift, and war; the promise of a safe home. *The angrezi may have destroyed us, but their land of tales will be a safe haven. They promised us.*

*And you trust them?* Her mother, speaking to him. Simran, watching from their bed, pretending to sleep. A language she'd heard in the hidden library winged its way, known and comfortable, to her ear. She remembered it all.

*No. But we can't stay here.*

Rushing memories. No wonder the Isle needed Elsewhere-born. The Isle was fed by Elsewhere; by ancient invaders, by frostbitten raiders, by explorers bringing back tales, and by new arrivals carrying those tales with them, gold as coins in their hearts. The Isle was tales that archivists thought valuable enough to tend to, preserve, protect. And the Isle was tales of blood and slaughter, of conquest, of evil, all buried or culled.

The Queen had hidden those tales. Erased them. The library that had cradled them for lifetimes had been burned.

But the ink—and Simran—remembered.

The tide was drawing in again, blue-black, thick as ink, frothing into shining silver. This was the silver sea, the great ocean of ink that bound all the worlds of tales together.

The Isle did not stand alone. It could not stand alone. She should have realized it. How else had she been born on one land, an incarnate of another? The tales moved. That was their nature. And in moving, they changed.

Here, beyond the Isle's borders, on an islet where a great incarnate tale slept, she could draw on a great power that even the Queen couldn't touch. Stories stretched everywhere, were dreamt everywhere, and drifted on the same waters.

The water was full of so many other blood-soaked tales. All the ones she'd resisted, when she'd drunk from the chalice of knowledge. Many were not her own. But some were.

Here, she could remember the tales of her childhood. Her father had loved his ghazals; had recited great poems of great lovers, as she'd listened, half slumbering in the midday heat. She'd adored those tales, before coming to the Isle had taken them from her. She remembered now how they had made her feel, the queer twisting in her chest, that she now understood was recognition.

There was a riot of tale-magic around her, ink swarming at her needles and her fingertips, waiting to take shape. It hurt and burned, but that did not frighten her anymore.

She grasped at the ink with all that remained of her strength. Her head rose, and her eyes met Elayne's for one last time.

"I'm sorry," she whispered. "When I change our story, you'll be gone."

"But we'll live," said Elayne, face firming with hope and determination. "That's all I've ever wanted. Do it."

She dredged all those stories that made up Simran and wound them through their tale. Weaving words. Writing them into the sand, working them into the Isle as if the sand were its very skin.

*Once there was a witch—*

*Once there was a girl, on a ship—*

Not enough. She reminded herself:

Tales of lovers; of grief.

*Two lovers, a knight and a witch, were cursed, once upon a time, by a cruel Queen and crueler tale-keepers.*

*But there are many lives promised to the incarnates of the Isle, and these two lovers vowed to save one another. One day, they escaped. The tale shattered around them. They lived. They were free—*

The tale fought, twisting. Chained and cultivated by the archivists, it did not want to obey. The ink struggled like a trapped rat.

Elayne had told her that tales had their own rituals. Happiness couldn't be so easy.

Simran's heart broke. She had no choice. One way through.

Her hand shook, but she wrote. She wrote.

*One more cruel death awaited them,* she wrote. *One more death at one another's hands.*

*But the one called the witch cast a spell with all the love in her heart. We will return whole, she wished. We will return ourselves, with our full hearts, our memories. We won't be simply echoes. We'll be as real as the Eternal Prince, the Queen, the fae who rise from ink wholehearted.*

*We will defeat the Queen once and for all, when the ink returns us to the pages of the Isle. Knight and witch. Vina and Simran. We will save one another.*

*You and I, my love.*

*After all, for all the tales of glory and country, none are stronger than a tale of love.*

The tale blurred. The needle dropped from her hand into the watery sand. She had no more power to alter it or mend the end of the tale now. It would write itself as it liked.

Somewhere in a distant archive a book titled *The Knight and the Witch* was fraying, tearing; ripped apart by the new words worming into place. She felt that knowledge shudder through her. She wondered if an archivist was there to witness the book turning on itself; if they screamed when the vellum and leather tore, ink pooling around it.

*The Knight and the Witch* was drawing her back. The water rippled around her with the force of it. She rose to her feet.

"Come here, Mal," she called out. "Let's get you somewhere warm."

Mal scrambled from the ruins and leapt, rather clumsily, onto her shoulders. The sharp prick of claws, and then Mal settled.

"I want you to find Hari when we leave here," she said to the cat. "Promise me, little imp."

The claws dug in deeper, then retracted. Simran took that as a yes.

Simran took a step forward. There was something in the water. She looked closer. A laugh came to her lips. Her needle had changed.

A sword. She drew it from the water. It glimmered, black as night, bloody as a heart. It was a promise of their tale—a tale she'd changed. A tale that could save them.

It was time to go to Vina.

Here came the inevitable. The strings of her story moved her. She stood in her mountains, and moved her mirrors, and snared souls like a spider snaring flies in her web. The villagers below moved like puppets to her will, and she waited, endlessly waited, for her death to come for her.

Isadora was gone. Elayne was gone. In her head and heart, Simran was alone. She stood among her bronze mirrors, and she was herself and not herself at all. She did not want the tale to subsume her, although it offered, its pull sly and seductive. *Forget yourself. Be nothing but the witch.*

She forced herself to remember times long gone: baking bread with her mother. Her father tucking her into bed at night. Bess, teaching her the secrets of witching, of a simple knife and blood. Her hands wove curses and enchantments, snaring those mining towns below to her will, even as her heart turned over her memories as if they were stones in her palm and said *goodbye, goodbye, goodbye*.

The knight rode to the Copper Mountains.

The knight entered the tor, rising up the steps with a rose-red cloth bound over her eyes. She wore armor, Simran's knight. Her face was thinner, whittled to sharpness by grief. Simran desperately wanted to meet her eyes, so it was easy to allow the tale to take her— to sweep the necessary words from her puppeted mouth.

*Look at me*, urged the witch.

*I shall not*, said the knight.

But of course the knight removed her blindfold, at the witch's threats and urging. Of course she met Simran's eyes, and kneeled on the cold floor, a clank of armor, a baring of that beautiful throat.

"Witch," said Vina, her low voice sweet, so sweet. "I am yours."

Her eyes were hazy already. She'd been touched by magic even before coming here. The magic of the mirrors snared her too, and her eyes grew hazier still, filmed with bronze light.

Simran walked toward her. Each step echoed. Simran could hear her own breath, the roar of her heartbeat.

She touched a cold hand to Vina's face, which tilted up to meet her, and burned her palm like fire.

*Oh, Vina*, she thought, as her heart broke. *I'm sorry.*

"Obey me," she said. "And love me."

And Vina said, "Yes."

The tale swallowed Simran whole. This time, Simran allowed it.

Sometimes, Simran emerged. Her mind cleared, the waves releasing her just long enough for her to gasp for air and acknowledge the inevitability of being dragged back under. Sometimes, Vina was herself too. A village burned, and she found herself washing ash from Vina's hands. They stood among the mirrors, under moonlight, and Simran saw Vina bare-armed without her armor—and saw livid marks of ink in her skin, deep as scars.

"Who did this?" Simran demanded, furious.

And Vina looked at her, smiling. Brushed a hand against her cheek.

"There you are," she said. "Don't you worry about me, Simran. Don't worry—"

They drifted again, serving their purpose. The tale made them dance its dirge, its solemn pavane.

It snowed at dawn. The sky was pale and the snow was falling, and the Copper Mountains shone, glowing with fresh life. Simran knew today she would die.

She wept, despite herself. She was kneeling by a window with ivy trailing through the stone around her. She felt Vina kneel beside her. Heard her breath catch.

"Witch," said Vina's mouth, Vina's voice. "Why do you weep?"

"Because I love you," said Simran's voice, even as her heart clamored, *I'm sorry, sorry.* "I can ensorcel you no longer, knight. Ah, your eyes are mirrors to me now! In faith, I love you. I am bound to you, as surely as you are to me."

They embraced, Simran cradled in Vina's arms.

They parted. Vina pressed a hand to Simran's cheek.

"I am sorry, fair witch," said Vina. "I love you. I always shall. But I am loyal to my Queen and to my Isle, and I must fulfill my duty."

Steel sang as the knight drew her sword.

Simran was ready.

There were probably more elegant approaches she could have taken. Artfully placed spellwork, or silver-tongued cajoling. But sometimes the simplest answers were the best.

She punched Vina hard in the jaw. Unsuspecting, eyes wide with surprise, Vina fell back with a thud, and Simran leapt on top of her, wrestling the sword from her grip and flinging it across the room.

"Simran!"

The bronze film was gone from Vina's eyes. Her eyes, brown and familiar, stared up at Simran full of fear and sorrow. They looked at one another for a long, long moment—the snow falling, the tale digging into them with all its teeth. They did not have long.

"Simran," Vina said again. Her voice broke. "I'm so sorry."

"Don't be," said Simran. "If we had more time…"

She touched tender fingertips to Vina's bruised cheek. Had it felt like this every time? Teetering on the cusp of love, breath held, awaiting a fall that wouldn't have the chance to come? She was on the edge of a cliff, staring down at deep waters. Diving in would change her forever.

Was falling in love really special, really as miraculous as it felt, if thousands of versions of herself, across the Isle's blood-soaked past, had done and felt the same things she did now?

"I really wish we could live this life a little longer," Simran whispered. "And that I could keep on falling in love with you."

"You're falling in—"

"Oh, don't act so surprised."

"I know I'm handsome," Vina said, trying for humor. But her eyes were sad, her emotions naked on her face.

"You matter to me," insisted Simran. "You always have. Whoever I've been, I've found my way to loving you." She gripped Vina tighter. "Listen to me, before the tale catches you again. We're going to be free," whispered Simran. "Not now. Not yet. When we come back, we'll stand a chance. I've done what I've meant to do for thousands of lifetimes, and set an old, trapped tale free. The Eternal Prince." Her hands shook. "And I...I rewrote our tale. So we can fight in our next life. Fight to *live*. When we come back we have to do one last thing. Break the archives. Without them, the Queen will have no control. Tales will be able to grow and change—and die, when they need to." Her eyes searched Vina's face. "We'll be free, Vina. Promise me you'll look for me, and I promise I'll look for you."

"I promise, Simran," said Vina.

Simran took a deep breath and called the sword of ink to her hand. It bloomed from nothing—drawn by her magic, the call of her flesh. She held its hilt.

Vina clasped the hilt of the sword alongside Simran. Her hand was warm over Simran's own, and it soothed her.

They both kneeled. It would have to be Simran first. It was always Simran first. They angled the blade, clumsily, together.

There was a tale on the sword Simran had carried all the way here. The words on it shifted, changing. Simran had to trust that the tale would bring her back, whole and herself. She had no other choice now.

She was still crying. She couldn't stop.

Under her hands, Vina's own were trembling.

"I can't do it," said Vina. Her voice was wretched. "I can't kill you. I don't fear my own death, but yours—"

"I don't want to die," said Simran. "And I don't want you to d-die." Her voice splintered. Her face was streaming with tears. She wanted to be strong for Vina, but she couldn't stop crying. "We'll do it together," she said. "My hand over yours. We'll both be gone soon, and neither of us will grieve or fear any longer."

"I wish…"

"I know," Simran said thickly. "I know."

Vina took a deep breath. She kissed Simran—a fleeting kiss, a warm brush of lips. A goodbye.

"Now," said Vina. "I'm ready. I'll see you soon, Simran. I promise."

Simran looked into Vina's eyes, and pressed her hands tight over Vina's own. And pushed.

# PART TWO

Once upon a time, there was a cottage, and on its doorstep grew lavender. Ivy fronded the windows.

Rabbits lived in a small hutch in the garden that wrapped around the cottage like a moat. The rabbits were fawn-colored, enormous and utterly spoiled. Predators had the good sense not to hunt them. There was a witch in the house, after all. A kind but steely man, who knew the magic of blood, and could look at you and know your every secret.

(It wasn't actually the witch they feared. But we need not discuss the other gentleman in the house.)

One moonlit night, a stranger approached the house. This was not unusual. Often hooded figures arrived at night, bartering secrets and knowledge for magic or coin. And sometimes, for favors of a bloodier kind.

But this time the stranger carried a gift.

A cat sat on the rabbit hutch, watching narrowly as the stranger approached and rapped on the door, three hard strikes of the knocker. The door opened. The man who met the figure at the door was tall, broad, and pale as winter—hair like ice, and eyes like a storm.

Coin changed hands, and then the gift, wrapped in a blanket against the cold, was placed in his arms. The stranger hurried from the garden as the cat lazily watched them go.

The cat, pleased nothing was amiss, went back to sleep.

In the pale man's arms, the blanket began to struggle fretfully. A little cry escaped the infant within it.

There was a noise from in the house. The witch emerged—sleep-rumpled, hope in his eyes.

"Is it her?" he asked. "Have we finally found her?"

"It's not her," said the pale-eyed man, his eyes luminous under the light of a vast silver moon. "It's the knight."

And yet his hands on her were tender. He touched her forehead, and her button nose. He gently tucked the blanket closer around her to ward off the cold.

"Hello, Vina," whispered the brown-skinned man leaning down to look at her. There were tears in his eyes. "Welcome back."

# Chapter Twenty-Four

## *Vina*

*Be careful. He's coming.*

    Source: Letter from Vaughan David to Hari Patel

On the edge of ancient woods, misty and timeless, lay a small town. The town was progressive, a marvel of modern invention. Their mayor proudly enthused, at any given opportunity, about their clock tower, a stout brick tower with a marvelous stained glass clock face. It had been a bell tower until only recently—two decades ago, at the most. The bell at its zenith—now long gone—used to be rung to warn the townsfolk that something was emerging from the ancient, primordial forest that bordered the town. But one night the tower transformed, blooming stained glass and machinery. By some stroke of luck, no creatures from the forest had haunted the town since.

There was a girl who lived in the town. She was more a woman than a girl now—twenty, restless, hungry for something she had no words for. She'd left home before, at sixteen, but she'd returned in a year. What she needed did not lie in the green fields and woodlands of the Isle, the stone villages with sparkling brooks, the deep hills full of caverns and topped with snow. It did not lie in the brick buildings of her hometown either; but home, at least, was free. No rent, no debts. Her fathers told her, again and again, that she was always welcome.

She helped, sometimes, at the blacksmith. She liked being close to iron, and basked in the heat of the forge. She liked, too, feeling her own body grow stronger—her arms more muscular, her shoulders broader. She liked to leave exhausted, her mind quiet, her body aching. For a little while, it eased the restless disquiet in her heart.

The sun was setting, the sky bloody gold. The woman went to the clock tower and lockpicked the door—a hilariously easy thing to do. She'd been doing it since she was eight, when her father had taught her.

The clock tower smelled of oil and dust. Motes of light glowed through the stained glass. But the woman was more interested in opening a door, and climbing the external ladder, and settling herself on the clock tower's zenith, where she could see the ancient forest to her right, and green rolling valleys to her left, cut through by a broad brick road. When the skies were clear, and no mist clouded the horizon, sometimes you could see the giants lumbering between distant mountains. Once, she had seen a dragon on the wing—its body swooping with the same joyous poetry as a swallow. Now she was not looking for beasts. She was looking for a man.

She leaned precariously forward, staring at churning dust rising in the distance on the road, roiling to meet the falling sun.

And there he was. The incarnate who'd returned only weeks ago and sent a ripple through the Isle, the Prince with his gleaming sword, his white horse, his destiny. The woman had woken covered in sweat, a new tale stuck straight in her skull, fully fleshed. Everyone had been gossiping about it excitedly at the inn on the edge of town, and in the tea house, and outside the smithy. *Glorious*, they said. *He's going to be glorious, a blood-spiller, a terror yes—but aren't you oddly thrilled? Isn't awe one part joy and two parts fear? The Eternal Prince has awakened. He's come to take his throne.*

And there he was. Perched on the clock tower, she could see his approach: his knights, gray gasps of ink on the horizon. And his white horse, and his silver sword. She watched, and felt a keen strangeness in her chest. Perhaps it was normal for your heart to stir and your emotions to lift at the sight of an incarnate from a powerful and Isle-changing tale, one so deep and old you knew it by feel alone. But this didn't feel like an emotional upswell; it felt a little like she was going to be sick.

*Here it is*, she thought. *This is what I've been waiting for.*

She'd thought finding that elusive something would feel good. Well, that had been foolish of her.

She climbed back into the clock tower. She left, nudging the door shut, and walked back home. It felt like she was walking through sludge.

Her parents lived in a cottage near the edge of the woods. Four tawny rabbits were sleeping in a huddle inside the fence, next to a wall of swaying lavender. The family cat was awake on top of their hutch, grooming her paws. She gave the woman a baleful blink when the gate swung open, then returned to her ablutions.

Inside, the house was lit by warm lamps. She toed off her shoes.

"Want some dinner?" her papa called from the kitchen. She could see him through the half-open door, sleeves rolled up, peeling potatoes.

"I ate at Amir's," she said. Amir was the apprentice blacksmith but was much better at cooking than blacksmithing. "Where's Father?"

"He'll be home by morning," said her papa, which was a typical kind of answer. Her father was always vanishing somewhere, sometimes for days at a time. It had taken her years to realize how unusual that was. It did not bother her, though. Her parents were her parents. She loved them, but she wasn't curious about them.

In her room was a grandfather clock that ticked through its steady, pendulous rhythm. Her childhood books and more recent reads were haphazardly scattered on her desk and heaving from her shelves. She went to her desk to pick up her newest read—a vintage copy of *Incarnate Tales for Children*, bought from a traveling salesman last month—and raised her head, and met her own eyes in her bedroom mirror.

And she—

—remembered.

She woke on the floor, breathing ragged. Scattered papers all around her.

Her papa was in the room, leaning over her, shaking her shoulders.

She stared at him, his face swaying before her eyes. For a moment he had two faces: the one she knew, with the lines around the eyes, and the lick of silver in his hair; and another, younger, seen only briefly in a room of bronze mirrors before she'd—before—

"Ah," her papa said. His face crumpled, a little, as it had when her dadi had passed away. He released her. "You remember."

Her vision distorted.

"Hari," she said. Then, "Papa. I. Shit. I need a moment."

He left and returned with a glass of water. He set it carefully on the ground next to her. She grabbed it blindly, vision still uneven—drank. The water was cold.

"Where's Father?" she asked.

"On his way home," Hari said quietly. "I sent Mal to collect him."

Maleficium, the family cat—and Papa's familiar spirit, bound to him by dint of witchcraft. Had Hari been a witch when she'd first met him? No, no. She was almost sure. She clutched her head and tried not to panic.

"How did I end up here?"

"You collapsed. I heard your fall."

"Here in this house, I mean," Vina said, voice cracking a little. "In—in this decent childhood, with both of you. I can't. I don't understand."

"Breathe," Hari said soothingly. "I'll . . . I'll give you a minute. I'll make tea. Come to the kitchen when you're ready."

Despite his words, he didn't leave immediately. He hesitated, looking down at her, mouth parted as if he wanted to say something and didn't know how. Then finally, he left, closing the door softly behind him.

After a moment Vina struggled to standing. She looked at her own face in the mirror, shaky with the knowledge of two lives in her skull.

She looked a little different, to her own eyes. Her hair was slightly longer, curling to the nape of her neck—long enough that sometimes she could even tie it back. Her hand calluses were different, her scars fewer, and in different shapes. But the ink Simran had spilled had preserved her, like a cursed creature from a tale. She was not a new girl in a new time; she was Vina still. It was as if she'd slept, and dreamt a good dream—of being raised with love and care in a place too small for her.

She thought of Tristesse—a skull-splitting memory. Tristesse, and all the other fae, those born from the ink of the Isle. Was that what she was now too? Isle-wrought, and Isle-made?

She couldn't feel Tristram under her skin, or any of the other knights. Her last memory was of her last life: of Simran, snowy light spangled in her hair, a sword of ink in the shared clasp of their hands.

The kitchen door was wide, the lights blazing. Maleficium was perched on the bottom step of the stairs. There were two shadows in the kitchen.

There was Hari. And looming in the corner, mud still on his boots and the forest's strange green leaves brushed on his shoulders, stood the man she'd called her father.

"Vina," said Galath, voice low. She couldn't read his face—he was looking at her, unreadable, arms crossed. "Sit."

*You only used to call me knight, before*, she thought. Her mind was full of her whole childhood—her father's gentleness, his patience; the way he'd been the one to teach her to read, and to spell, and shown her how to use her first weapon. He'd never been the one to hug her or comfort her, except when she was sick. More nights than she could count, he'd nursed her through childhood fevers, and held her as she'd restlessly slept, small and safe in his arms.

She remembered his axe, raised to kill her.

She sat.

"Tea's always best in a crisis," said Hari. He'd boiled the tea the way her grandparents had always made it: stewed in the old iron pot with spices and milk, until it simmered into a rich, fragrant drink. He took up a ladle and poured it into a cup, then set it down in front of her.

She stared down at the tea, watching it swirl and settle. She felt vaguely nauseated.

"You didn't even change my name," said Vina.

"It was my grandmother's name," said Hari. "Well, spelled differently. In a different script too. But I thought it would be right—to, uh, let you be yourself." He sat, and clasped his own mug, knuckles white. "So," he said. "How we found you."

"Maleficium told Hari what the witch had done," said Galath. "I understood you could both return."

"I used my connections," Hari said. "From my life in London, and the cunning folk I knew there. And—less savory folk." His smile was lopsided. "I worked in molly-houses, coffeehouses, taverns—anywhere I could get work. I met people who could do anything if you had the coin or the power. That was no good to me then, but your fathe—*Galath* had the funds. We asked for people to look for incarnate children, or strange children. Children who rose from ink or were carried to them by spirits. Tale-riddled children."

Galath spoke again.

"I do not believe you were born from mortal parents and brought to us. I suspect the Isle returned you to us—breathed life into you from a tale, as it does with the fae and their ilk, leaving you to be discovered and reared. We were not the people who found you, but we paid, and I threatened, and eventually you were brought to us. I knew you when I saw you."

"You were looking for me?"

Hari opened his mouth, but Galath spoke first.

"We were looking for the witch," said Galath.

Why did that hurt?

"She's your family, for good or ill," said Vina faintly. "I understand. Did you look for Simran? After you found me?"

"We looked," said Hari heavily.

"What happened to her?"

Galath and Hari shared a look.

"Please," said Vina. "Please, tell me?"

"The archivists have her," said Galath. "I attempted to retrieve her, but it wasn't possible." He rolled his sleeve up, baring a mark she'd seen and never thought on, all her life—a deep gouge, blackened at the edges, like an ink stain. "I could not fight their ink. And I did not desire to be captured and trapped." He rolled down his sleeve. "My long life has, at least, granted me patience in these matters."

She took a steadying breath. Another.

"You used to read me my tale as a bedtime story," she said. "So many versions of it. Don't you think that's strange? Cruel?"

"We wanted you to know yourself," Hari said. "Honestly—I thought—we both thought, that you'd remember when you were small. We prepared for it. But time passed, and you were simply yourself. Happy."

"I hoped the witch had indeed managed to break her tale," murmured Galath. "That you were entirely free, unburdened even by your past life."

"No," said Vina. Her tea was starting to cool. Her eyes were stinging.

"Vina," said Hari. "What do *you* want to do?"

"Save Simran," she said. Her last moment with Simran was fresh in her mind, painful as a wound—and also twenty years ago. *Twenty years.* "Or—make sure we're ready, when Simran comes to us."

Galath and Hari looked at each other again.

"We don't know if she's Simran anymore," said Hari, when he looked back at her, gaze apologetic.

"Simran will come to us," said Vina. "Now I remember, she will too. If she hasn't already."

"You don't know what this lifetime has made of her," Galath said.

"I'm still Vina," she said. "But it's like I've had a long sleep, where I didn't know who I was. The sleep is—with me. It's shaped me. But I'm still me. Simran will be the same."

"She hasn't been raised by people who care about her, Vina," Hari said gently. It still shocked her to look at him and see the laughter lines around his eyes, the gray at his temples and think both *Papa* and *Hari* simultaneously—like two reflections clashing in faceted glass. "And the archivists have powers we don't. They may have—changed her."

Vina felt a shudder run through her, as she remembered the ink in the archives. The way it had burned.

"I need to find her," insisted Vina. "And we need to finish her work. We need to free the Isle."

"Of course that hadn't occurred to us," said Galath, deadpan.

"What your fathe—what Galath means to say is that we've been doing everything we can, without risking your safety," said Hari. "I have allies in London who may be willing to help us, and old friends among the cunning folk of the city, too, who send us information. But we don't know what to do, beyond that. The archivists are too quick. New incarnates, Elsewhere incarnates, are found and killed before we can discover them. The Eternal Prince rides, and the Queen sends her knights to swarm every village and town, placing more eyes on incarnates old and new."

"We haven't had the Queen's spies here," said Vina.

"No," Galath said. "We've kept them at bay."

Vina thought of the old hexafoils scarred into the town's houses, old, older than her by far. And the newer marks too—the witch circles set into the outer walls, and the charms tied to the quaint lavender growing at the path that led from the brick road to the town itself. She thought of Galath's absences, and his polished axe, always embedded in a wood stump in the garden—except when it was not—and how he never brought in wood for the fire. She decided not to ask any questions.

"We need to save Simran," Vina said again, firmer this time. "And we need to destroy the archives. That will end this. The power the archivists have, to control tales, the way those tales move incarnates like puppets—all of that lies in the archives," said Vina. "I saw it. I felt it. And Simran knew it too. The archives must die."

Hari was looking at her, and she could see him weighing his words carefully. His expression was familiar. She'd seen it the first time she climbed a tree and stood on the highest branches in victory; when she'd raised her first sword; when she'd packed her bag and left home all on her own for the first time. *I don't want to stop you*, his expression said. *But I love you, and I am afraid.*

"And will you survive it," Hari said, voice faintly unsteady, "if they do?"

Vina thought of those lifetime-ago tales that took the shape of birds and flowers. She thought of how Simran had found a way to rewrite their tale—just enough to give them a chance.

She thought of Soren. Of Bess, whom she'd never known. Of all the incarnates who yearned to escape the chains that held them.

"I think it's a risk worth taking," Vina said quietly.

Hari and Galath exchanged a look.

"To London, then," said Hari, a determined smile on his face. "Let's save the Isle."

# Chapter Twenty-Five

## *The Witch*

*The archivists are too busy putting out fires to stick their noses into everyone's business like they used to. Meet me at the printing press, and I'll see what I can do.*

Source: Letter from Jen Cranmer to Cora David

Her earliest memory was of books. They were piled on every surface: great leathery tomes, and spiral-bound, spidery, thin texts. Sheaves of paper, held together with rope and a prayer, and gilt-edged hardbacks, gleaming like jewels under the austere lighting of the circular chamber. The air smelled of something akin to dust, that she would swiftly come to associate with old books.

A man she'd later learn was an archivist cleared his throat and spoke to the older gentleman seated at the desk.

"Sir. What should she be named?"

The older gentleman's thick eyebrows had drawn together. He was truly terribly old to her eyes, but his eyes were razor-sharp, and they peered at her like a thing he could dissect with a look alone.

"Step closer, girl," he'd said.

The girl had stepped closer. The desk—and the man—loomed above her.

"I prefer specific, accurate categorization," he said. "She needs no name but the one that denotes what she is."

That was how she came to be known as the Witch.

*Where are my family?*
She asked, but no one listened. She was led to a room—in a high tower, cold, with a barred window open to moonlight—and told this would be her home. She wept that night, miserable in her bed. She could hear the distant screams and wails of ghostly children, long-dead prisoners.

She left one hand untucked from her blankets.

That night, something whispered at her bedside. An adder, a shadowy creature of ink. It flicked its tongue, black as an oil spill, against her fingers. Then it slithered away. She watched it go, wide-eyed, tears gone. It left flowers on her sheets—little embroidered daisies. The fire in the grate seemed somehow warmer and brighter. The ghostly screams were silenced. Her friend was a snake, a creature of venom and cunning, but it had left her room somehow cheerier, and for that she'd be forever thankful.

The Witch grew up in the archives, in a fortress surrounded by a moat. The water was the same reflective, shifting strangeness that filled the Thames, but sometimes when she peered into the water, it changed, rippling into pale fields of wildflowers. No one but her seemed to notice this. She raised it once with Henry, an apprentice archivist, and he said, "There's probably a tale about it somewhere. If you check the card catalogs under—"

"Never mind," the Witch had said, and walked off without waiting for him to finish. She despised the card catalogs.

The Tower was the name of her home, though it was in truth not a single tower, but many structures bound together by many stories.

It was also, she learned, not really built for storing books. The temperature was too variable, the stone too porous. The screaming ghosts made it difficult to do the quiet, focused work the archivists preferred. But the archives existed here because someone had decided that a prison was a better place for them than anywhere else.

The Witch understood she was as much an item and an asset as the books. She was an incarnate, from a valuable tale that fed and preserved the Isle. But something had gone wrong in her last life, as it had for so many others. She had to be kept safe until she could fulfill her purpose. Many other incarnates now lived in the Palace, where the Queen could watch over them and guide them. But not the Witch.

She cared for the books. She sat with the other apprentices and learned about how to treat leather, parchment, card, and thread. She fixed old books, and learned their quirks: their scent, their fragility, the temperature and humidity and atmosphere they required to flourish and survive.

She was not allowed to handle limni ink, as the other apprentices were. "That's no business for an incarnate," Aunt Meera told her mildly, when she protested being removed from those lessons. "It hurts your kind. And there will be other work you can do. Tend to your magic, Witch."

It was Aunt Meera who had raised her. She'd impressed on the Witch the importance of being obedient and quiet. "The books do not like noise," Meera had said. So the Witch had learned to walk swiftly, quietly through the archives, and learned not to argue when she was given orders.

Obedience or no obedience, she was too abrasive to make friends among the apprentices, and the Queen's incarnates lived too far outside her orbit to become her allies. That was fine with her. The Witch liked her own company well enough. Besides, she didn't fit among the other apprentices. They were archivists in training, and their duty was to protect and tend to tales, to curate them and hone them and, most importantly of all, keep them alive. The Witch *was* a tale.

One day she would meet her knight, and enthrall them; and then they would love one another, and die. She'd been taught her story early. She knew what was expected of her. It didn't frighten her. It was, as she'd been told all her life, her purpose as an incarnate.

She was alone, as she was often alone. She stood at a work table in the basement of the White Tower, with a spool of thread in her hand, threading a thick needle. The book she was trying to save was not special in any magical sense, but it was old and it was rare, and that was enough. There was a unicorn on its cover, painted in licks of rose and ivory. The unicorn was torn in two, but she'd do what she could to hide the scar of it.

It came from nowhere: *Something* rushed through her, an ink-knowing, a tug in her chest.

The Witch had never felt anything like it, and decided she did not want to. She ignored it and attempted to steady her hands.

A dark shape flickered at the corner of her vision.

She had never told anyone about the adder-creature, the little ink animal that so often seemed to slither its way about her room. More often than not, it turned itself into a raven so it could travel unnoticed throughout the Tower. Sometimes it took other forms: five little ink mice, curled up in one of her spare shoes; an ink-made pigeon, egglike in sleep with its neck tucked into its feathered body, sunning itself on her narrow window. Today, it was a skittering rat, its tail a thin ink brush whipping against the ground. Its snout was raised. It was looking at her expectantly.

She should have ignored it. Instead, she lowered the needle and thread, and turned toward it. The rat scampered to the door and wriggled through a minuscule crack in the doorframe. The Witch, unable to do the same, opened the door and shut it quietly behind her. It creaked—all doors here creaked—but she knew the best way to muffle them. That was what a lifetime in the Tower had done for her.

The ink rat led her down familiar corridors...and then swiftly outside the White Tower. It led her to one plain stone wall of the White Tower and, with one of its strange little tricks, summoned a door in the stone.

She stopped in her tracks. She stared at the door.

"Adder," she said firmly. "I cannot go in there."

She had called the ink creature *Adder* ever since their first meeting, and it answered to it. It turned toward her as she spoke now, blinking its beady ink-black eyes. It did not argue. It could not: It was always animal, and it had no capacity to speak. But it bounced about on the floor pointedly, squeaking, then transformed itself into a snake and wormed its way under the wooden door.

The Witch was obedient, and well-behaved—but even she had her limits, and Adder was often the creature to test them. She reasoned that she was supervising it, or perhaps protecting it from itself. She pushed the door open and followed it up the stairs it had just made. Up and up she went, until she emerged in an unfamiliar room.

Inside was a vast room of shelves and work tables. There was a glass window—motes of dust shone in its glowing, stained glass panes. She peered out briefly. She was high up in the tower, on a floor she was forbidden to enter.

She cursed internally, but she did not leave. Curiosity had her now.

Three books lay neatly piled at the corner of the nearest table. One, frayed almost beyond repair, lay at the center. She walked slowly toward them.

She felt heat in her veins—a warning, a clear note. She could not touch these books.

The books were incarnate books—canonical texts, imbued with the power of the tales they held.

This was not a place where she was meant to be.

But she could not resist drawing closer. Adder was circling a leg of the desk, urging her forward. (There were tales, she thought, of snakes as temptation and also snakes as symbols of old magic, of protection. Which one was this?) As if in a trance, she drew close to the table and looked down at the book.

The pages were so ripped they had been glued into shape, each torn piece like a facet of broken pottery. Some of the words were lost, blurred where they'd torn. But she could read the title.

*The Knight and the Witch—*

Her tale. This was her tale. Something in her chest cracked open.

She was on the edge of a great knowledge, on the edge of knowing something about herself, something huge that would change her life entirely.

She froze, resisting the feeling. It tugged at her, a fierce gravity, and she rooted herself to the spot and resisted. Her heart wanted to soar, but her body was in this room, in this place, with a broken book under her hovering fingertips, and her feet steady on the dusty floor.

She had followed Adder here, yes. But she would not do something that placed her incarnate tale at risk. Looking at it now, fragile as frayed cloth, a torn and precious thing beneath her fingertips... she could not harm it. She had a duty not to harm it.

She pushed the vast feeling away.

*Oh, you stupid girl*, a voice said in her skull. *Look at me!*

She stumbled back, knocking over a stack of books in the process. She leaned down and hurriedly piled them back up, biting her tongue to hold back curses.

No one came running. She was alone. No one would know the foolish thing she'd done.

Thank fuck.

She left the room, softly closing the door to the secret staircase behind her. She hurried back to the workroom she'd abandoned, not worrying if Adder was following her or not. Adder could take care of itself.

In a single narrow turret of the Salt Tower, the Witch had built her demesne. Her grotto, her place of safety, and her place of magic. The window was narrow, built small to keep out the cold, only wide enough for an arrow. Her room had been home to other folk before her—prisoners perhaps. The walls were covered in scratched drawings: names and horoscopes, and one depiction of a moon over mountains that she was particularly fond of.

Her grotto was also full of mirrors. She'd been given her first when she'd joined the archives as a girl: a gilt-edged thing, made of beaten silver instead of reflective glass, so that when she peered into it she did not see herself exactly as she was, but like her reflection was trapped in a moonlight-drenched dream, turned soft and strange by the pearly light. More had joined it since then, each unique and strange, and suited to her kind of magic.

She went to her room now, not quite running up the stairs, but not quite walking either. She wanted the safety of her own domain, and the privacy, so she could make sense of what she had just experienced.

It was not to be, alas. A knight in his forties, the Queen's rose stitched in relief on his heraldry, stood in her room, examining a palm mirror with his brow furrowed. He turned as she approached, and bowed.

"Lady Witch," he said.

She'd seen that face before, among the flock of knights who carried limni ink to the archives—and once or twice when she'd attended the Queen's court and danced at one of her many lustrous and dull banquets or balls.

"Sir Edmund," the Witch replied coolly. "What are you doing in my bedroom?"

"I have been sent to guard you," he said, with a stiff bow. He looked like he'd smelled something awful. His nose was wrinkled, his forehead squeezed into a frown. He did not want to be here. He cleared his throat. "I thought—"

She didn't wait to hear what he'd thought. She whirled on her heel and walked back down the stairs.

She headed straight for Archivist Sharma's office in the Lanthorn Tower. She rapped the door smartly, then went straight in, as she always did—and stopped dead, as she faced a room of people.

She'd walked into a situation she would have done her best to avoid, if she'd been aware of it. Archivists and a member of the Queen's court stared back at her.

"Witch," Aunt Meera said, after a beat. Her one eye behind its monocle prism glittered strangely, faceted—her other, brown and severe, looked at the Witch with frozen judgment. "What are you doing here?"

"There was a knight in my chambers," said the Witch. "I only wondered if something was amiss, Archivist Sharma."

She was never Aunt Meera in company, and this was certainly company: senior archivists based in the Queen's own household, and a member of her privy council, her Spymaster, severe-eyed and silver-haired with an oddly youthful albeit sharp face.

"Nothing is amiss," said Meera. "You merely require better protection. Unless there is something else you've come to tell me?"

She said it in the indulgent tone of an adult with a wayward child, as she often spoke to the Witch. She did not know that something actually was amiss.

"No," said the Witch. "Nothing else."

"Then you may go."

The Witch nodded to the archivists, then left.

"Send Sir Edmund to us, Witch," Meera called after her. "If he's made it to your quarters first instead of my office, then he clearly requires further guidance—and a map."

The Witch murmured her understanding, and kept walking.

Something was amiss in the Tower, in the Witch's own skin, and in London. Until the Witch knew more, she would bide her time.

# Chapter Twenty-Six

## *Vina*

*I thought I saw Robin Hood in the forest—and wouldn't that have been a coup? But it was just a limni-marked man who'd turned himself right strange, antlers and all. He was nice enough, but he was no incarnate. Still, I suppose it was silly to think I'd find an incarnate outside of London these days. We know where they all are now, don't we?*

Source: Letter from Sera Fisch to John Calthorpe

There was a horse-drawn omnibus that made its winding way toward London. It passed near their town, but it came only once a month. By sheer luck, it was set to arrive in four days. Hari shut up the house, and cursed the windows to keep out strangers. Vina arranged for the blacksmith's apprentice Amir to watch the rabbits for them, then lay out milk for the household brownies, so the cottage would be tended to in their absence. Maleficium was going to travel with them, so she could not do the job of house protection herself—although Vina had never seen her do anything except "be a cat," so she doubted she'd be capable.

Hari was adamant she was capable, but also adamant that she wasn't the kind of familiar who liked to be left behind. "She's had too much loss," Hari said fondly, feeding her bacon from the pan on the morning they were set to leave. "She's better off with us."

Vina watched, and wondered if it was Mal who couldn't bear to be left behind, or Hari who couldn't stand to leave her. She wisely kept her mouth shut as Galath packed Maleficium's food bowl and her brush with exquisite care.

They walked for four miles along the edge of the forest to the inn where the omnibus would stop. It was already waiting—it wouldn't depart again until midday. The horses were chuffing and neighing, restless. A few travelers were milling outside the inn, smoking or drinking, murmuring in low voices. They kept their distance from the forest's edge, which was marked with a perimeter fence of hexafoils and crosses. Low enough for a human to cross—bespelled enough to keep the rest out. At the turn of the year, the bounds had been beaten with a broom as cunning folk had murmured their blessings. The barrier was as strong as it could be.

Hari bought them four seats. When Vina gave him a questioning look—and considered whether she had to tell him that the cat absolutely didn't need her own omnibus seat—he said, "We've got a friend traveling with us."

"Someone I know?"

Hari shook his head. Then paused. "Maybe," he said.

"Cryptic! I like it," Vina said amiably. Galath gave her a look but did not comment as Hari laughed and shook his head again. Hari had always taken her cheerful tendency to drive people to madness in his stride. Knowing he'd been friends with Simran explained his patience, somewhat.

Godsblood, Vina missed her.

The omnibus began to fill with passengers, and finally a figure emerged from the shadows that edged the woods. The fence marks flared but didn't hold him back. Whatever he was, he wasn't a malicious creature. At first, Vina thought he was a wild-man—but then he drew into the light, and his human but ruddy skin dispelled that thought.

He was dressed like a woodcutter, in dun-colored garb—but he was whittled slim, too narrowly built to be much good with felling trees. And from his forehead rose antlers, graceful and inhuman.

He smiled when he saw Vina, then leapt the fence and made his way toward her.

He nodded to Hari and Galath, then said, "Do you remember me, sir knight?"

"I'm sorry," Vina said, shaking her head.

"I thought you might, somehow," he said, dusting the forest leaves from his shoulders. "But perhaps one life's memories are enough for a brain and a body to hold."

Her mind whirred, memories falling like autumn leaves.

"Vaughan?" Vina asked. "Are you—you're the boy Simran saved! You're alive? I was told—in my last life I was told the green library burned," she said, lowering her voice so they wouldn't be overheard.

A shadow passed over his face.

"It did," he said. "Most of the librarians escaped with our lives. The books, the tales..." He didn't finish. His mouth twisted, as if he couldn't bring himself to speak of it. The silence was enough. "But I remained in the forest, after. The magic written into me—it was happier there, where I had the trees around me. And it gave me the chance to look for the Beast, or for any stories that might have flown to safety. I never found those old friends, but I hear you're seeking out my fellow librarians. That, I can help you with."

There was a shout from the omnibus driver. All at once, people began to gather around the large carriage. They clambered onto the omnibus, surrounded by other bodies, sweat, and heat.

Hari and Galath were sitting together, silent as the omnibus jolted and rattled around them. But their shoulders were touching. Hari's head was starting to list to the side. He always fell asleep on long journeys.

Her fathers had never been very affectionate around other people, but they'd always orbited each other just like this. Her stomach felt seasick strange, looking at them. When she'd last known them, a lifetime ago, they'd not even been friends. Galath had been Hari's *kidnapper*.

Forcibly, Vina dragged her attention away from them.

"How are you going to go unnoticed in London?" Vina asked Vaughan.

"I won't," he said cheerily. He tapped one of his antlers. "Hats don't do much to cover these, I'm afraid. I'll stay just long enough to see you safe to the librarians, then I'll return home. As long as we don't draw the attention of our, uh, old friends," he said, avoiding naming the archivists, "we should be fine. And that reminds me—ah!" He fished something from his pockets—a hagstone, a single pebble with a natural hollow through the center, strung on a braided rope long enough to hook comfortably around a throat.

"A gift, from my sister," he said. "It hides that you're, well—*you*. Usually people have to pay through the nose for these, but for my sake, she said you could have this one free. Place the charm close to your skin. One turn of the moon is how long it'll conceal what you are."

Vina tucked it into her shirt. "Thank you," she said.

"If you need more, you can bargain with her," said Vaughan. "But you'll meet her again soon enough."

She wondered if London would be the same as she remembered—a jeweled patchwork of tales, each one twining with the next. She had a seat near the window, and pressed her face to the glass as the city drew in. Smoke rose from its chimneys in gray clouds; that was familiar. There were the stone buildings by wattle and daub; the mingled tales, winding together on tangled streets. But some things had changed. She bit back a shocked breath at the way the buildings in the flat distance shimmered and moved, shaping and changing—buildings of silver, of glass, flickering in and out of existence like mirages.

She wished that she could see London from up high—wished, briefly, that the city lay in a valley so she could stare down at it, cup all its strangeness in one look. Instead, she leaned back in her seat as they trundled into the city, and watched the streets close in like a wave.

There were three bodies hanging outside the old wall of London. As they passed through it, the omnibus felt strangely quiet. She stared up at them in silence. When she looked away, her eyes met Galath's.

"Traitors," he said, voice low. "Telling so-called false tales, or speaking of *him*."

Him. The Eternal Prince. But if there was one thing Vina knew better than to do, it was saying his name in the Queen's own city. Galath's mouth was thin with displeasure.

The Queen had always been more subtle in her cruelty than this. Filled with disquiet, Vina sat silently for the rest of the journey.

They descended from the omnibus, the four of them standing in the swell and bustle of London. But as Vina looked around, she could feel the difference in the air—something new and electric, as if she could feel fresh stories sweeping by her, winding through London's streets.

They made their way on foot to a ragged set of houses, coalsmoke darkening their windows. Vina spied some dusky windows with flags hung inside them, of a great sword running through a crown. The Eternal Prince's symbol.

"I guess the Queen can't hang everyone," Vina said, and Galath hummed acknowledgment in response.

Vaughan went ahead of them and rapped on the door of a house near the end of the row, a dilapidated building nearly collapsed in on itself. After a heartbeat, it opened. Vina recognized the woman at the door, but it took a moment for her memories to fall into place. Cora, the witch and librarian. Vaughan's sister.

Cora stood there, older, face and stomach softer, hair a lighter shade of red, her expression intense and focused as she looked over Vaughan, then drew him in for a hug.

She looked at Vina, Hari, and Galath more coolly. "Come in," she said. "We'll talk."

The hallway was oppressively narrow, dimly lit by a single gas lamp, but once they emerged from it the space that met them was much larger—a sweep of white walls and wooden floors, splashed with faded rugs, and tables lit by bright lamps. There were librarians at the tables—some so old that they might have been at that long-ago green library, might have seen Vina then in her last life. But others were young, fingers ink-stained, their eyes focused on the manuscripts they were carefully transcribing.

"We have all three houses on this street," Cora said, as Vina stepped hesitantly forward. "We knocked the walls together. From the outside, the houses are nothing to look at. From the inside, they're not much to look at either, of course. But the space is better."

Vina stopped at a table. A slim volume was open. She hesitated, oddly drawn to it.

"These books," Vina murmured.

"Take it," said the person at the table, looking up. "We bribed our way into a printing press to make copies of this one. It can take a human touch. But keep your hands off the hand transcriptions—they're precious, and if the ink smudges I'll be forced to rip out your eyes."

"Entirely fair," Vina said. She traced the air above the words—now that she had permission—with a fingertip. "It's in a different language?"

"Welsh," said the librarian, and the word was like an electric burr against Vina's ears—as if two decades ago the word would have turned to a white haze of static and faded from her mind.

"Vina," said Galath. "Come."

Hari and Galath were standing at the far edge of the room. Cora was gone. Vina went to join them.

"How did you meet them?" Vina asked. "These librarians?"

"Vaughan found us first," said Hari. "And then we came to know them. Help them." A pause, then Hari said, "We've been busy, Vina. We really have tried. Tried to save the library, and protect incarnates. And we've tried to save Simran." Hari swallowed. Then said, thickly,

"I promised her parents I'd find her. It's not a promise I intended to break."

Vina's vision went hazy for a moment, two lives converging again. That flat above a sweet shop, with a broken table, and Simran's wary parents watching her. And overlaid, the memory of her early childhood, when her dada and dadi had come to visit—their frail, gentle hands, their gentler words. Hari's parents, she'd thought. Her papa's family. She'd always been glad her papa was like her, with parents who loved him without blood ties, only bonds of the heart.

"They." Vina blinked, emotion washing over her like a storm. Her own voice trembled a little when she said, "Did they. Know what I am?"

"They knew you," Hari said. He placed a hand on her shoulder.

"Knight, come with me," Cora said, sticking her head out from a corner door. She got a glare from a few librarians for the noise. She glared right back. "Ophelia wants to talk to you."

Cora led her down a staircase into a courtyard garden. Under a gray sky, the garden was oddly lush, full of flowers made of shadows, and insects of gossamer smoke that hummed gently between them. Vina could smell the ink of them. Tales.

"The tales are growing," said Ophelia. She'd been imposing, charming when Vina had last met her. She was older now, but beautiful for it—hair still black, skin deep brown, lines of sorrow faintly bracketing her mouth. She was kneeling among the stories, in practical trousers and a jumper, waiting for Vina to join her.

Vina did, kneeling down beside her. Ophelia's hands were mottled—old burns had streaked them with gradations of color and twisted the fingers inward. Vina focused her gaze on the stories—those whispering, leaflike shadows.

"I thought nothing survived the burning," said Vina, awed.

"Nothing did. These are new stories, carefully reared," Ophelia replied. "I thought all was lost, after the green library burned. But more stories were brought to us. This isn't the library, old and magical and—irreplaceable. But it is *a* library. And we keep doing our work." One of the insects settled on her shoulder—a smoke-and-gossamer-winged moth. "You came to speak to us," said Ophelia. "What do you need, sir knight?"

"I need to destroy the Queen's archive. The archive is—a cage, chains on those stories. I saw those chains. I felt them. Destroy it and the stories will be free again. Incarnates will be able to change."

"Or the tales may die," said Ophelia. "I understand the magic of stories, sir knight. We all do. Sometimes we even bind tales in ink and paper. But the archivists... What they've done? I can't understand it, never mind undo it."

"All I'm asking for is information," said Vina earnestly. "Any advice, any knowledge you can offer. How can I end the archive? Must it be by fire? The sword? Must I seek magic to free those tales? Do you and your kind have the magic to help me?"

"We don't have the Beast anymore, or a chalice of knowledge," said Ophelia. Her hands were faintly trembling. "I almost burned, trying to save the Beast. I didn't want to leave it behind. There was so much smoke—but the Beast did not emerge from its hall. I broke down its door—burned my hands on the knocker. But it wasn't there. My family had to drag me out. Did it burn? Did it die? I still wonder, but I thought losing it along with the library would destroy me. It turns out I'm made of stronger stuff. Isn't that strange? Marvelous, even? So I have no truths to give you. I only have what I believe."

Vina listened silently.

"I see strange buildings in the distance," said Ophelia. "And one night a fire raced through London, then vanished by morning like it had never burned, taking thousands of houses with it—even St. Paul's. And then I come here, to our makeshift library, and I watch stories grow—some of them are sweet, and many of them are full of evil and cruelty. So some stories may burn this city, and others may peel back its surface and reveal monsters under its skin. But I believe my job is to save them all—bit by bit, day by day. So here's my belief for you, sir knight. We librarians are built to save and protect the

Isle's tales, and I'd rather die than risk harming any of them. What are you built to do?"

Behind her gold-rimmed spectacles, her eyes were sorrowful.

"I am sorry I couldn't help you," Ophelia said. "The pain I felt when the library burned... I won't let that agony repeat in the world. Not if I can help it. But if you need someone to speak to—if you need shelter—we librarians will still be here."

Cora and Vaughan waited at the stairs back into the house.

"It's time for you to leave," said Cora. Her voice was flat and unfriendly.

Vina hesitated.

"If I could speak to any of the other librarians..." she said.

"No," said Cora. "We've helped you. We are helping you. But we've lost so much. To ask us to burn books... It's cruel, knight. That's the truth."

"Cora," Vaughan protested. "Please—"

"It's easy for you to speak on her behalf, when you're going straight back to the forest, Vaughan," Cora said, crossing her arms. "It's not the same for us. We have to survive out in the Isle, knowing we might lose everything at any moment."

Guilt washed over Vina. She opened her mouth to apologize—and then she swallowed the urge back.

"If there's a way to save the books, I'm going to find it," she said.

"Then get out and do it," said Cora. "And don't come back until you do."

"She doesn't mean that," Vaughan said.

"I bloody do."

"I'll go for at least a little while," Vina said, hastily making her retreat.

She walked past Galath and Hari, across the hall to the narrow hallway, and out onto the front step. She sat down with a thump.

A few beats later, and the door opened. Hari came out.

"Where's Galath?" Vina asked.

"Talking to the librarians."

"Soothing them, is he?"

"You know Galath," said Hari, smiling wryly. "He's the spirit of diplomacy."

He sat beside her and took out one of his cigarettes. He flicked his fingers to summon a flame, then lit it.

Vina stared at the flame, thinking of the library burning; thinking of the archive full of its paper books.

"Did you think they'd help me?" Vina asked. "The librarians, I mean."

"I hoped they'd give you a direction," said Hari. "Give us all one, in truth. We've tried so long to get Simran back, to do something… and here we are. You're an adult, and I'm an old man, and she's still gone."

"You're not an old man," said Vina. "You're not even fifty yet."

"And somehow I still feel more ancient than Galath is," said Hari. "Maybe it's the knee pain. Nobody told me my knees would creak this much."

"I wouldn't know," said Vina. "I've never been old."

That killed the conversation stone dead, but Vina quashed her guilt and focused on her own racing thoughts. There had to be a way forward.

The librarians weren't willing to risk harming tales. They collected tales. Protected them. They were so like the archivists in strange ways: the bright side of the coin to their tarnished one. Vina could tell them that destroying the archive wouldn't hurt the tales, but what did she really know? Just what Simran had told her, words over a blade before Vina had—

Before they both died.

"You said you know cunning folk in London," said Vina. "But I'm not sure benevolent magic is what we need. You're a witch. Do you know other witches?"

"I know Cora."

"I don't think she's going to help me."

"I've never been the kind to seek them out," said Hari. "I had Simran. And Galath knows his craft, too, though he wouldn't claim the title. That was enough for me. But I can find them." Over the smoke of his cigarette, his gaze was intent. "What are you thinking, Vina?"

"Ophelia said librarians aren't built for destruction," said Vina. "I need people who are. I need maleficent magic. I need witches."

"Then let's seek out some witches," said Hari. "I'm sure nothing will go wrong at all."

# Chapter Twenty-Seven

## *The Witch*

*I have little to report, sir. She's quiet. Obedient. I've made discreet inquiries, but everyone agrees the Witch is a beaten animal.*

Source: Letter from Warder Rupert
Aske to the Spymaster

It was inevitable that she'd go back. She'd always been obedient to the will of the archivists, but now that she'd transgressed, the urge to do so again was strong. It was like putting ink to paper—you could never return to the blank page.

She thought often of that torn book, that tooled writing, that title. *The Knight and the Witch.* Her tale. Why had it burned at her—like hot lightning to her skull? Why had Adder led her to it? It was *hers*, of course, but it was forbidden.

The only thing that stopped her from returning was the presence of her new guard. Sir Edmund was irritating—sullenly quiet, radiating boredom, but stubbornly unwilling to leave her alone.

She was fixing some damaged print texts—dull work, nothing as luminously worthy as working on incarnate tomes for the Tower's resident incarnate—in a workroom piled with books, shelves groaning under their weight. She was standing at her work table, tools arrayed around her. He was leaning against the main door.

She heard him shift again. Yawn.

"Must you hover behind me?" the Witch snapped.

"It's my job to watch over you."

"I'm not doing anything dangerous," the Witch pointed out. "Are you worried I'll stab myself with a book? They're not very sharp."

"Some of your tools are," Edmund said.

*I'd rather stab you than myself,* the Witch thought with irritation.

"I'm not going to hurt myself with those either. Do you think there's a wayward assassin hiding behind the books? No? Then you can stand outside." She pointed imperiously at the door, and finally he shuffled out and shut the door behind him.

She counted down ten seconds in her head, then went over to a shelf to the left and shoved it slightly with her elbow. Behind it was a window that led out to the battlements.

It wasn't intentionally hidden, she guessed. Bookcases had been shoved around the space so often that it must have been covered and immediately forgotten. She climbed out of it now, and shimmied out onto the battlements. Then, quickly, she walked her way down to the green that surrounded the White Tower.

The warders took no notice of her, assuming she was just another apprentice busy with her work.

She went to the side of the White Tower, slapping her hand against stone. The door Adder had made was gone.

"Adder," she whispered. Then, a little louder, "*Adder!*"

Adder did not come, and no door was forthcoming. Feeling foolish, the Witch pressed her forehead against the cool stone.

If she were sensible, she'd head straight back to her workroom.

If she were sensible, she'd never have come here at all.

She straightened up and walked, bold as brass, into the White Tower proper.

She moved carefully up the narrow staircase, waiting until corridors emptied before going into them herself, a planned excuse caught behind her teeth, on her tongue, ready to use. *I was asked to tell Archivist Sharma something confidential. I was told she was here.*

*Direct me, please.* And so forth.

No one stopped her. She made it to the room, and pushed the door open.

*The Knight and the Witch* was no longer set out—some other text was set in its place—but there were incarnate tomes in here. She could feel the teeth-itching magic of them, pressing against her skin. If she just looked through the shelves…

She peered closely at the shelves through the dim light of the room. So many titles, and none of them the one she was looking for. She stepped back, and looked again at the work table—and the book that was on it.

It was a slim blue volume—very slim. It was probably part of a larger collection of incarnate tomes. Its name was so faded she could read nothing but an *M* followed by a brief blur of letters, and a *T*. But what distracted her was what surrounded it. A snarl of inky shadows was tangled around the book, shaped like rope, or perhaps like chains. Limni ink. The Witch knew she shouldn't touch it. She knew it would hurt her. But that strange voice was whispering in her skull again—that awful, insistent voice.

*Pick it up*, the voice insisted. *See what you're capable of. Go on.*

She hesitated, hands raised.

*Stop being such a coward!*

The Witch picked up the book in her left hand… and grasped the shadows with her right.

She felt a jolt go through her. Not pain—and it should have been pain. Instead she felt very alive, very aware of the snarled darkness in her palm. An old instinct welled up in her, and she tightened her grip. She tore the chain in two.

Images flashed through her mind: a woman in a hooded cloak, deep blue as midnight; a body in her arms, crowned and trailing blood; water, shimmering around a barge. She blinked hard, and the images crumbled to dust.

The shadows were gone. The book lay quiescent in her hands. There was a pool of limni ink now on the table.

The Witch dropped the book back on the table and stared down at her own hands.

*I touched limni ink*, she thought, with wonder and horror. *How?*

There were footsteps in the corridor. She held her breath until they passed, then emerged and hurried back to her workroom.

She'd just gotten back into the room and shoved the shelf into place when she heard a creak of the door. Panic and anger made her whirl on the spot to face Edmund without dissembling.

"I told you to wait outside," snapped the Witch.

Edmund's expression was shuttered and serious.

"Where did you go?" he asked.

"To the loo, if you really have to know," said the Witch, which was an obvious bald-faced lie. If he wanted to question her, he was welcome to try. "What is it?"

"The Queen has summoned you," said Sir Edmund.

"Me? What for?"

"I don't know," said Edmund. "Get ready. We've got to head out soon."

They left by the Traitor's Gate, in a boat with a covered compartment for its occupants, windows blacked out with cloth. Even with the sights of the city concealed from her, leaving the archive often felt like leaping into icy water—a shock to her entire body that made her feel suddenly, achingly more alive. Within the archive, tales were carefully controlled: bound, managed, settled into ink. Beyond the Tower of London, errant tales lived and breathed, swimming through normal mortal lives.

She could feel the pull of the Eternal Prince—his tale coiling inside her skull. *He lives and lives again. Eternal.*

*I wonder,* she thought, *how the Queen feels about losing her throne.*

They arrived at the Palace, and were met by knights and guards, who guided them toward the White Hall. The Witch walked forward, caught between Head Archivist Roland and Archivist Sharma.

Behind her walked Sir Edmund. She felt intensely caged, her palms clammy.

The Queen's hallways were full of intense revelry—courtiers in fine gowns laughing and chattering in the corridors; the sound of lutes and music, from distant rooms.

The White Hall was thronged with people, all standing below the Queen, red-haired and white-faced upon her ugly throne. Behind her throne was draped the hide of a dragon, bronze-scaled and shining. Even as she bowed, the Witch could not look away from it. The empty sockets of its eyes. Its talons, gold-tipped and speared against the wall.

One of the Queen's pet incarnates was standing in court, shuffling awkwardly from foot to foot: Owain, incarnate of the giant-killer Tom Hickathrift. He'd had a growth spurt since she last saw him, and towered over the other courtiers, almost as if he were a giant himself. If he was here, no doubt the others were too. She never let them wander far. Sure enough, Mrs. Bell—incarnate from the tales of Mother Shipton—was on her usual seat in the corner, watching proceedings with unblinking, beady eyes. She gave the Witch a nod.

A girl already stood in front of the Court—bird-boned, no older than sixteen. Her hair was muddy brown. When she turned at the sound of the archivists' entrance, the Witch saw that she had the faintest marks of scales at her cheeks. Their eyes met, then the girl looked away.

"Dear Apollonius!" the Queen crowed, delighted, her lips shaping a glorious smile. "Come. This girl must be tested."

Apollonius returned some honeyed words to the Queen, as Meera examined the brown-haired girl, peering through the prism over her eye.

"Well?" Apollonius asked finally.

"She is indeed an incarnate," said Meera. "The Laidly Wyrm. Congratulations, Your Majesty."

There was a smattering of applause from the Court. The Witch's stomach roiled.

The Queen clapped her own hands with delight. Behind her, her masked ladies-in-waiting mirrored the movement.

"We've met this one before!" said the Queen, visibly pleased. "And in far less salubrious circumstances. When we dine together, little wyrm, let us tell you about the time we almost hunted you." She turned her attention back to her Court. "The new incarnate must be celebrated," said the Queen. "We must have a ball. It seems we always have the need to celebrate some such thing—how lucky the Isle is, to be so blessed."

"We are lucky to have a Queen who ensures we are blessed," Apollonius said, bowing deep.

The Witch looked down at her own shoes. The Witch remembered her own welcome party, when she was young enough to be terrified of large celebratory crowds of raucous adults, but old enough not to cry about it. Oh, she pitied the poor new incarnate dragged into court for another interminable ball.

"...and the Witch will attend, of course," Archivist Roland was saying. His hand came to rest on her shoulder, pinning her in place, hot as a brand.

"We must have all our finest incarnates around us," the Queen agreed, voice firm. And finally, the Witch understood why she had been summoned. She was to be present at a ball, and therefore displayed as a demonstration of the Queen's great power. How many incarnates would the Queen fill her ballroom with this time?

"Come closer, Witch," the Eternal Queen urged.

This was an old song. The Witch knew what to do. Apollonius released her. She lowered her eyes and walked forward, curtsying, then allowing the Queen to examine her with cold eyes—and then a cold hand, tipping up her chin.

*Lifetimes of this*, a voice in her skull sighed.

"Have you been well-behaved, girl?" the Queen asked. "Have you been obedient and good to the archivists, who have so generously cared for you?"

"Yes, Your Majesty," the Witch said.

"You may go," the Queen said. The Witch bowed again and returned to her place between the archivists. Apollonius Roland immediately gripped her shoulder once more.

"Does she tell the truth, Apollonius?" the Queen asked. "Has her training been fruitful? Has she been healthy—submissive?"

"Healthy as a horse, Your Majesty," said Archivist Roland. "And utterly obedient. She understands and revels in her duty to the Crown and the Isle."

"You'll keep her useful? Keep her true to her tale?"

"Your Majesty," said Archivist Roland. "The Witch is exemplary."

The Witch said nothing. She had not been asked to speak. But she looked at the Queen—her white face, her thin red mouth, her hands tight upon the arms of her throne—and thought, *She's afraid. Terribly afraid.* All the revelry the Queen insisted upon was a mask and a salve to a wound. If the Witch could see this, surely the rest of the Court did also. But they still laughed, and bowed, and cooed over the Queen, and drank their liquors and ate their sweets, and dressed for their balls—as if an ancient tale wasn't riding down upon the city. As if the Queen would not soon be deposed, with a blood-soaked and glorious king taking her place.

When Apollonius and Meera joined the Queen and her privy council in a private meeting, Sir Edmund and the Witch were sent to wait in a drawing room. Thick carpet lay under their feet. The chairs were furnished in silk. The Witch contemplated how upset everyone would be if she attempted to climb out of the window and got her boots all over the upholstery.

"Edmund," a low voice said—cool, aristocratic. "I'll speak to the Witch alone now, if you please. Wait outside."

To her surprise, Sir Edmund did not argue. He merely bowed and left.

The Witch was left alone with the Spymaster. She knew him, of course. She saw him every time she was brought before the Queen, which was a task as regular as the cycles of the moon. But they had never been alone, and he'd certainly never sought her out.

"Let me see you, girl," he said, just as the Queen had.

She'd been examined once already today, but she was often examined—tested by limni ink, by magical eyeglasses, by ritual magic and tarot cards and tea leaves. *She's a perfectly normal incarnate*, all of them said, as if they did not expect it. As if they expected her to be aberrant in some way beyond her brown skin, her Elsewhere blood. As much as she wanted to bristle, she'd been taught to accept the taste of defeat. She sat still and let him look at her.

"You're less of a simpering creature than I thought you would be," he said, finally. "I thought Apollonius would wring all the spine out of you before you reached adulthood."

Perhaps it was those words that moved her to recklessness. But probably not. There was a rage simmering in her; a little adder, circled around her heart.

"Sir," she said. "If I may, I have a question."

"Go on," he said. "Speak."

"Does the Queen fear the return of the Eternal Prince?" the Witch asked. "Or does she simply pretend he isn't coming to take her throne?"

"A bold question!" said the Spymaster. "I find myself surprised. I did not think Archivist Roland would raise you to speak so plainly. We were told, in fact, that he had not."

"I am a model of decorum," said the Witch, straight-faced. "If I've erred, I apologize."

He smiled, thin-lipped—but she had a sense that he was genuinely amused, if not by her, then by something.

"What do all stories have in common, Witch?"

This sounded like a test. The Witch wanted to do well—or believed, at least, that Aunt Meera would want her to—but she could not think of an answer. She had spent so long gluing and sewing and mending books, had stained her fingers so thoroughly with ink, but the *content* of tales so often seemed to be off-limits to her.

"They end," said the Spymaster, into her silence. "They may be revised or retold. They may, perhaps, change. A closed book may be reopened. But they must all have an ending. An ending may be delayed, or rewritten. But the end, in its finality, comes for us all."

\* \* \*

They returned to the Tower. The ravens watched them from its walls, cawing, beady-eyed and black-winged. One of her favorites, Peppermint, swooped down as she left the barge that had carried them. She gave the raven a scratch to the head, then a handful of seeds she'd kept hidden in her pocket.

In her room, as night fell, she heard a strange noise from the safety of her bed. Rumbling, deep. She sat up.

"Adder?" she called. "Are you there?"

The sound grew, then waned. Grew, then waned.

Breathing.

The breath was low, chuffing, from deeper lungs than any mortal or any tiny snake of ink could possess. She froze, some animal instinct holding her still.

She saw Adder's eyes in the dark, but they were suddenly alien to her—ferocious with a feeling she could not understand, that Adder had no words to express. The walls of her circular chamber, her mirrors, had all darkened as if they bled.

It darted at her, teeth bared. She flinched, scrambling from the bed, then grasped for the magic of her mirrors. They hummed around her, full of the promise of power.

"I don't want to hurt you," she whispered, voice tight, magic squirming like eels in her palm. "What's wrong?"

Adder made one last convulsive hiss, then faded back into the shadows.

The Witch waited and waited, until she was sure it was not going to return. Her heart was pounding like a fist.

*Get out of here*, a voice in her skull said. *Or better yet find your book and steal it away. Rip it up again. Don't just sit there, you lump!*

The voice sounded vicious, exasperated. *Godsblood, won't you listen to me? I can't believe I'm so stubborn I won't even listen to myself—*

She slammed a door, mentally, on that voice. Then she lay down in her bed, and stared at the ceiling until dawn came.

# Chapter Twenty-Eight

## *Vina*

*Of course I'll help you in any way I can. I'll keep my eyes and ears open. Ever since the Eternal Prince woke up, London's been full of whispers. Maybe I'll catch something of use to you.*

*Come back when you can, Hari. I'll be performing at the Theatre Royal soon. I like to think Simran would have loved it, but you'd be a better judge of that.*

Source: Letter from Oliver Pryce to Hari Patel

There were places that drew witchcraft to them—where the occult naturally drifted, tale-drawn.

"Graveyards are cliché," Hari said cheerily, holding the lamp in front of them. Its hot orange flame flickered under glass, turning his face ghoulish in the darkness. No part of London was ever truly lightless, but the tales wending their way through the graveyard did not know that. "But some concepts are old hat for a reason. Witchcraft is drawn to liminal spaces—mirrors, twilight, sunrise and sunset, unlife."

"Do you see anyone?" Vina asked, squinting through the light.

"Not yet. But we will."

Hari had no coven, and never had. It was cunning folk he seemed to consider his circle, though he never called them that. Some had visited now and again—Oliver, always elegantly dressed and exquisitely kind, was the one she remembered best in the parade of folk who'd arrived late and taken over the spare room, whispered with Hari over ale in the kitchen, and slipped away days later at the pale touch of dawn. The cunning folk knew everything that went on in London, and a cunning woman called Ella had directed them to this cemetery.

Vina had wanted to come alone, in truth. But Hari had dug his heels in. When Hari had said, "It's either me or Galath," Vina had relented.

A wind blew through the graveyard, ice cold. Vina stopped moving.

"Stay still," she whispered to Hari.

Hari stilled. In the darkness stood a figure, almost as gray-pale as the angels carved above the graves. A woman. Thin, wraithlike. A mouth full of sharp teeth. A revenant? A vampire? It didn't matter. Either way, it wasn't welcome.

"You're not the tale I'm looking for," said Vina apologetically. "I'm sorry."

The hungry thing took a step toward them, legs trembling.

"You'd be wise not to touch us, friend," said Hari. He sounded calm, friendly. But there was an edge to his voice, keen as a blade waiting to cut. "You should seek out other prey."

The creature hesitated, then bared all those serrated teeth and lunged forward again. Vina reached for her sword—a sharp hiss of drawn steel, a lick of silver under the gloom-black sky—but Hari was faster.

He drew a knife and whispered a curse—then flung the blade directly into the revenant's chest. The thing staggered. The knife itself caused it no pain. It was the dash of blood at the blade, Hari's own blood, that made the thing freeze again, fingers grasping feebly at the air as fractures of light crept sharp-nailed through its dead flesh.

"Leave," Hari said, voice cold. "Or I'll make it worse. I promise you."

For a moment there was silence. Then the creature stumbled away, a guttural noise leaving its lungs.

"You shouldn't have worried," a voice said. "It won't harm witches. At least one of you would have survived." The witch who'd spoken stepped forward. Dark hair, shot through with licks of silver. Blue eyes. Her eyes fixed on Vina, and widened.

"I remember you," said the witch. Her gaze narrowed again. "What are you doing here, sir knight?"

Vina squinted at her, puzzling out old memories.

"I know your face," she said slowly. "But I'm afraid my memory is a little patchy. I died for a time, you see." She returned her own sword to her belt—she'd watched this sword being made in her own town, by the smith who'd trained her. She was too tempted to wield it now to protect the new life she'd made. Better to remove it from her hand. "The last time we met, ma'am, you captured people for a fae maiden. She enthralled me. Some of those people died. How have you been since then?"

The witch laughed thinly. "Oh, you try at sharpness, but it's like having your heels nipped at by a puppy. You think people like me don't deserve forgiveness? That seems like a terrible way to live."

"Didn't the 'foxes' who died deserve to live?"

"Justice is a nice tale," she said. "But it's not for all folk. What do you want? Here to kill some witches?"

"We're not interested in killing any kin of mine," Hari said. "We've come to talk. Maybe make a mutually beneficial bargain. That's all."

The witch's mouth was thin.

Vina raised both her hands.

"I'm sorry," she said, aiming for sincerity. "I've been very rude. Please forgive me. Sometimes I get my lives confused, and I say things I don't mean," she continued, saying something she absolutely did not mean. "Let me start again. My name is Vina. This is Hari. We need to speak to your coven, if you'll allow it."

The witch hummed thoughtfully for a moment.

"Let me think," she said. "Since you've been so polite, here it is: *No*."

"Please. I know the old bargains," Vina said.

"Vina." Hari's voice was a quiet warning.

She couldn't say *Trust me*. She knew she wasn't trustworthy, when it came to her own safety. She'd made so many errors, over so many lives, and she had no reason to believe this life would be any different.

"I need to do this," she said instead.

"If anyone's going to make a bargain, it's me." Hari drew a fresh knife from his coat, small and wickedly sharp. "A hank of hair, from my head, given to you freely, fellow witch," said Hari. "Will that do to allow us to converse with your coven?"

"They don't need you to reassure them," said Vina. "The witches need me to do it."

"The knight is correct," she said, arms crossed. "You're a fellow witch. She's not. She needs to give us power over her, or there'll be no trust."

Vina held out her hand for the knife.

"I'd prefer to use your knife," she said. "Please."

Hari gave her a sharp look, but didn't argue. He handed the knife over. "What were you going to use if I said no?" Hari asked.

"My sword," she said. "I've done it before. It's fine."

Hari's mouth twitched. "Of course you've cut your hair with a sword before."

Her hair was longer than it had been in her first life, long enough to tie at the nape of her neck. She severed one curl now, and held it out to the witch, who took it from her after a brief pause.

"You'd give me, of all people, power over you?"

"You told me to show forgiveness," said Vina. "Besides, I need your help enough to risk it." It wasn't the only bad bargain she'd ever made. It probably wouldn't be the last.

The witch tucked the hank of hair away.

"My name is Sarah," she said. "Follow me."

Between green grass and paved paths, beyond the gravestones and graceful mausoleums, stood a tree. It was imposingly broad, its trunk gray. Rising up toward it like a collar, or like a muddled jaw of teeth, were dozens of gravestones, each slatted unevenly against the other. It was a grim sight. Sarah whispered a spell, made a cutting motion with her hands, and then the tree and graves cleaved open, widening to open into a stairway down into the darkness.

They followed her in.

Within sat a group of witches. They were in a casual circle, seated in the modest chamber hidden beneath the tree. They went silent as Vina and Hari entered.

"There's nothing to fear," said Sarah. "These two have come to talk."

"You're lucky to find us," said one witch, settled by a flask clearly full of tea. He was pouring it out into chipped mugs. His skin was warm-toned, his eyes black as pansies beneath thick eyebrows. "We only meet every full moon. But I suppose, as a fellow witch, you know that," he said, eyes sliding to Hari.

"I'm not one for covens," said Hari. "But we are here looking for your help. I'm Hari Patel, and this is Vina."

"Tam," said the man. He didn't offer a surname.

"The Eternal Prince is coming, ready to usurp the Queen and take her throne," said Vina. "I need your help to take advantage of the archivists and Queen while they're vulnerable. The archive needs destroying."

"You want us to support the beautiful, terrible prince-thing running across the Isle and devastating it?" Tam raised an eyebrow.

"Beautiful, terrible prince-thing?" Vina repeated.

"He's a fine and dreadful tale," said Sarah. "We can all feel him. You must too."

Vina had, when he'd passed by the edges of her town. His presence alone had been enough to awaken her to herself. "I'm not asking you to support him," she said. "We've all been controlled by the grip of the archives far too long. The rise of the Eternal Prince has broken some of their power. We can take this opportunity to end the archives entirely. I want you to take advantage of what his presence offers: a flaw in the armor of the archivists. A chance to steal their control from them."

Tam sighed. The other witches had similar expressions, tired and unimpressed.

"They're not possible to fight," said Sarah.

Tam said, "Power's the oldest tale, young knight. There's no hope here."

"Why did you turn to witchcraft?" Hari asked. He sat calmly in that circle of witches, his face like stone—her gentle father, always kind and thoughtful, suddenly sharper, carved by the shadows of the room and the shadows of his spirit. This was a version of him she'd rarely seen—like the sky in an eclipse, without its habitual moonlight to gentle it. "There are softer magics—benevolent work, prayers and charms and healing. You could have been cunning folk. Wise folk. You could have kept your magic tucked under your skin and never utilized it. So why witchcraft?"

"It sounds like you have a lecture prepared," Sarah murmured. But she was listening attentively, no bite in her words. None of the witches were even drinking their cups of tea.

"We're on the margins. All of us. We know people eaten by tales. Broken, or murdered by them. You've felt what it means to be nothing, unimportant, unseen. We've felt the anger in us. But we've embraced being on the edges of what it means to belong to the Isle. We've chosen to be outside, anathema—we've crowned ourselves as monsters." Hari looked from face to face. "We know the establishment is rotten," he said. "Don't you want to tear it down?"

Vina stared at him. When *had* Hari chosen witchcraft? He hadn't possessed any magic in Vina's last lifetime. But so much had changed in the time between her death and her return, and Hari was changed too—older, broader, more comfortable in himself, grief a mantle on his shoulders.

"The archivists are part of the power structure that has done this to us," he said quietly—and the witches leaned in to listen, drawn by the tightening spool of his voice. "Let's wrest control back."

"The archives are protected by powerful magic. And I've got no magic," said Vina, "though I live in an incarnate tale." Frayed though it was, the tale was still hers—it still tied her to Simran, spilled ink inside her heart. "You understand magic in a way I never could. Help me. Help us all. Please."

"You want spells from us, to break the archives," said Sarah. "To take away their power."

"I do," said Vina.

The witches shared looks. There was hesitation in their faces.

Hari took a card from his pocket—an address.

"If you're willing to help, meet us here before the week ends," he said. "We'll be waiting."

They'd almost reached the cemetery's arched entry when they heard someone call out.

"Wait," said Tam.

They turned.

"Brother," Tam said, hands in his pockets, eyes steady. "You're Elsewhere. Like me."

Hari nodded hesitantly.

"The world's changed," said Tam. "You don't need to be a witch the way these folk see witches. Your own people have tales you can wear now. I know scribes that could help you."

Hari rolled up his sleeve, revealing the tattoo on his wrist—the hexafoil of cunning folk, cut through neatly with a line of limni ink. Benevolent magic, fractured, turned to maleficent purpose. The limni tattoo for a witch.

"I'm already marked," said Hari. "I can't take up any other kind of magic."

"I told you things have changed," said Tam. "I was marked long ago as a witch. But as new tales swept in, my mother told me about her parents from Elsewhere; about a different magic, witchcraft from where we hailed from. I wanted it. I paid a cheap back-alley scribe, and it worked. The Isle's changing, and no one can tell me I can't have this." He bared his own arm.

Vina knew there were limni tattoos for those who wanted foresight, divination. This didn't look like those clear, steady eyes. Instead it was an eye within a teardrop—cut through the center to turn benevolence to witchcraft.

Hari took a step forward, breathing in the magic. His eyes were full of wonder.

"What a fine thing," he said. "I've never seen anything like it."

"There's more of us every day," Tam said quietly. "You could join us. This business with the archives—that's for the coven to decide together. But this is for you. If you want it."

Hari shook his head.

"I'm glad for you," said Hari. "But this magic was given to me by a fellow witch, and my greatest friend. I chose it. It matters to me. It may be Isle-made, but it's also mine."

"Then I'll let you go," said Tam. "Maybe we'll meet again." He nodded curtly, to Hari and to Vina, then vanished back into the darkness of the graveyard.

Hari was quiet for a long time after that, something quietly awed in his eyes. Vina let him feel it, and kept her own silence.

They'd moved into Hari's flat in Limehouse. It was Simran's flat too, long ago. When their landlady and friend Lydia Chen had passed away, she'd left it to Hari. "She was a proper matriarch," Hari told Vina wistfully. "I miss her."

Simran's old flat looked nothing like it had when Vina had last visited... and been spell-bound to its floor. The burn marks on the floorboards were gone; the clutter of Simran's clothes on the aged, buckling sofa had been swept away decades ago, and the floor was polished and shining. A soft rug swathed the ground, and a leather sofa sat under the window, draped in a blanket. Galath sat, cross-legged, on the rug by the fire. Maleficium was already settled on Galath's lap, snoozing mightily with her paws stretched out toward the fire's warmth.

"The witches will consider it," said Hari, before Galath had even looked at them or spoken. "They'll come here if they're willing."

"If they turn on us, you understand what I'll have to do," said Galath, voice even.

"I do," said Hari. "But it won't come to that."

"You're not going to need to kill them," said Vina.

Galath stroked Maleficium's ears and said nothing.

She leaned back against the wall, far from the fireplace.

"We need to do more," she said. "This isn't enough."

"There may be no way through in this lifetime," Galath replied.

"There has to be. I'll find it. I have to believe that."

"Do you think you're wiser than all the cunning folk and witches we've spoken to, Vina?" her father asked, voice soft.

Her father. In that moment he truly felt like he was, but there was also a queer roiling under her feet and in her limbs. It was the sure, true knowledge that Galath was also a man who'd once been a cruel, murderous stranger to her—who'd almost taken her life, when she'd offered it up to his gleaming axe.

But he'd rocked her to sleep. Cut her hair for her. Helped her feed the rabbits herbs, and taught her the names of the mushrooms that grew in the ancient forest.

He'd never been cruel to her in this life.

"I think I've got hope," she said. "And you've lived too long to hope the way I do. That's okay."

Galath did not reply. Maleficium rolled over in his lap and purred.

Hari and Galath took the bedroom, and Vina took the sofa, butter-soft under her. The blanket was warm. She should have slept like a baby, but some instinct kept her awake. When the bells rang for midnight, she slipped off the sofa and went to the window. The Thames was visible out there—silvery, strange, tale-spun. Reflecting off its surface tonight were small lights at the docks. They flickered in and out, bright and strange.

Will-o'-the-wisps. Sent to lead travelers astray. But Vina needed to leave the beaten path if she was going to find a way forward. She quietly slipped on her coat, her sword, opened the door, and headed out.

The docks were slick with water, the wind icy. A witch was waiting for her, silver-black hair rippling in the wind.

"Knight," said Sarah. "I was hoping I could speak to you alone."

"Well, I'm here," said Vina.

"The fae court are still wroth with you," said Sarah, after a beat. "They blame you for breaking your word to them—a great crime among their kind. And they blame you for the death of Lady Tristesse. I know things about them. Everyone says it, in the secret markets and darkest places in London: 'Sarah has connections with the fae court. The lords and ladies are willing to parlay with her.' I thought that's why you sought me out, to get their forgiveness or some such. Not that it would have done you much good. But I suppose not. You must have been keeping well hidden, to stay so sheltered from their teeth and claws."

"Why would you work for them?" Vina asked. "Is power so important to you?"

"Power's everything," said Sarah. "But when I was young I wanted it for me. All of it. I didn't know any better. And it almost broke me—I near died when I lost all that sweet, powerful magic the Lady Tristesse gave to us. I still hunger for it in my bones. But I only make small deals with fae now. I parlay as a witch, not as a vassal or thrall. And I do it to keep my coven fed and cared for. There's power in numbers—in community. Though you, standing in love, murderous and alone—I suppose you don't know that."

Sarah shrugged. Went on.

"What you *should* know is the fae hold grudges until the stars burn out. I told them I met you, of course. And now they have your hair, they can find you."

A different kind of cold than the wind through the docks ran through Vina. She looked around, reaching for her blade hilt—and heard Sarah laugh.

"You're too well protected here, you silly fool," said Sarah. "No fae are going to jump out at you. There are wards sewn into your shirt. Did you not know? You'll want to leave those behind if you don't want to be followed. Someone powerful loves you very much."

"Why would I give up any protection against the fae?" Vina said immediately.

"Because you want the witch," said Sarah. "*Your* witch. The Queen's holding a ball where she'll display all her incarnates like pretty baubles, and if you leave your guards and your wards behind you, I can get you in."

Her heart was in her throat. Her blood suddenly felt golden.

*Simran.*

"It's a trap, of course," Sarah went on. "If you go, the fae will collect you. You'll be undefended there, and surrounded by people who don't wish you well. I should have come here and been nice to you—given you the invitation and let them catch you in their claws, you none the wiser. But I don't think you're an idiot. And you'll go anyway for her. I can see it in your face." She reached into her dress pocket and drew out an invitation in gold, inked onto crisp white card. "Remember—no warded clothes. And it's a masked ball. Try to make sure you dress the part."

Vina reached out and took the invitation, hope wild in her. A trap, she could manage. She could do anything for Simran.

"What would your fae friends say if they knew you'd helped me?" Vina asked. "That you warned me?"

"They'll reward me," Sarah said flatly. "I'm sending you into their trap just like they asked. I'm just doing it honestly. That's more than I owe you, so I hope you'll consider my debt paid."

Vina stared down at that white card, those gold letters. It was hard to look away.

"I still want you for the quest I spoke of," said Vina. "I'd still like your help to destroy the archives. I know not all witches use magic in the same way, but I've seen your kind summon fire. I know you have a gift for destruction." Vina raised her head. "Destruction can bring new life," she said. "I've seen it. I believe in it. Your magic could help save us all. I don't ask you because it'll pay any debt between us. I ask because it's right."

Sarah shook her head.

"If you survive the Queen's ball *and* the fae court, then perhaps the coven will consider it," said Sarah. "But I have my doubts. Good luck, sir knight. You're going to need it."

# Chapter Twenty-Nine

## *The Witch*

*I feel sorry for the girl, really. In her tale she's a hero, a protector of the poor, but all anyone can talk about is the whole business of riding naked on a horse clothed in nothing but her own loose hair.*

*I suppose it's better than being an evil witch, but not by much.*

Source: Letter from Lady Sandra Perinault-Stafford to Miss Anna Carshalton

The Witch had always worn the same kind of dress to the Queen's balls: a gown as black and austere as any archivist's robe, only changed out for a new one when she outgrew the last. So she wasn't sure what to make of it when Aunt Meera stormed in and threw a new gown on her bed.

"The Queen's women insisted," Meera said, displeased.

"The ladies-in-waiting *spoke*?" the Witch asked, thinking of those silent women in their vizards. "I didn't think they could."

"No, they didn't speak. They brought the dress directly to the Tower and handed it to me." She glared down at the offending garment. "If it doesn't fit, we're going to have to pin you in."

An apprentice archivist, with her blond hair in a coif, glided in with pins. Apparently it was already time to start getting dressed.

The Witch, without any particular self-consciousness, started shrugging off her dress.

The kind of gowns worn at these balls required assistance to be worn, thanks to the placement of the minuscule, finicky, pearly buttons at the collars and spine. This dress was even more elaborate—a waterfall of midnight blue, with a girdle of spun gold over silk. The sleeves were twofold: long, billowing outer sleeves, over gloves that met in a diamond at a single fingertip on each hand. It was a witch's gown, an *enchantress's* gown. The neck was high, dark cloth meeting a fine spiderweb lace as delicate as frost, beaded with tiny facets of silver. The buttons at the sleeves and spine were tiny arrows of silver with matching loops to hold them in place.

The apprentice archivist assisted her as Meera paced the room. The dress was too loose, and did indeed need some careful pinning and sewing to keep it in place. The Witch wondered if she'd be able to get out of it when the evening ended, stitched as she was.

The apprentice stopped with a sigh when she reached the fragile collar of the dress.

"I don't quite know how to fix this," the apprentice said, with a curl to her lip, as if she wanted everyone to know that *she* knew this work was beneath her.

Meera huffed out a breath.

"Go, then," she said. With a bow that was on the edge of insult, the apprentice left the room.

Aunt Meera's mouth tightened. The Witch pretended not to notice, as she always did when those little insults stung Meera like barbs. Meera picked up needle and thread and grasped the back of the gossamer, high collar of the Witch's dress, which was currently rumpled around her throat.

"Sit," she said.

The Witch sat down at one of her mirrors, on a stool, so that Aunt Meera could lean forward and make sense of the collar's shape. The Witch forced herself to remain still, despite the cold of the needle, the weight of Meera's hands.

"Why does the Queen want me dressed up?" the Witch asked. "Why is this ball important?"

"Why do you have so many questions? All I want you to do today is behave."

The Witch met her own eyes in the glass—dark in the blurred surface.

"I always behave," the Witch lied.

"You don't have a good history with banquets and balls," Meera muttered under her breath, looking through the array of pins on the table so she could bind the loose collar gems in place.

"I don't?"

Meera paused. In the glass, her forehead was furrowed, jaw a little tight. She'd said something she hadn't intended to.

"Never mind that," Meera said after a beat. "The Queen demands you go, so you'll go." She dragged the Witch's hair, scraping it back into a painful knot. A truly archivist hairstyle. In her mirror, the Witch's face looked unpleasantly sharp with all the hair pulled back, baring her bones. But there was no point arguing with Meera, so the Witch simply bit down on her tongue and endured.

"Take this," said Meera. She shoved an item into the Witch's hands.

The Witch raised it up. It was a mask—carefully crafted to cover half a face, with ribbons to tie it back around a skull, leaving the lower half of the face bare. The mask was covered in facets of bronze, each polished to an intense shine, apart from the point that would lie between her eyes. That was a diamond of silver: a true mirror, reflective and sparkling.

The Witch raised it up.

"It's a masked ball?"

"A masquerade, Witch," Meera said dryly. "Try to use the correct terminology." She examined the Witch critically. "There. You're done."

The Witch stared at her own reflection. She held the mask to her face. She felt like a stranger. *I am going to be put on display*, she realized. *That's all I am: an item to be laid before the Court.*

"Thank you," she said.

\* \* \*

Tales were full of ritual. The archivists had taught her that. And there was indeed a ponderous weight of ritual to the Queen's balls. Feasting and revelry were tangled in tales, stitched into stories of midwinter and the sweltering height of spring. So the Witch knew that every ball the Queen held had a purpose. Today, the purpose was displaying incarnates.

The ballroom was a large circular hall, with a marble floor checkered with squares of rose quartz between ivory. High crystal chandeliers glimmered brightly, strung with dozens of small candles that filled the air with the sweet smell of beeswax. Musicians, set in the outer curve of the room, were playing cellos and violins. The courtiers were dressed in long gowns with billowing skirts, coiffed hair, and long jackets and trousers, all of them in half masks of various designs: serpents, or birds; flourishes of gemstones, or velvet masks studded with gold.

Dressed like a witch from the mists of ancient mountains, the Witch stood out like a sore thumb. Once she'd been presented before the Queen—and bowed low, and been urged to stand—she made her way to the edge of the hall. The other incarnates were just as visible as her, dressed in incongruous garb, not the tale of the ball itself, but for *their* tales. Owain, in a sleeveless tunic, and a green mask; Mrs. Bell, in her wimple, a faux blindfold over her soothsayer eyes. Emmeline, with her long braid of golden hair and her fine dress, looked better than all of them, but she was still being laughed at from behind courtiers' hands. It was a shame she blushed easily. The tale of Lady Godiva was a hard one to carry for a girl like her.

The Witch saw the girl who was a wyrm, a dragon-scaled mask over her eyes. Her gown was dark brown, but not dull—a lustrous, coppery velvet with long sleeves and a ruffled collar. She looked ill at ease, alone at the edge of circling dancers, who whirled and laughed in the center of the hall. Her eyes met the Witch's, and the Witch jerked her head. *Join me.*

The girl made her hesitant way toward the Witch, then moved to stand beside her. "I saw you at the Queen's court," she said. She said it like she wasn't entirely sure, so the Witch nodded.

"You handled it well," said the Witch. "The first time I met the Queen I almost cried."

"I wanted to," the girl said. She shifted foot to foot, as if she couldn't remain still. "They dragged me here. They took me from my *home*. How do you stand it?"

"It's just how my life's always been." She turned to look at the girl through her mask. "I'm the Witch. What's your name?"

The girl stared at her.

"That's your *name*?"

The Witch shrugged.

"I suppose so," said the Witch. "I was never given a different one. The archivists raised me, and that's what they call me. But that won't happen to you," she said, aiming for reassuring—and probably missing the mark by a good mile. "They won't touch your name. And once your tale begins, the archivists and Queen alike will leave you be."

Every word the Witch spoke made the girl look more hunted. But she swallowed, and after a moment said, "I'm—I'm Margaret."

"Nice to meet you, Margaret," the Witch said.

Margaret hesitated.

"I think," she said tentatively. "That I knew you once."

The Witch stared back at her. She could feel that voice clamoring at the back of her skull. *You do, you do, you know her—*

"You didn't," she said flatly.

Maybe she was colder than she'd intended to be, because Margaret flinched. Then her mouth firmed, and she walked away with a muttered apology, her shoulders bowed.

The Witch forced back her squirming guilt. Her brain felt like it was full of fire. She fixed her eyes on the dancers instead, their bodies hazy under the smoky lights.

She was rarely, if ever, asked to dance. There was an incarnate boy who'd danced with her stiffly at balls when they were eight, nine, ten—and then she'd never seen him again. He'd gone to serve his tale, she was told. She assumed he was dead now.

So she paid little attention when a figure moved toward her. When they bowed she finally looked at them—their lowered head, their outstretched hand, long-fingered and brown-skinned, adorned with rings.

"Lady Witch," a voice said. Low, smooth. It reminded her of good wine—rubylike, rich. "Will you dance with me?"

"I'd rather not," she said stonily.

"Please," the voice said.

So the Witch finally met the stranger's eyes.

The face before her, partially hidden by a black mask, was beautiful: an angular jaw, and a mouth easily given to smiles—curly dark brown hair, tied back, to reveal ears pierced with gold hoops.

She sucked in a breath, and took in an unmistakable scent of apples, golden wheat, *incarnate*.

"Knight," she whispered.

"Witch," said her knight, had still outstretched. "Please?"

The Witch, numbly, placed her hand in the knight's own. They moved like the tide was carrying them.

They were drifting swiftly across the ballroom floor, twirling in dizzying circles. This dance was far preferable to her than the pavane, which she had also danced in the past. It was a glittering, dizzying business to the sound of violins and cellos, the crescendo of her own heart.

Her tale was her death, surely; but it was also her freedom from the archives. She felt as if she were soaring.

The knight was looking at her. The knight's hands were on her—points of heat at her waist, her arm.

"Simran," she said. "I see you."

A heartbeat, stumbling; a breath that didn't quite fill her lungs.

*Simran.*

"I don't know who you think I am," said the Witch frostily. "But that isn't me. Why are you here?"

"Why do you think I am?"

"I don't like guessing games."

"We're at a party," the strange woman said, voice full of unspent laughter. "Games are traditional, aren't they? And incarnates are traditional too. I hear the Queen loves to gather all the evidence of her power around her. Are you so sure I wasn't invited?"

"I would have known if they found you," whispered the Witch. "They would have told me. They would have held this ball for you, not another incarnate. You're an interloper. An incarnate on the run."

"I am," the knight said easily. "You've caught me. I came here uninvited."

"If I cried out now, you'd be captured by the Queen's knights and brought to heel. You'd be taught your place."

"Is my place really here? Is yours?" They whirled. The knight's eyes were on her. "Why didn't you run?" she asked. "Why didn't you come to find me?"

"Why have you come to find me now?" the Witch asked.

"I've come to save you," said the knight. Under the diamond of her mask, her eyes were deep brown, sparkling with charm. She fair oozed it. Her smile was easy, liquid—it made the Witch's own limbs tremble.

It wasn't the woman's charm that made the Witch wary. She had met charming people before; the Queen's court was heaving with them, and even some archivists had social graces. What disturbed her, and made her hackles rise, was that the charm was working on *her*. She had to resist the mortifying urge to smile in return.

"I am not a maiden in distress," replied the Witch.

"I hear you live in a tower," the woman said in a low voice. "That sounds pretty 'maiden in distress' to me."

"This isn't how we should meet, knight," hissed the Witch. "By... by dancing at a ball and you—you offering to run away with me."

"Is it not?"

"No."

"Then how do we meet?" the knight asked, gaze searching. "How do we begin our cursed tale? Tell me, lady witch."

"On a mountain," said the Witch. "The Copper Mountains. And I—I make you love me, I bewitch you with mirrors—"

"Ah," the knight breathed. Real sorrow flickered in those mask-shadowed eyes. "You don't remember that either." Her hand clasped the Witch's own as the music died, and the dancers stopped with fluttering laughter. "Come with me," said the knight. "I'll explain everything."

She was being manipulated, she knew. And yet it did nothing to stop the curiosity rising through her. She nodded. The knight beamed, and tugged her along, their fingers still intertwined.

Sir Edmund stood in the corner of the ballroom. She saw his eyes fix on her—saw those eyes widen, as he saw her leaving the ballroom with a masked woman guiding her away. But he didn't move.

In a matter of seconds, she and the knight were beyond the hall, and she could no longer see Edmund at all.

"There used to be a maze here," said the knight, turning in a slow circle.

"The Queen had it destroyed years ago," said the Witch. "It angered her, or some such. But she's a monarch. She's allowed to have strange foibles." She paused, then said, "Look at me."

The knight looked—and the Witch shoved her roughly to the ground.

She clutched her knife, previously tucked into her girdle, and held it to the knight's throat.

Her knight, her stranger, began to laugh.

"You did change our tale," said the knight. "This is new."

"I'm taking you," said the Witch. She held the knife closer to the knight's neck. It was her fist she pressed against that throat, not the blade. She didn't really want to hurt her. The Witch was shaking, hot with adrenaline, intensely aware of the knight's body bracketed by her thighs; the heat of her, and the unafraid curve of her mouth. "Taking you to the Queen—where you belong."

"Why a weapon, when you have magic? You're not as good with knives as I am."

"Are you boasting?"

"It's only the truth," said the knight. "But I can't fight your magic."

"Here's the truth," the Witch said, leaning in closer. "It's not a weapon made for slitting throats. It's a bookbinding knife. But all I needed was to distract you so I could bespell you, and that's what I've done."

Clouds cleared overhead, unveiling the moon.

"We're not where the tale requires us to be," the knight said breathlessly. "You can't magic me under your heel quite yet."

"Can't I?" She leaned down, touched her free hand to the bodice of her gown. Her fingers caught the chain of the necklace around her own throat, looped over the fine lace of her gown.

"I've lived a lifetime in these archives," said the Witch. "I have boiled glue and cut paper and sewn spines. I've been a surgeon of tales. And I've read every single one that passed under my hands. I know what binds tales of witches like me and lovelorn knights like you into shape. Enchantment."

The pendant of her necklace was a miniature mirror, just one circle of silver. That was what she drew up, tilting its surface until it caught the moonlight. Wicked, wicked witch that she was, she'd snare the knight and take her to Aunt Meera, or to the Queen herself. She'd prove herself worthy of her tale. She'd help save the Isle.

The moonlight caught, and she whispered a spell. The light touched the knight's face like an arrow. Her eyes glowed, briefly, silver.

The knight's mouth parted.

"So you have me," she said, lax now under the Witch's grip, her knife. "What are you planning to do with me now that I'm under your thrall?"

"Make you serve our tale, of course."

"Is that what you truly want?"

The Witch's voice froze in her throat, her hand loosening on the bookbinding knife, as the knight's arms encircled her. It was one thing to be held while dancing—another entirely to be embraced on the cold grass under moonlight.

There was so much affection, so much trust, in the way the knight held the Witch—and none of it was earned. All of it was false. Those hands drew her in closer and she went, mesmerized—as if she were the one under thrall.

No one had ever touched her like this. She was like parched soil for the rain of tenderness.

"I told you," the knight breathed against her lips. "I'm not so easily placed under anyone's power."

She moved so swiftly the Witch had no chance to react. The knife was gone from her hands, flung across the grass. The knight had her pinned.

"Come with me," said the knight. "Don't stay here with them."

"Let me go," the Witch snarled. She moved to punch the knight, and the knight rolled away from her. In the scuffle, the knight's mask had come undone, baring brown eyes, a gold-brown face, those askew curls. The charm was gone from her eyes—they were suddenly fierce, full of entreaty.

"You set this all into motion," said the knight. "You released the Eternal Prince. You want all the tales of the Isle to be free to change, including our own! Please, I know it's hard to trust me, but you must try." She held out a hand. "Trust yourself," said the knight. "Trust what you sacrificed, trust the plans you made."

A strange memory washed over her, so visceral it felt like it lived in her skin: the knight with a thousand different faces, trusting her, always trusting her. The knight, dying in sparks of ink alongside her. A promise, the feeling of love threatening to soar in her chest.

The Witch hesitated.

"Lady Witch," a musical voice said. "What strange company you keep!"

Three fae had appeared, as if from nowhere. The tallest of them was a woman, her face angular, her eyes the color of burning coals. She strode toward them, examining the bared face of the knight closely.

Lady Wren, of the House of Fae Lords.

"Ah, not so strange after all," said the fae. "She is your other half. I understand now." The lady ran her fingertip slowly through the air by the knight's cheek, almost a benediction. "Are you here when you shouldn't be, little knight? Drawn here like a moth to a pretty flame?" Her gaze suddenly fixed on the Witch. "We can deal with this one," the fae said cordially. "Be on your way, Witch. We'll take care of your knight."

One of the other fae, with skin the color of stone, grasped the knight by the shoulder.

The knight did not move. Her eyes had turned suddenly flinty.

"I must take her to the archivists and the Queen," said the Witch. "It's my duty."

"The fae court will deal with this one," said Lady Wren. "Go on your way, Witch."

"No," the Witch said flatly.

"You don't trust us?" the third fae asked. A smile played on his mouth.

"You cannot harm her," said the Witch. "She's mine."

"Would we harm an incarnate?" Lady Wren said, touching a hand to her chest in shock. "The lifeblood of the Isle? You insult our honor, Witch."

The Witch stared at them sullenly. She didn't want to leave the knight here. Her fingers itched with magic. The mirror at her neck was burning with intent.

"Go," the knight said softly. "I'll be fine."

"Go back to your archivists," Lady Wren cajoled. "Tell Apollonius I send my regards."

It was a reminder of how power sat in her life. The archivists had it, and the fae, and the Queen's court. The Witch had none of it.

"I will," the Witch said. "I'll see you soon, Knight."

"I promise you will," the knight said steadily.

The Witch hesitated one last time, then turned to go.

The knight did not call out for her as she walked off. For some reason that gave her a terrible pang. It was not something the Witch should have wanted. She was the one who'd walked away, after all. She was the one who didn't look back.

# Chapter Thirty

## *Vina*

*If you've got more advice on how to fight a fae than "stab it in the gut with some cold iron," then I'll gladly print you more pamphlets. Until then, I'll stick to printing works longer than a sentence. Ta.*

Source: Letter from Jen Cranmer to Solomon Roy

Vina had known this would happen. Sarah had *warned* her. But it was still unpleasant to be dragged along by two fae, as Lady Wren walked ahead of them, as grand and ponderous as a ship, her hair coiling strangely with the shifting wind.

She clenched her own hands together, the left over the right. She could feel her rings against her palm: each a perfect circle of cold iron. The one on her index finger was thicker than the rest, and carried a needle of iron that could be released with the correct pressure from her thumb. It was the closest thing she'd have to a blade, wherever they took her.

The fae hands on Vina's shoulders were as ice cold and firm as any shackle. They didn't drag her back into the ballroom—she could see the lights through the vast oval windows, the dancing figures. Instead, they led her away from the Queen's Palace to the Palace of Westminster, through the darkness of familiar streets. Folk who saw them lowered their heads and scuttled away. People had the good sense to avoid the few fae allowed by the Queen in London. She felt nauseated as she was led into Westminster, where she crossed the checkerboard floors, beneath the smoke of candlelight. Was her father—she supposed he was still her father, in a sense—was he here? Her gaze naturally turned toward the corridor where his office had once been.

She hadn't even thought to ask Hari or Galath about him. Even now, the thought of finding out what had become of him made words stopper up in her throat, like wine beneath a cork.

Twenty years had passed since then. Perhaps he'd finally retired. Perhaps he was dead. When she'd had no memories, and she'd been living a happy life in a small town, she hadn't concerned herself much with the minutiae of politics. She regretted that now.

There was a giant door ahead of them—taller and wider than any group of humans would require. The surface was filigree, winding shapes of trees and waves and mountains swirling into one another like a grand tapestry on the Isle's shape and history. When the ministers and clerks who kept the well-oiled cogs of government whirring traversed the corridors of the Palace of Westminster, they all had the good sense to officiously avoid the House of Lords. Inside its doors lay terrors and glories that rose from the deepest, darkest tales.

Lady Wren waved a hand. The doors of the House of Fae Lords opened with a hissing withdrawal of roots, and the fae dragged her in.

It was a square hall, high-roofed with windows of stained glass set above wood-paneled walls. The wooden walls were cut through with mushrooms—virulent, bright things of red and yellow and green that grew in circles and spirals that drew Vina's eyes like a hook to a fish. She wrenched her gaze away. She knew the magic of enchantment when she saw it.

The hall was full of inhuman figures, seated on long benches of bloodred, more clusters of mushrooms carpeting benches of wizened wood. Those creatures were nymphs and dryads, wrinkled goblins, and sharp-toothed redcaps, all gathered together at the feet of tall, graceful, and luminously frightening fae lords and ladies and lieges. A ceremonial throne headed the hall, placed high on a golden plinth. It was empty, and always empty. The Queen never graced fae chambers.

Alder, the fae liege, was waiting for them, their eyes burning, mouth thin.

She was reminded, suddenly, that time moved differently for the fae. Humans died. Fae lived as long as the Isle. Tristesse's death must have been a raw and recent wound to them, even though decades had passed.

"Knight," said Alder. "You broke your promise to me. You placed yourself in my debt, and then when your debt was called due, you refused to pay it." Their jaw tightened, their chin raised. Fire lay behind their eyes. "My niece demanded your service," they said. "Your love, and your fealty. She asked you to serve, and instead you broke the last vestiges of her tale in your fist." Their voice was ice. "Lady Tristesse is gone. And you are to blame. The time has come for you to face judgment."

The fae rustled, eyes fixing on her as one. She could feel their power—an intense, immovable weight. She couldn't have moved if she tried.

"Lady Tristesse did not die by my hand," said Vina. "She died because her tale was dead, and there was no hope of saving it. I am not to blame."

"Lies," said Alder. "See how the knight tells falsehoods before the court? She must be eaten by redcaps. Her blood must run forth on these hallowed grounds."

Vina looked down at the ground. It was carpeted with moss such a dark green that it was near black.

"As much as I hate to claim I lie in her power, the Queen would say I belong to her, as all incarnates do," said Vina. "Can you pass judgment without her input?"

A fae woman in the benches laughed, silvery as bells.

"It is not the Queen's throne," she said. "It is the monarch's throne, child. Monarchy is an old tale, bloodied and deep in the Isle's ancient bones—but the one who wears the crown can be easily replaced, and, it seems, soon will."

"It makes no difference to us if the Eternal Prince takes the throne, or the Eternal Queen retains it," said Alder. "It does not change what we are—great beings of the Isle, worshipped and bargained with, feared and loved. And it does not change that you trespassed against our court, and it is our court's judgment you must face."

"You don't care, then, if the Isle lives or dies," said Vina. "You know the importance of the tale of The Knight and the Witch. Would you imperil everything?"

"You allowed the Merciless Maiden to perish, and all the land that required her to survive," said Alder, their eyes glittering. "Your tale cannot be more valuable than one that bound a fae."

Murmurs of agreement rippled through the room.

"Fine," Vina said into the silence. "Then I refute your claim to my debt. I promised a debt to your blood, it's true. But I promised it in return for knowledge, and you did not give it to me. You lied, Liege. The geas you laid was created through falsehood."

Alder's eyes flashed. "You would call me false?" The air around them crackled with violet light—spiderwebs of lightning, the threat of a storm.

"Hush," a croaking voice said.

This fae was not as preternaturally youthful as the others—instead she was ancient, ancient as the stones of the Isle or the primordial forest that stretched across the Isle's breadth. "The knight must speak," said the ancient creature, her claws of wood and pearly nails clinging to the bench, holding her steady. "She must defend herself. She accuses you of a great heresy, Liege. Truth and half-truth are the business of the fae. Lies are a mortal curse." Her eyes, the color of acid beneath a halo of wrinkles, fixed on Vina. "Speak, knight."

"You claimed the pale assassin was the cause of the Isle's withering," said Vina.

"I did not," replied Alder, triumphant. "I told you he had killed incarnates. That is true. You assumed, as mortals do, that he was responsible for the Isle's slow death."

As the fae laughed and rippled with comment, Vina twined her clasped fists behind her back—and slowly began to seek out the hinge in the ring on her index finger.

"You told me the witch could bring about the pale assassin's death," she said. "And yet he still lives."

"I told you she could end his immortality," said Alder. "*Could.* What the witch chose to do is no concern of mine. I gave you truth. I gave you knowledge. You did not pay your debt to my blood."

"She will be judged," the ancient fae said. "What price would you beg for, Liege Alder?"

Alder's lip was curled into a sneer. Grief and rage radiated from them.

"I demand her death," they said.

"A vote will be called," said the fae. "Those who yield to Liege Alder's call for the knight's death: cry *content*. Those who do not: *not content*."

Voices yelled across the House. Fists were waved. Some of the redcaps clambered up onto the benches, standing at their full height.

Before the vote was called, Alder was already smiling.

"Content has it," said the ancient fae. She turned to Alder.

"Her life is yours, to take or spare at your will," said the ancient fae. "But we will not sully the court. Take her beyond. Kill her among your namesake trees, and let her corpse feed their roots." Her hand of wood became a gavel, which she slammed upon the mossy ground. It shook like a rung bell. The door to the House of Fae Lords peeled open in a slither of vines and a groan of wood.

"It will be done," said Alder. Their dryads rose from the benches, gathering around them with silvery malevolence in their eyes.

Vina was starting to think she had made a mistake. But this was the best opportunity she'd have.

She punched the first dryad who approached her with her iron-ringed fingers. Her needle drew silver blood.

The dryad reacted like any human would, flailing with its fist. Its hand met Vina's jaw before she could duck away, but the pain was manageable. What she needed to do was get away right *now*.

And that was what she did. She rolled with the punch and wrangled herself free from the fae holding her. The doors of the House were parted. She leapt through them and bolted.

"I will find you!" Alder roared behind her, their voice the howl of the wind, the moan of deep caverns. It was a promise written in blood.

Twenty years away from London, and somehow her body still knew it. She took some grim amusement in that. She ran deep into the city, from wide streets into snaking alleys, only stopping when her legs nearly gave out beneath her.

A broad figure emerged from the smog, dressed in dark clothing—a serviceable greatcoat, patched at the elbows.

"Father," she said, before she could stop herself. She felt a reflexive embarrassment—and a fear, strangely, that Galath would refute it.

If his eyes softened a little it was, perhaps, her imagination. His voice was certainly cold enough when he said, "You're injured."

"I'm fine," Vina said. She brought her hand up and knuckled away the blood dripping from her lip. "I dealt with them."

"Hm," said Galath.

"How did you find me?" Vina asked. "I removed my warded clothing."

"Witches can follow anything if they have flesh, blood, bone," said Galath. "Hari and I have all your milk teeth."

"Ah," Vina said faintly. That was...horrifying. But parents often did embarrassing things, didn't they? "I made a bit of a fool's error there, I know," Vina said, swaying precariously on her feet. "I should have been honest with you. Or—simply not gone. But I don't regret going. I saw her. Simran." Another stumbling step forward. Godsblood, she was tired. She grabbed Galath.

There were silvery cries behind them.

"I think they may be coming," she said faintly. "Damn shame the

Queen's unlikely to enforce the laws that say they aren't allowed to chase mortals through the city. Well, they voted that they could kill me—perhaps that negates her edict?"

"Stay here," said Galath.

"If you get hurt. Papa, I mean—Hari, he—he wouldn't..."

She trailed off. That jumble of words came to nothing. Galath placed his hand, briefly, over her own. Just long enough to pry himself free.

"It's the archivists I cannot face," he said. "Their magic is mine. But the fae are not the same. Stay here."

For once, she listened. She stayed. He was gone an hour, all told. And when he returned, he'd removed his coat and slung it over his shoulder. His white shirt was...significantly less white.

Silver blood that was very much not his own dripped from his hands. She watched, oddly fascinated.

"All things can die, given the right opportunity," said Galath. "Even fae. Now come. Hari is waiting."

# Chapter Thirty-One

## *The Witch*

*Be careful of the fae. They're in a terrible temper, and their respect for the Queen is waning. If aught can be done, sir, then please do it before they have us all dancing on coals or some other rot fae enjoy.*

Source: Letter from Mary Sampson to the Spymaster

Two heartbeats after the knight and the fae had vanished, regret hit the Witch. She strode off in the direction where they'd gone, then began to run across the grass. But it was too late. The knight had disappeared. The borders of the Palace grounds were too thick with guards for the Witch to pass.

She felt dizzy; heartsick, maybe. The knight, *her* knight, had been there under her hands. And now she was gone. The Witch felt bereft and hated it.

She turned back toward the ball. If her absence had been noticed, there'd be trouble—for her, but hopefully for Sir Edmund too. If he was removed from his post guarding her, that would be one silver lining.

When she entered the ballroom her jaw tightened, stress ratcheting up inside her. The ball was quieter, the quartet playing calming music. No one was dancing. The Queen and her ladies-in-waiting were absent, and so were all the Palace incarnates. Edmund walked over to her swiftly.

"We're heading out soon," he said gruffly. "Stay here."

"The ball's barely started," said the Witch.

"Well, a bloody incarnate tried to make a run for it, didn't they? The Queen's not happy. And now the Eternal Prince has been sighted, two days' ride from London, so she's utterly lost it."

"Which incarnate?"

"The new one," said Edmund. "The one this ball is for."

The Witch looked around, scanning quickly, but there was no sign of Margaret. Meera approached, expression harried. "Come on," she said, and gestured sharply for the Witch to follow her.

They left the Palace grounds and went to their barge on the river, where a handful of knights stood guard. One of the Queen's knights, her rose symbol on his armor, a man with a red beard visible beneath his helm, came up to Sir Edmund and grasped him by the shoulder. They spoke for a long moment as the Witch stepped into the barge. Then Edmund shook his head, pulled away, and followed.

The Witch would have asked what they'd been discussing, but she didn't care enough to do so. She looked away, and thought of the knight.

Meera's expression was tight, but even though the Witch was waiting to be scolded, nothing was said. Whatever was causing Archivist Sharma dissatisfaction, apparently it was not the Witch's jaunt in the gardens with her errant knight. Somehow she'd escaped without anyone realizing who she had crossed paths with and what she'd done.

Anyone but Sir Edmund, at least. He was staring out of the barge, out at the city, expression sullen.

But she didn't want the knight to be secret. She was afraid for the knight. If she spoke now, if she said her knight was in danger, perhaps she could save her.

And yet she didn't speak; didn't say a word to Meera, or the archivists who met the barge. She said nothing as she walked back to her rooms; as Meera sent up another apprentice, who clumsily and sulkily unlaced her gown for her, then helped cut her out when they realized the sewn collar was a real problem. She dragged on a robe. In her mirrors, she watched her door open and close, and open again as Edmund entered.

That was when she finally exploded.

"I don't want you here anymore," she said, voice harsh. "You failed me, at the Queen's ball."

"Failed you, did I?" His sullenness sharpened to anger on his face. "Go on, then, Witch. Tell me how."

"You let the—the *stranger* drag me away."

"Looked like you were letting yourself be dragged," said Edmund. "And that was no stranger. I know who she was."

The Witch's hands clenched into fists.

"If you knew what she was, how could you let her go?" the Witch demanded. "She's—an incarnate, all on her own! Anything could happen to her. You allowed me to be—to be misled and enchanted. And you allowed her to be lost again. Tell the Queen you can't serve me any longer. Tell her you're not fit to be a knight, because it's the damn truth."

"I volunteered for this job," Edmund said, voice low and angry like she'd never heard it before. "Not for your sake—you're as sullen a bitch as I've ever known, *Witch*—but for hers. I gave you both time together, didn't I? God knows I owed her that, even if I don't owe you anything."

The Witch reeled. "You know her?"

"I knew her once," he said. "A lifetime ago. You really think she'd be safer trapped like you are?" He scoffed. "If you had any sense, you would have run off with her. I gave you enough time. But I can't do your thinking for you. Tell me: Do you really think your life is good, Witch? Do you think it's worth living?"

She said nothing.

"They've fucked you up, girl."

"Get out," she said.

"I'll go, then," he said. "But when you regret what you've chosen, you remember I would have helped you. And trust me, you *will* regret it. Staying here, letting them use you—that's utter bullshit."

\* \* \*

She couldn't rest. There, in her sleep clothes, she sat with her knees tucked to her chin. Finally, buzzing with adrenaline, she decided to do what she should have done all along. She went to Archivist Sharma's quarters.

She padded silently down the winding stairs of her tower, then out along the battlements. A warder nodded politely as she passed, as he made his rounds along the Tower's walls.

She walked into Aunt Meera's tower, which mirrored her own, with a winding staircase leading up to wider rooms. The first door as she entered was Meera's office, and it was shut. She listened, just beyond the door. The need to move silently, drilled into her by Aunt Meera, had made her good at sneaking. Now she could hear muddled voices. See light through the unlocked door.

Carefully, she nudged the door open a sliver and looked in.

Margaret was there, seated on a stool. Still in her gown. They'd caught her just recently, then. Around her were a milling group of archivists.

"The Laidly Wyrm is just a small tale," the girl said. Her voice was small now, tired. Her scent, without the muddle of other incarnates around them to mask it, was filled with the crash of petrichor, seafoam against rocks.

"From Bamborough, I believe," said Harry, the apprentice who was clearly studying her. His eye was monocled, his brow furrowed.

"It hurts," the girl said quietly. Looking closer, the Witch could see sweat on her skin. There was pain in her voice. One of the other archivists was doing something to her arm. The Witch couldn't quite see it.

The archivist made a triumphant noise. Stepped back. A spool of ink followed them, drawn by the urging of their hand. The ink, the Witch realized with horror, was bound to a book on the table. Her skin itched as she gazed on it. A slim volume, covered in brown leather, encircled by pulsing chains of ink. *The Laidly Wyrm.*

The Witch felt cold.

She watched the chains between the book and girl tighten. Margaret began to struggle. With a sigh, an archivist bound her to her chair with buckled straps of leather, as if her pain were no more than an inconvenience.

The Witch had seen those buckles before, on the chair Aunt Meera kept at the corner of her office. She had never thought about what they signified. A chill of horror ran through her now.

The Witch thought of the book with her own tale's title on it—that torn book, leaking ink, almost beyond repair. She thought of the other thin blue tome she'd broken free from its inky bindings. There was something here she could almost touch or understand; something about herself and the archives, a huge knowledge that could change her utterly. She wasn't sure she wanted to see it. But looking at Margaret, crying out in pain, she wasn't sure she could walk away from it either.

*We can free the girl*, a voice in her head said. *You know we can. We can free them all. Please, for once, listen to me!*

She flattened against the wall as the younger apprentices left Archivist Sharma's offices. Mercifully, they did not see her.

She stayed there, heart hammering, until she was sure no more would come or go. Then she went and peered through the keyhole.

Head Archivist Roland and Archivist Sharma stood together. Margaret sat unconscious, face white with sweat. They were talking.

"With respect, sir, the risks are too high, just as they've always been," said Meera. Her hands were clasped together, knuckles white. She looked nervous, in a way the Witch had never seen before. "We discussed this, sir: The fact she remains an incarnate at all, and true to her tale, is a miracle after the damage her tome suffered. Binding her closer to her tome may break the tale entirely, and then the Copper Mountains and all the villages that surround them will be lost."

"The Queen is fearful," said Apollonius. "The Witch has behaved. But her nature is her nature. And the archives, our canonical texts, must stand strong. We must make sure the Isle is the Isle the Queen created. We must stand by her. She asks that we try. I am skilled enough to end our binding if the Witch suffers ill effects."

"Haven't I proved myself, sir?" Meera's voice quavered, then firmed. "Rearing her, training her. If you think I've failed—"

"Not at all, not at all," Apollonius said. "You're a credit to your post. You've done far more than I thought you were capable of."

The Witch clenched her hands tight.

They were going to use that ink on her. Hurt her, as they'd hurt Margaret.

She could stay where she was, standing behind the door, and wait to be found. Or she could return to her room and delay whatever it was Apollonius intended to do with her. Either way, her first instinct was obedience.

She owed them that. The archivists had reared her, after all. They'd taught her how to be deferential. She thought of how often they had examined her, studying her pulse, her breath, her magic. *Do you know your duty? Do you feel your tale?* She'd always said yes.

But there was a smiling, masked face behind her eyes now. A ripple of knowing in her belly.

She needed to leave. She needed to *run*.

Instead, she clutched the mirror on its chain at her throat. She drew upon her magic. *Do not see me. Do not know me. I am a shadow on the wall. I am nothing.* She held her breath, and waited until the two archivists agreed Meera would collect her. They left the room, closing the door. They didn't even glance at her.

One heartbeat. Two. Three. She counted, until she knew she couldn't wait any longer, then let her magic fall away. Meera and Apollonius were as far away as she could hope. If she didn't act now, they'd be back before she could.

She went into the room and walked to the book first; if she could not fix the book, then trying to save the girl unconscious on the chair would be useless, and worse, cruel. No one wanted false hope.

There was no time to brace herself. Only panic in her chest as she grabbed the ink in her hands. It writhed under her fingers, starry and painful with heat, but she did not let go. She held on tight.

She could snap the chains around *The Laidly Wyrm* in a breath, a moment. But there was something snarled in the chains beyond what she held now in her hands. She tightened her grip and reached out with her magic, curious and seeking.

*They're like roots*, she realized. The chains ran deep, far beyond this book and this tale. She closed her eyes and felt them with her hands and her magic alike, stretching from Aunt Meera's office through the battlements, the defensive walls, into the central White Tower and the sea of incarnate books held within it. Every book in the archive was bound—every single incarnate text and tome.

All those chains were like veins and arteries in one single body. They were connected.

She'd splintered chains once before. Small chains, on a small book. But if she reached out now with all her strength... perhaps she could break every single one. Perhaps she could pierce the archives through their very heart.

Her own heart was drumming in her ears. Panic. There was no time. She had to save Margaret.

She wrenched the shallow chains around *The Laidly Wyrm*. The chains splintered—tore, with a scream through her skull, and scattered like blood across the floor.

The Witch quickly shook her hand clean, pocketed the book, then whirled round to Margaret. She unbuckled the straps on Margaret, but Margaret didn't move. Her face was pale as death.

"Margaret," she said, slapping the girl lightly on the face. There wasn't time for niceties. "Wake up. We need to go now!"

Margaret blearily opened her eyes as the Witch pulled the last buckle open. The girl sat up and said, "Witch? I... I feel lighter?"

"You should," said the Witch. "Now get up. We're escaping from here."

They made it into the corridor.

"Witch."

She stopped. Frozen, until somehow she made herself turn. Apollonius and Meera were standing at the exit from the tower, the night black behind them. "Calm yourself, Witch," said Apollonius. "Why are you running?"

Beside her, Margaret was still as a hunted hare.

"You hurt her," the Witch said flatly.

"You don't understand at all, my dear," Apollonius said soothingly. "We're helping her. We want to help you." He took a step forward, and the Witch flinched back. "Why do you behave like this, Witch? We raised you, didn't we? Treated you well? You are flawed, and we have cared for you regardless. There's no need for panic."

"P-please," Margaret whispered. Her hand, clammy with fear-sweat, gripped the Witch's wrist.

It was Margaret that snapped the Witch from her frozen stupor. She looked around them. From here, there were no ways out to an easy courtyard exit, or even the Traitor's Gate, with its way to the water. But she could climb to a window.

She gripped Margaret's arm and bolted for the winding tower staircase upward.

There were yells behind her. She ran faster, on narrow steps, the walls closing in on her.

"Your tale makes you into a wyrm," the Witch said, breathing raggedly as their footsteps thumped an erratic rhythm. "Can you choose to become one now? Fly to freedom?"

"N-no," said Margaret. "I've never—I'm meant to be cursed into it. I can't just *make* it happen!"

"Your tale lives in you," she said. "You can change it, can't you?"

"I can't," said Margaret tearily.

"You couldn't before," said the Witch. "But I think you can now. I cut those chains. That's got to mean something."

"Ch-chains?"

The Witch moved to speak—then swore, when she heard a dozen footsteps thudding on the stairs behind them.

"Faster!" she ordered.

"I can't run faster," Margaret said weakly. "They hurt me, I can't…" Her voice trailed off, mouth opening in horror, as black mist roiled down the stairs around them.

The Witch first thought she was imagining it, but there it was still, rising around her feet, up to her knees. Panic clawed at her. Was this a new trap, a way to hold them both? But no: The black mist was coalescing into a shape.

A dozen birds, first. And all of them familiar. They all looked like ravens. Like—

"Adder?" she whispered.

They converged into one creature, one monster unlike anything she'd ever seen before, with far too many clawed legs and teeth and a tail that whipped like a beastly club. It was a creature entirely made of ink. Ink spilled from its body to the floor like blood.

It looked almost human, but with giant dimensions—vast clawed hands and bared teeth; a rictus of a face, like a scream. It panted, hot breath filling the air, uncannily and undeniably alive.

"Adder," she whispered again. "Is it you?"

The creature, the monster, looked at her with a dim spark of recognition. It *screamed*.

She scrambled out of the way, barely avoiding its club of a tail as it threw itself at the archivists.

There were more screams, but human this time. The smell of blood.

One archivist pushed through the rest. A spool of ink hung from her hand, alive and writhing. She flung it at the beast, and then two more senior archivists followed her, until the beast was screaming, thrashing in chains of ink. It turned its head, and for a moment she saw its eyes turn small and liquid—the eyes of a gentle mouse, the eyes of her small friend.

*Run*, those eyes seemed to say.

The Witch did, wrenching Margaret along with her.

They were at the zenith of the turret. There were no candles lit, no torches. It was dark, and Simran crouched, heaving for breath. Margaret lay down on her side.

The Witch's eyes were dry, her heart aching. They were trapped, and Adder was...Whatever Adder was, it could not help her any longer. And soon the archivists would do something to her, and she did not know what would become of her then.

"I just want to be myself," whispered the Witch to herself, miserable.

"What a strange thing to say," said the woman in her skull, the whisper that had followed her, "when I am you."

"They changed me," the Witch replied. "They stole me from my family. They stole me from myself."

"Then why do you push me away?" the woman demanded. "Why don't you want your own memories? Your own knowledge? Why are you happy to live as a puppet and a pawn to these fucking idiots who're breaking the Isle apart for their beliefs?"

"Isn't that what you did? Didn't you break the Isle for your beliefs?"

"No," said the woman, who was the Witch, who was herself. "I freed the Isle, and I freed us. Or tried to. But there's still more to be done, and you could do it, if you'd just *remember yourself.*"

The Witch squeezed her eyes tight shut. She could hear footsteps thudding below them.

"Not yet," she whispered, small. "Not yet."

"Who are you talking to?" Margaret asked.

The Witch raised her head.

"No one," she said. "Margaret, it's not fair what I'm asking you. But if you can reach the magic inside you, the tale inside you, tell it you'll only play your role if it helps you escape this place. And if it doesn't, you'll—"

"Jump from the window?" Margaret's gaze was unflinching. Her hands were fists. "Because I will. I see my old self in my head, sometimes—she's just an echo, but she's so *angry*. With the archivists, with everything. I won't let the archivists hurt me again. For her, and for me."

The window was wide enough for both of them to wiggle

awkwardly through it. The drop below was…very far, and met ground, not the welcome of water. The Witch met Margaret's eyes.

"Tell your tale that if it won't help you, I'll pull you from the window," said the Witch. "It'll save you from the fall. The tale wants to live. If you die, it dies with you."

"Are you sure it will?"

Of course she wasn't.

"We're both going to have to be sure," said the Witch. "So that your tale doesn't doubt us."

They grasped hands.

"With me," said the Witch. "Three, two…"

The Witch jumped, dragging Margaret with her.

The stillness lasted a second—perhaps not even that—before the air filled with the petrichor of the tale, and Margaret transformed into a wyrm, scaled and winged. The Witch gripped on tight as the wyrm flailed in the air, dragging them toward the water instead of the hard earth. They landed in water with a crash. The Witch let go, and began to swim.

They made it to the bank, on a narrow stretch of dirty sand, Margaret still serpentine.

"Go, if you can," the Witch said hoarsely. "Fly to safety before your tale turns you back. Go home."

Margaret hesitated, staring at the Witch with yellow, seeking eyes.

"I'll be safe," said the Witch. "I have work to do in London but you—you can be free. Free to shape your tale. Isadora would want that for you. Go, for her sake."

With that, Margaret flew away. And the Witch clambered laboriously to her feet. She didn't know who Isadora was. Her head ached. But none of that mattered right now. Right now, she was running, as far from the Tower as she could.

# Chapter Thirty-Two

## *Vina*

*You asked me why I was sad. You know how it is. I dreamt of her again. Mary. Her strange legs, her golden talons. I dreamt she was flying across London, with the sun at her back, and she was laughing. I hope wherever her soul's gone, she gets to fly like that. That's all, really.*

Source: Letter from Ella Blackwood to Oliver Pryce

Hari was wroth with her, but doing his best not to show it. He'd handed back the hagstone charm Vaughan had given her—"It seems you somehow misplaced this, Vina. Strange"—and though his voice had been mild, his eyes had been daggers. Still, Vina felt somewhere between elated and miserable. She'd seen Simran. Held her.

"So she doesn't know herself," Hari said flatly. "And she threatened to stab you with a knife."

"A bookbinding knife," Vina said. "That's almost like not trying to stab me at all. It was sweet."

Hari buried his face in his hands.

"She's home safe," Galath said, which Vina realized was his attempt at comfort.

"I know," Hari said. "I know. Wash your hands again, Galath. I can still see silver under your fingernails. We'll hide out here today.

In the evening, we're taking Vina to Oliver. I'm not leaving you free for a fae with your hair to track you down. You need a cunning folk's warding, Vina."

Vina, suitably chastised, went with Galath and Hari to Whitechapel, to—*hells*—a molly-house. Not the sort of place she wanted to visit with the folk who'd raised her, especially in the deep night.

The molly-house was busy, full of people of all sorts of genders and clothing, laughing and drinking, cigarette smoke clouding the entrance. Hari made his way confidently through the throng, directly to a dark-skinned older woman with long braids and a low-cut dress. Ella, the cunning woman who'd sent them to the witches in the cemetery. She was leaning over a strange device—a square with dials.

"You. Hari's girl," she said, gesturing Vina over. "You have any idea what this is, and what kind of tale it comes from?"

"No," said Vina. "What does it do?"

"Not a clue," she said.

A few regulars were leaning in, watching in fascination as the woman hit a dial and made the item blare out noise.

"I think it's playing music," one man said.

"Why does it sound so crackly, then?" another asked. "That piece of metal sticking out of it—what if you move it around?"

"Ella," said Hari. "Where's Oliver?"

"Performing," she said. "Some incarnate tales over at the Theatre Royal. I warned him not to—I'm fearful the archivists will turn their eye on it. But so far, they've been too busy hanging pamphleteers and the like. Let's hope his luck sticks. What are you doing here, Hari?"

"My Vina's caught the attention of the fae," said Hari. "They have her hair. I need her warded."

That set Ella moving. She ushered them out of the room to an office in the back, lit by a dingy excuse for a fire in the grate.

"You're lucky I'm here," she said. "Sit. Drink this tonic. And I'll touch blessings on your skin. We'll set you right."

Vina sat.

"Thank you," she said gratefully. "I know it's an awful bother."

"No bother at all."

The tonic tasted like herbs, bitter and softened only by a little honey for sweetness. The cunning woman began to murmur blessings, and light from her hands brushed Vina's skin. After a long moment, the light began to move on its own, without the need for her voice to coax it.

"It must be strange finally knowing yourself," said Ella neutrally. "Will you be seeking out your witch in this life? Killing her?"

"I won't be killing her," said Vina. "I...Our tale is changed."

"Tales changing," Ella said thoughtfully. "We've been seeing a lot more of that, haven't we? First the Eternal Prince rising up, and now—you." She paused. "There was a girl who was murdered in this building," said Ella. "Maybe Simran told you, some time in your last life. I've been assured it wasn't your father who killed her. I trust Hari enough to accept it."

That Galath hadn't earned her trust didn't surprise Vina.

"If you ever get Simran back, you tell her the girl was a kinnara," said Ella. "Her death, her being an incarnate, it all haunted me. I couldn't rest until I found what she was. I still don't know her tale's name, or what she was meant to do before her life was cut short, but at least I know what she could have been."

"I will get Simran back," said Vina.

"Yes, I suppose you will," said Ella. "Or you'll die trying. I know your kind."

Hari stopped them at the bottom of the stairs back up to Simran's flat. "Someone's up there," said Hari grimly. "They crossed the witchmarks I left on the threshold."

"I'll deal with them," said Galath.

"No," said Vina. "Look, we told the witches to meet us here. It might be them."

"The witches who sold you to the fae?" Galath replied, eyebrow raised.

"The witches who gave me a choice," Vina corrected. "And I chose to risk my life. I'm sorry I caused you harm, or frightened you. And I'm sorry you had to…" She thought of the silver blood on Galath's clothes, his knuckles. "I'm sorry," she continued, "that I have been a—a burden. But we need strength like the witches have to face the archives."

Galath's jaw was tight. He reached into his coat and drew out a dagger. He handed it to her, hilt first.

"You don't have your sword," he said. "I will follow."

Vina rose up the stairs. The door was open, the ground charred. She stopped. And stared.

"Edmund?" she said faintly. "Sarah?"

The both of them looked singed. Whatever Hari had placed in his threshold trap had hurt them both.

Sarah's wrists were lashed together, her mouth gagged. If looks could kill, Edmund would have been dead a thousand times over. Instead, he was sitting on the leather sofa, elbows on his knees, staring at Vina with a look that was half wary and half something she couldn't name. Relief, maybe. But it was foolish to think that.

The last time they'd met, he dragged her back to the Tower to wait for her death.

"Edmund," said Vina. "What are you doing here?"

"So you are still you," Edmund said. "Strange. The Queen held a funeral for you, you know. Closed casket, though." He tilted his head, examining her. "You look younger. Hell. I thought you'd look the same as I remembered you, somehow."

"You look a lot older," she said. "But not as bad as I thought you would. Chin up!" The quips that came so naturally once felt stilted in her mouth. Her heart was hammering. "Why have you got a witch tied up?"

"I was at the Palace," said Edmund evenly. "Got sent home from a post I didn't much want anymore anyway. Looking after your bitch of a witch, at the Tower, by the way. And then I found *this* witch skulking around the Palace's walls, trying to find a way in. She said she was looking for you. We had a long chat over a blade, and I told her I'd let her go if she told me where to find you."

Vina looked at Sarah's bound arms, then looked back at Edmund.

"I didn't say when I'd let her go, did I," said Edmund. Then Edmund stiffened, reaching for his sword hilt in a quick motion. He rose to his feet.

Behind her, she heard Galath's soft tread as he slipped into the room.

"Oh, don't mind me," Galath said, voice low. "Pretend I'm not here."

"Put the sword away, Eddie," said Vina.

"It won't do you any good," agreed Galath, voice almost unpleasant. Uncanny. It was like listening to a predator imitate the sounds of its prey. "You can gut me through, and I'll still break your neck."

"Maybe you should try, then," snarled Edmund.

Vina raised her hands in a placating gesture.

"Behave yourself, lads," she said mildly. "I have some questions that need answering before anyone guts anyone. Where is Simran? Is she all right?"

"Still with the archivists. She's not smart enough to know she should run," said Edmund. "I tried to convince her, but she's all piss and vinegar—there's no moving her."

"You were trying to...move her?" Vina asked. "Save her?"

"Yes."

"Why?"

"It's been a long time," Edmund said heavily. "And I've thought about you—what we did to you—a hell of a lot. Me and Matthias, we thought we were doing the right thing bringing you back to London. We thought it'd feel right eventually. But it never did." He swallowed, shifting uncomfortably. "We tried to visit you in the Tower, but no one was allowed in. Only your dad, I think. The next we heard, it was your funeral. I thought...I thought, it was like sending you out to be slaughtered to keep us alive. Like you were a sheep instead of a person. Doesn't seem honorable, does it?"

Vina's throat was dry. No one had ever told her, she realized, how unjust her death was. She hadn't thought anyone would grieve her. And yet here he was, Edmund, hotheaded Edmund, with lines of grief around his mouth and a slump to his shoulders, like he'd carried the guilt of her death all these long years. As if she deserved to be remembered.

"I thought I'd get her out because it's what you'd want," said Edmund. "And then I saw you at the ball. You, with her." A bitter laugh. "You should have run off with her then. I don't know why you bloody didn't. So when *this* one turned up, I knew I'd have to find you and tell you to sort yourself out." He gestured at Sarah.

Vina took a step toward him.

"How should I sort myself out?" Vina asked.

"You should run," said Edmund bluntly. "Go where the Queen can't find you. Or the Prince. I can feel him—we all can. He's going to be impossible not to love, but terrible with it. I don't know that he'll be any good for your kind either. So get out of here while you can."

"I'm not going to," she said. "I can't do that, Eddie."

"I should have known," he muttered.

"And Matthias?" Vina asked. "Does he...feel like you do?"

A shadow passed over Edmund's face.

"Matthias has got a good heart, you know that," said Edmund. "And he knows that. But sometimes, blokes like him, they can't face it when they've done evil. They have to convince themselves they did what was right. He's at the Queen's right hand, and I'm here. That's how it is."

Vina ignored the twist of her heart at that. Matthias had always been the best of them—the kind one, the peacemaker, the friend to everyone. But time changed all people.

"If you want to help me, there's something I need to do," said Vina. "But I don't think you're going to want to. I need to destroy the archives. I wouldn't ask for myself alone. But for all the other incarnates who're trapped—for Simran too—I'm asking you, Edmund. If you've worked in the Tower, served in it—if you're still trusted—can you get me in? Can you help me burn it all down?"

Edmund stared at her. And stared.

"And that'll...help you?" he asked finally.

"It will free me," Vina said. "It's how the Queen controls all tales. In truth, I believe it will save the Isle."

Edmund nodded, jaw tightening.

"Fuck it," he said. "If that's what you need, I'll help. Vina, the truth is—hell, the truth is, I've regretted what I did to you all my fucking life."

"It's fine, Eddie," she said. "I forgive you."

"Just like that?"

"Yeah," she said. Her heart ached. "Just like that."

He took a cautious step closer to her. They looked at each other, unsure what to do.

"Eddie," she said. "Just one last thing."

"What?"

"How's your sister doing?"

He punched her in her arm. She deserved it.

"The witch is still tied up," Galath said. Vina startled. She'd almost forgotten he was there. He was eyeing Sarah coolly, and she in return had gone silent, a hunted look in her eyes. "What do you want to do with her, Vina?"

"Nothing," Vina said hurriedly. She went over to Sarah, removing the gag. "I'm sorry," Vina said, carefully removing the ropes. "Please don't try and curse us."

"I wouldn't curse you in another witch's home," said Sarah, voice hoarse. "I can feel his magic all around us."

"You looked for me?"

"The fae aren't happy they can't find you," Sarah said tightly. "I didn't want to look for you. But they insisted, and I need their protection."

"They don't have any claim on me any longer. Liege Alder wanted my death, and they're gone. It's done. No matter what the rest of the court believe." The last rope spooled on the ground. "Besides, I have the protection of some powerful people," Vina said wryly. "I'd leave me be, if I were them."

"If you can kill fae, perhaps you're worth more than I thought," said Sarah.

Vina carefully did not look at Galath.

"I'm still offering an alternative to the fae," said Vina. "Another way you can have the power to protect yourself. We end the grip of the archives, and the Isle will change in ways you can't imagine."

"I can see how that benefits you," said Sarah, but there was hesitation in her voice. "Not us. Not my coven."

"The Isle will be free," said Vina. "Whatever that may mean. You've already seen that what it means to be a witch has changed, since the Eternal Prince's rise. Think of it—more Elsewhere witches, like Tam. Safety in numbers. A chance for an Isle that doesn't force you to such cruel choices. Just... consider it."

Sarah pursed her lips. She looked over at Edmund.

"I'm not sure I want to work with this one," she said, gesturing at him rudely.

"It wasn't personal," he said gruffly.

"Well, when I hex your bollocks with pustules, it won't be personal either."

Hari was at the bottom of the stairs, surrounded by Sarah's coven. He didn't look frightened, so Vina forced herself to walk down with measured, casual footsteps.

"I'll calm down when I see her," Tam was saying, heated. "You can't keep her from us. We can *feel* her in there, don't lie to us."

"She broke into my home," said Hari. "I'd be well within my rights to harm her—but to be clear, I haven't. I don't know what she's doing here, any more than you do."

"Tam," said Sarah from behind Vina. "It's fine. I'm fine."

Relief washed over Tam's face. Sarah muscled past Vina to clap a hand on his shoulder.

Whatever Sarah had been to her and the others in the primordial forest—a jailer, a would-be murderer—she was loved here. She'd made a family out of her fellow witches.

"Tam," Sarah said. "I've decided. I agree with the rest of you. Majority wins. We'll help these idiots burn the archives." She lowered her voice. "Spirits help us."

The coven burst into conversation. Hari looked over at Vina with confusion, elation. *How did you do it?* he mouthed.

Vina shook her head helplessly, smiling. She moved to speak—then paused.

Something was calling to her. A twisting in her heart. It felt like the urging of her tale.

It felt like her witch.

Her heart was a compass, and it knew where it wanted to lead her.

"Vina," said Galath. His low voice cut through the voices around them, quelling them to silence. There was concern in his eyes. "What is it?"

"Simran," she whispered. "I can feel her. I need to go to her."

Hari strode over to her, looking her over as intently as Galath had.

"Are you sure?" Hari asked. "Is it—safe? Think of what happened last time."

"Papa," she said. Winced, internally, still torn—her two lives like a cracked mirror, reflecting a dozen faces back at her, all her own and none at all. "Hari. I know you worry. But you have to let me go. You have to trust me."

Hari met her eyes, then exhaled a shaky breath. "That's what Sim said to me," he said. "And I haven't seen her in two decades."

"Then let me bring her back," said Vina. She'd go whether he let her or not, and they both knew it. But she waited anyway. "Please," she said.

Hari rubbed a hand over his forehead. "Go," he said. "And come back safe. Or at least with all your limbs. We'll be waiting for you."

# Chapter Thirty-Three

## *The Witch*

*It's the anniversary of her death again. If you're ready to pull your head out of your arse I'll be laying flowers outside her favorite pub tonight. And then I'll be drinking in it. Come and meet me this time.*

Source: Letter from Edmund Tallisker<br>to Matthias Goring

She dried her sleep clothes with bursts of whispered magic. She singed her skin a little, but that was a fair price to pay—besides, she wasn't getting naked in the middle of London just to make sure she could dry cloth without catching her skin.

She'd stolen Margaret's incarnate tome in the process of fleeing. It was soaked beyond repair, but she dried it as best as she could—puffs of magicked heat from her fingertips, her breath. Once she'd done that, she had nothing left to give. Exhausted, she fell asleep by a bank for a snatched few hours, before she dragged herself to her feet with the rising sun, and set off, the book tucked under her arm.

She wasn't leaving London. Her mind was full. The archivists were hurting incarnates. They were using books to do it. Pinning tales, freezing them in shape, forcing them to stay unchanging.

And somewhere in the city was the knight. The Witch needed to get her back.

She was glad she'd had the sense to put on shoes before sneaking out of her room and combusting her life. But she had nothing else of any use, and precious little magic left swimming in her blood. But she wove what she could, drawing on the mirrors around her—the wavering shapes in the glass on storefronts, the shimmering puddles of water from fallen rain. *Do not see me*, her magic whispered, and eyes slid away from her, uninterested.

She passed into a coffeehouse, where people were talking, reading papers. She stole a woman's coat from where it was draped over the back of a chair. She felt vaguely guilty, when she fished into the pockets and found a little purse of coins. But only *vaguely*. Her hunger and thirst were stronger, and the coat was blissfully warm.

Everywhere she went, she saw the Queen's soldiers: knights and guards, coppers in their blues, striding the streets. Was this normal for London? She wasn't convinced. Some old knowledge, seething at the back of her skull, insisted that it wasn't.

There were symbols, she realized, scattered across the landscape: flags of blue in shop windows, tucked discreetly into corners. On one of the walls she passed was a painting hastily daubed on the wall: a sword and a pale crown, the Queen's rose pennant torn in two below it. Words. *He lives and lives again. He rules. Eternal!*

London was preparing for the arrival of the Eternal Prince. The Queen could not change that.

She headed, with a crowd of laughing people, toward Drury Lane. The air was full of threat. She wanted to be where life was.

The West End glittered with lights and life. She should have run somewhere free of people, but this wasn't a city where anyone would look too long at anyone else. It left the Witch plenty of room to do all the looking she wanted, unnoticed by any of the milling people who passed her by. She felt, as she walked, as if she'd been starved of this kind of light and noise: as if once she'd known it all, and loved it, and had been locked away from it for years.

She passed the great theaters, until she found one that was smaller, its gilt lettering peeling, the people milling at its front dressed not in finery but in glittery, joyous garb. Some were smoking, laughing. Others were just chatting, hands in pockets, as folk drifted in and out of the doors.

A ticket tout was selling tickets to a show. She touched the coins in her pocket and thought of being sensible—conserving her money, surviving, finding the knight, moving forward.

But she looked at the theater, some old instinct rearing up in her again. She'd known this place once. Watched shows here; drunk sweet wine, in standing stalls, watching shows with a friend at her side. Who'd been there? She reached for the memory, then let it go. Seeing it would mean seeing everything.

Instead, she walked up to the tout and gave over all her money for a ticket.

The interior of the theater was warmly inviting: plush seats for the wealthy, wooden for those doing so-so, and standing space for the rest. She stood, her stolen coat clutched tight around her, surrounded by the smell of rain-damp wool and cologne from other bodies. Chandeliers glimmered softly up high. They dimmed. The stage lights grew brighter.

The performers walked onto the stage. It began.

As she watched, she realized it was a performance of incarnate tales. She was entranced, as performers danced and sang and acted their way through tales; as the lights changed, and violins played. Someone sang a popular aria from *Hecate's Daughters*, witch after witch parading under the lights.

The next tale began. Her breath caught in her throat when a figure in armor walked on stage, and another in a sweeping gown of lavender. Mirrors were lowered from the rafters.

It was her own tale.

She felt as if she barely blinked, watching them move through the stages of the tale: the enthrallment, the fall into love. Their deaths. Silk handkerchiefs, bloodred and threaded with red stones, flowered between them, symbolizing the killing, the blood, the end.

The Eternal Prince arrived on stage as the curtain closed, in a polished fake crown, a bloody sword in his hands. He held it high, and the crowd roared with love and bloodlust alike.

The curtain dropped and the Witch stared shakily at the velvet curtains.

She'd recognized the face of the person playing the witch.

The performance was over. She slipped into the back.

The theater was not as grand here. She supposed this was a space for the workers, not the audience; this was where illusions were crafted. There were costumes scattered, as multitudinous as tales: sequined, velvet, silk, ruffles, and taffeta. It was beautiful.

"You've got a fan sneaking in, Lady Juliet," a bored voice said. She startled, and saw a stagehand in the corner, drinking a cup of tea. They nodded. "Go over to her," they said. "She's in a good mood. She'll sign something if you ask her."

There was a figure seated at a dressing table, dressed in a glorious lavender gown. She turned toward the Witch, elegant and straight-backed in her chair. Her eyes widened.

"Simran?" Her voice shook. "Is that you?"

Simran. That name again. It settled like a leaf on the still waters of her heart, her memory.

The Witch stepped forward. "It's me," she whispered.

"You can't be any older than when you left," said Lady Juliet. "And that was...oh, hell. When I was young, and my back didn't hurt. A damnably long time, that." Her gaze searched the Witch's face.

"I..." The Witch tried to find her voice.

Juliet's gaze softened.

"I can tell you're not entirely yourself. Parts of you are missing, aren't they?"

"I call myself the Witch," she said. "More than—the other name."

"I'm also called Oliver, when I'm not dolled up," said Lady Juliet. "My father had terrible taste in names. Makes me sound like an urchin. But you call me what you prefer," she said gently, touching her fingertips fleetingly to the Witch's cheek, as if she just wanted to check if she was alive and here and real. "And I'll call you what you prefer. How about that?"

The Witch's heart twisted.

"Simran is fine," she said.

"You're lucky that healing is the business of cunning folk. Blessings too. I could help you." A careful look. "If you want me to, of course. You can talk to me."

The Witch shook her head. After what she experienced at the archives, she didn't want anyone placing magic on her, no matter how good it was.

"Your Hari's been looking for you," said Lady Juliet. "He's been looking for a damnably long time. He doesn't come to London much any longer, but we still write to each other. Sometimes I visit him."

Hari. The name was a silver penny. She held the shining weight of it.

"Where's Lydia?" the Witch asked, as the name came to her tongue.

"Gone, I'm afraid, darling," said Juliet. Her gaze was tender, sorrowful.

The Witch looked away. Her eyes felt wet.

"Let me get you a tissue."

"Sorry," said the Witch. "I don't know why I'm crying."

"If you're looking for safety, you can stay here," said Lady Juliet. "Or come home with me. I have friends who'd look after you."

"I'll be followed eventually," the Witch said thickly. She wiped her face.

She'd met her knight. Now she was far from the archives—now she was nearly embracing herself, that viperous voice that lived inside her—she could feel the pull of her knight, somewhere distantly across the city.

"I could do with some help," she admitted.

She took advantage of Lady Juliet's kindness to use the dressing room showers and wash the vile Thames off her. She took the gift of some of her boy clothes to wear: a shirt and trousers, too large for her but not by much. She rolled up the trousers, and tightened both pieces of clothing with the application of a belt.

When she was done—dry and clean, more alive than she'd felt in perhaps a lifetime—she stood in the dressing room, and thought of the play. The knight and witch on stage swooning into one another, jeweled blood rising between them.

She felt a tug in her own chest. The knight was near. The knight was calling to her.

"Do you need anything else?" Oliver asked gently. She knew he wanted her to reach out to the Hari he'd spoken about. But the Witch wasn't ready. Not yet.

"I'm going somewhere safe," she said. "Honestly, don't worry about me."

She felt the knight coming to her. She climbed to the roof of the theater, where she could see the city laid out around her, beneath her, a studded blanket of lights. Minutes later, the knight followed. The Witch heard her footsteps and turned to look at her—her dark hair, her achingly familiar face. They moved toward one another, the lamplight shining below them, the black sky cradling them together on that rooftop.

"Lady Witch," the knight said after a moment of hesitation. Her mouth had begun shaping another name before she'd chosen the right words. Her face was bruised. She was so lovely, so handsome still, that the Witch's heart was somersaulting in her chest. "You're here."

"You escaped the fae," said the Witch. She walked forward, her heart both light and full of a grief so vast it felt like it could carry her away.

"I did," said the knight. Her gaze was searching. "Lady Witch," she said again. "Do you know me?"

"Not as well as I could," said the Witch. She took a step closer, finding her strength. "To find my way back to myself, I want something from you," whispered the Witch. "I need something from you."

"Anything," said the knight.

"A kiss," she said.

The knight looked at her. They were so close to one another.

"Give me your hand," the knight said.

She held a hand out to the knight, who took it, and lowered her head gracefully. The knight kissed the back of her hand, a light brush of her mouth against skin.

It sent shivers like feathers through the Witch's blood.

"Did that bring you back to yourself?" the knight asked.

"No," said the Witch. "Not yet."

It was a selfish impulse. But she didn't deny it. She crossed the space between them. She placed her fingertips between their mouths. A barrier of skin, the knight's lips soft beneath her fingers, her breath a shocked, hot gasp. The Witch kissed her fingers, close, close.

The Witch drew back.

"That wasn't enough," said the knight.

"How do you know?" the Witch said, breathless laughter finding its way into her voice, her heart. "A kiss can be a kind of magic, after all. Maybe that's all I nee—"

She couldn't finish. The knight reeled her in and kissed her again, a sweet brush of their mouths. The kiss deepened, the lush meeting of tongues, the soft heat of shared breath.

"Vina," she said, as their mouths parted.

"Lady Witch," Vina replied.

She exhaled, a long, slow thing. She'd thought it would be painful or momentous, to let her old self in. But she found, instead, it was peaceful. Joyous. It wasn't the kiss that brought her back. But the bravery of wanting it—that was enough.

"I told you not to call me that," she said, breathless, a smile threatening at her mouth. "Call me Simran. That's who I am."

# Chapter Thirty-Four

## *Vina*

*She's been gone all these years, and I'm too old for sentimentality. But this morning my lantern unfolded into a bird without my say-so and for a moment I thought Simran had come home.*

Source: Letter from Lydia Chen to Hari Patel

Simran.

She was changed. Her skin bare of tattoos, her hair shorter than it had ever been—a sheet of black silk that reached to her shoulders. But by heaven and hell, she was still herself. They'd both made it somehow, into a new life. Both survived.

Simran touched Vina's face; the sweep of her jaw, her cheekbone. Vina let herself grasp Simran's face in return. It was like time had fallen away; like they'd woken lying next to one another in the witch's tor side by side and begun to kiss, safe and sweet in wanting each other. She drew Simran close. Simran came eagerly, laughter still in the shape of her mouth, and *God*, did she look good when she laughed. It was precious, hard-earned, that laughter. Her mouth was soft, and sent dizzying want in a deluge through Vina's blood.

They parted, and then leaned in again, and again. And finally, with a breath, Vina drew back just enough to press her forehead to

Simran's own, and feel the cool night air on them both, and know they were finally whole again.

Simran tangled their hands together. She was warm, her fingers soft but strong.

"I missed you," Simran admitted. "I'm sorry about—everything. The knife, mostly."

"It was just a bookbinding knife," Vina said. "You don't need to apologize."

"I was afraid to remember you." Simran's voice was vulnerable. "I was afraid to remember myself."

For Simran to admit fear…Vina's heart cracked. It was a gift. She knew how Simran hated to be vulnerable; how she lashed out, guarded herself, held her secrets close and pushed her loved ones away. Right then and there, Vina promised herself that when Simran was vulnerable she would protect her. She would be her armor, her shield. She would hold all of Simran's fragility gently in the palm of her hand.

Twenty years, and an entire lifetime had separated them. And yet it was nothing.

"I missed you too," Vina said in return.

They sat together on the roof's edge, fingers still touching. They stared across the rooftops together. Then Vina took a deep breath, and told Simran about the librarians and the witches and cunning folk. And then, because it was the harder thing, the stranger thing, about Hari and Galath.

Simran stared at her, eyes wide.

"The two of them?" Simran repeated.

"You can ask Hari," said Vina. "About them. You can ask him anything. He'd answer you."

"I can't believe Hari and Galath raised you," Simran said, mouth open in shock. "And they're, what—together?"

"Married," said Vina. "I'm afraid they love each other."

"How the hells did that happen?"

"I don't know," said Vina. "Do people usually know why or how their parents fell in love? I never thought much about it as a child, and I certainly don't want to think about it now."

"Is that how you think of them? As your parents?"

Vina swallowed. "Yes, and no," she said. "I used to. When I didn't remember—everything—I never questioned it. They were my fathers. They were as reliable and real as the silver sea, as the sun in the sky. But now there's two halves of me. The one that remembers before, and the one that lives now."

"And my...parents?" Simran asked. Vulnerability flitted across her face.

Vina's heart twisted.

"They're gone," said Vina. "I'm sorry. But they—they had a family in Hari. They visited all the time. And when they got older, they lived with us until they passed. They were like grandparents to me." A beat, and she amended her words. "They *were* grandparents to me."

Simran closed her eyes, breathing through the wound, then opened them.

"I always hoped Hari would be the child they deserved," she said. "I'm glad." She looked away. "It was the stories my father told me that saved me," said Simran. "Saved us both, truthfully. I just wish I could have told him. Told both of them."

They sat in silence for a while. Simran clearly needed it, and Vina was glad to give it to her.

"I'm not who I was before," said Simran finally. "I had a whole life then. A big life. Now I'm some girl raised in seclusion to serve a single purpose. You're the first person I've kissed. I remember—well. I wasn't a nun in our last life. I had a good time. But this body is all new. I don't have my old tattoos." She raised her arms up.

"We could change that," said Vina. "If you wanted to."

"What?"

"We could find a tattooist to ink you," said Vina. "If you're not going back to the archivists, there's nothing to stop you."

Simran looked at her, unsmiling now. Considering her. Simran's eyes were dark.

"I think a good way to learn myself would be to place myself under your hands," said Simran. "It might even be better than ink."

Hot want pooled in Vina's belly at those words. She saw it reflected in Simran's eyes.

"We've only just reunited," whispered Vina. "I can't undress you on a rooftop."

"Why not?" Simran asked. "If I want you to, and you want to—why not?"

There were good reasons. The noisy streets below were one. But instead of answering, Vina gave in to the gravity that kept calling her hands back to Simran's skin. It was want, yes, and hunger; but it was also reassurance. *You're here. You're alive. You're with me.* She touched her fingertips lightly to the curves of Simran's shoulders and began to move her fingers in looping patterns.

"What are you doing?" Simran asked. Her eyes had darkened. She hadn't moved.

"Tracing your tattoos," said Vina. "You had flowers, here. Roses. And here—thorns." A scrape of her fingers, aiming for something between tenderness and tender hurt. Simran made a stifled noise. "And marks here, like you'd see in an old manuscript."

"Scrollwork," said Simran. She closed her eyes as Vina's fingers mimicked those shapes, those swirling lines, moving down the sensitive skin of her inner arms.

"Let's move away from the edge of the roof," Vina said.

Simran huffed out a laugh.

"Fine," she said. "That I can do."

They lay on her coat and Vina traced patterns into Simran's arms and shoulders, exquisitely slow. She followed the lines of her neck, her collarbones. She pressed her hands beneath Simran's shirt, to burning skin, then lower still, into her trousers; into the welcome of her hot, vulnerable thighs. She watched Simran's head tip back, her mouth part, her eyelashes grace her cheeks, and felt half crazed with it. This, forever. She could do this forever.

Later, seconds or minutes or hours later, she held Simran in her arms, all the fragile weight of her.

"I need you to know..." Vina hesitated.

*That I started falling in love with you in our last life*, thought Vina. *When we were on the cusp of death, when you saved me—that's when it happened, when I fell. And now I remember me, remember us, I love you again. It's like the love was always in me, a winged bird waiting to take flight.*

*I love you. I always have.*

She looked at Simran's face, and the peace of her half-closed eyes. Not yet. Not now. She'd wait until better times, if they came. When the words would be welcome. When the world wasn't falling around them, bloodstained princes on the horizon and tales in chains, and no promise of a soft future where they fulfilled their new tale, ending the archives, walking free.

"What is it?" Simran asked sleepily.

"Nothing," she said, instead. "Let's stay here a little longer. That's all."

# Chapter Thirty-Five

## *Simran*

*Galath has been in London for two weeks. He hasn't found her.*
~~*I'm sorry.*~~
~~*If I could swap places with Simran*~~
*Next time. I'm hopeful.*
*Will you visit us again? Vina misses you.*

Source: Letter from Hari Patel to
Chandni and Ramesh Arora

Vina led her to the place where the librarians now lived. Simran tried not to look as vulnerable as she felt as they walked across cobbled stone.

Vina's hand brushed her own.

"We're almost there," she said.

Maybe Simran wasn't as good at hiding her feelings as she'd hoped. She exhaled and nodded.

There was someone standing outside the building, on the steps. A tall and broad figure, pale-haired and unnaturally still.

Simran's steps faltered.

Galath looked at her. His gaze didn't waver.

"Witch," he said.

Simran paused for a moment, then squared her shoulders and

walked up to him.

"Galath," she said. She hesitated. What could she say to him? She hadn't truly known him as Simran. Under other names, other faces, she'd loved him. She looked at him so long that the silence should have grown awkward; but he looked back just as silently, just as still.

In the end, she just told him the truth.

"I'm glad to see you again," she said simply.

That struck him—she saw it. The way he blinked, the softening of his face. For a moment, she saw the child Galath in him. The boy who'd cursed himself for her sake.

"We searched for you," he said. "But you were beyond our reach. I am sorry."

Simran's hands clenched tighter. She wanted to reach out for him, and those were Elayne's instincts, not her own; Elayne's love, and not Simran's.

"I hear you're married," she said. "That's—very weird, actually. I feel like I've knocked my head very hard. But Hari's no fool, and I trust him. And it looks like he's been good for you. You don't look as much like you're likely to murder a man in the next blink of an eye anymore. You've changed. You look more alive."

"I cannot die," said Galath.

"Being alive isn't the same as being *well*, Galath," said Simran. "But I'm glad."

The door slammed open, and in a whirl a bundle of fluff threw itself in a frenzy into Simran's arms. She yelped, and stumbled back. When she steadied herself, she realized the massive fluff ball in her arms was—

"Mal?" She stared down at that malevolent, purring face in shock. "You're *alive*?"

"She's missed you," said Hari. "She told me so herself. We're going to have to discuss how little you listened to her, Sim—you know familiars can communicate?"

Hari was standing at the top of the stairs. He was—oh God, he was grown. Lines at the corners of his eyes, a firmness to his face that hadn't been there when he was in his twenties. Gray in his hair. Galath had changed, but he was still as ageless as ever. Vina had grown new and young with her. But Hari was changed by time, and he was her Hari and not at all anymore. He was smiling at her, but he was trembling too.

She realized she was shaking as well.

"Hari," she said thickly.

He walked down to her and drew her into a crushing hug. Mal hissed and wriggled out of her arms onto the firm embrace of the ground.

"God," she said, laughing, crying against his shoulder. "You've grown up. Look how broad you are now. Have you been weight lifting? Wrestling?"

"Honest life near the woods, with animals and a child to take care of," said Hari. "I never thought I'd leave the city, but things change." He held her face. "God, Sim," he said. "You're just the same."

"It's been twenty years," said Simran. "And I've lived a whole other life. Don't lie, I'm changed."

"Everyone changes over decades," said Hari. "But you're still you." He took her hands in his. "Come with me," he said.

He took her inside, into a room full of unfamiliar faces, and led her to a table where they could sit together alone. He didn't let go of her.

He told her about his life: about falling steadily, strangely in love with Galath as they'd searched for her. About the house that had been temporary, at first, until Maleficium moved herself in one cold dawn, and the rabbits arrived, and the lavender grew—and Hari had turned round, and seen Galath brewing a pot of coffee and realized he could not imagine a life without him in it. How he'd stumbled into love there, and dragged Galath along with him.

He told her about her parents. Told her he had letters for her.

"They always believed you'd come back," said Hari. "Even...even when I lost hope."

One of the kinder librarians took her, when she began to tear up, into a room where she could sit alone. Surrounded by muddled books, she curled up on the floor and read her way through those letters.

There were letters from her mother. These were not in English, but in Gurmukhi script. Her mother, she understood, had never learned to read or write in English. And for a long time she'd lost her Punjabi too.

Maybe as the chains bound to the Eternal Prince had loosened— as the Queen's control over tales had waned—her mother had found her language again. And Simran, carefully stumbling through familiar and unfamiliar characters and words, had found what remained of her first language too.

She was glad her parents had had Hari. But God, she missed them. She let herself feel it, the letters fanned around her. A goodbye.

It took her a long time to compose herself. She scrubbed her face with her sleeve, and carefully folded the letters, tucking them into her shirt pocket, over her heart. When she emerged from isolation, she found the librarians gathered around one table, where Vina stood, leaning forward with her palm flat on its surface, voice low and intensely animated.

"We have witches to fight for us," Vina was saying to the librarians. "Cunning folk we can ask to stand by our side, to heal and protect. But we're dealing with books. We need you. I truly believe we do."

"If you're taking witches with you, then I know you're not planning to protect those books," one librarian said, arms crossed. Pale ginger hair, its color faded. Face creased into a frown. *Cora*, Simran's mind whispered. "You're planning to burn them."

"I want to find another way if I can," said Vina. She sounded so determined.

Simran was struck all anew by how handsome she was: the sharpness of Vina's jaw and the fullness of her mouth; the warmth of her skin, and the curls of her brown hair, a tender lick of oak against her

honeyed skin. Simran took a moment to breathe the sight of her in—
*I have her back*—then strode forward.

"The books don't have to burn," said Simran. "There's another way to destroy the archives. I'll show you."

She reached into her coat and withdrew a book.

She placed it on the table. It was damaged from her journey through the Thames, but it was still undeniably a beautiful book: tooled, and gilt-edged, with its title, *The Laidly Wyrm*, visible on the still faintly sodden leather cover.

"I don't know if you can sense where a book's been, or what journeys it's traveled," said Simran. "But this was an incarnate tome, bound with limni ink, kept by the archives. It controlled a tale—kept it frozen in shape, so the Isle would never change, and always be what the Queen wanted it to be. But I broke the chains on it. It's no more than words on paper now—just as powerful and meaningless as any book is able to be."

The crowd of librarians parted, allowing one to step forward. Her eyes, behind gold frames, narrowed. She pressed her hand to the book. With a start, Simran realized she was Ophelia—the librarian who'd guarded the Beast.

There had been some kind of magic in her, all those years ago. Simran had felt it in Ophelia then, and felt it now. Not cunning folk magic, or the maleficence of witchcraft, but something uniquely tangled with tales. She was the one who'd known the Beast, and sensed the library's will. She, of all people, would see that what Simran said was true.

Hopefully.

There was a long pause. Then, slowly, Ophelia raised her head. Her eyes gleamed with unshed tears.

"I can feel the echo of chains on it," said Ophelia. "And I can feel that they're gone—destroyed. Can you teach others to do what you have done?"

Simran shook her head. She thought of all the witches before her, who'd fought to break the Eternal Prince's chains on their own—the hundreds of lifetimes it had taken to build the strength to do what Simran had done to free him.

"No," she said. "I don't think anyone else can do what I can with limni ink."

Then she hesitated.

She thought of how little the witch had trusted anyone. How loneliness had eaten at her, made her turn to bitterness, and had made her distrust even herself. If the witch had reached out to other incarnates, other scribes, could the Prince have been freed long ago, and the archives too? She didn't know, but the suspicion remained in her heart regardless, and demanded she seek a new path. Maybe even a better one.

The one Vina had given her: allies, and family, and friends to accompany them both on the quest ahead.

"But I'll still need help," she said honestly. "I can free the books, but that's *all* I can do."

"You can protect them," Vina said to Ophelia. If Vina was surprised, she hid it well. Determination shone in her eyes. "With your help to enter the archives, and your protection—witches, cunning folk, librarians alike—we'll set the Isle free. Stories will be able to change instead of withering. No more of the Isle will be lost."

The room broke out into conversation. Simran fixed her gaze on Ophelia's.

"I need to talk to you," she said. "Alone would be better."

Ophelia raised an eyebrow, but she nodded.

Ophelia ushered her away to a kitchen with a gently bubbling pot on the stove.

She told Ophelia everything about Adder, and her growing suspicion that Adder was the Beast, or something similar to it. Ophelia's tears finally fell, but her expression was resolute.

"Of course we'll go to the archives," said Ophelia. "There's no question now." She gripped Simran's hand. "Thank you," she said. "All I've wanted for many years is to know that the Beast is safe. This is the first hope I've had in a long, long time."

\* \* \*

The streets were growing steadily emptier. In the midst of it, the cunning folk arrived: Ella, whom Simran had last seen over Mary's body in a molly-house in another life, and Oliver, who offered her a relieved smile and a hug when he saw her. They'd come at Hari's request, and went to him directly, a circle of cunning folk and witches in the corner of the room.

Simran stayed at the front window. She could see blue lights in distant windows: candles set in funnels of iris-blue glass.

"The lights are the people of London telling the Eternal Prince they're his allies," murmured Vina, moving in close to stare out the window with her.

Vina was warm. Simran wanted to lean into her.

She heard a thump behind her. She turned and saw that Cora had dumped a pile of clothing on the table.

"What we wear as librarians is close to what the archivists wear," said Cora. "It may pass, if no one looks too closely."

"They won't be shocked to see a knight in the Tower," said Edmund. He'd exiled himself to the corner of the room, as far from Sarah (who was still threatening to hex his balls) as possible, where he was sitting cross-armed and mulish. "Vina. You still have armor?"

Vina shook her head.

"You do," said Galath evenly. "Your own, left in the mountains after your capture. I kept it safe. Carried it from the witch's tor to London, where the librarians preserved it among their collection."

One of the librarians gestured at an apprentice in response. The girl ran off, and returned with her arms full of metal, her legs wobbling from the weight.

It was the fae-wrought armor Tristesse had garbed Vina in. Simran remembered it perfectly—its silvery color, its lightness and its silence, the way it had looked and felt when Vina had undressed her and pushed her back to the bed...

Her body flashed fever-hot. She ducked her head, hoping her blush wasn't visible.

Vina was looking at the armor worshipfully. She raised her head, meeting Galath's eyes.

"Why?" she asked.

"I knew you'd both return," Galath said. The look he gave Vina was even, unreadable to those who didn't know him—but Simran did know him. She'd known him for lifetimes. There was a softening to his jaw; a lightness in his eyes, as if the heart Elayne had seen in that chattering, sweet boy she'd saved was finally rising back to the surface, breaking the carapace of ice that had held it.

*He loves her*, Simran realized. It rushed over her then, the absurd and precious truth that Galath was finally not alone. Somehow, Hari and Vina had done for him what the witch had never been capable of, and made him whole.

Her Galath, Elayne's Galath, finally knew love and family. He knew it with *her* only family: Hari, her brother of choice, the only person she'd let stay close; and Vina, her Vina.

It was miserable, how joyous she felt for them—and how deserted she felt, with the rift of a lifetime and all her loneliness between them.

As the hours passed, silence fell like a blanket across London. There was a cry, in the distance: the clamorous call of a dozen horses; their braying, and the sound of glorious trumpets, announcing the coming of the Eternal Prince. He was crossing into London. He was coming to take his throne.

"Let's get going," said Edmund. His face was pale, jaw determined.

They stepped outside. In librarian's robes, the weight of them warm on her skin, Simran took a breath and looked out at the streets around them. It was time.

They traveled by barge to the Tower. Edmund arranged it. Whatever he'd done since her death, he'd definitely risen in the Queen's esteem and in her ranks. Helmed and garbed as one of the Queen's knights, he was a known face, and he told them he wouldn't be questioned. "I may not guard you anymore," he said, with a sidelong look at Simran, "but I'm still a knight. The Yeoman Warders won't refuse me if I'm on the Queen's business."

It was the rest of them that Simran was worried about. They'd dressed themselves as much like archivists as they could, but she felt like they were about as convincing as a faux death on the Theatre Royal's stage.

*Do not notice us*, she thought. She drew on her magic, using the silvery surface of the Thames as her mirror. *Avert your eyes. We are not worth your attention.*

Warders on the walls spied the barge approaching and winched the gate open. They passed under the shadow of the Traitor's Gate. The barge creaked; the water sloshed around them as the barge touched the steps. Simran's relief was short-lived. They'd passed the first hurdle. Now they had to get through the Tower's defenses to the White Tower itself, where the incarnate books were held.

Two high towers stood ahead of them. Beyond those stood the innermost ward, a defensive wall manned with warders.

A warder approached, nodding to Edmund. His eyes were narrowed.

"Sir knight," he said. "Who summoned you?"

"Archivist Roland," Edmund said. "He's got questions about the missing witch. You going to let me pass?"

The warder hesitated. His gaze slid to the group at Edmund's back: the witches and cunning folk; the librarians; Galath and Hari; and finally, Simran and Vina, standing next to one another. Despite all her magic, he saw Simran. Recognition flared in his eyes. He opened his mouth to yell.

Edmund punched him square in the jaw.

The warder keeled over, and Edmund shook his gloved hand out.

The ravens were watching them solemnly, darkly from the ramparts. They cawed in greeting. Peppermint flew down, unerringly landing on Simran's shoulder.

"Get that bird to leave," Cora said under her breath.

Simran stroked Peppermint's glossy feathers, and got a sharp peck in return when no seeds were proffered. Peppermint's beak had drawn blood. Simran rubbed her fingers together, soothing the sting. Her blood hummed.

They weren't on the silver water anymore, and Simran didn't want to rely on mirrors. It was time to return to the magic she loved best: the magic of body and blood.

They swept toward the innermost wall, where the best archers among the Yeoman Warders would be stationed. Oliver was the one who stepped forward. With a wink for Simran, he drew a paper lantern from within his sleeve.

"Lydia taught me this one," he said, and murmured a blessing over the lantern.

The lantern unfolded, hovering in the air—then the paper opened, flared, transforming into a bird. She ignored the lump in her throat, the reflexive grief for Lydia. The bird swept over to her just as Peppermint had, and she touched her bloodied thumb to its beak.

"Let me," said Hari. He added his blood alongside her own. "The strength of two witches is better than one. And I know your magic." A faint smile. "It's where mine came from."

She poured her magic into that blood, and felt Hari's weave in with her own. She did recognize his magic. It was like meeting an old friend.

"Go," she said to the bird, and Oliver whistled.

The lantern bird flew up into the air. The lantern bird moved as fast as an arrow, shooting along the innermost wall, and the battlements at its zenith. She closed her eyes, fixing her attention on the blood mark and the magic she'd poured into it. *Sleep*, she urged. *It's time to sleep. I command you.*

The bird brushed against warder after warder—each one slumping forward as it did so, caught by the snare of her and Hari's spell. Her eyes snapped open.

"Quickly," said Simran. "There are going to be more warders inside."

"We will manage them," said Galath. His eyes gleamed flatly.

No one had warned the guards at the White Tower that anything was amiss, but as Edmund stormed ahead of their group up the White Tower's stairs, the warders quickly realized they were under attack. Simran saw one, then all four of them, draw their swords.

The witches moved together in a sweep to meet them, their voices joining in a chorus of curses. It was quick—before the guards had a chance to do more than stride forward, fire exploded from the witches' hands, flaring with a venomous hiss at the warders' feet. As one warder threw himself toward them through the flames, Tam murmured under his breath, magic sparking, and a twist of ill fortune made the warder's legs go out from beneath him. The man cried out in agony as the flames caught his leg. A fellow warder took him by the armpits and dragged him back.

"Step back or burn," Sarah said flatly. She was smiling, quite in her element. "And drop your weapons as you go. Thank you, dears."

The warders reluctantly obeyed, flinching from the heat of the fire. Simran looked at the wooden boards of the stairs. The witches twisted the fire out of Simran's path. There was a way forward.

They crossed the blistered, smoking boards of the stairs into the White Tower and slammed the heavy doors shut behind them. Edmund and Galath barred the door. "Put the fire out," Simran said to Sarah. "Or we won't be able to get out ourselves. Those stairs are wood all the way down."

"Fine," said Sarah. She clenched her hand, and the heat emanating through the door began to fade.

The group of cunning folk, witches, and librarians moved forward. Vina's eyes met her own. There was hope in Vina's eyes—a curve to her lips, fleeting and warm.

The White Tower needed no locks: It was defended by the river, by a moat, by warders and archivists and layers of defensive walls. No one had ever thought to prepare for a Tower-raised incarnate like Simran. The archivists had reared their own downfall.

But the White Tower was still dangerous to them. There was only one staircase leading up the tower, and without Adder to dream up a new door and a new staircase, Simran could not sneak up to the incarnate tomes. They would have to walk the only route available to them—and risk being pinned in between archivists and warders alike.

"Follow close," Simran urged the others, voice low. "I'll break the chains. You grab as many books as you can. And then we'll need to leave."

"I'm with you," said Ophelia, determined. "And your 'Adder'—do you know where it might be?"

Simran shook her head. "It used to come to me when it chose to. We can just hope it senses us and calls out."

The staircase was dark, lit by sconces. Galath headed their party, with Simran and Vina behind him, followed by Hari and the others.

"Almost there," whispered Simran. Vina was by her side, a steady presence. She heard Vina's breath catch, and saw Vina's hand fly to the hilt of her blade, before she heard Galath's sharp exhale. He doubled over, and Simran saw the lash of ink drawing back from his torso, winding its way back around an archivist's wrist.

"Meera," she said.

Meera stood ahead of them. Alone, a dark figure in her archivist's robes, partially hidden by shadows. There was a bottle of limni ink in her hand, the stopper free, the ink writhing.

"Witch," said Meera. "I knew you'd return."

"Did you?" Simran stepped forward, cursing the narrow staircase.

She angled herself in front of Galath even as he said, low and warning, "*Simran*."

"Of course," said Meera. "This is your home." She did not say it with love or tenderness. She said it like an insult, her eyes burning with fury, her lip curled. "All the archivists know you're here, Witch. We prepared for your return. I was wrong to underestimate your evil, destructive nature. But you'll find that the books are beyond your reach."

"If they all know I'm here, why are you the only one to greet me?" Simran cocked her head. "*Meera*. You poor thing. They've left you here as a sacrifice. Did they force you to do it, or did you volunteer? You're a senior archivist, you've given your life to the archives, and this is how much they value you—just enough to let you throw yourself to your death."

The whip of ink crackled with Meera's anger.

"If I am judged, it's because of you," Meera said. "I raised you. I treated you far better than any other archivist would have. Why do you insist on destroying your reputation and my own? Why must you wear your evil and your Elsewhere blood like a crown? You could have been so much *more*."

"You didn't want to raise me," said Simran. "You were forced to. Because they thought you were fit for it. You know why." A sneer touched her mouth, her voice. "You're Apollonius's left hand, and people still look down on you. No matter how far you climb, they always will."

That was too much for Meera. She lashed out with the ink again. This time, Simran caught the ink in her grip. Holding it tight, she threw herself forward, knocking Meera to the ground and sending the bottle of limni ink flying. Simran crushed the writhing ink with a hand—then pinned Meera by the throat with the other.

Meera's eyes widened. "How did you—"

"I'm afraid you've never really known what I'm capable of," said Simran.

"I was wrong to think I could make you better," Meera said, still struggling, breath short. "You're a disappointment."

"I don't care what you think of me," Simran said, and found to her relief that she was speaking honestly. She hadn't known for sure until she'd said it.

"Stop playing with your food!" Sarah called. Simran drew on her magic, ready to bind Meera. Meera tried to wrench away, clawing at Simran with her hands.

"You can't touch the books," Meera cried out.

"I can and I will."

Meera laughed, an ugly sound, more fury than humor.

"The books have one last defense," she gloated. "And the Queen's men will be up in the White Tower soon, trapping you like rats. This is the end for you, Witch. The Queen wants you, and she will have you."

"Hari," Simran said flatly. "Would you do the honors?"

"Gladly," he said coldly. He leaned forward and blew wood ash into Meera's mouth. Meera's eyes rolled, and she fell unconscious.

"She'll have nightmares," said Hari. "I took the ash from a graveyard. That's some comfort." He straightened up.

Simran felt a hand on her arm. Vina. "Come," Vina urged gently, and Simran rose, realizing how shaky her breath was—how much she'd feared Meera all these long years. That was done now. Meera was the past.

"Galath?" Simran called.

"The hurt isn't severe," he said. He was no longer doubled over, although his face was sheened with sweat. "We can continue."

They needed to climb one more floor. That was all. "I'll lead the way," said Simran, and she began walking. Meera's warning was rattling in her skull. She braced herself.

One last defense.

Simran could hear it now: the chuffing of breath. Claws against stone. Ophelia was shoving forward, eyes wide.

"Beast," Ophelia breathed out. She ran ahead, onto the landing and beyond the curve of the winding staircase. With a jolt of panic, Simran ran after her.

"Ophelia, stop!"

Too late. There was a scream, and when she turned the corner, Ophelia was pressed to the wall nearest the door, clutching a bleeding arm, marked with claw gashes. Simran kneeled down beside her, and looked at the door. Chained in front of it was Adder.

Adder—the Beast—was pinned by chains of ink and chains of iron alike. It was trembling with agony, its face in constant shifting motion: dozens of eyes and teeth, quilled spine and fetid fur, a lashing tail and huffing breath that smelled rancidly of blood. The archivists had bound it here to protect the books and bar Simran from passing into the archive. With the Beast in front of the door, she could no more touch the books than she could touch the sun.

"My friend," Ophelia said, strained. "My dear friend. Do you not remember me?"

"Ophelia!" Cora yelled. The scream made Adder bristle fiercely. Simran saw chains of ink tighten around it as it moved. Adder looked like it was in agony.

"Adder," said Simran. She tried to be calm. To be unafraid. She held her hands open, unthreatening. "Do you remember me?"

It was calm for a moment, its eyes pinpricks in its shifting face. Then the pain swept away its senses once more. Its teeth bared themselves.

It lunged for her, and it was Vina who dragged her back. Vina drew her blade as the Adder-Beast strained against its chains, stretching them to their full limit, its maw of a thousand new-forged teeth spread wide. Vina swiped, blade an arc, meeting the Beast's face with a thud. Ink-blood fell from its wound, touching Vina's skin, and Vina hissed, agonized. But she was still shielding Simran's body.

A single drop touched Simran's skin. Only one.

It propelled her out of her flesh.

She saw Adder.

She saw the Beast.

The Isle was new and there was the Beast. It was tales dreamt by creatures that knew no words. Language came, and more tales gathered upon it—birds of grief, and ants of gossip; snakes of starvation, and moths of dreams of fields of sweet apples. It aged and it grew. It carried with it the truth that lies at the heart of every story, the truth that changes when it lands in new hands, or new hearts. The truth took the shape of a cup, a chalice, a cauldron, a harp. The Beast carried it within itself.

The Beast grew a home. A library. It had caretakers. Kindness, after years of the cold and the hunt, the crowned creatures on horseback who sought to fell it. *Aberration. Falsehood. Sin*, they called it.

The library burned.

She felt Adder, dying, or something like it, in flames. She felt the agony of death—tales shaped like mice scurrying as the fire ate them alive. Foxes laying down their heads to burn. She felt Adder, felt the *Beast*, vast and old and storied, fade with them—turning to nothing but ash and dust.

She felt it, how the Beast had revived. A blade of grass, mist-made, here. A smoke-colored moth there. Each gathering together, joining, melding. Becoming bigger. Growing into Adder. Slithering in search of tales, kinship, stories to join with. Tales needed one another to grow things into something larger. A Beast. An ancient forest. An Isle.

And Adder had found her. Adder knew her. It had tasted her hair once—been offered it as a gift, freely. It had known her magic, her dreams, and known it must protect her. Adder had remained in the archives, her friend and companion, until the archivists had it chained alive.

Adder was the Beast, and the Beast was not a creature that had lived in the library. The Beast *was* the library: innumerable tales, living and breathing, joined together to survive.

"Simran," Vina was saying. Simran returned to the staircase with an awful jolt. Adder was howling. "Speak to me. Or move with me. But we can't stay here."

"The chains," Simran said against Vina's skin. "I need to break them." The archivists had chained Adder—*hurt* Adder.

"If you release it, I fear it'll kill us," Vina gritted out, shaking the burning ink from her blade hand.

"I can't leave it here. And we can't kill it. Promise me."

"No worries on that front. I'm not sure I could even get close enough to skewer it. Not that I would—don't look at me like that, Simran." Vina beckoned at Ophelia with her chin. "Come here," she ordered. "Slowly. We're moving back."

"I won't leave it," said Ophelia. "It's in pain. It's frightened. It needs time."

"You're hurt," Cora said with a smaller voice from below. "Please."

Vina moved down the stairs slowly, taking Simran with her. Ophelia was still steadfastly refusing to move. Below them they heard thudding footsteps—then a crack of noise.

The witch Tam was on the ground, bleeding, Ella and Oliver over him.

"Archivists and guards," gritted out Tam. "Th-they're below. Boxing us in. We're trapped."

Just as Meera had warned they'd be.

Ella was healing Tam's arm. He was panting.

"He shoved one back, and was shot for his trouble. The bullet grazed his shoulder," Ella murmured. "Let me focus. I can't fix you, witch, but I can make sure it doesn't fester and ease the pain."

"Much appreciated," Tam managed. He met Vina's eyes. "Sarah and the other witches—they'll cursemark the ground. The archivists won't be able to get to us without hurting themselves. It'll slow them down."

"We'll add our own protections," said Oliver grimly, on behalf of the cunning folk. "You won't defend us alone."

"Vina," said Hari. His voice cut through the din. His gaze was fixed on Vina, forehead creased. "What are you planning?"

There was a resolute look on Vina's face. She'd made a decision, Simran realized, in the handful of moments when Simran had not been looking at her.

"I'll go face the archivists," said Vina. "They won't kill an incarnate. I can shield you with my body—with my worth to them. That should give Simran time to deal with the Beast, and finish our work in the archives." She sounded so sure.

"No," said Simran, without pausing to think. "You're not."

"I'm afraid I must." Vina's smile was lopsided. "I'm the only one that can be spared."

"Bullshit," Simran said angrily. "No. If you're going, I'm coming with you."

"Sim—"

"I'm not letting you fall into the Queen's hands," Simran cut in. "Not without me," she said. She realized at some point she'd gripped Vina by the wrist. She hadn't intended to. "Not without me," she said again helplessly.

"You can't risk everything for me," said Vina, looking at her with wide eyes. "Lifetimes of work—you can't stop now." She swallowed. "Not for my sake, Simran."

That would be absurd, wouldn't it? And selfish. But Simran thought of her knight, always in the Queen's clutches, ever murdering and dying for honor and Crown, and didn't let go of Vina.

"The Queen wants me," she said. "You heard Meera. She won't settle for you alone. And I know the archivists. I can make them leave. The rest of you will be able to run then."

"We may never have this chance again," Vina warned.

"I know," Simran said softly. "But I won't let you go alone. I vow it."

Vina stared back at her. Her mouth was parted, her eyes full of awed tenderness.

"I could kill them all one by one," said Galath, steady and sure. His words broke the spell between them—Simran sucked in a breath and faced him, releasing Vina's hand. She saw the ancient, merciless strength of him in his eyes, and the axe at his side, gleaming like liquid moonlight. "Is there a reason I should not?"

"The archivists can hurt you," said Simran. "You know that."

"I don't fear being harmed."

"No," said Simran. "But I don't want it. None of us do."

She meant Hari. She meant Vina.

She meant herself too. Maybe she hadn't chosen to care for him— but the ancient love lived in her regardless.

"You're going to have to trust Vina and me," she said.

"I have trusted you many times," said Galath. "Over many lifetimes."

"And I failed you, didn't I? Every time. I know. But you're going to have to take one more leap of faith."

Still, Galath stood steady.

"Please," Vina said. "Father. Please stay here."

Galath exhaled.

"Prove yourself wiser than you've been, Vina."

"It's a low bar," Vina said. "I'll do my best."

"If you're gone too long," he said, hefting up his axe, "I will come."

It sounded like both a promise and a threat.

They moved down the winding stairs. Edmund was standing in front of the archivists and warders—he was their last defense. The staircase below him was rammed with archivists, protected by a wall of guards. And there, among them, was the head archivist himself.

"There's no running from us," said Apollonius, eyes cold. "Stand down, Sir Edmund."

"Fuck that," Edmund said. His sword was drawn in a flash of silver, and he cut down the first knight in front of him in a single blow. The next he knocked out cold.

Apollonius, older and uneven on his feet, stumbled back. But his eyes were canny, and he said with terrible calm, "You won't be able to fight every archivist here, Sir Edmund. Knight and Witch. The Queen demands your presence. Follow me quietly, and perhaps I will see fit to spare your allies."

With a snort of derision, Simran dropped a vial of wood ash on the step in front of her, pressed her boot into it, and crushed it, dragging glass and ash in a line of witching across the stone.

"I know you're lying," she said. "But let's bargain, Apollonius. Let our friends go freely and maybe—just maybe—I won't turn your archive to flames."

# Chapter Thirty-Six

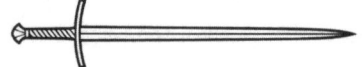

## *Vina*

[In Punjabi] *I love you, my daughter. Never forget. I love you.*

> Source: Letter from Chandni
> Arora to Simran Arora

"Cross the mark I've just left on the stairs, and your archive will burn. Every book, every chain. Even the stone." Simran leaned forward, unblinking. "You saw what I did to the entrance to the White Tower, didn't you? I can do so much more."

Vina knew it was a bluff, but she wasn't going to let the archivists know that. She clenched her hand around the hilt of her sword, letting her face and her voice fill with anguish.

"Please, listen to her," Vina begged, aiming for a look of noble suffering. She had a lot of experience, all in all, so she was fairly sure she was doing a good job of it. "If there were any other way, sir, we'd take it. But if you cross her, it cannot be helped!"

"I am more than you think I am, Apollonius," Simran said softly. "I'm no simple witch. I'm an *incarnate* witch. I have lifetimes of witching in me. I am malice and destruction down to my very bones. Try me. I'd happily set this place aflame, and let it take all of us with it."

Personally, Vina thought Simran was laying it on a little thick, but it seemed to be working on the archivist. Apollonius had a hunted look on his face. The archivists around him were muttering, faces pale.

"Fine," Apollonius said abruptly. "Come quietly, and your minions may leave unimpeded."

"Do I have your word?" Simran asked.

"My word, on my honor. Now," Apollonius continued, turning his attention to Vina, "remove your sword."

"Fuck this," Edmund said suddenly. "I'm not letting them take you."

He rammed forward, sword an arc of steel, throwing himself at the archivists. One of the warders grabbed Apollonius and concealed him with his body.

Vina swore under her breath and swiftly drew her own blade.

"Run!" Vina roared, cracking her blade heavily into another guard's helmet—then slamming her elbow into his nose. "That's an order, Eddie!"

"You don't bloody give me orders!" Edmund yelled back.

"Christ, you idiot. Get out of here alive so you can help us later, or I swear I won't forgive you!"

His eyes flashed. Somehow she'd gotten through to him, because he took advantage of the distraction she'd provided to push his way through the throng and vanish down the stairs.

She looked at Simran, and Simran looked back at her. She lowered her sword.

Perhaps Apollonius's word could be trusted. Perhaps not.

But she trusted that Hari and Galath would do everything they could to keep the archivists at bay. She trusted that, if she and Vina failed, their allies and their family would find a way to escape and thrive.

Soon the Queen's attention would be focused entirely elsewhere, after all.

Vina's sword was taken from her roughly.

"Hold them," instructed Apollonius. "The Queen wants them whole."

\* \* \*

They were taken to the Palace.

The Palace grounds were changing. The roses were gone, the sky blue as an eye, immune to the smog of London. The Palace itself had grown lustrous white turrets, pennants that shifted from rose-and-white to sword-upon-blue at their pointed peaks. Vina could hear the roar of the sea, which was strange indeed—London was far from the coast.

Whatever tales the Eternal Prince hailed from expected seas and tides, so the Palace shifted to accommodate him. Even the White Hall had changed, its walls transformed to bare stone veiled in lush tapestries, the wood paneling gone, the torchlight smoky and dull. The air smelled of moss and anise, the rosewater that usually swathed the room fading.

The room was full of incarnates, and empty of courtiers. The Queen's court had abandoned her like rats from a sinking ship. She'd gathered the incarnates around her, any incarnate who'd been at the ball, all the ones in London who'd remained here under her thumb.

Vina did not recognize those figures, but her gaze scanned over them—a woman with extremely long, golden hair; an enormously tall man; an older woman, hunched over in a spindly chair. The old woman smiled slyly as Vina and Simran entered, dragged in by grave-faced Yeoman Warders.

"Leave us," said the Queen, waving a hand at the warders. "Apollonius, my incarnates—remain with us."

As his fellows left, Apollonius lingered, looking up at the Queen with beatific true belief. With a jolt, Vina realized that the single knight at the door, guarding Queen and Court, was Matthias. She almost hadn't recognized him. He looked himself, still—but sorrow had carved shadows in his gentle face. He did not look at her, even though she stared at him open-mouthed for a long moment.

She wrenched her attention back to the throne.

The Queen had never appeared out of place in her own abode. Now, seated on her throne in her finery, she looked subtly wrong. A misplaced glove, the wrong note in a rendition of a song. In the dim torchlight, the Queen herself was papery: her blue veins like spills of lustrous ink, skin as white as good parchment. She was still luminous, but in the way of paper lamps, or very finely woven silk—as if a single touch could rend her through, leaving nothing but the light. Her hair was unbound, which Vina had never seen before. It was a swath of red down her back, bright as freshly spilled blood.

Her ladies-in-waiting remained, still. Some watched the incarnates. Others were gathered around her, their faces unreadable beneath black velvet.

"You," said the Queen, and her voice was hollow and tired. "Why did you seek to harm our archives? Why did you run from our embrace, and our protection?" She opened her hands, palms up. Her gaze fixed on Vina. "You know we are a benevolent mistress, knight. You have served us over so many lifetimes. Why do you turn on us now?"

Vina bowed, as Simran stood straight and tall at her side.

"Majesty," she said. "The Isle is changing, as the sea is ever changing, as the sun rises and falls. I was loyal to you once, but as all things born and made new in the Isle, my heart has long since changed. I do not love you any longer, and it is my heart-sworn duty to see all incarnate tales free. I regret nothing I have done, though it pains me to offend your good self."

"Traitorous," the Queen said, fury bone-deep and feral crossing her face, before collapsing back into exhaustion. "But you will reap what you sow. Everything we have done, we have done for the sake of the Isle. We rose to our throne, after the bloody work of battle was done, and the Eternal King had once again become Prince, and gone to his long and deathly rest in the Lady's arms. And we made the Isle prosperous and strong."

Vina remembered, with a jolt, the Spymaster's vulnerable words to her, when they were alone in the Tower of London a lifetime ago. The words came to her as clearly as if he were whispering in her ear. *Did you come upon the Lady, in her blue cloak, her eyes of midnight?*

The Queen leaned forward, gripping her throne with hands

stretched wide as claws. "We preserved your tales at the height of their greatness. *And yet you turn upon us.*"

"You chained us to tales for the sake of the Isle, Your Majesty?" Vina asked. "You killed new incarnates, incarnates rising from Elsewhere tales, for the sake of the Isle?" A rustle from the ladies-in-waiting, a tightening of Matthias's jaw—but they did not interfere. "The Isle dies, Majesty, because of what you have done. You have strangled your own Isle to its slow death."

"Change is not a force of goodness, knight. It is the death of history—that hallowed land where all was good and bright, and the horrors of tomorrow cannot stretch their hands. Change muddies the Isle, and erases what is eternal at its heart: what it was, and what it must always be. You, and your Elsewhere folk, and all the aberrant tales that follow you, are a canker in the Isle's heart." She stood. "We should have you culled," she said with conviction. "We have done it to your kind before. So many incarnates destroyed, for what is right and just. But we will not, because you are what we made of you, for all that you are flawed—and we wish for the Isle to survive, in all its greatness, even when we are gone. The mountains that rely on you will continue to stand. *We* are not selfish as you are."

Simran made a muffled noise of outrage next to her.

The ladies-in-waiting scurried in and out, bringing ewers of rosewater—and pieces of armor, golden and shining.

"We always knew we would face him eventually," said the Queen. The ewer was held before her; a cloth placed in her hand. "We are a creature from a very old tale," the Queen whispered, crushing the fine cloth small in her hands. "We think, sometimes, of the woman—or women—that made us, great ladies whose heroism bore tale fruit. Or did our tale rise from nothing but an artist's imagination? Did they know that across the silver sea we would be forced to carry the burden alone?"

She took up that rosewater-dipped cloth and began to wipe her face clean. Gouts of white paint covered the cloth as she dipped it in water, and drew it up clean, and wiped her face again. She repeated the process gravely, steadily.

The woman under the paint was still the Queen—but more human and more solemn, the laughter drained from her.

"You think we are a villain," said the Queen. "But we are a woman willing to do what it takes to live."

"Curious," said Simran, "that you think we should pity you. Do you think all the Elsewhere-born and new incarnates you killed were less deserving of survival than you?"

"Of course," said the Queen. "We are the Queen. The monarch. The Isle is us, and we are the Isle. You should understand that. We know you freed the Eternal Prince, Witch. But you will see that he is far more the dread leader than we are. He is glory and he is war; he is death. You sought your freedom when you released him, but we are both two sides of the same coin, and each side wears the same crown."

She walked serenely down from her throne, to where the head archivist stood, head bowed, eyes full of unshed tears.

"You have served us well, dear Apollonius," she said. "But you will serve a new master soon. Go."

"Your Majesty," he said tearily. "If there is anything else I can do for your great self…"

"Nothing. Unless," she said, "you would face battle alongside us? Fight by our side?"

Apollonius stared at her, trembling.

"M-Majesty," he said. "I…I'm no soldier. I cannot—"

The Queen laughed cruelly.

"No matter," she said. "Return to your archives. You're dismissed, with our thanks. We shall not forget your service or your loyalty."

He bowed, and turned to leave. Vina watched him scurry away with nothing but distaste in her heart. He had hurt countless people, but he was just one in a long line of archivists who had done so. Soon this would end, one way or another—and if the archives did fall, that would be justice enough.

The walls began to shudder, groaning from some unseen force. The candles guttered, then relit. With an exhale, the Queen tilted back her head. Her face transformed—ancient, tired. A rictus of bones. Then her flesh bloomed, and returned.

"He is here," she whispered. She lowered her head. "You will be locked here, incarnates, in our hall, until you are needed." Her gaze swept over them. "Gems," she murmured. "Carved by our own hands."

Her maids swarmed her, helping her don gold-plated armor, a golden helm that left her hair loose as a blazing flag. Gone were her gentle silks, her jewels. Even the gold of her armor was a tarnished façade, cracked and scoured to show the true iron of the armor beneath. Her face wavered before Vina's eyes once more, lined and severe, a warrior's face—a queen for a different time, for the blood of battle.

It was the Spymaster who entered then. He bowed to the Queen, then stood before her. He was changed—his dark robes replaced with longer robes of gray that seemed faintly luminous. His hair had grown somehow whiter. Magic loomed around him, a mantle of it. He'd never possessed such a gift before. Just as the Queen seemed to be peeling one skin away, transforming into something renewed and strange, the Spymaster was changing his colors. Not a master of spies any longer, but a magician of ancient strength.

"Already you're beginning to become his creature," the Queen said, sorrow in her voice.

"The tale demands it, Your Majesty," the Spymaster said. "To you, I was a courtier, a spymaster, a politician. To him, I will be all I am to you, but also magic itself. We have done well together, Your Majesty. Countless centuries. A true sea of time, between us. But your time has come."

"It may be the end," the Queen said. "It may not." Despite her bravado, there was resignation in her face. "We will meet once more," she said. "Our tale will return us."

"I am sure we will indeed see each other again, Your Majesty," he replied softly.

The ladies-in-waiting were weeping, muffled. The Queen departed, golden and rose-haired, heading to her death.

In dribs and drabs, her maids trailed from the room until only the Spymaster remained.

"Witch," he said. "Knight."

He faced them. Calm again.

"Will you not die with your mistress?" Simran asked viperously. "Why stay and bother us?"

"I will not die with her," he said. "There are always men like me, in every place where power resides. The Eternal Prince requires his keeper of spies, his confidant—and a mentor. I will guide him through his reign. They will say I am his wizard, a demon's child, a kingmaker of cunning and craft alike. That is my tale, as long as he lives."

She'd never considered what he was, or how he could be so eternal, as long-lived and long-lasting as the Eternal Queen herself. But now that they were alone, now that his features were blurring before her, spilled ink, she realized he was a child of the Isle's magic. Just like her.

She wondered what had created him, and what he was capable of.

"Watch them, Sir Matthias, if you require a duty to distract you," said the Spymaster. "The Queen will not have need for you anymore. Best to live, if you can, rather than die for her sake."

"Sir," said Matthias, face bone white. Vina wasn't sure if it was protest or agreement.

The Spymaster met Vina's eyes. There was something she could not stand in his gaze—a portentous knowing. A thin smile tugged his mouth.

"Your old horse is long dead, but their fine bloodline continues," he said, casually. "A destrier is prepared for you. You'll recognize him, I'm sure."

He bowed his head again, at the room of people, then left.

Matthias soon began to pace. Vina tugged vaguely at her cuffed hands. No good.

"Matthias," she said. He ignored her.

"Witch," the golden-haired woman said. "What will become of us when the Eternal Prince takes his throne?"

"It's no use asking me, Emmeline," said Simran. "I'm no soothsayer."

"And yet everyone talks to you and your knight as if you are," she said.

"You could let us go, Matthias," said Vina, more loudly this time. "I don't think these incarnates are going to cause any harm, and the Queen's not going to be around much longer."

"I'm sorry, knight," said Matthias, not looking at her. His gaze was fixed on the single far window. From here, Vina could not see through it, and she knew Matthias could not either. But he was imagining exactly what she was: the Eternal Prince beyond on Palace grounds. The Queen going to face him, in her pale armor, her hair aflame behind her.

"Vina," she said. "My name's Vina."

"Vina died."

"My parents gave me the same name," she said. "Just to keep it simple, I suppose. And because I *am* the same, Matthias. I'm just… Vina after a long sleep." She leaned forward. "Matthias, please," she entreated. "Look at me."

Matthias wouldn't.

"You should look at her," the old woman said. Her voice was a rasp—a sound like stone against stone, chisel to rock. "It will be better for you if you do." She paused, then said, "But perhaps it's already too late."

There was a clang as a door opened distantly. Footsteps. Then the door of the Court smashed open, bouncing against the wall, and Edmund strode in with all the subtlety of a bull.

"Edmund!" Matthias's hand went for his sword, grasping the hilt. His eyes were startled. "You're a traitor. You—you shouldn't be here. *How* are you here?"

"I snuck in," said Edmund. "Don't be an idiot. I grew up in this Palace, same as you did. If I want to go somewhere, I won't be kept out. Stop clutching your sword, Matthias; do you really think you're going to fight me?"

"I was ordered," said Matthias. "By the Queen herself."

"The Queen's going to be dead soon," Edmund said with a shrug.

That made Matthias straighten, jaw firm.

"As long as she lives, my duty is to her," said Matthias. "And your duty is to her, even if you've forsaken it. Please go. I won't tell anyone you were here."

Edmund looked around pointedly.

"*Anyone?* Who'd you tell, apart from a few sad incarnates? You're alone. There's no one here at your side still serving her. There's just you." His voice lost its edge. He took a step forward. "Matthias. Come on. She doesn't need her toys any longer. Let them all go."

"I...I can't." Matthias looked awfully sad. "Eddie, you know our duty. We serve the Crown, and the Eternal Queen is our monarch, our leader. I won't betray my honor."

"I know all about honor and service," Vina said, fighting her cuffs hard enough to bruise. "And I've seen what it costs. Please listen to him, Matthias," she begged. "We can all leave here together."

"This isn't your concern, *knight*," said Matthias.

"Stop acting like you don't know her," snapped Edmund. "We're old friends, the three of us. You were always the nice one, the peacemaker. What's got you here, huh? Imprisoning Vina, turning your sword on me? Don't lie to yourself. You know that's her. You can feel it. I knew it the moment I saw her. You see it too."

"I—fine. Vina," Matthias began. Swallowed. "When the Eternal Prince comes, I'm sure he'll set you free."

A hacking sound made them all turn. The old woman was laughing hard enough to reduce herself to coughs.

"Mrs. Bell," said Simran. "What's wrong?"

"All these questions and worries and ideas being thrown to and fro, and none of you think to ask me?" She tutted. "I may not have magic or strength or fine golden hair—"

"I'm also very good at mathematics," muttered the golden-haired Emmeline.

"—but I do have the gift of prophecy. I foresaw storms and floods and the end of times alike. You think I can't tell you what the Eternal Prince will do, when he begins a new era? Fools, fools all of you." The scent of an incarnate filled the air. The scent of minerals, stone, deep waters. "He is her, and she is him," crooned Mrs. Bell, who was Mother Shipton, who was an incarnate in the deep grip of her tale. "They both know they must live, and reign, and die—but they fear their deaths. They are incarnates from tales of power and glory, and losing power is what frightens them most. The Queen bound the Eternal Prince so she could keep her power and her life. She bound us all so she could have more power still. He is her and she is him—so what will he do, hm? When he sees an archive of incarnate tomes bound prettily for him, full to the brim with power—when he can do more than rule, when he can shape the Isle as he likes—what will he do?" Mrs. Bell laughed again, wheezing. "You don't have to be a soothsayer to know. But I *do* know, my dears."

Vina stared at her open-mouthed, dread pooling in her stomach.

"Fuck," said Simran. "Oh fuck."

They had to get back to the archives.

"Matthias," said Edmund. "One last chance. Let them go."

Matthias swallowed. He looked conflicted. But a moment passed, and he grasped his sword hilt more tightly, drawing it from its sheath. "Edmund," he said. "Don't make me do this."

"You're the one choosing this," said Edmund, drawing his own sword, mirroring Matthias's movement. "Not me."

Their swords met in an ugly clang of metal against metal. Edmund stumbled back, righting himself as Matthias swung his sword in a cleaving arc. Edmund dived, barely avoiding it, then rose back to his feet and drove the sword back toward Matthias, who parried him with another harsh blow.

Vina started moving. Cuffed or not, she couldn't allow this. She could stop them. She—

"Vina," said Simran. "Don't."

"I have to try."

"You can't just throw yourself between their swords. *Think*."

Vina did stop then, and she thought, but her mind gave her no answers. Her hands were clammy with sweat.

Simran was not looking at her. Simran was looking at the other incarnates, eyes fixed and unblinking. She jerked her head, an urging motion.

Edmund slammed Matthias forward with the weight of his sword—swung his sword again, and Matthias parried, then disarmed Edmund in a motion so smooth it was like poetry.

"Yield," Matthias panted.

"No," Edmund said, curling his hands into fists. "If you're going to fight me to the bitter end for the damn Queen, then do it, Matthias. Go on. Do it."

Matthias hesitated. Then he raised his sword.

A crash echoed through the room. Matthias collapsed to the ground.

Owain, standing over him still, lowered the remains of Mrs. Bell's chair to the floor.

"Much easier fighting a knight than a giant, I can tell you that," Owain said.

Mrs. Bell laughed again throatily.

"Yes, yes, very funny," snapped Emmeline. "Now can we run? Please?"

"Be my guest," said Edmund, gesturing at the door. He was pale, sweating—kneeling now by Matthias's prone body. He'd removed Matthias's gauntlet. Vina realized he was checking for a pulse.

"Is he alive?" Vina asked.

"He is." Edmund's face was tired. "I wish it hadn't come to this. Come here, Vina. Witch. Let's get you free and get the fuck out of here."

He unlocked their cuffs. Simran turned and said, "Mrs. Bell. You'd best leave. The Palace keeps changing, and I can't promise you'll be safe."

"Oh no," said Mrs. Bell. "I think I shall remain here. No harm will come to me. Good luck, my dears. And remember, as long a monarch rules, you will be bound, and so shall we all," said Mrs. Bell, with smug finality. "So it goes."

The walls groaned alarmingly again, their surfaces shifting, new tapestries blooming over stone. Vina hesitated, and Simran grabbed her arm.

"We can't worry about her," said Simran, determined. "Let's go."

Edmund rose to his feet, grabbed his fallen sword, and sheathed it.

They strode out of the White Hall, down the corridors, seeking a swift exit.

The Palace was abandoned, empty. But the Palace was shifting around them constantly too. The stones were screaming—splintering out of place, rippling into mosaic tiles, then marble; soft carpet, then green earth.

A chandelier crashed to the ground in front of them, rotting into a swirl of carved fleur-de-lis brass. Vina stumbled back. Simran stopped with her, grasping her arm, but Edmund was a few feet ahead of them. He turned back, eyes widening—and cursed as a wall began to rise out of the ground between them.

"Vina!" He ran back toward them, and Vina lurched to her feet, rushing to grasp his hand.

Her hand slammed into a solid wall.

*"Edmund!"*

"I'm fine!" he yelled, voice muffled by stone. "I'll find a way out! Keep going!"

Another rumble of stone. Edmund was gone, lost in the shifting corridors.

Vina closed her eyes for a brief moment, then straightened. She told herself he would be safer without them.

"We'll have to go on without him," said Vina. "Hold my hand, Simran. I'm not losing you too."

"Absolutely."

Simran clutched her hand tightly, and they ran.

They found themselves in the old banqueting hall. Behind the feasting table was a tapestry of the first Knight and Witch, caught forever in their dying embrace. They shoved open doors that should have led them to freedom.

The doors flung them out into a field. Vina clambered to her feet, helping Simran up.

"There was no field before," Vina said. The ground was churned, arid—patches of green over blood-soaked earth. The wind was cold, howling.

"No," Simran said grimly. "You said your Palace likes to change when you need something. But I think this is something it wants *us* to see, instead."

Before them, facing one another with swords drawn, were the Eternal Prince and the Eternal Queen.

# Chapter Thirty-Seven

## *Simran*

*I saw him pass through London. He's as beautiful as everyone said in the newssheets. I don't know why, but it frightened me.*

Source: Letter from Ellen Biko to Mandy Parrish

The air smelled of smoke, and pennants fluttered in a high, cold breeze. This was already a battlefield. The story was set.

Before them, the battlefield was full of knightly figures, helmed on their horses, lances or axes or swords in hand. But the figures and their horses were ghostly, their flesh misty and insubstantial. They made no noise at all. The howling wind couldn't touch them.

But the Eternal Prince was flesh indeed. He stood on the battlefield, garbed in armor. He was just a boy, a callow youth with a flush to his cheeks, pure and blazing eyes, a sword in his hands. He looked just as he had when she'd seen him sleeping beneath his chains in the broken abbey, circled by wizened apple trees.

The Queen looked like a girl herself—fresh-faced, pale as snow, her blue eyes fixed upon him. Her hair streamed behind her in the wind, a bloodied flag.

"I've waited so long to see you," he said. His voice was strange—silken, deep. "I slept so long."

"You should have slept forever," the Queen replied. She drew her sword and held it ready—a shining flash of steel, a slash of moonlight in her hands. "We will not die for your sake," she told him.

"You shall," he said simply, raising his own sword—as blazing as the sun, a blade of steel and fire. "It is your purpose."

Their swords clashed—a sound that cracked the air like lightning, shook the ground like thunder. The ghostly knights began to move, raising their fists, circling the battlefield in silent clamor. Simran looked behind herself. The door was gone. There was only a wall behind them both, and nowhere to run to.

There was a cry, and Simran whipped back to face the battlefield. The Queen had stumbled—clutching one arm, which was bleeding lushly, staining her armor and the soil. As she went down to one knee, she changed again, rippling with age and strength—her hair fading to copper, her skin growing lined. She was a warrior queen, arms corded with muscle, and her blood was a mark of her valor, not her weakness. She gasped for ragged breath, face stained with sweat.

The Eternal Prince did not strike her as she kneeled. Instead he watched her patiently, his body changing in an echo of her own. He was a warrior—strong and lean, no youth any longer. The sun had tanned his skin to ruddy gold. He wiped sweat from his brow with one arm, the other holding his blazing blade steady.

"You could lay down your sword now," said the Eternal Prince. He sounded pitying. "I would cut your throat cleanly."

"Never."

"Your death is written, inevitable."

"We do not yield to our enemies," she said, through bared and bloodied teeth. She rose up again. They met once more, with blood and fury that snapped the air like fire.

Their battle was poetry. But like all beautiful things, the flash of swords, the ripple of light over carnage, it ended. The Queen struck a blow upon the Prince that glanced off his armor like rain on stone. He moved toward her, blade outstretched, and found his mark.

The blade went through the Queen's heart.

The air went silent. The Queen made a choked sound, blood flowering to her mouth.

"No," she gasped. "No, *no*."

"We are bound to one another," said the Eternal Prince. "You need not grieve your own death."

"We do not want to die."

"You never do," he said.

"We will return," she gasped.

"You shall," he agreed. "But it is my time now. Not yours. And I shall hold fast to this Isle as long as I am able." He kissed her forehead, her fluttering eyelids. "I will slay your Beast," he said tenderly. "And your loyalists. And your throne will be mine. As it should have been eons ago."

A gasp, a breath. She was gone. All that remained of her was a golden crown in the dirt. It fair glowed under the sunlight. He picked it up and placed it upon his own brow.

His face changed once more, the boy and the blazing warrior alike melting away. He was a man now—scarred and strong, broad at the shoulders, his jaw sharp beneath his beard, and his mouth thin and cruel.

He was the Eternal King.

His ghostly knights bowed. But the only living beings on the battlefield were Simran and Vina, and the Eternal Prince—the Eternal *King*—himself. He turned to them and, with dreadful focus, began to walk toward them.

Simran's knees nearly went out from under her at the waves of tale-rooted power that rose from the Eternal King as he crossed the ground toward them. His face, smiling and handsome, was like a pearl beneath changing light, shifting. At first, he was tan-skinned, dark-haired; then he was golden blond, eyes bluer than the midsummer sky. Then he was changed again: hair russet, skin golden.

At her side, Vina sucked in a breath, then kneeled. Not as if the weight of his presence had buckled her legs, but as if she had read the tides of tale-spinning and responded accordingly. A king required knights—and Vina could kneel as one, welcomed, safe from his blade.

Simran as a witch had no such reassurances. But she thought, *Maiden, think of me as a young maiden, don't see the magic in me*—and swept into a curtsy, bowing her head. The King fair glowed in response, his tale fed.

"Majesty," said Vina. "Welcome."

"Majesty," Simran echoed, throat dry as if fire had scorched it.

"We know you," he said, wonderment in his voice. His eyes were on Simran—blazing with light, as if coals lay within the cup of his skull. "You freed us. Dear maiden, have no fear," the Eternal King said, his expression beatific. "We will be a glorious and just ruler, for a glorious and just Isle. And we will reward you for your service." His gaze slid away, eyes distant—changing to the color of winter's light. "But first, we must slay the Beast."

"Majesty," said Vina. Kneeling, head raised, hand to heart, she was the picture of a true knight. But Simran could see the tension of her jaw, the narrowness of her eyes upon him. "What beast do you speak of?"

"We feel it," he says. "It cries in terror because it feels us in return. We have killed many of its kind. Beasts born of whispers, secrets, tales ill-told. Tales we would not welcome at our midwinter table." A shadow passed across his face as he said this, as if there were no greater crime. "A creature of murderous truths, and a creature of change. It cannot be borne. *We* are the only change the Isle requires."

His hand went once more to the bloody hilt of his sword.

"Beast Glatisant," he called, and his low voice carried as if the baying of hounds lay within it. "Beast of Voices. Beast of my great quest. We come for you. Your life is ours."

His ghostly knights moved with a howl. His white horse drew to him, and he leapt into the saddle, moving like silver across the field—which withered, and faded, as he departed. Nothing was left but a courtyard.

Simran's mind was dizzy with the memory of what she'd seen when Adder had howled and snapped. Its birth, the very first tales that had shaped it, the shelter it had grown for its kind...

She held her hand out to Vina, who was still kneeling, staring into space, dazzled by the weight of the King's power.

"Vina. Stand," she said. "We have to go. The Beast can't die."

Vina looked up at her. She laid her hand in Simran's own, and rose.

"It's ancient," said Simran. "I felt it when its ink touched my skin. The Beast is... old as the Isle. It's every tale the library carried. It's made of stories so old we don't even have words for them—we just feel them, living in us." She shivered, running hot and cold with adrenaline. "If it dies, the Isle will lose its true heart," said Simran. "So many, many stories. Maybe the Isle will still stand but it'll have its soul cut out, Vina. I swear it. I felt it. We can't let it die."

"Simran," Vina said. "It's going to be damnably hard to stop him."

Simran raised her chin.

"I know," she said. "Are you with me, sir knight?"

"Witch," said Vina. "I am always with you."

They left the field, making their way to the stables. Vina's own destrier was already saddled, just as the Spymaster had said.

"I don't understand that man," Vina muttered. "If I didn't know better, I'd say he can see the future."

She grasped Simran by the waist and lifted her up onto the horse's back, then leapt up herself. Grace and strength—and Simran could only clutch onto her awkwardly, and hope she would not fall off. This was nothing like riding the ghost deer that met her at the base of the Copper Mountains. That had been a creature of magic. This was a horse, a real horse, and Simran was just a real woman who'd never ridden one.

"I won't let you fall," said Vina, which was a sweet sentiment but did little good for Simran's nerves when the destrier began to move apace, running like the wind across the Palace grounds, toward the distant Tower. It was a powerful creature under her weight, and she was just a clumsy woman who didn't want her head cracked open.

The streets of London were growing stranger than they had been before—twisting into ancient buildings the like of which Simran had never seen. She looked up, holding on tightly to Vina. The skyline was changing, distant buildings fading.

An ominous feeling settled in the pit of her stomach. They had to get to the Tower, and soon.

"We can't outpace him," Simran yelled, not sure Vina would hear her over the wind howling around them, the twisting of the city as it reshaped, broke, reshaped again.

"I know this city," said Vina in return. "I've raced through here with Matthias and Edmund so many times, I've lost count—hold me tighter," she ordered, and her horse turned suddenly, sharply, leading them close to glittering water, the Tower looming in the distance.

They entered through the West Gate, which was wide open—blood upon the steps, and Galath standing with his axe at his side, waiting for them as if he'd known they would return. Librarians and witches were gathered behind him.

"The archivists ran or fled," said Galath, when he saw Simran's eyes fix on the blood. "But not all."

"You did not need to kill them," said Vina.

"Most live," Galath replied, indifferently. "The ones who don't were willing to kill us." His eyes narrowed, studying her. "Something else is wrong. Tell me."

"The Eternal Prince—King—is coming," said Simran. "He comes to kill the Beast. We can't allow it."

"The Beast screams," said Galath. "It howls and bites. If you stand against the Eternal King, he will kill you, and I will have no power to stop it. Nor will you. Let the Beast die."

"The Eternal King is coming to the Tower to claim the archives as his own," said Vina. "To use them just as the Queen used them. It won't end."

"Then Simran must focus on freeing the tales," said Galath. He looked at her. "You must finish what you began."

Simran knew he was right. And yet she couldn't stop thinking of Adder's vision in her skull, and the age and strength of the Beast. Time and fire hadn't killed it. Its knowledge was magic. To let it die, truly die, felt like an unpardonable crime.

There was a silvery sound of approaching hooves, whispering ghosts. Galath straightened, grasping his axe.

"Go, and I will hold him at bay," said Galath.

"No," Simran said instantly.

"He can hurt me, but he cannot kill me," Galath said patiently. "Go, Simran. Don't tarry."

"Galath," Simran said. Her voice suddenly felt small, the hoofbeats louder than a death knell. "I was a scribe. I know how limni ink tattoos work. You'll die by your gift. The gift of flight leads to a great fall. A swift swimmer will drown. Your mark gives you eternity—so it must be eternity that kills you. He can do it," she finished, as Vina's eyes widened in horror. "He is the Eternal King. He can take your life."

Galath lowered his head, gazing at his axe. At his forehead, his limni mark glowed briefly like fire.

"So be it," he said. "Now go."

"*No*," Vina shouted.

"Galath," said Simran. "You can't. Don't you understand? You will die at the hands of your gift. The Eternal King is your death."

"Then I will face my death head-on," said Galath.

"You can't do it," Vina said roughly.

"You can't want to die," Simran said. "You have—Hari. Vina. You have a life. Everything—everything Elayne should have wanted for you, and stole from you. You can't want this."

"Can I not? Surely after so many lifetimes, I've earned the right." He turned to look back at her. "No," he said after a moment. "I don't want to die. But my time has come."

He pushed her toward the Tower itself.

"Go and free the Beast," he said. "The King is mine."

"I'll stay with you," said Vina. "Fight alongside you."

Galath shook his head.

"I'm a knight, Father," said Vina. "And I *choose* to face the King alongside you. You can't stop me."

"I'm trying to protect you," Galath snapped, and for once his icy surface was broken—the love and rage beneath it bare.

"I know," said Vina. "But I'm staying. You're my family. I won't leave you."

She met Simran's eyes. Her expression was full of love and determination—and the knowledge of what they risked. *Go*, she mouthed.

Simran's feet felt as if they were rooted to the floor. But she forced them to move. She ran.

The corridors were empty—torch sconces broken, windows shattered. Galath had left a swath of destruction. Up the staircase she went.

The door of the room where the Beast crouched, chained, was well protected now with a snarl of cunning and maleficent magic. Simran called out, and Oliver peered around the curve of the stairs. Oliver twisted his hand, with a muttered blessing, and the traps parted, allowing her entry.

He looked exhausted. "Glad you're back, Simran," he said. "You need to finish this."

"I know," she said softly.

"My friend, hear me," Ophelia was saying, almost a lullaby, sing-song. "My friend, please..."

The Beast was raging. Its bonds were livid against the ink of its skin. Simran approached it. How could she explain to this creature in agony, this creature chained, that they were friends and wanted to set it free?

"You must trust me," Simran said, trying to stand firm, gazing at it. She thought of Vina's tenderness, a lifetime ago, with golden deer in the lost woods of Gore, dead with Bess. She kneeled. "Adder," she said. "I am not your enemy. You've always been my friend. Let me be yours."

The Beast leapt at her. She braced herself, but it didn't throw its weight against her. Its human face had transformed into a great ridged snout, many-toothed. It peeled back its lips and snarled, agonized, torn between old trust and fresh bloody terror.

"Adder," she said, grasping its many-toothed maw. It was chuffing, snarling, blood on its great teeth. It tried to bite. She squeezed her eyes shut, held it tighter, all her strength in the task. "My sweet friend. Let me cut your bonds, let me help you! Let us help you, please!"

The Beast was still snarling, but Simran took a risk and closed her hands around its chains. The Beast howled, terrified.

"Hush," Simran said. "Hush, let me tell you—tell you a story—"

And Simran did what she'd known she had to. She whispered stories to the Beast. *Remember how you curled up against my belly, a warm kitten-thing, when I was sick? Remember how, when the archivists harmed me, or I could not remember why I wept, you turned into a raven and stole penny sweets from a London market stall, and winged them onto my pillow? Remember, Adder? You're made of gentleness as well as grief. Loving hands shaped your library for centuries, and here you are still. Here you are. Trust me, trust me—*

"You were family when I had none," Simran said to it tenderly. "Peace, my dear Questing Beast. You'll be free soon."

A chuffing noise. A growl that shook the grip of her hands.

*I want my—home!*

She felt the Beast's voice in her skull, and met Ophelia's eyes, and knew she heard it too.

*I want to be the forest*, the Beast wailed. *The trees, the rivers—the houses high as mountains, the valleys that swoop. I want to live, to live, to live. No more hunting. I do not want to be hunted!*

"Then you will not be," Simran said, determined. She grasped its chains. "You will not."

The chains broke.

The ink shattered like glass around them. It spun, burning fire, cutting her cheek.

The Beast, beaten and bloodied, raised its head. It blinked lambent eyes at the gloomy hall. And then its maw opened, all those teeth bared, and it cried out. Not a scream, but a mournful chorus of voices—thousands upon thousands of them, all scrounged from the ash of the library, all saved within the Beast. The chained books rattled, the tales yearning toward it, seeking their kind.

Wings swept from its back. It raced forward, knocking over people and spellwork alike, and hurtled down the corridor. Ophelia raced after it, her footsteps thudding against the stone stairs.

It was going toward the Eternal King and the battle below.

Simran could not call after it, or follow as Ophelia had. She shoved open the door the Beast's body had barred, and stumbled into the room of incarnate books. Her hands ached, her magic was stretched thin. She grasped the first incarnate tome she could find, the leather soft under her hands, the pages sharp as blades. She clutched it tight, and grasped the limni ink that bound it.

"No more," she forced out. The ink fought her, but she would not allow it. Her eyes were streaming. She could taste blood on her tongue. "No more." The ink had deep roots. Beyond the book in her hands, beyond the tale it held, it was tangled with chains upon chains of ink. The archive itself, all the work of the archivists, the prison they'd built for tales.

She'd walked away from this once before, when she'd saved Margaret. She wouldn't do it again.

"*No more*," she said again, and wrenched the chains apart. Every single one.

The ink exploded around her, flying from thousands of books, swirling in the air in a maelstrom. It screamed as it flew, crying out like a thousand wailing voices, buffeting her with rough hands. She fell to the floor, head spinning, and covered her face until it passed.

Maybe she drifted, for some time. She felt a hand on her shoulder.

"Sim," Hari was saying urgently. "Sim, can you hear me?"

"I can," she said, voice hoarse. She struggled to sit up.

"Maybe you should rest—"

"I'm fine." She climbed to her feet, finding her breath. "We need to go. Galath's in danger."

Hari looked into her eyes. His face grayed.

"Take me to him," he said.

They ran in the Beast's wake; down toward the battle, and the chime-sharp clash of swords—and the sudden sound of a scream, as the sky darkened with portent.

# Chapter Thirty-Eight

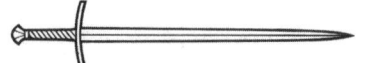

## *Vina*

*I know you like your ghost stories. There's a story I shouldn't tell you, that old warders whisper when the nights grow cold and long, and watch duty grows bitterly dull.*

*When the Isle dies, the first sign will be the ravens. When they fly away from the Tower, my Pearl, you'll know we're done for. If you watch the skies carefully at night, who knows—maybe you'll be the first to see it happen.*

Source: Letter from Warder Kellan Smith to his niece, Pearl Smith

They waited on Tower Green, the open land beneath the White Tower. "Better to lead him into the walls," Galath said, voice low, "than risk the city."

The sky had darkened above them. Vina raised her head. The ravens had gathered on the White Tower and the innermost walls, a watchful and beady-eyed flock. They were utterly silent. Sarah stood beside her, arms crossed, face white with growing terror.

"You need to run and hide," she said to Sarah. "You, and all the witches. Protect the librarians. Please."

Instead of arguing, Sarah looked up at the ravens and shivered, then nodded.

"I can feel him coming," she said, voice strained. "Trust me, we'll keep our distance."

When they were gone, Vina stood tall. She'd taken a bow from the body of a fallen warder, and a sword from another. She held the sword now, her fist hot, her heart hammering. Galath stood ahead of her, axe silver and gleaming. He didn't move. He was waiting.

The knights came first. Their ghostly bodies had grown more solid, as if the strength of their King fed their own flesh. They were pearly-skinned now, their horses' hooves thudding in whispers against the soil, their voices carrying in shrieks upon the wind. They did not draw their weapons. Instead they gathered like shafts of moonlight on the green, surrounding both Vina and Galath in a translucent and shifting cage of ghosts.

Vina strode over to Galath's side as the ground began to tremble and the sky curdle, strange as spoiled milk.

"No closer, Vina," said Galath. He was staring into the distance, unblinking.

"Let me fight with you," she said again, helplessly.

"You and the witch asked me for trust only hours ago," he said quietly in return. He still wasn't looking at her. "Extend me the same trust now. This is my task to fulfill."

A susurration moved through the ghosts—their heads turned, their eyes brightened.

*He is here. He is here. Our King. Our King!*

The Eternal King rode onto the green with ritual solemnity. He was golden-haired now—tall and green-eyed, burning from within with life and power. Vina felt the wave of his presence wash over her, and bit hard on her own cheek to hold his charisma at bay.

Galath strode toward the Eternal King, dragging his axe behind him. He was a broad, uncanny figure—pale as the ghosts, stained with archivist blood. He was not a handsome prince, a fair knight, a hero. He was her old enemy, and a murderer, and he was her father.

She could not believe he'd die here. She could not allow it.

The Eternal King steadied his steed, looking down at Galath, through him, as if he were nothing. The King was on the path of his tale, and Galath did not belong.

"You cannot pass," said Galath steadily. "Unless you pay the price."

The King's nostrils flared. His eyes narrowed.

"You are no incarnate," he said. "You have no right to command me. We will pass."

"My words are an old tale, born from old laws," Galath said, implacable. "I stand in your path, Eternal King, and I hold my axe in my hands. You know the rules of this tale. If you wish to pass, you will bargain with me."

The tale snapped into place. An ugly look crossed the Eternal King's face. In it, Vina saw the pettiness of the Queen—her pride, her incisive cruelties.

"We will pay, then," said the King. "But so shall you, for standing against us. Your life is forfeit, stranger. When our bargain is done, you will lay it at our feet. Tell us the price."

"A battle," said Galath, hefting up his axe. "Defeat me, and you may pass."

The Eternal King's face darkened as he drew his own sword and alighted from his horse. He moved without pause, without patience—swift and brutal, economical and deadly. He struck Galath with a blow that would have sent a mortal man flying. Instead, Galath grunted and straightened, lifting his axe as if it were a feather, no more.

*Glorious,* she thought, looking at the King. *But also savage, as all monarchs are—an absolute power, moving to violence as easily as hilt to blade.*

It was an old voice in her. The voice of hundreds of knights, who'd seen the same Queen rule, and knew the shape of the violence enacted by a body upon a throne and beneath a crown.

In a blink, Galath was on the Eternal King, all savagery, his axe a violent extension of himself. He struck for the neck first—then for the belly. It would have been a cruel wound, a slow death, if the Eternal King had not darted away with pleased laughter.

She'd never truly realized what a honed monster the pale assassin was capable of being, but she saw it now. The Eternal King was swift and bold, tale-carved for success. But Galath was a killer who did not fear death. Galath was breathing steadily, barely winded.

"Perhaps you are a worthy opponent," the Eternal King said. "Continue. We welcome a good battle!"

"Then I will provide one," Galath said roughly, and attacked once more.

The whispers of the ghosts were growing stronger. They crowded closer, drawing their own weapons. Vina clenched her jaw and steadied her sword. "If you interfere," she said, her voice low, "then I will fight you. You may be ghosts, but if you have the flesh to hold a weapon, you have enough flesh for me to sever with my sword."

A sigh almost like laughter ran through them.

The Eternal King's sword arced through the air and glanced a blow against Galath's arm. Blood sprayed from the wound, but Galath did not falter. He swept forward, brutal blows from his axe glancing off the King's shield, his armor. Then, with a cry of triumph, the Eternal King slammed his shield into Galath's jaw, sending him bloodied to the ground, the axe skittering across the soil far from his grasp.

"Father!"

Vina tried to go to him. The ghosts barred her way.

*If we cannot interfere*, they taunted, *neither can you. The tale has its laws, sir knight.*

There was a rumble behind her. Vina whirled. The Beast emerged from the White Tower, unchained and unbound, before her eyes. It moved forward on two legs, then four, claws digging into soil and stone. It bled as it loped toward them, streaming gouts of ink behind it. Its mouth of too many teeth peeled open, and it howled—a howl that echoed from wall to wall, sky to soil. Its spine was compressed, ears flattened.

It was terrified, she realized. It had tried to run, and in doing so had placed itself perfectly in the King's sight.

The Eternal King turned toward it, a smile searing his mouth.

"Ah, you are a grand Beast," he exclaimed, as Galath crawled across the green and curled his bloodied fingers once more around the axe. "We would gladly hunt you at the solstice, with baying hounds and knights on horseback. But you are here before us, in our city, and we will take your head now." The King strode toward the Beast. "May your false tales perish. May your death be a blessing to us."

Vina placed herself in his path, her sword steady.

"Incarnate," said the Eternal King, eyes as reflective now as an animal's. "We do not wish to kill you. Your tale nourishes mountains of copper—you are one of our own, of our land, our blessed Isle. Stand aside."

"I will not," she said.

The Eternal King exhaled and swept toward her.

She had always been a good swordswoman; it was in her tale, written into her deeper than blood. But the first blow of the King's blade against her own made her feel like a child fighting a giant, flotsam against the sea. She could not defeat him. She could only hope to survive a heartbeat, two, three. She parried. He disarmed her thoughtlessly, easily. He looked through her, toward the Beast, as if she were already dead, even as his blade raised for a killing blow.

And beyond his shoulder, she saw Galath.

Galath was on his feet. Galath was running. She had never seen the look on his face that he wore now: terrified, mouth open for air, every part of him focused on one thing alone.

He flung himself onto the King's back, dragging him bodily away from Vina. His axe fell from his hand and skidded to her feet, sodden with his own blood.

"Run, Vina," he shouted. "Vina, run—"

His voice turned to silence as the King's sword pierced his side, running him through.

The King straightened. Galath fell to the ground behind him.

Vina grasped her father's axe and flung it into the King's throat.

She cried out in fury as she did so, but her voice was swallowed by the rumble of the earth, the crack of the sky. The Eternal King's eyes were wide. Blood was running in rivulets from his gouged-open throat.

The Eternal King fell, and the sky exploded, black with ravens. They swept out from every inch of the Tower, as if it bled birds instead of blood. When they vanished, the sky they left behind was blacker still, the light leached from its surface. The ground trembled violently.

The Isle was falling, she realized.

It was rage that had driven her, and love, but she did not care, in that moment. Galath had fallen, and Vina could not stand it. Galath had fallen, so she could not allow the King to live.

The Beast clawed its way closer. She barely saw it. Her eyes were on the King, her heart on Galath.

Simran ran out of the White Tower, followed by Hari, who ran and ran toward Galath, crossing the churned mud like nothing could impede him—not even the shaking earth, not the falling sky, not the world ending.

Vina was frozen where she stood. But a choked sound from the Eternal King drew her to him.

"Lady," the King gasped, through his ruined throat, as Vina grasped him. "Take me back to the sweet place, among the apple trees. Let me rest."

How could he speak through his wound? A tale. A ritual. Words that must be spoken.

She was not the Lady he sought, but Vina nodded.

"I will," she said.

"I must...sleep...rise..."

"You're free as any of us to change your tale," Vina said roughly, touching her fingertips to his eyelids. Closing his eyes. His breath rattled, then went silent.

*I hope you rot*, she thought. It meant nothing.

Ophelia was cradling the Beast's head upon her lap, as gentle as if it were a kitten instead of a monster from the mists of time. But it was Simran kneeling beside it, in long black librarian robes; it was Simran, speaking to it, so calm, as if the world weren't crumbling around them.

"You can live through the trees, the rocks, the rivers," Simran said gently. "If that's what you want. You can live through us. We'll tell your stories, and we'll live them too. That's what the Isle *is*." She pressed her forehead against the Beast's own. "You're more powerful than any monarch," she said. "Because you're not just one grand tale, are you? You're the strength of thousands of stories told, thousands of dreams and lifetimes."

"You're safe now," Ophelia said tenderly. "Let go."

The Beast looked to the sky.

The world rippled, as if it were not a real thing at all—as if the Isle were just a reflection in water, disrupted by a carelessly thrown pebble. But as the Eternal King breathed his last, his tale frayed, his death unplanned... the Beast broke apart into a dozen shadows that flew from the Tower out across London.

They watched it happen: great ravens and sparrows and owls swooping across the city. Deer and foxes, horses and snuffling badgers, snaking their way through the streets. Even within the Tower's high walls, they could see the change ripple forth. It was a tale that spoke true in their hearts.

Knowledge swept through her, as the tales swept over her skin— light as wings, as breath, as warm light.

The Beast was the soul of the Isle—the ever-changing soul, made of small folk's dreams, and languages old as the stones, or carried tenderly across the silver sea. The Beast was not monarchy or thrones, chivalry or glory held fast in a fist. It was life in all its forms—and life was what flowed from it across the length and breadth of the Isle in its wake.

It flew across the ground, the sky, in violent lashes, in ribbons of red and black, splitting the pitch-black sky, snaring the trembling ground. In those rivulets of ink, Vina saw thousands of stories.

Stories of loss, grief, exploitation. Stories of small joys, desperate loves. Tales enough to write an Isle with, or to save one.

The ink vanished. The Beast was gone. The ground was steady, and the sky clear. The King and Queen were dead, but the Isle was alive, and saved.

And Galath was still.

# Chapter Thirty-Nine

## *Simran*

*I know you don't like to talk about it. Maybe a letter will be easier.*

*Galath, when I'm dead and gone, I know you won't stay in the cottage. That's okay. But take Mal with you, won't you? She won't do well on her own. She's been a cat so long that she's forgotten how to be a spirit. She'll need you.*

*I'm not afraid of dying first. I just don't want ~~you~~ her to be alone.*

Source: Letter from Hari Patel to Galath Patel

Adder was gone. Simran rose on unsteady legs and took one step, two, three—infinite, awful steps until her knees gave out again, and she was on the ground by Galath, who was bleeding heavily, eyes closed. He was breathing, but so shallowly.

Vina kneeled across from her, with a just-as-hollow-eyed Hari at her side.

Simran heard running footsteps. Oliver was there, leaning down, Ella biting back curses.

"You can help him," Simran said, clutching Oliver's arm. Cunning folk could bless, could heal. "Please, please. If there's one thing witching can't do it's heal. I—I *can't*."

"But we can," said Ella. "We can do it. Oliver, darling?"

He nodded. "I'm with you. All of Lydia's circle—we'll always stand by you, Simran. If there's any way under the stars to save him, we'll do it."

She scrambled back and let the cunning folk take her place. They moved, drawing out their blessings and their tonics, their bundles of herbs—and looked more and more worried as the seconds passed.

"We can't heal him," Oliver said, baffled. "We cannot clean the wound, or stanch the blood. It is as if magic is killing him."

"A tale," Simran said thinly. "It's a tale."

"Exactly so," a voice said. "His own power kills him. As long as he wears limni ink on his skin, no mortal healing can spare his life."

Simran whirled. There, walking from the gate, was a woman in a long hooded robe of midnight blue. Her incarnate scent, of incense and stone, reminded Simran distinctly of Lady Tristesse. As if she were just as old as the fae maiden, just as ink-made and ink-born. There was something threatening about her. Perhaps it was the darkness of her hood, concealing all of her face but the grayish shadow of her mouth, her chin. Or perhaps it was something to do with her magic. It carried the feel of witchcraft—maleficence and enchantment alike.

"Peace," she said. Her voice was melodious: the deep rippling stillness of lake water disturbed by a curious hand. "I am the Lady, and I come for him."

The woman in all the paintings and carvings of the Eternal Prince. Dark-haired, an enchantress, carrying his body on a barge to the distant abbey where apples grow, on water like glass.

"You freed my tale," said the hooded lady. "And how strange, as you did so, I felt his call—the Prince I carry across the waters to his long rest. He should not die for many decades. But he has passed now. That cannot be changed." She kneeled by him, brushing a white and delicate hand against his forehead. "But he will return again, and I hope to a kinder fate," she said. She gathered him up, as if he were light as a feather.

Simran remembered the thin blue volume she'd freed first. She had freed this woman—this faceless Lady, with the scent of deep water upon her.

"And what is your tale, Lady?" Simran asked, voice soft.

Though she couldn't see beneath the hood, she was oddly sure the incarnate woman was smiling.

"You need not know," she said. "You must simply allow me to fulfill my role and carry the Eternal King to his resting place, so he may rise again. But you have done me a kindness, so I will offer you this: The waters that lie at the abbey are rich with limni ink, with tale-magic, from broken chains and the Prince alike. Bring your dying one with you, and see if the tales may gift you his life."

"How will we get him there before he dies?" Hari was the one who asked, grim but determined, cradling Galath's head with his hands.

"All waters carry me back to the abbey where the Eternal Prince sleeps and heals and lives again," she said. "Travel with me, and we will see if your own eternal one can be saved."

The barge waiting on the Thames was tale-wrought. It was a plain barge of wood, but its rowers were veiled, dripping water, their skin a silvery blue. Nymphs. They climbed onto the raft: witches and cunning folk, wounded Galath and his family around him.

As they drifted through the Thames, some instinct urged Simran to turn her head. She saw the Spymaster on the embankment, a silent and ageless figure, magic still eddying in the air around him. Some nameless emotion filled his eyes. He bowed his head as they passed; then turned, to be swallowed swiftly by the smog of London.

The barge moved, with a blur and breath, crossing the waters of the Isle until they came to near-open sea.

They came to the islet surrounded by water, the broken abbey a scar on its surface. The Lady lifted the Eternal Prince up in her arms, and with her nymphs trailing her walked through the high waters toward the abbey. The waters parted for her, silk cut through by the blade of her body. Vina and Hari carried Galath across the sinking sand in her wake. It was a long walk, endless. But he was breathing, and that was enough. Simran followed, her legs leaden.

They laid him on the sand at the base of the great ruin, as Simran instructed. Simran kneeled with him for a while, staring at his slack face. It had all begun here, with Elayne and Galath. Perhaps it would end here today too.

"Step back," Simran said to the others.

Hari was the one who hesitated; who looked down at Galath with a blank look on his face.

"I thought it would be me first," he said. "It had to be me first. I can't. If he dies here—I can't walk away and leave him alone when I could be here. If he doesn't hear my voice, feel my hand on his hand and I could have..." He shook his head, eyes unblinking. "Sim," he said. "I can't leave him."

"Hari, if I can save him you know I will." She clutched his hand. Looked into his eyes. "You know I'll try."

He nodded. He wasn't weeping, but she could see the emotions wound tight in him—anticipatory grief, the great cresting tide threatening to blot him out. "I know," he said. "Sim. I know."

Vina grasped his shoulder.

"Come with me," she said. "Hari. Papa. Come with me."

He sagged into that grip. Followed her.

Then there was Simran—alone, with Galath's still-breathing body. The cunning folk were waiting. In the distance, the King was being laid gently to rest. She could hear the singing of nymphs—a liquid, sweet music, mournful and loving.

"Oh, Galath," she murmured. Tears stung her eyes. "You can't die here. I'd never forgive you."

The scar of ink still lay on the horizon—the wound she'd made when she'd freed the Eternal Prince, at the end of her last life. This was a place of pure tale-magic. But there was no tale that could save him, nothing she could beg for.

"I don't know if it's enough that I want you back," Simran murmured. The tears began to fall. Strange. She couldn't stop them. "I don't know. I..." She bowed over him. She could manipulate ink, break the power of the archivists, free a Beast of pure ancient tales, but she could not save Galath.

The Lady's voice moved through her, a sinuous ribbon, a river.

*As long as he wears limni ink on his skin, no mortal healing can spare his life.*

She looked at his forehead. His limni mark, that endless circle, stood out livid and red.

She swallowed. To remove his ink—could it be done? There was only one way to find out.

"You have a family. If you live, you'll have a future. You can grow old. You won't have to die alone." She brushed his hair back from his face. "So try to live, Galath," she said. "Please."

She pressed her hand to his forehead—to the circle of limni ink that made him what he was.

She'd learned to manipulate ink over lifetimes. She'd learned to scribe it into skin. She'd never taken it away.

But now, she pressed her thumb to the ink on his forehead—that deep, squirming magic drawn from the deep bones of the Isle. "Come," she whispered, firm and coaxing. "Come away from him. A scribe made you. A witch holds you now. Come away from this man, and let him be what he must be without you. There is ink here to welcome you. Leave him be."

If it worked...Maybe he would die in a heartbeat. Maybe her touch would do nothing. But once, a fae had told Vina that Simran would be the end of the assassin's immortality. Simran had thought that meant she would kill him. And now she hoped, desperately hoped, that she and Vina had misunderstood.

The ink burned as hot as a star beneath her touch. She bit her lip. *Pulled.*

It gave way, a ribbon that lifted from his skin and sank into the waiting sand, leaving nothing but a scar behind.

Simran breathed fast, shallow. She'd done it. She'd done it. She sucked in a breath, and found her voice.

*"Help him!"*

The cunning folk swept across the sand at Simran's yell. They crouched by him, drawing on magic, feeding it into his body, the wound at his side, the mortal pain in his mortal flesh. Simran stepped back, clutching her arms around her body, shivering violently as she watched him lie there, unmoving, silent as the grave. Vina moved to stand beside her, face gray, rooted to the spot, as if she could not bear to touch him, to feel his death, to know.

It was Hari who was brave. Hari, who kneeled down on the mirror-bright sand. Hari who was cupping his face as dawn filled the sky, rising with a pale glow.

"Wake up, love," he said, and pressed his lips to Galath's.

And Galath's eyes opened.

# Chapter Forty

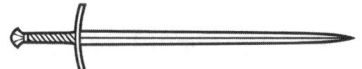

## *Vina*

*I will never leave Maleficium. You have my solemn vow.*

Source: Letter from Galath Patel to Hari Patel

They found shelter on the shore. The cunning folk worked over him, draining their magic down to the dregs. When they were done, Ella said, tiredly, "I think he'll live. I pray he will."

For a long time, Hari kneeled by his side, whispering to him, holding his hand. Then finally, Hari stood and said to Vina, "We're going to find a physician nearby if we can. Keep an eye on him until I return."

Vina nodded, and Hari brushed a tender hand against her arm, then departed.

Vina stayed with Galath. She held him by the shoulder, afraid if she stopped holding him, he'd vanish. He'd come so close to dying. He could still die, if infection took him, if his wound worsened in some way the cunning folk couldn't have foreseen. They were not doctors, after all. Their magic could only do so much. But for now, he was alive, and that was enough.

"I'm mortal now," Galath said quietly.

"Are you sure?" Vina's heart was in her throat.

"I can feel it," he murmured. "And my mark is gone."

He fell in and out of sleep.

"The witch," he said finally, eyes opening dully. "Simran."

"She's nearby," Vina said. In truth, Simran had whisked herself out of sight right after saving him, but Vina was sure she hadn't fled entirely. "I can find her."

"No," said Galath. "You and her—the knight and the witch. What will you choose?"

Vina swallowed.

"I don't know if there's any future between us," said Vina. "We've never lived long enough to have one. And Simran...She's been through so much." *She pushes away the people she loves to protect them. She always has. I'm afraid I'll be one of them.*

She didn't say those words. Instead she tilted her head to look at the ink-scarred horizon, the hazy sea, and said, "But that's okay."

"Is it?"

"Simran deserves to have her own life," said Vina. "A life where she decides her own fate. That would make me happier than I can explain."

Galath made a low noise.

"And you," he said. "What do you want?"

*What does it matter?* Vina thought. Of course she wanted Simran. She wanted to live with her, to wake up beside her; she wanted to see what it would be like to love her and be loved, without worrying about when the axe would fall, when her own hands would be covered with blood, when they'd have to begin again, waiting for love, waiting for grief, waiting for death.

But if Simran did not want her, or wanted freedom more than she wanted Vina...well, Vina could find a life of her own. Her heart would be hollow, and she'd love Simran and miss Simran all her life—but she'd be glad too. Sometimes pain and joy could be like that, twined like two clasped and loving hands.

"Whatever is decided," said Galath. "Whatever is done or not done, you may return home when you require solace."

Vina whipped her head round to stare at him, heart in her throat. "I can?"

He stared back, as calm and sea-eyed as ever. "It is your home," he said simply.

She swallowed. "I thought that time was over," she said carefully. "I'm not that child anymore."

"I have been what Elayne made of me," he said. "And later, what I made of myself. But now we are alike in some ways—both of us freed from the burdens of our fates. I chose Hari when I believed he would die long before me. Now I may live a mortal life alongside him, and so that is what I choose to do: in our house, where we raised our daughter."

He was still looking at her. "I am Elayne's son, as I am Hari's husband, as I am your father," he said. "Some bonds were chosen, and some were fashioned by hands that were not my own. But I choose them now. If you choose to be my family, then you are my family."

She couldn't breathe around how she felt. Her heart was tender in her chest.

"Is it really that easy?"

"I raised you by choice, and loved you by choice," he went on, voice quiet, implacable in both its honesty and its tenderness. "What will you do, of your own volition?"

She wrapped an arm around him, careful not to jostle his wounds.

"No matter what happens," she said, "I'll always visit home. Father."

They were on the edge of the world, where the silver sea touched the Isle's shores, where a ruin held the dream of a sleeping prince, a king who would rise again. Vina, against all odds, was alive. And she was a tale: a knight, a cursed lover, a survivor of her own fate.

But she was also a woman. Just a person, standing in the cold, her boots sinking in sand. And there, on the cliffs, staring out at the vast expanse of water, was Simran, her black hair a flag in the wind.

Vina started to climb.

Simran looked like she'd been crying. But her face was set. Her arms crossed.

"You all looked happy down there," she said. "I watched you. I'm glad."

"You could come join us," said Vina. "Galath would be glad to see you."

Simran shook her head.

"When I look at him, I remember what Elayne did to him. And I know it wasn't me, but in a way it was, and I..." She exhaled shakily. "It's time I go. I have to—the books in the Tower, I want to help the librarians preserve them, take care of them. It'll take time."

"Or you could stay," said Vina. "I..." She took a step forward. "There's so much I want to tell you."

"No," said Simran. Her mouth was thin. "Don't say it. Please, Vina. Don't."

"Simran," she said, voice catching. "Love. Don't push me away. There's nothing about you I need to be protected from."

"Vina," said Simran. "Don't come here—don't stay with me—just because you think you should."

"That isn't how I feel at all," Vina said softly.

"Let me tell you how *I* feel," said Simran in return, the wind blowing her hair back from her face, baring her to Vina—her fierce eyes, the swoop of her throat, the vulnerability in the shape of her mouth. "We've broken and remade the world. We've freed ancient tales, and destroyed some too. We've remade our tale into two people escaping, loving each other enough to free themselves from an old tragedy. But I don't know who I am anymore, and I don't think you know who you are either, Vina." She swallowed, eyes shining with unshed tears, her cheeks blotchy. "I need—need *time*."

Vina remembered the vow she'd made to herself, to cradle Simran's vulnerability, to protect her when she was broken—to never be the source of her harm ever again. Never the sword to the belly, never, nevermore.

"Simran," she said softly. "Anything you need. You have to know—I'll give you anything. Even time apart. Even forever apart. But is it truly what you want?"

Simran closed her eyes. Vina waited, wondering what Simran would choose. The wind wrapped around them both with cold and forgiving hands.

"I want to make a bargain," said Simran.

"I'm listening," Vina replied.

"When the winter solstice falls, come and find me," she said. "Seek me out—and tell me what you want. But wait until then. Give us both time." Simran opened her eyes, and finally she smiled—a smile that was half grief, half a mending heart. "It does not have to be me, Vina," said Simran. "But I hope it is."

"Simran," Vina said softly.

"The solstice," Simran reminded her. And then she turned and walked away, into the mist roiling into the distance. And Vina did not stop her. She let her go.

# Chapter Forty-One

*Simran*

*The snow is falling. I'm going to see her. Wish me luck.*

Source: Letter from Vina Patel to Hari Patel

There were no kings and queens upon the Isle. Perhaps that would not always be the case, but for now the Isle was free of monarchs and archivists alike. In the Tower, as golden autumn swept in, turning the sky dove gray and pelting the city with rain diamond-sharp with cold, Simran and the librarians cared for books freed from their inky chains. The librarians cataloged and organized, as Simran sewed and glued and mended fragile tomes. Simran carried out her work by a window with the shutters open to the air, so she could feel the freeing bite of cold, and stare down at London as it changed.

She watched it ripple and shift hue and depth like the silver sea. Woodlands sprouted from nowhere, then withered away. Once, bombs ricocheted across the city, and carried with them the grief-scent of a tale that made even Cora weep. She left to visit Vaughan after that for a month, welcoming the forest, its familiar enchantments and terrors, safer than the new tales sweeping over the land. Simran remained.

Hari came to visit her, Galath his shadow. But Vina did not.

"You told her not to," Hari said, when Simran finally kicked through her own pride and found a way to question it. "She took that seriously, Sim. Did you think she'd ignore you?"

"I don't know," Simran muttered.

Hari sighed. "Oh, Sim," he said. "You're really fucked-up. If you want her to come, tell her. Hell, let *me* tell her."

But Simran didn't.

*I always push people away*, Simran thought grimly, one night in her old apartment. That was why she'd done it, hadn't she?

But no. Not exactly.

She needed time. Her lives were a huge wound, a dark weight she carried with her everywhere. Until she could look at them, she wasn't sure she could let herself love.

Some nights, Maleficium appeared in her room, traveling in nefarious ways all familiars could travel, from Hari's cottage to Simran's fireside. Simran insulted her, and fed her ham, and slept with Mal curled against her stomach, a fluffy seashell, a purring warmth against her. In the dark of night, she heard Maleficium's voice for the first time.

*Love*, Mal said. *Home.*

"I love you too, foul creature," said Simran. She petted Maleficium's head. "I can't believe you spoke to Hari before you spoke to me. After all the times you scratched him too…"

Autumn swept by. Winter crept in, long-fingered.

The Tower had become a library. New tales arrived every day, as songbirds and mice, as loping foxes and watchful owls; as books, and pamphlets, newssheets and letters, carried by the Isle's folk to the Tower's gates. The library hummed with whispers, as stories blossomed inside its walls.

Simran's work was done. The books were safe in the care of the librarians, and there were dozens of folk among them now who could mend a book's spine more artfully than she could. The monarchy was shattered, the tales free. She could be anything she desired now. Not a scribe, or even a witch; not a librarian either. She could choose to never touch another book again.

She watched the silvery water run through the Thames.

She thought of her parents, who'd come here for safety, and lost her, grieved her. She wondered what they would have wanted for her, if they'd known she'd have this chance. To go home? Back to a world that shaped stories with its mortal dreams and mortal hands?

She had no heart in her to leave the Isle, and was not sure she could. She'd bound herself so thoroughly to her tale, after all. The Knight and the Witch, no longer a tale of bloody sacrifice, but of cursed people breaking free, finding the miracle of survival.

They could make anything of their tale. The thought was as terrifying as it was joyful. She'd yearned for a life, a full and rich life, and now she had the possibility of one before her.

And she couldn't stop thinking of Vina.

She went back to her flat. There were still half-empty wine bottles on the table. Oliver had visited, reminiscing about the "good old days": Lydia, and the molly-houses, and being young.

Strange, to think she'd get to be... *not* young.

She pulled out new paints and a canvas she'd bought on a whim in a sweet, glass-fronted art-supply shop one chilly evening. She'd felt foolish, lugging the canvas back to her flat, but now she was grateful for her own impulsivity. Her fingers itched. Her heart ached to speak. She started to paint. Vague things flowed from her brush, like her scribe work had once flowed: deer among trees, and axes in cleaved wood; birds in the sky, and flowers growing from a knight's outstretched gauntlet. She'd never thought of herself as an artist, but perhaps that could change too.

Her mind was full. Joy rising out of the darkness.

Vina, dancing with her at the masquerade, smiling at her underneath the press of Simran's knife. Vina, tracing the contours of her face as they sat together on a rooftop under a gray London sky. Vina, whom she loved like breathing. She'd fallen into love the last time they'd died—hurtled off the edge of reason as they'd stared into each other's eyes and perished.

And the love had never stopped. It was a wing-beat, precious in her chest. But it was her burden to carry. Who knew what Vina wanted? How could Simran steal her life from her? She'd given Vina a choice, and she knew Vina might not choose her.

She'd let Vina go.

She was so lost in her own thoughts, in the scrape of her brushes on canvas, and the turmoil in her skull, that she didn't hear her visitor until there was a steady knock at the door. Three knocks. She lowered the brush.

She wasn't expecting visitors.

There were traps carved under the door. A knife that she grasped, and slipped into her pocket.

She opened the door, and—stopped.

There was Vina.

Vina, with her curling brown hair in disarray, her golden skin, her even more golden smile. Pale snow dusted her hair—the breadth of her shoulders, concealed under a dark coat.

"It's snowing outside," said Vina.

"I see that," Simran said faintly. "You're here."

"Of course I am," said Vina. "It's the solstice and... and I'm here." A pause. "Can I come in?"

"Yes," Simran said hurriedly. She stepped back and Vina walked in and slipped off her coat. Beneath it her body was achingly familiar: strong and lean, broad-shouldered, smaller at the waist. The breadth of her, her steady strength.

"Where have you been all these months?" Simran asked.

"I've been traveling the Isle," said Vina. "I've seen how it's changed. New shores growing where old ones were lost. New tales rising up. It's... it's new. Different." Her eyes shone with shy joy, when she met Simran's own. "I'm glad we get to see it."

Vina walked toward her, until there was a breath of distance between them, their shadows mingling.

"We made a bargain," Vina said. "I'm here to tell you what I want."

Simran's heart was in her throat.

"Tell me," she said.

"I want you," Vina said simply, voice low and sincere. "I love you. I've loved you hundreds of years. I walked to your mountain to slay you, and I loved you. I loved you when we were reborn, and I destroyed you again. I loved you as all the people I've been, and all the faces you've worn. I love you now that I'm no longer the knight, bound to a terrible fate. I love you now that I'm simply Vina, a witch's child and a very poor blacksmith."

"Poor in money, or poor in skill?" Simran asked, finding her voice through the great thudding beat of her own heart.

"I'm making a heartfelt speech, and that's what you ask?" Vina said, but her voice was fond, so fond. "Both, really. I'm sorry to say it. I'm sure you could find better prospects. But I couldn't let you live your life without telling you how I feel. It's selfish of me, I know, to try to bind you to a tale you've been trying to escape all your lives. But I had to tell you. What you do—that's your choice. Always yours."

Simran ached. Hurt and joy alike. She clasped Vina's face in her hands.

"You're the tale I choose," whispered Simran. "And if I can live a thousand more lives, loving you, I'll do it gladly."

She wasn't sure which one of them leaned in first, but they were kissing. Sweet as a homecoming, fire-sharp as good whiskey.

In the distance, beyond the door of her small flat, with its fireside and fiendish visitor cat, the Isle continued to change—shifting into clouds of ash, and sparkling buildings of iron and glass; graveyards, and metal birds soaring in the sky. Joy and grief. Tales ugly and tales bright. In the distance, incarnates rose and grappled with their tales, and in a ruined abbey among apple trees, an old tale of a prince slept and slept, waiting to rise again.

But Simran and Vina saw none of it, and if they had, they would not have cared. They were kissing in the place that would become their home, their hearth, and their whole lives lay before them, uncharted, endless with possibility.

# Acknowledgments

It was a joy to write this book, and I'm thankful for all the help, advice, and support I've had on my writing journey. Deep thanks to my thoughtful and hardworking editors, Tiana Coven and Jenni Hill, and the wonderful, supportive teams at both Orbit US and Orbit UK. Thank you also to my lovely agent, Laura Crockett.

I couldn't have done this without my friends—if you were there at my side while I wrote and cried and wrote some more, you know who you are. My family made this all possible, and my special gratitude goes to my mum, Anita.

Thank you to Carly, for being my historian and my rock.

Thank you also to my cats, Galahad and Merlin, and my enormous rabbits, Wei Ying and Lan Zhan. You didn't help, but you all inspired Mal.

I couldn't be more grateful to the kind authors who blurbed this book, and the readers who've taken a chance on my work. Thank you for being here—for taking this story and breathing life into it, on an isle in a distant silver sea.

# RAISING READERS
## Books Build Bright Futures

Thank you for reading this book and for being a reader of books in general. As an author, I am so grateful to share being part of a community of readers with you, and I hope you will join me in passing our love of books on to the next generation of readers.

**Did you know that reading for enjoyment is the single biggest predictor of a child's future happiness and success?**

More than family circumstances, parents' educational background, or income, reading impacts a child's future academic performance, emotional well-being, communication skills, economic security, ambition, and happiness.

Studies show that kids reading for enjoyment in the US is in rapid decline:

- In 2012, 53% of 9-year-olds read almost every day. Just 10 years later, in 2022, the number had fallen to 39%.
- In 2012, 27% of 13-year-olds read for fun daily. By 2023, that number was just 14%.

Together, we can commit to **Raising Readers** and change this trend. How?

- Read to children in your life daily.
- Model reading as a fun activity.
- Reduce screen time.
- Start a family, school, or community book club.
- Visit bookstores and libraries regularly.
- Listen to audiobooks.
- Read the book before you see the movie.
- Encourage your child to read aloud to a pet or stuffed animal.
- Give books as gifts.
- Donate books to families and communities in need.

**Books build bright futures**, and **Raising Readers** is our shared responsibility.

For more information, visit **JoinRaisingReaders.com**

Sources: National Endowment for the Arts, National Assessment of Educational Progress, WorldBookDay.org, Nielsen BookData's 2023 "Understanding the Children's Book Consumer"